IT'S A LOVE THANG

Reon Laudat

St. Martin's Paperbacks

NOTE: If you purchased this book without a cover you should be aware that this book is stolen property. It was reported as "unsold and destroyed" to the publisher, and neither the author nor the publisher has received any payment for this "stripped book."

IT'S A LOVE THANG

Copyright © 2002 by Reon Laudat.

All rights reserved. No part of this book may be used or reproduced in any manner whatsoever without written permission except in the case of brief quotations embodied in critical articles or reviews. For information address St. Martin's Press, 175 Fifth Avenue, New York, NY 10010.

ISBN: 0-312-98302-6

Printed in the United States of America

St. Martin's Paperbacks edition / September 2002

St. Martin's Paperbacks are published by St. Martin's Press, 175 Fifth Avenue, New York, NY 10010.

10 9 8 7 6 5 4 3 2 1

RESERVATIONS AT MOTEL HELL

Kenny-Wayne's pad was not the spacious apartment Ebony had envisioned, but a tiny room—a '70s psychedelic nightmare . . . decorated with a soul brother in mind, circa 1974. Ebony gathered up her favorite Mickey Mouse–print cotton pajamas and marched to the bathroom. A few minutes later, she returned to find Isaiah on his knees, hovering over a garment bag stretched out on the floor, so unzipped and unbuttoned, he might as well have been naked. His shirt parted, revealing the fine dusting of hair. It fanned over those sculpted pecs and narrowed to a dark line that disappeared inside his pants. His belt buckle dangled and clinked, drawing attention to his fly. *Lordy, the man is fiiiine!*

"The bathroom is all yours if you want to change." She cleared her throat when her voice came out in a rusty little croak.

"Change? Change into what?" Isaiah said.

"Your jammies, of course."

"I don't wear jammies."

"What do you sleep in then?" An odd mix of edginess and excitement heightened with Ebony's curiosity. "Boxer shorts?"

"Nope."

"Briefs?"

"Guess again."

"The altogether?"

"Yup. Commando, baby. Buck nekkid as a jaybird. . . ."

*To my wonderful husband,
Peter F. Laudat, with all my love*

ACKNOWLEDGMENTS

My heartfelt appreciation to:

My parents, James and Yvonne, for love and encouragement.

My grandma Sara, for the same, but with the best darn mac 'n' cheese in the world on the side.

My oh-so-cool editor Monique Patterson, who saw my fiction writing in the roughest stages, but wanted to work with me anyway.

Cincinnati Enquirer columnist, Jim Knippenberg, who is *not* a nudist, but happens to have the best nudism research file that he was more than happy to share.

IT'S A LOVE THANG

CHAPTER 1

Ebony MacKenzie wheeled her weathered Escort along Shangri-La's driveway, half expecting to see naked people dotting the surrounding green.

Instead a smattering of birds, squirrels, and assorted insects reveled in the warmth of a late-May morning. The car crawled ahead. Her heart rate accelerated. Nestled on acres of virgin forest and verdant meadow, Shangri-La Naturist Retreat appeared to be a world unto itself. A half-mile and a long lush row of Ohio buckeyes separated its vine-threaded entrance from Interstate 275 and the rest of civilization.

Ebony's mind had been made up—until reality drop-kicked her square in the gut: she might have to get naked!

After the forty-minute orientation tour all visitors were required to strip down to their birthday suits if they chose to participate in Shangri-La activities or mingle with Shangri-La guests. The unseasonably hot spring day, reminiscent of July, hardly made dropping trou more appealing. Why couldn't Reuben Renfro have more conventional pastimes? Golfing, fishing, water-skiing, heck, even big-game hunting and bungee jumping were preferable to what awaited her beyond the five-foot-high electronic fence encircling Shangri-La. Dread lodged in her throat, but a determination to focus on the positive kept the car rolling forward. She refused to lose her nerve. Renfro was as good as hers, she vowed, pressing onward. Maybe, just maybe, she'd timed her arrival just right. With a flick of her wrist, she checked her watch again. Renfro, scheduled to appear at noon, would arrive in exactly seven minutes. She'd wait five before alerting the staff. That would buy thirty-eight minutes for snooping around. That is, if she managed to ditch her Shangri-La guide.

She pulled up to a speaker on the driver's side of the narrow gravel path, then announced herself. She glanced around, surprised by the nearly full parking lot on a workday. Obviously nudists or rather naturists—the preferred term—didn't clock in at real jobs. After the gate parted she entered to claim one of the few open parking spaces.

Tucking a small reporter's notebook inside her oversized fanny pack, she made her way toward a canopied area as instructed by the posted signs. Soon an approaching golf cart with an elderly driver rattled in the distance. The engine putt-putted as it approached. An old man wearing nothing but a bath towel cinched around his waist, sarong-style, navigated the cart, which came to an idling pause in front of Ebony.

Unnaturally white teeth, tube socks, and sneakers glowed against a backdrop of sun-roasted skin. "Climb aboard!" the old man bellowed then whisked her off toward the administrative office.

"I'm Bernie Herman, but everybody calls me Pops." He smiled, tipping his sun visor. Look Ma, No Tan Lines! gleamed across the bill in bold iridescent letters.

Ebony found her voice and a weak smile. "Uh, er, nice to meet you, Pops." Unsure how thoroughly he'd secured his towel, she had to decide where to aim her gaze. Between the greenery and the gravel path before them, she focused on his silvery blue eyes with laser precision.

"You picked a great day for an orientation tour. One of our new members is due for a dedication ceremony. I'm sure you've heard of Reuben Renfro."

Had she ever. "The Ice Cream King, right?" The words eased off her lips, though the mention of his name sent her adrenaline rampaging. Reuben Renfro—the man behind this madness. She had become obsessed with the eccentric multimillionaire after promising to deliver his exclusive to the *Cincinnati Examiner*. An editor at the award-winning daily newspaper had practically promised her a job if she could pull this off. A full-time staff position at the *Examiner* would mean she could kiss the *Butler County Bee* goodbye. Hacking for the rag of a weekly had taken its toll. At the *Examiner* she could tackle bona fide journalism and cozy up to a fatter paycheck. Those extra bucks would go a long way toward easing the strain on her family's finances.

She'd latched on to the idea of going after Renfro, undeterred by the equally determined pack of print, radio, and television reporters who had done the same. Neither Renfro's power nor infamous distaste for the media had intimidated her. He might have parlayed his granddaddy's two-truck milk delivery service into an international ice-cream empire, but when all was said and done, his life story was just another puff piece. Hardly a notch up from the Porta Potti scandal she'd exposed on page 1 of the *Butler County Bee* after last year's Veterans Day parade. But Renfro was a means to a desperately desired end.

The scoop required savvy investigative reporting, well-placed sources, and even her undercover tag—Elaine, her middle name. No Bond Girl panache there, but at least she'd never made the cover-blowing mistake of not answering to it.

Undercover tactics were one thing. No-cover tactics were another. The possibility of infiltrating a compound full of naked weirdos to get to Renfro had never occurred to her until earlier that morning, when she discovered he was to appear at Shangri-La at noon. She'd jumped at the chance to get a crack at him. Who knew when another hot tip would fall in her lap again?

Pops broke her reverie. "Shangri-La's brimming with a lot more excitement than usual today. A man as successful as Mr. Renfro should give the place an air of respectability."

The administrative office, housed in a dome-shaped, burnt-orange stucco building circled by purplish puffs of barberry shrubs and large leafy hydrangeas, popped into view in the clearing just ahead. The driver bounded out, skirted the grill of the cart to the passenger side, and extended his hand to assist Ebony. "Trudie, the manager, is inside. Hope you enjoy your visit." Pops took off toward the group of towel-clad people playing volleyball on a vast square of sand a few feet away. *Yes!* Ebony hadn't been as happy to see so many towels since Kmart's last Martha Stewart white sale. She hadn't encountered one butt-naked person yet. Maybe this wouldn't be so bad after all.

A brassy blonde with dark roots waited at the door. *So far, so good.* She wore an oversized Shed Your Threads T-shirt that reached mid-thigh. "Nice to meet you, Elaine," she said with a Kentucky-fried drawl, then extended acrylic talons for a shake. "I'm Trudie. We spoke on the phone."

"Hello." Ebony scanned the surroundings. Those in the office were busying themselves with mundane tasks, wearing more terry—tied wrap- or sarong-style. A petite brunette with a Betty Boop tattoo on her left shoulder answered the ringing phone at the reception desk. A sunburned guy with a screwdriver in hand and a tool belt swinging precariously low over his towel-covered hips tinkered with a VCR atop the old Motorola in the corner. In the recreation room to the right of the lobby Ebony heard tinkling laughter and the staccato click-clack of two chubby young women engaged in a vigorous table tennis match.

"Have we met before?" Trudie asked, studying her thoughtfully. She cocked her head to one side. "You look familiar to me."

"No, I don't believe we have." Ebony's cover would be blown if Trudie made the connection to the head shot published along with Ebony's newspaper columns. That photo made it too doggone hard to do undercover work, but she couldn't persuade her editor to get rid of it. Donning some sort of discreet disguise in the future might not be a bad idea. Her best friend's Star Jones wig collection was probably as good a place as any to start. She made a mental note to call Yolanda about it.

"So, you're thinking of joining Shangri-La?" Trudie lifted a clipboard and pen off a nearby counter.

Still uneasy about misrepresenting herself, Ebony avoided making eye contact as she served up one of many fabrications necessary to get the job done. "Sounds like fun."

"Have you ever been to a naturist retreat before?"

"No."

Trudie quirked a penciled-in brow as if she could see right through her. "Why now?"

Ebony evaded the woman's hawklike gaze and feigned interest in the cheesy watercolors of nude people adorning the wood-paneled walls. "I've always thought I'd enjoy the freedom of being unencumbered by all of this." She plucked at her blazer and the sateen tank top underneath it.

"You can always walk around in the privacy of your home without clothes. Why join a naturist retreat?" Trudie grilled her.

Ebony hesitated a moment too long. Waltzing in to poke around without someone poking back was obviously out of the question. Forced to look the manager in the eye, she replied, "Well, true, but . . . but . . . here I wouldn't be confined to indoors. I'd love to feel a soft breeze and the warm sun on every inch of my skin." She gestured toward one of the watercolors. "Like the happy folks frolicking in these pictures here."

Trudie went through the motions of a smile, clearly unconvinced. "We're a family resort. All sorts of good solid citizens of the community are members here—young, old, doctors, lawyers, teachers, housewives, even business tycoons. The atmosphere is clean and respectable. We can sniff out people who come here looking for . . . for . . . something other than what goes on here, if you know what I mean. There's tennis, volleyball, swimming, hiking, camping, and wholesome parties and get-togethers that all ages can enjoy. This is not nor has it ever been a swingers' or singles' club." Trudie stabbed Ebony with an accusatory glare.

The manager had obviously misinterpreted nervous energy as something lascivious, dirty, improper. Ebony squared her shoulders. She was a class act. She looked it in her navy business suit. Didn't she? Her skirt grazed her knees with unrelenting appropriateness and the scoop-neck tank barely skimmed her modest curves. She fumbled to button her jacket, but the bulging fanny pack strapped to her waist prevented that. She dropped her hands and bristled at the woman's nerve. Unlike bra-less Trudie, Ebony wasn't serving up bobbling boobs like Jell-O jigglers. But indignation would not get the best of her. "I understand," Ebony said, dulling the sharp edges from her tone. "Sounds like just the sort of place I'm looking for." She smiled with as much sincerity as she could muster to ease Trudie's suspicions. It appeared to be working. The stern lines of the manager's savagely tanned face softened.

Ebony fiddled with a vase of wax daffodils on the reception counter. "Speaking of activities. Mr. Herman, uh, I mean Pops, mentioned that there was something special going on today."

"Ah, yes. Reuben Renfro, one of our new members, donated a beautiful bronze fountain to the grounds," Trudie said. "We're having a special dedication ceremony as soon as he arrives."

"Isn't he here already?"

"No. I'm afraid he's been detained by business. He promised to get here as soon as he could, though."

Ebony chewed her bottom lip. Of all the dumb luck. She checked her watch, then the wall clock, which was about five minutes too fast. Its tick resonated throughout the room like a time bomb. The countdown had begun. Thirty-five minutes until strip time.

"As I told you on the phone," Trudie explained as if reading her thoughts. "You're allowed to keep your clothes on for the guided tour, but if you want to stay longer to take part in the festivities you'll have to disrobe." She went to the wall shelf with her rubber flip-flops slapping the ceramic tiles. She removed a folded white square and held it out for Ebony's inspection. "You'll be given a towel like this one. Shangri-La rule number one, no bare bottoms are to touch any of the furniture, for sanitary purposes, of course. And besides, flesh sticking to vinyl can be dreadfully unpleasant in this heat. Rule number two, the towel is usually for sitting, but we're making an exception today. Mr. Renfro requested that we all cover up for his wife's sake. It seems Mrs. Renfro hasn't wrapped her brain around the Shangri-La concept just yet. Poor dear, probably has deep-seated body-image issues. She'll come around eventually. But in the meantime he really wants her with him at the dedication ceremony. So today, and today only, you may fashion a wrap with your towel. Soon as Mrs. Renfro departs after the ceremony, it's business as usual."

Ebony nodded, relaxing her grip on the towel in her hands. All the creative twisting and knotting in the world wouldn't make it adequate coverage.

"You can leave your towel here for now, but should you choose to stay, I'll go over the rest of the regulations before you're set loose on the grounds." Trudie waved at a short, balding man passing by. His slight frame barely managed to support the belly bulging over his towel wrap. He had spindly legs with bony knots for knees and boatlike feet tucked in chunky Teva sandals. "That's Lars Washington, one of our oldest and most generous members."

Reuben Renfro. Now Lars Washington. Two of the most successful African-American entrepreneurs in the country were members of Shangri-La. Ebony shoved the towel she hoped she wouldn't need back on the shelf.

The man nodded his greeting, then scooped a soccer ball from a cardboard box of sports equipment before heading back out the door.

"That's *the* Lars Washington of Sole to Soul Shoe Factory?" Ebony asked, watching him depart.

"One and the same. In the Shangri-La brochures we could boast about our multimillionaire members, but we chose not to. Part of Shangri-La's appeal is when you step behind these gates and strip down; we're all the same. There's very little social class distinction. Nobody is judging you based on what you're wearing. There's something so liberating about that. Don't you think?"

"Great," Ebony replied on autopilot.

"It's tour time, then!" Trudie jotted down a few notes on

her clipboard. "Hmmm. Let's see, we'll start with the campsite, then we'll work our way back to the rec room."

A crowd had congregated around the pool and fountain. Ebony hoped Renfro had arrived. "Can we start with the pool instead? I'd love to see your new fountain."

Trudie paused to consider the detour. "I guess that wouldn't be a problem. We're going to have a contest to name the fountain. The winner gets a free one-year supply of Mr. Renfro's best-selling flavor, Mega Mocha Chubby Chip!"

"Is that so?" Ebony replied, thinking the last thing a nudist needed was a truckload of free ice cream.

When they reached the fountain Ebony gaped, blinked, then gaped again. The monstrosity of metal was the most hideously phallic thing she'd ever seen in her life.

"The history of naturism is very rich. Benjamin Franklin was a naturist, you know," Trudie prattled on. "Mr. Renfro commissioned the sculpture, but he let us submit ideas to the artist for the design. He hasn't seen it yet, but we think he'll be quite pleased with the concept, don't you think, Elaine?"

"Well . . . uh . . . It's very . . . um . . . interesting."

The brunette with the Betty Boop tattoo darted toward the pair. "Trudie! You're not going to believe this! The ice sculpture just arrived, but instead of getting the replica of Michelangelo's *David* we ordered, they delivered this god-awful no-neck bird they're claiming is a swan. It looks like a duck! Obviously somebody screwed up, but the deliverymen won't take it back and they're demanding the balance of the bill!"

Trudie sighed, turning to Ebony. "I should've known it would be too much to hope I could pull this day off without a hitch. You stay right here. Feel free to grab a bite and a drink. I'll be back as soon as I straighten out this mess."

"I'll be just fine." Ebony restrained the duplicitous grin threatening to curl her lips as the brunette took off with Trudie in her wake. Shangri-La members circled long tables topped with a smorgasbord of meats, cheeses, fruits, and crudités. Two fully stocked bars flanked the buffet. Blending in was out of the question. Ebony's navy suit demanded attention against the palette of flesh tones and white terry. She reached for a fistful of doughnut holes with rainbow sprinkles. Popping one inside her mouth, she caught the rear view of a magnificent male physique near the fountain. It wasn't like her to gawk, but she boldly catalogued his assets—the long sleekly muscular legs, broad V-shaped back, diamond-cut calves and wide, wide shoulders. His towel hugged slim hips and a taut tush, making what she couldn't see all the more tantalizing. Her mouth watered. She popped another doughnut hole then decided he had to be some sort of sexual deviant. He was into group nudity, for crying out loud. Probably a few fries shy of a Happy Meal. She wouldn't be surprised if he had piercings in the most inconvenient places and a couple of large, disgustingly suggestive tattoos. When he turned to chat with the obviously enraptured female at his side, Ebony caught a glimpse of his profile. For a closer look, she took a few steps forward and joined a cluster of chatting women. No precious metals or body graffiti broke the smooth expanse of warm sepia skin. The neatly groomed moustache anchored by a shadow of a goatee gave a smoldering edge to a face almost too pretty to be male. But that physique of his, layered with well-honed muscle, inspired fantasies involving honey, 103 ways to savor honey, to be exact. Her gaze climbed the stairway of his deeply chiseled abs. One. Two. Three, four, five. *Hot Dang!* The man was the proud owner of the legendary six-pack. And his chest ... Sculpted golden-brown heaven, she marveled before trying to snatch her attention back to the business at hand. Renfro. Yes, making a connection with Reuben Renfro. But instead Ebony strained to block out the cackling women to eavesdrop on Six-pack's conversation.

"I'm going to get a drink. Would you like something?" asked the woman with the boom-boom curves standing beside him.

"Allow me," he replied in a rich, deep timbre perfect for whispering sweet-and-naughty nothings.

"No, I'll get them. I need to chat with Stan the bartender anyway. What would you like?" The question came fully loaded with a coffee-tea-or-me option.

"Surprise me." He winked.

Ebony nearly choked on her third doughnut hole when the handsome stranger's gaze locked with hers. Something magnetic zigzagged between them. Her belly fluttered. Her breath snagged in her throat. His light brown eyes bewitched her. She definitely wasn't at Shangri-La for that! Turning on her heel, she scrambled like a skittish cat and crashed into a billowy bosom.

Trudie clutched Ebony's shoulders, breaking her ricochet. "Elaine, are you all right?"

"Yes, I'm fine." Ebony eased out of the grip, adjusting her jacket and fanny pack. "Will the dedication ceremony start soon?"

"Trudie! Trudie!" Betty Boop accosted the Shangri-La manager again.

"What now, Debbie?" Trudie heaved a sigh heavenward. "You're the assistant manager, you know. When are you going to start assisting? I can't handle everything."

"I know, but it's Mr. Renfro. He's on the phone in your office. Line one."

"I'd better take that. I hope he's not canceling on us." Trudie anxiously checked her watch, then turned to Ebony. "Debbie here can show you around."

"I'd like to wait if you don't mind." Ebony plastered on a meek smile. "I'm more comfortable with you."

"Oh, all right, I guess it'll be okay if you wait here for a few more minutes." Trudie took off again.

"Take your time." Ebony hadn't recovered from the stranger so handsome he had to be trouble, but she refused to remain distracted by his six-pack. She didn't care how yummy he looked or how long it had been since her legs felt all noodly like they did when she first laid eyes on him. Nor did she care that he had made her insides somersault. Something nobody had done in a long, long while. She was there to work and it was high time she got to it. Renfro hadn't arrived yet, but she didn't believe Shangri-La was as squeaky-clean as Trudie insisted. Ferreting out any freaky-deeky happenings was an excellent way to repay Stella, a pal and *Bee* co-worker, for passing along the tip about Renfro and Shangri-La. Stella was always hungry for scandalous morsels for her Deep Dish gossip column.

A few feet away on a grassy patch, the two plump perky women who were playing table tennis earlier had moved on to a heated badminton battle with Pops. Most Shangri-La members, including those who had been working in the office when she arrived, were now cavorting on the lawn or around the pool and fountain. Ebony headed for the main building to do a little sleuthing.

CHAPTER 2

Isaiah Malone scoured the patio for the woman in navy blue. With that softer-side-of-Sears suit, pleather pumps, and uncompromising bun of microbraids, she was hardly his type. Tall, angular, and damn near regal, when built, babelicious, and defiantly buck wild was more his style. Still, he continued his search, convinced he'd seen her before though he couldn't recall where.

"I'm back. Did you miss me?" Desiree, the woman who had been shamelessly flirting with him, returned carrying two bright crimson drinks with little umbrellas sprouting from them.

Isaiah accepted the offered drink with one hand and adjusted the jumbo safety pins securing his towel with the other. He couldn't believe he'd been reduced to wearing the damn thing, but he wasn't about to blow an opportunity to get to Reuben Renfro simply because he refused to part with his jeans. Landing this interview was his ticket to a full-time staff position at the *Cincinnati Examiner*, but most importantly a little professional respect. The excitement of gallivanting all over the globe freelancing alien abduction and three-headed-baby stories for the *International Inquisitor* and the *Weekly Tale Tattler* had lost its appeal. He hadn't expected his first foray into legitimate journalism to land him smack-dab in the middle of Shangri-La. But here he was at a festive gathering with nothing but a scratchy towel between him and complete humiliation. And all because that *Examiner* editor had made it clear that landing the Renfro profile was the only way he'd overlook Isaiah's tabloid background.

Once Isaiah accomplished what many others had tried and failed, that editor and all the rest who had looked down their noses at him would have to admit they'd been wrong. That thought strengthened his resolve. He sipped and winced as what must have been wild cherry Kool-Aid spiked with rubbing alcohol seared a path down his throat.

"Too strong?" Desiree asked, reaching to retrieve his cup. "Can I get you something else?"

Isaiah wheezed, swallowed a cough then shook his head. "Nah, I'm cool. Just prefer my liquor to slide down a bit smoother, that's all."

Not one to bypass an opportunity to add an entry to his little black book, he couldn't help noticing Desiree wasn't half bad to look at. Not bad at all. A nice full figure eight. Thick. Like a woman should be. Toned and firm, but she hadn't aerobicized all of her feminine softness away. Rarely did he get to perform such a thorough appraisal of the goods before the wining and dining. That towel of hers was so short, one hiccup would expose all her secrets. But he decided not to go for her phone number this time. While he'd admired the centerfolds in *Playboy* from time to time, the idea of other dudes ogling *his* woman's private parts would drive him crazy. Call him a hypocrite. But besides that, he was a real sucker for lush bee-stung lips and Desiree's all but vanished when they stretched into a smile. Now the woman in the navy blue suit ... She had quite a kisser on her. A real cushy pair that inspired a marathon of heated fantasies. It was painted a sassy shade of red on a face otherwise devoid of makeup, so she obviously knew that her mouth was her most striking feature.

"Thanks for the drink," Isaiah said. "Hey, did you happen to see where the woman in the blue suit went?"

Desiree pointed. "In the main compound over there."

"Excuse me." Isaiah pivoted in that direction. "I'll be right back."

Ebony slipped inside the recreation room relieved. She'd managed to elude Trudie, who was still ensconced in her office on the phone.

Snooping was next to impossible to do so Ebony slouched on the leather cushions of a worn La-Z-Boy recliner. This *had* to work out. Her family counted on her. Her younger sister needed help supplementing her academic scholarships and government grants. No way was Ebony going to let Kenya sink into debt with student loans or work ragged trying to juggle a load of classes and a full-time job as she had. With night courses squeezed between two work shifts, it had taken Ebony twice as long as most people to earn a bachelor's degree. Then there was their grandmother to think about. Granny Mac, who'd recently moved into Kenya's old room, brought her cantankerous disposition, Bruce Lee video collection, pint-sized hound from hell, and the balance of her medical bills that weren't covered by Medicare and Social Security along with her. But with a position at the *Examiner* Ebony believed she could make it all work. Her mother had been too scattered and overly emotional to hold on to any job for long, so Ebony took over the role of primary breadwinner when her father died almost a decade ago. A huge responsibility for a girl of seventeen, but she'd quickly honed an impressive knack for stretching a buck.

Ebony stood and caught a glimpse of her reflection in a mirror on the wall. Her lipstick could've used a touch-up, but she wouldn't bother. She usually saved cosmetics for special occasions. That day she had worn Brazen Berry lipstick, blush, and nail polish samples only because Granny Mac had insisted. Her grandmother had flaunted an impish grin as she presented a plastic bag bulging with miniature containers pilfered from Taffi, Ebony's friend, neighbor, and Mary Kay representative. Ebony flopped on the chair and loosened the strap on her fanny pack until she heard Trudie's flip-flops heading for the front door.

IT'S A LOVE THANG

Ebony tipped from the rec room to find the lobby clear. Two doors led to opposite hallways. She chose the left one and ended up in a Tex-Mex-style kitchen. Nothing out of the ordinary there—except the broken-down juke box and the pop-bottle-cap-studded Frigidaire. A velvet Elvis portrait from his Vegas days hung near an old smashed penny clock. Studded white jumpsuit and pork-chop sideburns. A scratching noise drew Ebony's attention to another door. She turned the knob, peeked through a slit of an opening, and found a pantry chock-full of dry and canned goods. The kind packaged in the party-sized containers found in those discount warehouse stores. A giant box of Cheez-Its on the floor sprouted a tiny gray tail.

"Knock yourself out, little fella," Ebony said to the rodent who had burrowed its way inside the box. Those Hostess Ho Hos tucked away on the top shelf were calling her name. Light-headed with glee over her discovery, Ebony paused, drew in a deep breath and willed herself to resist temptation. She'd already eaten two sticky buns for breakfast and several doughnut holes from Shangri-La's spread, which had already pushed her beyond a reasonable sugar allotment for one day. She had to take control and get a handle on her sweet tooth at some point. Maybe tomorrow. She surrendered, peering up at the box to gauge whether a chair was needed to reach it.

The shelf's warped, fraying wood and loose joints were much too rickety to disturb, but the craving got the best of her as she latched on to its edge anyway. Dust rained down and stung her eyes. The shelf creaked in protest, but if she was careful she could still peek inside at the big box of chocolate delights. No one would miss the one she considered swiping. Hoisting herself up on tiptoe, she gingerly tilted the box.

"Lose something?" asked a deep voice from behind.

Ebony reeled back and lost her grip on the box. A shower of individually wrapped snack cakes pelted her head. She whirled around and recognized Six-pack from the pool area. Then the Ho Hos box and rotting shelf plummeted toward her. Six-pack shoved her toward the box of Cheez-Its. The frightened mouse skittered between her feet. The agile Six-pack avoided flattening the rodent and caught the wayward plank before it bashed Ebony's brains out.

"Are you all right?" she shrieked, grasping the sturdy doorjamb. "I'm so sorry!"

"I'm fine," he managed, pitching the plank to the floor and wiping bits of wood and chipped paint from his towel wrap.

"Are you sure?"

"Yeah. Just took me by surprise, that's all. You all right?"

"Yes, thanks." Ebony's hand flew to her chest, where it felt as if her heart would hammer through. "Goodness, you scared the bejeezus out of me. You should never sneak up on a person like that."

"Especially when that person is snooping, right?"

She'd been busted, but she took a stab at shifting the focus. "You're hurt." She pointed to the clusters of splinters piercing his palms.

Six-pack looked down as if he'd just noticed them. "I think I'll live."

"They need to come out—now." Ebony grabbed his arm and led him toward the picnic-style wooden table. "Sit." She gestured toward the matching bench. Obviously stunned into submission by her take-charge manner, he did as told. "Splinters can wreak major havoc and cause infection if they're not removed quickly and properly."

"Is that so?" His dark glossy moustache and goatee circled a brilliant smile.

"You don't have to be all macho about it. The smallest injuries—paper cuts, hangnails, splinters—can hurt like heck," she told him in the gust of a single breath. Her hands fluttered about her fanny pack and removed a slim vinyl case containing a deluxe Swiss Army knife. She flicked past the mini corkscrew remover, magnifying glass, pliers, can opener, toothpick, file and cigar cutter until she came to a set of shiny tweezers.

Six-pack eyed the Swiss Army knife. "Does that thing come with a Batman decoder ring, too?"

"I feel really bad about this." Still flustered by a riptide of guilt, Ebony ignored the crack and turned his palms upward for closer inspection. She plunked down on the bench next to him and began removing his splinters. Blocking out the awe-inspiring ridges of his bare torso and lean blocks of chest flesh was impossible. She fumbled the tweezers.

When he leaned forward to scoop them up, the slit in his white towel wrap widened a bit—exposing just enough of his hard, etched thigh to send her pulse rate on a wild tear.

Six-pack moistened very kissable-looking lips with his tongue just before flashing her a rascally smile, gleaming and white. "Here you go." As he passed the tweezers back his thumb brushed over hers. The small gesture, charged with sensual promise, sent a current bolting through her body. So intensely sensitized everywhere else, she felt dizzy with awareness. His gorgeous body was so close to hers. The innocuous friction of her nipples against the textured lace of her Wonderbra drove her batty in a wanton sort of way. Reining in uncharacteristically raunchy thoughts, she gulped and went back to work on the needlelike bits of wood sprouting from his palm.

"This is really sweet of you." His honey-colored eyes fringed with satiny jet lashes bored into her.

"Seeing as how I almost got the stew knocked out of you, helping with these splinters is the least I can do."

"I see." Six-pack shifted as she plucked and his towel parted a tad more. More polite conversation might have been an effective diversion. But she doubted idle chatter about the weather, the stock market, or even simple introductions would suffice. Besides, tagging this ultimate female fantasy with a name might somehow detract from the titillating surrealism of the encounter. Her best friends, Yolanda and Taffi, were going to flip when they got wind of this.

Ebony sneaked a peek at the muscle definition around his knees, a sure sign he was also the proud owner of a rock-hard butt. The mental image made her tingle. His knees parted a bit more, almost in invitation, or so she hoped. Ebony guesstimated that seven splinters later that towel of his would be split wider than a Broadway stage curtain on opening night.

She plucked faster! So fast she fumbled the tweezers again. This time they landed between Six-pack's bare feet.

"I'm such a klutz today!" She squatted to the floor as ladylike as a slim skirt would allow. That's when it hit her. She kneeled at feet attached to a body that would make any woman bid *adios* to her morals and good home training. And it didn't help that he seemed to be staring as if he could see right through her tank top and blazer.

"Are you always so quick to take such a . . . um?" He cleared his throat. "Submissive position with men you don't know?" Mischief glittered in his eyes. "And if so, you're my kinda woman."

"Yes, no, I . . . um. I mean . . ." Make it quick, straight to the point, she thought, lunging to retrieve the tweezers. She lost her balance then braced herself using his knees to break her fall. Her face loomed *way* too close to his danger zone for someone who refused to French-kiss until the fifth date. The room spun around them. She looked up, their gazes locked and loaded until—

A wail of disapproval ripped out of nowhere. Trudie stood in the doorway, hands clutched to her chest, mouth stretched in a giant O. "Why, I never!"

Ebony, stunned to a freeze-frame, realized how incriminating things looked. She *was* crouched at this towel-clad stranger's crotch. Her lips wiggled into a nervous smile. Her voice came out all quivery and high-pitched. "Hi, Trudie. It's not as bad as it looks."

Minutes later Isaiah and the woman in the cheap blue suit sat in Trudie's office like juvenile delinquents in detention. He checked the safety pins on his towel. In the kitchen earlier, modesty had been the last thing on his mind, but he was relieved Trudie hadn't got a gander at the goods usually reserved for private showings. Now the woman in the blue suit . . . He had to admit, he'd entertained thoughts of flashing her something to talk about.

"I knew something wasn't right about you two the moment

I laid eyes on you." Trudie's lips contracted as if pulled tighter and tighter by some invisible drawstring. She bounced from one to the other, scolding them and pacing the length of her smallish office. She whirled toward Blue Suit and pinned her with a look of total disgust. "And you, with all your highfalutin talk about feeling the soft breeze and the warm sun on your skin. That's obviously not all you wanted to feel," she harrumphed, zooming in on Isaiah's groin area.

Straightening his towel wrap, Isaiah crossed his legs. Unrepentant, he tried to get comfortable on the cool molded-vinyl chair. He refused to give Trudie the satisfaction of pleading his case when he knew no matter what he offered as an explanation, he'd get the boot.

"But Trudie . . ." The woman in the blue suit tried reasoning. "I know it looked bad, but if you'll just let us explain. What you saw isn't really what you saw."

Trudie harrumphed again.

As his partner in crime shifted her body, Isaiah felt the caress of her heat and caught a whiff of the same soft soapy fragrance he had enjoyed as she kneeled at his feet. He had rather enjoyed that view from the bench, the perky curves of her sweet breasts and the way her skirt stretched over a deliciously rounded bottom.

Florence Nightingale with tweezers surged to her feet with her own affronted look. "You couldn't possibly think that I was engaging in some sort of . . . of—"

"Disgusting sexual act that's still illegal in some states," Trudie cut in, wagging a finger. "Don't try to play innocent with me, missy. I know what I saw." She tried reining in her anger and plunked on the seat behind her desk. "Elaine, Isaiah, I sense big trouble and Shangri-La doesn't need this. We have enough public relations nightmares as it is, with people thinking we're all perverted sex fiends."

Elaine. Isaiah searched his brain for a connection as he regarded the woman in the blue suit. She was fine, just not in that flashy sort of way that usually got his double takes. With the exception of that bluntly sensual mouth, her dark beauty was subtle. Had she not been the only fully clothed person among a throng of towel-clad nudists, he might not have noticed her at all.

"But . . ." Elaine looked to him for alliance. He brought a finger to his lips to shush her. She should know it was useless to try to explain.

"You two needn't hold your breath for an invitation to join any time soon," Trudie said, confirming Isaiah's hunch.

Isaiah merely shook his head and chuckled to himself at the absurdity of the situation and he couldn't resist getting in one last jab. "What's the matter, Trudie? All bent out of shape 'cause you didn't get your chance to play crouching tiger, hidden dragon?" Isaiah winked.

Trudie stood ramrod straight and pointed to the door. "You two, out! *Now!*"

CHAPTER 3

Trudie sent Elaine on her way, but she reluctantly granted Isaiah just enough time to retrieve his clothing from one of the coed changing rooms. Reuben Renfro was obviously a no-show for the little shindig given in his honor. Isaiah took consolation in that.

Once freed of that rough terry towel, Isaiah felt less like Tarzan and more like himself. A pair of loose jeans never felt so good. He adjusted the collars on his sport jacket and silk shirt before stepping aboard the golf cart, where Pops greeted him with an apology.

Pops revved the putt-putt engine. "I dropped Elaine off a few minutes ago." He manipulated the small gearshift on the cart's floor. "I like her. Reminds me of my granddaughter—pretty but with a no-nonsense way about her. I find Trudie's accusations hard to believe." The cart lurched over a huge bump on the gravel road.

"You know what they say, believe half of what you see, none of what you hear," Isaiah replied.

"Oh, yeah, of course."

Just before they reached the canopied pickup station Isaiah removed his shades from his shirt pocket to block the wallop of the midday sun. The cart stopped and he stepped out.

"Again, I'm so sorry this didn't work out. Take care," Pops tossed out before heading back to the festivities.

"You, too. Later." Isaiah offered a no-hard-feelings rap to the side of the cart then turned to search for his Mustang. He'd crossed two rows of vehicles when someone called out to him. Elaine emerged from the bench under the canopy.

"Hey, I thought you'd be long gone." Isaiah couldn't deny the pleasure percolating inside at seeing her again.

"I couldn't leave without thanking you again for helping me out in the pantry and I wanted to apologize for what happened with Trudie." She brought a slender hand to her forehead to shield the relentless rays. "I'm sorry I got you thrown out."

"It wasn't your fault." The heat from the sun and that somethin'-somethin' simmering between them forced Isaiah to shuck his jacket. "I think Trudie was gunning for me as soon as I got here. Apparently single young men are always suspect." Her flawless skin reminded him of fudge-cookie dough—rich, dark, and velvety. Her eyes were wide and eager. And those lips . . . As if on cue, Isaiah prepared to shift into flirt mode, but his circuits were jamming. Silence wedged between them. Awkward, tongue-tied, he felt his lips move, but nothing came out. He'd had his share of knockouts before, but none had ever had that effect on him. While he couldn't put his finger on it, something about this one was different.

Fortunately, she spoke up. "Apparently single young women are suspect, too. I got beat over the head with the same this-isn't-a-sex-club preamble."

"Really?"

"Really." She chuckled. "Excuse me for prying, but you don't look like the Shangri-La type. What are you doing here?"

"And what's the Shangri-La type, may I ask?"

Elaine shrugged. The sweetest dimples dotted her cheeks. "Let's just say I don't know what it is, but I think I know what it isn't."

"I could say the same thing about you."

"Thank you. I think I'm flattered. Shangri-la is way too out-there for me."

Isaiah kinda dug this lady in the cheap blue suit with the kiss-me-crazy lips. He considered asking her out, but something held his ever-ready pickup lines hostage.

"Why are you here?" she asked again.

"Hey, let's back up a minute. I don't believe we've officially introduced ourselves." He extended a hand for a shake. "Isaiah Malone."

She accepted it with a nice firm grip. "Sorry. Forgot my manners. Ebony MacKenzie."

"Oh, it's *Ebony*? I could've sworn Trudie and Pops called you 'Elaine.'"

She merely shrugged again and smiled, with a hint of white teeth nipping at a sexy lip.

"Your face looks familiar." Isaiah flashed his best ladies' man smile.

"Maybe you've seen the photo they run with my columns in the *Butler County Bee*."

"Ah, the *Butler County Bee*," he echoed. "That's interesting..." Perhaps he had seen her photo there. He'd picked up the humdrum community weekly once or twice while scanning the local classifieds for a good deal on a used car. More than likely, he'd spied her before among the posse of reporters dogging Renfro, but he hoped it wasn't so.

Before he could question her, a silver stretch limousine, wheels straddling the narrow gravel road, cut two fresh tracks in the grass. Sunlight reflected off the glistening MEGACHP license plate attached to the rear bumper. The windows were tinted, but Isaiah knew Renfro was inside. Isaiah clenched his fist as exasperation heated his face. "I don't freakin' believe this," he ground out, then swore under his breath. He had been damn close to finally making contact, but now he had to watch his best opportunity in weeks glide right on by.

"Oh, no!" Ebony lamented, watching the limo cruise toward the cluster of Shangri-La structures and vanish behind a shield of Ohio buckeyes. "Renfro!"

Isaiah eyed her warily, donning his mask of battle as his

suspicions were confirmed. Both were obviously casting their lines for the same big fish. Isaiah spoke first. "So what's up with that? You seem ticked off all of a sudden."

"You hardly look or sound like the happy camper yourself. And you didn't answer my question before. What are you doing here and why were you just cursing up a blue streak a moment ago?"

The soft rustling and swaying of wind-blown trees and the chirping of birds punctuated the thick quiet. They stood like gunslingers with itchy fingers at a showdown. That fiery somethin'-somethin' instantly extinguished.

Isaiah decided he might as well lay his cards on the table in hopes that she would do the same. "I'm a freelance investigative journalist, hoping for a crack at an exclusive with Reuben Renfro for the *Examiner*."

"You work for the *Examiner*?" Ebony seemed rattled by the prospect. "I've never seen your byline."

"No, I repeat. I'm a freelance investigative journalist. The Renfro piece is my pitch for a full-time staff writing position at the *Examiner*. If I get Renfro, I get the job."

Isaiah didn't think Ebony's demeanor could get any chillier, but damn if it didn't plummet to subzero. "Is that so? Just so happens I'm here for Renfro, too. Only I'm not just hoping for a crack. I'm going to get it *and* that staff position at the *Examiner*." She hitched her chin with a smug look that said, "Deal with it."

Isaiah usually liked feisty confidence in women, but not from one who had set her sights on the prize that had his name written all over it. "And how do you plan to do that? I mean, seeing as how you just got us tossed out of Shangri-La."

"Ooooh, so now it's my fault?" Ebony latched both hands on her hips. Defiance rioted in dark eyes that had been soft with gratitude before. "That's not what you said a minute ago. You were the one who sneaked up and startled me. I wish that shelf had crowned you on the head after all!"

"So you could sneak a peek under my towel while I was out cold, eh?"

"Sneak a peek?" Ebony's eyes bugged as she gasped. "You

couldn't possibly think I tried to help you with your splinters as an excuse to leer at you."

"Well, you got awfully close to my—"

"You're arrogant, rude, and lewd!"

"Rude and lewd?" Isaiah chuckled with condescension. He played cool, but in less than five seconds she had managed to thoroughly piss him off. He couldn't help goading her. "Loosen up, baby. I know you can do better than that. Let a brother have it in choice street words he won't forget."

Her face tightened with angry lines. He watched the muscle at a corner of her jaw twitch, the rapid rise and fall of her chest, and waited for her to rip into him again. Instead she pulled in several calming breaths. "Look, I'm not your baby." Her tone crisp and composed. "And I don't have time for this childish nonsense. Now if you'll excuse me."

She tried to skirt him, but he reached for her arm and considered apologizing. He had let his temper and intense competitiveness get the best of him. "Wait."

"Don't touch me." She jerked away, nailing him with a withering stare. He retracted his hand without hesitation, sensing he had pushed her too far. She adjusted the bulging fanny pack strapped around her waist and tugged at her lapels as if to get her bearing then stalked off to a little Ford hooptie-mobile at the other end of the lot.

CHAPTER 4

Isaiah slipped inside his own ride and headed back to town with thoughts of that Ebony chick on his mind. So she thought she'd beat him to Renfro? No way was someone at a sleepy little weekly called the *Bee* going to scoop him. He would relish showing that little *Lois Lame* a thing or two. Once within Cincinnati city limits he considered his next move. Renfro was obviously a bust for the time being and it was too nice a day to spend cooped up at his apartment in front of a computer. He reached for the cell phone in his glove compartment. Maybe he'd buzz that little massage therapist who had slipped him her phone number at the Zodiac bar the other night. She was a hottie, but definitely a space case. Maybe Shelly. Nah, too husband-hungry. On their first dinner date, she'd sketched a wedding seating arrangement on the back of his menu. Shereen? Too difficult to scrape off. Rendezvous with her tended to run on for days. Then there was Diandra. She knew the rules and was always good to go, but she lived on the West Coast. He clicked off the phone and chucked it back inside his glove compartment with disgust. He really wasn't in the mood for a date anyway. He considered calling his older brother, Tarik, whose neighborhood was just a few blocks up the road. He retrieved the phone, dialed a number, and boomed, "What's up, bro?"

"Same ol' same ol' with me. But listen, I just got off the phone with the old man," Tarik told him. "Guess what? He just signed up for flying lessons."

Tarik always seemed to be privy to the latest updates on their father's life. A pang of jealousy nearly made Isaiah run a red light.

"Hey, why don't you swing by? I was just thinking about throwing some steaks on the grill," Tarik said. "Your timing is perfect."

Isaiah's thoughts lingered on the news about the flight lessons. Their father had talked about learning to fly since he and Tarik were boys.

"So are you coming or what?" Tarik prompted. "There's a bottle of Heineken with your name on it." Isaiah could feel his brother's smile radiating through the phone. Tarik genuinely wanted him there, but he wondered about their father. Isaiah was in no mood to feel like the family screwup that afternoon. "Is Dad coming over?"

"C'mon, dude, he's not here, all right?"

Isaiah reconsidered that U-turn he was about to make. "Yeah, I'm on my way."

He veered off at the exit and drove through a clutch of residential streets until he reached his brother's cul-de-sac. As a kid Isaiah had resented Tarik because their father preferred his sibling to him. Though only three years apart, the brothers hadn't been particularly close. Tarik, who excelled so effortlessly at every damn thing he attempted, only reminded Isaiah of his own inadequacies. But as an adult, Isaiah knew he shouldn't hold anything against his brother.

Isaiah, and Isaiah alone, had hurled their father off the deep end. Isaiah had brought shame to the family's illustrious journalism legacy, which dated all the way back to the Underground Railroad. Malone men, former slaves, had escaped to the North and published freedom-fighting bulletins to help the cause. A great-uncle had been among the first minorities to become an executive editor at a major metropolitan newspaper and a great-aunt who had headed the African-American Journalists Coalition national trade organization.

Isaiah's father had won a Pulitzer Prize for his national coverage of the civil rights movement. Tarik had had impressive stints at the *Wall Street Journal* and the *Chicago Tribune* before following in their father's footsteps to head the journalism department at a local college. Isaiah's career highlights: double-page spreads with the shrieking headlines—"*Spider Monkeys Raise Slain Missionaries' Orphaned Babies!*" and "*Studmuffin Potbellied Pig Sires 1,651 Potbellied Piglets!*" But if he landed the Renfro exclusive and the *Examiner* gig, all that was going to change.

Once in Tarik's shaded backyard Isaiah made his way to the patio while his brother went to the garage to gather more of his fancy grilling accouterments. The plan had been to hoop it for a couple of hours then chow down on steaks. Tarik fancied himself king of the grill. He lived for throwing T-bones and New York strips on his beloved "forty-eight-inch-15,000-BTU-dual-range-top-stainless-steel barbecue with its integrated smoking system, built-in rotisseries, and solid-gold bezel knobs."

He and Tarik were having a good time, talking trash and throwing back Heinekens, until their father, Mr. Pulitzer Prize, showed up.

Isaiah, who had been casually rocking his deck chair, let it rest on all four legs. His posture snapped erect as he plunked his beer bottle on the glass-top table. "You called him over here." Isaiah cut a hostile glance at Tarik then watched their father stride up the paved driveway with the impassivity of a king. Tall, handsome, and silver-haired, George Malone had that distinguished thing going in spades, even when dressed in a short-sleeved oxford shirt, beige Bermuda shorts, and loafers sans socks. He'd been lauded as a brilliant journalist and columnist with an impeccable nose for the news and a flair for writing prose that sang. As a father he'd been judgmental, mercurial, and self-righteous. And his favorite pastime was clowning his youngest son.

Tarik leaned toward Isaiah. "Yeah, I did, but—"

"Man," Isaiah grumbled, shaking his head. "What did you have to go and do that for?"

"The three of us need to spend more time together. Just give it a chance. All right? For me?" Tarik pleaded.

Isaiah finally felt closer to his brother. He risked alienating him and ruining the progress they'd made, but Tarik tried his patience. Things would not get better between Isaiah and their father over hot steaks and cold beer.

"All right." Isaiah sighed deeply. "But as soon as he starts getting in my shit, I'm outta here."

Isaiah felt every muscle and tendon in his body tighten. He reached for his beer and took several cool gulps.

"How's it going, fellas?" George Malone had a lit pipe clamped between his teeth as usual and a brown paper bag in his arms. "Brought dessert. Stopped at the little bakery a couple blocks away and got us a pecan pie. Not just any pecan pie, mind you. But one like your grandma Virgie used to make—an old-fashioned Karo dark syrup pecan pie."

Tarik gave them a wide smile as he turned to head for the house. "I'll get another knife and some clean plates."

George took the seat across from Isaiah. "So, Tarik tells me you're active in the local chapter of African-American Journalists Coalition now."

"Yeah, he thought it would be a good idea to mix and mingle with other young professionals," Isaiah replied, then quickly shifted the conversation away from anything that could segue into a full-blown debate about journalism. "Tarik tells me you're taking flight lessons soon. Cool. You've talked about doing something like that for years. Glad to hear you're moving ahead on it." Isaiah wiped his hands on his jeans, unsure whether his palms were moist from anxious sweating or the frosted beer bottle.

"Yeah, can't wait." George shifted the pipe from one corner of his mouth to the other.

For as long as Isaiah could remember their dad had smoked the same special blend—three-quarters McClelland 2050, one-quarter vanilla. The sweet woodsy aroma took him back to his childhood. Sunday mornings and the newspaper, fat with glossy sale circulars and extra sections. Eight-year-old Isaiah just liked the colorful illustrations in the comics. He and Tarik would often squabble over them, but George soon put an end to that, suggesting the best reader of the two should get first dibs on the section. Isaiah, no match for his older, smarter brother, would relinquish the paper without taking the challenge, sure to lead to another humiliating defeat.

George went on about the flight lessons, speaking around his pipe's stem. "It's going to be expensive as hell, though."

"But worth every penny," Isaiah replied with genuine interest. As long as they lingered on aviation, things should be fine. "After you pass the course, think you might even try to buy your own plane?"

"Maybe . . . Who knows? I believe in dreaming big."

"I hear ya." Isaiah placed his beer on the table again and reached for the basketball wedged between a leg of the table and a chair. To keep his hands busy, he began dribbling it between his knees. "Wonder what's taking Tarik so long with those plates?"

"I think he calls it giving us some time alone." George tapped the bowl of his pipe with a finger. "I hardly see you at all these days. How about we go a few rounds of one-on-one? Winner gets the first slice of pie. Loser gets to watch, then wash the dishes."

"Make-it-take-it?" Isaiah felt his muscles relax and he released the breath he had held since his father arrived.

George nodded, pressing out the smoldering contents of his pipe with the stamp-sized thingamajig he removed from his pocket. He rested both on the tabletop.

"You're on." Isaiah smiled, then came to his feet, still dribbling the ball. His father followed him to the rectangle of asphalt where the basketball hoop and backboard were perched overhead. "Age before beauty. You get to go first." Isaiah passed the ball, relishing the companionable vibe between them.

He still had misgivings about his father's mellowed mood. What had Tarik said to him? He supposed it really didn't matter. He'd go with the flow. George reached out to him for once. He had to be grateful for that.

George made a clean basket from the three-point mark. He went in for a second with Isaiah shadowing his moves. George quickly faked left, then shot from the right to score again. Isaiah didn't hustle or play his best defensive game, but his mind wasn't on winning—just savoring this rare no-hassle time with his father.

When George scored his third basket he crowed, "C'mon now. I know you're not going to let an old man whup your behind." George's maneuvering became increasingly aggressive as his elbow jabbed Isaiah's ribs.

"Just letting you warm up. Just a warm-up." Isaiah lifted his hands high over his head to block a shot when George shoved him so hard, Isaiah's ankles wobbled a bit before he regained his balance. George fouled as if he had something to prove. Isaiah could wipe the asphalt with him. Really school him on the ways of take-no-prisoners street ball, but refused to turn what was supposed to be a nice game of one-on-one into another metaphor for their dysfunctional relationship.

"Guess you're about as good on the court as you are on the career tip, eh?" With more excessive force, George butted his hip against Isaiah's and made another shot. "I use the term 'career' loosely, of course." A smile settled on his face, but that all-too-familiar edge crept into his tone.

Isaiah's demeanor frosted over. He knew more verbal swipes would follow. Why had he believed this encounter would be different? He knew what would follow so he'd beat him to the punch. "So I guess you've seen my latest piece: 'Man Coughs Up Twenty-Pound Hair Ball,' huh?" Isaiah said, all fake grin and false bravado. "My personal favorite."

Isaiah thought he saw George wince. He knew as well as anyone how ridiculous his *International Inquisitor* assignments were, but would it kill his father to give him a damn break every now and then? He wanted to reveal his efforts to switch to mainstream journalism, but decided to hold off, reasoning the impact would be greater if he could announce that he'd actually landed the job. He'd wait and try his best to ignore his father's salvo of insults in the meantime. But that didn't mean he had to let him get the best of him on the court. Isaiah swooped in like an NBA superstar and took possession of the ball. For the next few minutes he swiftly fancy-footed around George and scored point after point to win the game without breaking much of a sweat. By the time Tarik returned the tension between Isaiah and George had settled in for the afternoon. Isaiah, who had lost his taste for steak and pecan pie, tossed Tarik the ball. "I'll catch you later, man."

Isaiah headed toward the gate.

"Wait, you're leaving already?" Tarik looked surprised.

"Yes and you know why."

"But—"

Isaiah lifted a hand to cut him off. "Save it. I know what you were hoping to accomplish and I love you for trying. It's on me now. I know what I have to do to get through to him." Isaiah watched their father shoot basket after basket.

"At least take some of this food home with you." Tarik led him back inside the house, where he wrapped and packed up enough steak, grilled corn, and pie for several meals. "You all right?"

"Yeah," Isaiah replied though his stomach twisted. "You go on back outside with Dad. I'll let myself out." Isaiah gave Tarik a reassuring slap on the back.

"Call me later this week. I got tickets to the next Reds game."

When Tarik left, Isaiah passed through the living room to exit the house. He caught sight of the curio cabinet filled with family photos, memorabilia, and Tarik's many academic and journalism awards. Isaiah no longer begrudged his brother's successes as he had when he was boy. Tarik had always been pretty cool as far as older brothers went. He'd even gone out of his way to try to help Isaiah study.

At first neither of them could understand why Isaiah sucked at schoolwork—especially when he seemed to be trying so hard. But grade school had been one long humiliation after another. After a while he began to routinely complain of stomachaches to get out of going, but their father had the uncanny ability to tell when he was faking it. Consumed by feelings of failure and inadequacy, Isaiah had decided if he couldn't be as smart as the other kids, he'd force respect by being the class cutup. He'd usually end up in the principal's office, but at least he was spared the cruel, condescending laughter.

One earnest effort to read stood out among his most painful memories. He'd inadvertently substituted the word "God" for "dog." God rolled over and fetched a bone. God played dead. Classmates cracked up as if they'd never heard anything so funny. And his teacher, who thought he was up to his usual games, had sent him marching down the familiar path to the principal's office. Only that time, he had been suspended for unruly behavior and an ever-growing list of disciplinary offenses. Remedial reading classes had been recommended to boot. The embarrassment sent his father over the edge. "You're a screwup and you'll never amount to anything!" George had ranted during that drive home from Isaiah's school. "Why can't you be more like your brother?"

Educators finally diagnosed Isaiah's alphabet-soup problem when he turned fourteen. The discovery was akin to someone switching on a light in the darkness. Einstein, Dickens, Shakespeare, Yeats. He could rattle off a long list of legendary and talented dyslexics. People with dyslexia had average and even above-average intelligence, he was told. Isaiah had struggled to believe this, but found it difficult when his father obviously didn't. The great George Malone had been an ace student from grammar to graduate school. George simply couldn't fathom how he, a man of superior intellect, could have sired a dummy like Isaiah.

But after years of dogged hard work, Isaiah caught up to students his age and graduated at the top of his high school and college classes. His dyslexia had been reduced to a manageable annoyance. He still had trouble balancing his checkbook. He was lousy with directions. His spelling was laughably bad, but computer spell-check and copy editors fixed that. Freelancing for the tabloids not only afforded him the flexibility he craved and an opportunity to thumb his nose at his high-minded, Pulitzer-obsessed father, but he could dispatch his stories by phone to copy clerks who took dictation when needed. He had it all worked out. Just when he thought he'd proven he could face his demons and beat them down, he couldn't get a handle on the compulsion to make his father sit up and take notice. Unsure whether landing the *Examiner* job was enough, he had to give it a shot, he resolved, as he headed to his car for the drive home.

CHAPTER 5

"Grrrr," Ebony ground out as she brought her trot on a treadmill down to a brisk walk. "I could've strangled him." A dose of endorphins usually lifted her mood. After leaving Shangri-La she'd bypassed the *Butler County Bee* newsroom for a pit stop at Spunky's Funky Gym. But after a forty-five-minute jog her emotions were still boiling over. She didn't like the effect Isaiah Malone had had on her. He had pressed—no, jabbed—her darn buttons like no stranger had before.

"Dude sounds like something else." Yolanda, one of her closest friends and workout partner, strolled into her cooldown on a neighboring treadmill. "But let's get to the real deal here. Is the brother fine or what?"

Ebony didn't respond. Rhapsodizing about Isaiah's sexy honey-brown eyes was pointless. And his body. *Lordy, that body!* Darn lethal and more than enough to drive any woman to distraction. She lifted the towel from the treadmill's console and looped it around her neck. "He's an arrogant jerk. What difference does it make what he looks like?"

"Oooh-la-la," Yolanda lilted. "Looks that good, huh?"

"Geez, I don't know." Annoyed by Yolanda's prodding, Ebony released a put-upon sigh. "I guess he's all right. I mean, if you go for that type." Ninety-nine percent of the female heterosexual population with half-decent vision would.

"If he's fine, there's a chance all this heat is not just because he pissed you off." As usual, what popped into Yolanda's brain soon popped out of her mouth. "Maybe you want him and he wants you."

"I just met the man." Ebony managed to keep her voice from scaling higher octaves in frustration.

"Chile, please, popping chemistry ain't hardly about clocks and calendars," Yolanda insisted, challenging Ebony to get a darn clue. "It's either there or it ain't. Trust me. He wants you."

"What he wants is to work my last nerve." Ebony tilted her plastic water bottle and squirted a stream inside her mouth. "And besides, I doubt that I'm his type anyway," she muttered. "He's one of those oh-so-cool brothas. Much too slick and a tad too hip-hop for my taste with his trendy jeans and fashion-forward designer shirt."

"Trendy jeans and fashion-forward designer shirt? And what would *you* know about that?" Yolanda gestured toward Ebony's gray sweatpants and oversized gray T-shirt mottled with sweat circles as exhibit A. Definitely a stark contrast to the scraps of leopard-print Lycra cinching Yolanda's own curves.

"I know enough. And besides, I come to the gym to work out." Ebony plucked at her T-shirt. "This is functional workout wear."

"And the rest of your wardrobe couldn't possibly use a little more flash, sass, and razzamatazz? Am I hearing you right?"

"I don't believe in wasting a lot of money trying to keep up with every fashion trend that strolls down the runway. That's all." Though she was a sucker for sexy lingerie, her choice of undies was certainly none of Yolanda's beeswax.

"I'm just messing with you, girl. If anybody can rock those Jaclyn Smith separates, it's you," Yolanda teased.

"Okay, Gucci's hoochie, but remember, a designer label on a too-tight, too-short, too-skanky outfit doesn't make it any less tight, short, or skanky."

"Whatever." Yolanda flapped one hand, breezily dispensing

her version of touché. "I don't think you should write off . . . What was his name again?" She pressed the button to halt the rolling treadmill belt beneath her feet then sat on the gym floor.

"Isaiah. Isaiah Malone."

"It's been a long time since I've seen you so hot and bothered over anyone." Yolanda darn near quavered with enthusiasm. "Correction. I've *never* seen you hot and bothered over anyone."

"I am *not* hot and bothered!" Ebony huffed. "Must I look at every man I meet as a potential opportunity?"

"I think the sistah doth protest too much." Yolanda chuckled knowingly, pretzeling her torso left then right in a thorough spine-splintering stretch. "Aaah, that feels good." She sighed and scissored her legs as far apart as physiology would allow and eased her face toward the floor. "Gumby ain't got nothing on me."

Envy seized Ebony. Though she was the cardio queen, her own joints would snap, crackle, and pop like Granny Mac's if she attempted anything beyond the basic warm-up and cooldown maneuvers. "You're a chiropractic nightmare. You know that, don't you?"

"Careful. That green is clashing with your gray."

"If the good Lord meant for me to touch my toes, he would've put them on my knees," Ebony quipped.

"Hey, don't try to get all off the subject, Miss Thang. About this dude. He really has you going. You're touchy and snippy today. You're usually so cool, calm, and supersensible."

Ebony joined Yolanda on the floor. "And that's a bad thing because . . . ?"

"I didn't say it was bad. It's just that I kinda like this feisty side of you. All fired up. The two of you . . ." She snapped two fingers with long lacquered nails. "It's on. Mark my words."

"Don't you think you're making a whopper of an assumption? We didn't exactly part with grins, smiles, giggles, and laughs."

"With both of you going after the same story, your paths

will cross again. And no telling what could jump off then."

Exasperated, Ebony folded into an unexceptional hamstring stretch as she told herself that Isaiah Malone was nothing but trouble. She did not need to get involved with someone who could blow her chances of getting that Reuben Renfro exclusive first.

"Hey, you want to see Mystic Sensations with me and Taffi tonight?" Yolanda asked as she ogled a buff guy in a tank top and shorts who sprinted by, butt cheeks riding high and hard as bowling balls. "We'll grab a bite first then head over to the jazz club on the riverfront."

Ebony stood up and balanced on one leg for a front thigh stretch. "Uh, well, I don't know if I can make it. I'll have to check my planner."

"Here we go again." Yolanda released a heavy sigh. "You never can make it."

"I've just been a little busier than usual, that's all, with my job and trying to freelance on the side." But Ebony had also been spending most nights at home watching videos, playing Scrabble, and refereeing spats between her mother, Jolene, and Granny Mac. The pair couldn't agree on the color of tap water if their lives depended on it. They'd squared off in an ongoing war of in-law wills since Ebony's mother and father swapped "I dos." In Granny Mac's eyes Jolene was never good enough for her son, Buster. His death had only intensified the animosity between them.

Yolanda would not drop the Mystic Sensations idea. She trailed Ebony to the women's locker room. "C'mon, girl, it's about time you got out of that house and had some fun with people your own age. You're gonna dry up baby-sitting your mama and Granny Mac every night. When was the last time you got out? And Taffi's last Mary Kay party doesn't count."

Yolanda and Taffi believed Ebony's dedication to family bordered on obsession. She'd heard it all already.

"I swear, Ebony. You really oughta . . ." Yolanda's chatter slowly faded.

Taffi and Yolanda just didn't understand, Ebony mused idly, twisting the knob on the combination lock securing her locker. She couldn't fault them for that. She hadn't confided in anyone about the details surrounding her father's death. She couldn't handle the awkwardness that would follow. Yolanda and Taffi would try to assuage her guilt with insta-advice about "the disease to please" gleaned from Oprah. A couple of counselors had tried to help Ebony sort through her feelings about the accident, but she had stopped attending those sessions soon after they began. She didn't need their well-meaning but empty psychobabble. She already knew what had to be done. The only thing that kept her from sinking into pitch-black depression. Her mantra: take up the slack. Fill the void. Her family had suffered a devastating loss. All because she had been too distracted by a boy and a silly school dance to act responsibly. The squeal of fire-truck sirens still hurled her back to that night she'd returned from a high school homecoming celebration to find her home engulfed by flames and surrounded by half a dozen emergency vehicles. Her mother and Kenya had been unharmed. But her father, who had been trapped in his basement workshop, died from severe smoke inhalation from the fire. A fire that Ebony soon discovered had started with the lit cherry-scented votive candle left unattended in her bedroom. Since then her first priority had been to be there for the rest of the MacKenzies, to provide for them the best way she could. To that end, she needed that *Examiner* job. Shangri-La had been a waste of energy. She tried to erase the mental image of a towel-clad Isaiah Malone. Now was not the time to get distracted by titanium abs and pecs and—

Yolanda waved a hand before Ebony's face. "Hey, you, where did you go just now?"

Ebony blinked, then opened her locker to remove her gym bag. "I know where I can't go and that's to see Mystic Sensations tonight. I couldn't if I wanted to. I've got to get up early tomorrow to head up to Grundie." She checked her watch, then dropped on the tiled floor to remove her cell phone from her fanny pack stashed inside the gym bag.

"Don't tell me. Checking up on your folks again?"

Ebony made the fifth call home that day. "You know how

they are. Those two cannot be trusted alone for too long." She punched the redial button and waited for a ring. When her mother answered, they exchanged greetings. Granny Mac had gone to a prayer meeting at the church, which put Ebony's mind at ease. She had a couple of extra hours to shop. "Hey, Ma, do you need anything from the grocery store?" She removed a notebook and pen from her fanny pack. "I'm making a pit stop there, but I'll be home in time to play a few rounds of bid whist before *The Jeffersons* reruns. And don't forget to take the chicken out of the freezer so it'll be thawed and ready to bake when I get there. You know how I loathe zapping it in the microwave."

Yolanda rolled her eyes and shook her head.

Ebony clicked off her cell phone and tucked it away. "What?"

"You treat those two like children. Next you'll send them to bed with no dessert when they don't behave." Yolanda stopped yanking a sweatshirt out of her own gym bag. "So you're going to Grundie tomorrow, huh? Why are you going all the way up to the sticks . . ." Her words trailed off. "Wait. Let me guess. Reuben Renfro. Right?"

Ebony stood and began removing her damp sweatpants. "You've got it."

"I'm surprised that man hasn't had you arrested for stalking."

"Believe me, I can think of a dozen things I'd rather be doing. But Grundie is the site of this big three-day paintball tournament. Word has it Renfro signed up. I've got to hand it to him; with his bent toward the colorful, quirky, and kooky, no one can ever accuse the man of being dull."

Yolanda began peeling out of her leopard crop top. "Paintball?"

"You know, that silly war game. Grown men, and, I'm ashamed to say, a few misguided testosterone-envying women, get decked out in camouflage duds and armed with toy air guns. They run around like raving lunatics splattering each other with paint pellets."

"Whop-dee-do," Yolanda said dryly as she jiggled the handle of her locker. "Some folks get to have all the fun. Well, at least it'll get you out of town and a much-needed break from the family for a few days."

Ebony sighed. "As bad as I need this shot at Renfro, I'm a little nervous about leaving Ma and Granny Mac alone for that long. I just hope the house is still standing when I get back."

CHAPTER 6

The next morning Ebony caterwauled to a Patti LaBelle tune as she guided her Escort along a small curving two-lane road. She'd been blessed with the kind of crystalline Friday perfect for a road trip and a new opportunity to latch on to Renfro. Just what she needed to put that Shangri-La flub-up behind her.

The highway leading to Grundie had been thick with traffic. Patches of flat, barren fields and monotonous billboards were the only distractions. But the plotted back route was virtually traffic-free and scenic. Ebony tried approaching this paintball adventure with a lot more confidence. Her knowledge of the game was limited to what could be gleaned from a couple of brochures, but how hard could an adult version of Capture the Flag be? She shrugged off all niggling doubt, cranked up Patti, and tapped out the beat on her steering wheel. "Ooooh, oooh, oooh . . . I gotta new attitude."

Just up the road a tall broad-shouldered vagrant caught her attention. Drawing closer, she slowed her speed to match his purposeful long-legged stride, then rolled down the window on the passenger side. "Isaiah?"

He stopped, sucked in a deep breath, and stood there, relief washing over his face.

"What happened? Why are you walking?"

"My car conked out on me. She ran out of gas." Isaiah stepped closer to her Escort. Sweat beaded on his golden-brown skin, darkening the armpits of his burgundy short-sleeved shirt.

"Is that so?" A singsongy lilt lifted her voice as her lips curved into a sinister smile. She took far too much pleasure from his mishap. But it didn't take a rocket scientist to figure out where he was headed and why. So much for her hot Renfro tip. "Well, Grundie is about eighteen miles up the road here. Hmmm, walking at a nice clip, you might get there before nightfall."

He released a dry chuckle. "You're kidding me, right?"

"I know you're not headed to Grundie for the tourist attractions. I'd be aiding and abetting the competition if I helped you out," she taunted him, knowing full well she didn't have it in her to desert him. "But if you asked real nicely, with lots of cream, sugar, and cherries on top, I just might be persuaded to reconsider."

"Forget it." Isaiah clenched his jaw and resumed his march onward, too proud for his own darn good.

"If you'd rather walk . . ." Ebony gunned the engine, well, as much as one could gun an old Escort. Her rear tires kicked up a cloud of dust as she took off. About half a mile up the road, she checked the rearview mirror. Isaiah had stopped in his tracks, waving a fist at her. She jammed on the brakes and shifted to a zippy reverse until the car flanked him again. Smiling with the mischief she felt, she asked with feigned innocence, "Forget something?"

"I can't believe you were going to leave me here like that." While he seemed to struggle to maintain his cool, his nostrils flared and his words came out in jerky little spurts. "Just go on and kick me to the curb, then."

She replied so sweetly she hoped it set his teeth on edge, "All you had to do was ask for a ride."

"No, you wanted me to *beg* for a ride. I'd hotfoot it to Timbuktu first." When agitated, his eyes darkened and the planes of his cover-boy face took on a virile intensity.

"Were you waiting for an engraved invitation?" Ebony reached over the seat to lift the lock on the passenger side.

"A little less gloating would be nice."

"You think I'm gloating? Ha! That's rich coming from you. So are you getting in or not?"

Isaiah grumbled, scrunching his long legs inside the tight interior.

"Something wrong?"

"Adjusting to your little Hot Wheels here, that's all."

"A walking man oughta be real careful what he says about this Hot Wheels." Ebony stole a sideways glance at him. The temperature inside the Escort rose a few nonweather-related degrees. She nixed turning on the air conditioner. Too obvious. His proximity and the scent of his perspiration mingled with cologne made her hyperaware of him. "So, you ran out of gas, huh?"

"Yeah, sometimes I get a little too distracted to notice—"

"Something as insignificant as a gas gauge," Ebony interrupted him with more than a hint of condescension. "You're not a details sorta guy, huh?"

Disregarding her crack, Isaiah pressed his lips together and sucked in a deep breath. "Had to leave her on one of the smaller roads that branches off from this one."

"Can happen to the most conscientious among us—especially when preoccupied. And I'm sure you were very preoccupied. You're on your way to Grundie, right?" Ebony paused. "On a mission, perhaps?" The mission to screw up her plan to connect with Renfro first.

Isaiah secured his seat belt over his brick wall of a chest and broad shoulders. "Yeah, I'm on a mission. I'm just dying to see the world's largest rutabaga on display in the town square."

"My, but it sounds as if somebody forgot to pop his happy pill today," Ebony chirped, hoping he found her perkiness grating.

"I seriously doubt you'd be Suzie Sunshine if your car conked out on you when you were already late then you had to hike it a few miles in the blazing heat."

"Late for what?" Ebony needed to hear him say it.

"As if you didn't know. The paintball tournament. Renfro. This weekend he's mine." Isaiah poked his chest for emphasis.

"Not if I get him first." Ebony reached inside the glove compartment for her sunglasses then pushed them over her eyes, the gesture a symbol of the shield she needed to erect between them.

They rode in rigid silence until they reached Grundie and Pac 'N' Snac, a rinky-dink convenience store with two ancient gas pumps out front. She plotted her next move. She'd done her good deed for the day. She had every right to ditch Isaiah's butt right there and get back to the business of sniffing out Renfro. Isaiah had been remote and sullen for most of the ride and he'd climbed out of the car without tossing so much as a thank-you her way.

Inside the Pac 'N' Snac Isaiah quizzed the store clerk so he could make arrangements for alternate transportation, but had little luck. Taxi service appeared to be out of the question. He quickly shopped for the toiletries he forgot to pack during his mad dash for Grundie. He pitched a toothbrush, a minitube of toothpaste, and mint-flavored dental floss inside his handheld shopping basket. As he passed the large glass storefront, he caught sight of Ebony scowling at him from the front seat of her car. That woman had one funky attitude on her.

Still simmering from the tension-laden barbecue at Tarik's the day before, the last thing Isaiah needed was the company of an ill-tempered female balancing a boulder-sized chip on her shoulder. They'd obviously gotten the same lead on Renfro again and that had pissed him off, too. But he had to admit that that little coincidence ultimately worked out in his favor. She couldn't have shown up at a better place at a better time, whacking twenty miles off his unexpected hike and rescuing his bunions from the unyielding wrath of a too-new pair of Cole Haans. He watched her twine a microbraid around one finger. The day before, the braids had been corralled in a tight bun. Today they'd been freed. There must have been a jillion of those things on her head. The glossy ropes cascaded past her shoulders. They gave her the exotic appearance of an African queen in spite of the denim overalls, Spunky's Funky Gym T-shirt, Reeboks, and ratty little macramé bracelet she wore. She was attractive without trying very hard. She obviously didn't put herself out primping and preening. Again, she appeared to be free of war paint. Though he dug the berry-colored lipstick she'd worn the day before, her kisser was just as sexy sans artificial coloring.

"Hey, mister, we've got a four-for-one sale on ice scrapers." The clerk behind the cash register barged in on Isaiah's thoughts, pointing to a prominent display situated on the counter. The clerk had a pleasant smile, neatly trimmed blond hair, and a white shirt pressed and starched so crisply it appeared to be fashioned from construction paper.

"Ice scrapers? It's May," Isaiah pointed out.

"Hence, the four-for-one special. What a bargain!"

"I'll pass." Isaiah pitched additional items inside his hand-held basket as he moved toward the checkout counter. "I'm looking for a place to crash for a couple of nights. Any recommendations? Hotels? Motels? Inns? What's Grundie's best?"

"Got one inn in town, the Bluebird," the clerk told him. "You can try there, but it might be a long shot. We've got a lot of out-of-towners in for that paintball tournament, but who knows? You might get lucky."

"Directions?"

"Just get back on the road out there, heading north, then take the right on Elm then a sharp left on Boll Weevil."

After memorizing the directions Isaiah paid the clerk and made his way toward the exit with his stash, which included an empty gas can. When he stepped outside he immediately felt Ebony's arctic glare. But he had a little something in his bag that was guaranteed to thaw her out.

Resentment simmered inside Ebony as she watched Isaiah mosey out of Pac 'N' Snac as if he had all the time in the world. It would serve him right if she made him eat her dust again. Who did he take her for, anyway? Boo-Boo-the-chauffeuringfool? He could get a taxi. Why waste valuable time driving him back to his car when she could get at least a good hour's jump on him? But instead of seizing the opportunity, she snapped, "Aren't you going to say thank-you?"

Isaiah set his gas can on the ground and ambled over to her window. Her gaze roamed from his lips then to his fingers as he worked three buttons at the neck of his shirt free. Rivulets of sweat trailed from the curve of his jaw, convened at his Adam's apple, then pooled in the deep crevice dividing artfully carved pecs.

Isaiah bent from the waist to stare at her from the driver's side. "I was going to say thank-you as soon as we got back to my car." He moved in close. So close she noticed luminous flecks of gold in his brown irises.

The prince of presumptuousness had a lot of gall. "*We* are done, as far as I'm concerned. This is the end of the road. You're on your own, buddy."

"So you're just going to leave me stranded out here?" he asked, as if the very idea were akin to eviscerating helpless kittens.

"Get a taxi."

"Look around you. Grundie makes Mayberry look like Vegas. I could walk back to Cincinnati in the time it's going to take for Melvin, the town-mortician–notary–cab-driver, to head this way. He's in the middle of embalming the Widow Tillery so I don't think he can help me out."

She lifted one brow and sniffed. "How do you know all that?"

"The store clerk told me. Apparently this is Melvin's day to work the funeral home. You see, I did try to make other arrangements so I wouldn't have to detain you any longer," Isaiah told her. "Look, I understand if you have to leave. I'll figure something out. You go on ahead." He reached inside his bag and removed a package of Hostess Ding Dongs. "Thought you might need a sugar boost right about now." He passed Ebony the snack cakes and a liter bottle of water to wash them down.

"Tokens of your appreciation or a bribe?" Ebony wanted

to appear hard and in charge, but she reached for his offering anyway.

"Look, I appreciate what you've done for me so far," Isaiah offered with some reluctance. "Especially under the circumstances."

The package of Ding Dongs was two days past the expiration date, but she didn't make an issue of it. He appeared rumpled and humbled. He played the pity card. She watched him trudge to the pumps. Where was the trumpet wailing taps? As he filled the gas can with premium unleaded something nudged her conscience. Would she ever sprout a spine? She sighed with resignation and shouted at him, "Hurry up, would you? I don't have all day!"

He went back inside Pac'N'Snac to pay for the gas then settled on the front seat of her car again.

"How did you know about my sweet tooth, anyway?" Ebony asked, trying to make polite conversation.

"All those doughnut holes you scarfed down at the Shangri-La buffet table and the way you risked life and limb to get to that box of Ho Hos gave you away."

Ebony unwrapped the Ding Dongs and took a greedy bite before starting the engine. The cake disappeared in three bites and the second separated from its wrapper before they rolled away from the Pac 'N' Snac.

Isaiah stared at the road ahead. "Got quite an appetite on you for such a skinny thing," he tossed out as a droll afterthought as they headed down the road.

Ebony rolled her eyes, but couldn't launch a counterattack with a mouthful of cake. She wasn't used to all this verbal jousting and jabbing. She found it draining, but strangely exciting at the same time. With them both in Grundie hot on Renfro's trail she'd get her chance to even the score.

At the Mustang Ebony discovered an empty gas tank was the least of Isaiah's automotive troubles. The car wouldn't start with a full tank and required a tow to the town auto shop. By the time they reached the Bluebird Inn where she had reserved a room, night had fallen and the last of her patience skidded away.

"Let me get this straight." She pinched the bridge of her nose then dragged in a deep breath. "Every room in this place is booked?"

"Yup." The desk clerk's hair glistened with a juicy Jheri curl and one front tooth gleamed with a gold cap as he sat riveted to the portable television on the counter and a round of *Wheel of Fortune*. "Buy a vowel, fool . . . *E* . . . *E*."

Ebony tried to get his attention again. "Excuse me, but I have reservations. You do too, Isaiah, right?"

"Well, not exactly." Isaiah had been leaning on the counter, quietly taking in Ebony's exchange with the desk clerk.

"What do you mean, 'not exactly'?" Ebony asked. "When I told you I had a room here and you asked to tag along, I assumed you had reserved a room here, too. Where do you have reservations, then?"

"I don't recall actually telling you I had reservations," Isaiah split hairs. "I just figured I'd find some place to crash after I got here."

"Don't tell me." Ebony clucked. "It's that thing you have against handling details, right?"

"I wasn't even sure if I was going to show up for the paintball tourney at all. If all had gone as planned I would've hooked up with Renfro yesterday at Shangri-La. That is, if *somebody* hadn't gotten me thrown out. When it looked like I had to come to Grundie after all, I figured I'd wing it on the sleeping arrangements. But sounds as if I'm not the only one who has to wing it." Isaiah gestured toward the desk clerk. "Right, my man?"

"Yup," the clerk said. He finally stood, pried his gaze from the television and looked at Ebony. "When you didn't show up or call by three P.M., we rented the room you reserved. A lotta people in for that paintball thing, you know. Most of them ended up in hotels in nearby counties. You might try Marion or Grant County, but forget about Potts. They're having their big Garlic Festival this weekend. I doubt you'd find anything open there. Oh, and you lost your deposit, too.

Thems the breaks, I guess." The clerk turned his attention back to the TV screen. *"H . . . H . . . H."*

"Them's the breaks?" Ebony prepared to rip into him, but Isaiah grabbed her arm and dragged her away from the counter. "Hey, chill, would you? This guy might be useful."

"Useful? I doubt it." Ebony crossed her arms across her chest. "He can't seem to pull himself away from that stupid game show long enough to do anything," she ranted. "I don't believe this! It's like something out of the dang *Twilight Zone*. And it's all your fault!"

"So it's like that now, huh?" Isaiah bit his bottom lip, then hammered her with a hard, assessing look. "You think I actually emptied my gas tank on purpose then broke my alternator belt on the off chance that you'd happen by and pick me up? You're tripping big time."

"Well . . ." Ebony drew the word out. The accusation was ludicrous, but her nerves were frayed. She wasn't in the mood to fake rationality.

Isaiah stayed calm enough for both of them. "Look, I know you're ticked off. I don't blame you, but let's consider our options."

"I'm not going all the way back home." Ebony knew she had a tendency to sound too shrill when perturbed so she tried to take it down a notch, but failed. "That's almost a three-hour drive and I refuse to sleep in my car after the day I've had."

"Those options don't exactly appeal to me, either." Isaiah approached the desk clerk again. "Hey, man, I don't believe I caught your name."

"Kenny-Wayne Cobb."

"Kenny-Wayne." Isaiah leaned against the counter. "Got any suggestions for us? Maybe there's a boardinghouse or something around here."

"One boardinghouse in town. Already booked up," Kenny-Wayne told them before falling under Vanna White's spell again. *"J . . . J . . .* For the big money! Big money!"

"Speaking of money." Isaiah pulled his wallet from a back pocket and removed some bills. He slid them across the counter. "You sure you can't come up with something else?"

When Isaiah plucked a few more bills and placed them on the counter, he finally had the desk clerk's undivided attention. "Gimme a minute to check something." Kenny-Wayne stepped away to use the phone on the opposite end of the counter. He dialed a number then turned his back to them as if making sure they couldn't eavesdrop on his secret conversation. After talking for a few minutes he walked back over to the counter. "You're in luck. I live at my uncle's place. For double the inn's standard weekend rate you and your lady can have my pad over Uncle Waymon's garage. I'll sleep on his sofa bed in his den."

Ebony opened her mouth to explain that she and Isaiah were not a couple and that sharing accommodations was out of the question, but Isaiah closed the deal. "We'll take it." He slid the bills toward the clerk.

"Wait a minute!" Ebony reached out, slapped her hands on the money to block the transaction.

Isaiah dragged her away from the desk again and reasoned in a stage whisper, "Look, you don't have to drive back to Cincinnati tonight or sleep in your car now, and an apartment over a garage sounds a helluva lot better than a sleeping bag in a garage, doesn't it? We're two adults. I know it'll be a challenge, but surely you can control yourself enough to share accommodations with me for one night. Maybe we can come up with another arrangement tomorrow."

"Control myself?" She gasped in disbelief. "Don't flatter yourself, mister. Kenny-Wayne, his uncle, and you could be ax murderers for all I know! I don't even know what I was thinking when I picked you up, a gosh-darn hitchhiker!"

"I *wasn't* hitchhiking." He got in her face, brows rushing together, jaws clenched. "I was *walking* to town before you came along."

"A hitchhiker who was parading around practically naked the day before! A perverted, ax-wielding hitchhiker! Maybe that ax is hidden in your duffel bag! My god!"

"Get a damn grip," Isaiah said, clamping onto her shoulders and giving her a little shake. "*You* could be the ax murderer for all I know. But I'm dog-tired. I'd be willing to take my chances with Dahmer and Bundy right now."

A rumble of thunder and a clamoring downpour suddenly shook the inn's roof. A piercing beep drew their attention to the severe-thunderstorm warning scrolling across the bottom of the television screen.

Ebony threw her hands up in supplication. "Will this nightmare never end?"

Isaiah turned toward the desk clerk. "Guess we'd better get directions to Uncle Waymon's house, huh?"

CHAPTER 7

Kenny-Wayne's pad was not the spacious apartment Ebony had envisioned, but a tiny room—a seventies psychedelic nightmare with loud neon colors and roaring animal prints dueling for dominance. A dusty stereo system with an eight-track tape deck, turntable, and towers of vinyl LPs cluttered most of the space not occupied by the waterbed. The place had been decorated with a soul brother in mind, circa 1974. Sun-faded Kool and the Gang, Lola Falana, Dr. J, and big-fisted Black Power posters were tacked to the walls. A purple fishnet drooped from the ceiling. Four tired beanbag chairs sagged in one corner. The room reeked of rancid athletic sneakers and stale green-apple incense. Dirty laundry spilled from beneath the waterbed.

Isaiah dropped their bags on the grimy shag-carpeted floor. "Well, I guess beggars can't be choosers, right?"

"Ewww." Ebony crinkled her nose. Using an ink pen from her fanny pack, she lifted a pair of Fruit of the Looms off the bed as if they were toxic waste and tossed them on a stack of *Bodacious Black Booty* magazines in a corner.

"It's a little ripe in here." Isaiah chuckled and brushed a finger under his nose. "But I've seen and smelled worse. One hovel in San Juan comes to mind."

"This place is disgusting."

"Hey, you don't want to insult our hosts." Isaiah cracked a window. "How's that? This is the best I can do without letting too much rain inside."

Moist cool air squeezed through. Ebony removed a can of antiperspirant from her overnight bag. "Maybe the baby powder scent can mask the smell of funky feet." She coughed as a misty cloud formed. "That bed looks like it has fifty kinds of cooties in it."

"Cooties?" Isaiah shook his head. "I haven't heard that one since third grade."

Ebony sprayed in the bed's direction. "What do you think the chances are of getting a clean set of sheets?"

"Judging from the piles of dirty clothes all over the place, I'd say slim to none." Isaiah pointed to a door. He walked over and opened it. "A john. If the toilet's operable, we're in business." He stepped inside, flushed, and stepped back into the room. "No flood. So far so good."

Ebony proceeded to dress one of the bed pillows in the brand-new Howard University sweatshirt that her sister Kenya had mailed to her a couple of weeks ago.

Isaiah stared in disbelief. "What the hell are you doing now?"

"You don't think I'm actually going to put my face on that pillow, do you? This makes a sturdy barrier." Ebony tucked the pillow inside the shirt and tied its gray sleeves together.

"Wuss."

"If the idea of wallowing in Kenny-Wayne's drool, dandruff, and Scary Curl juice doesn't turn you off, you're braver than I am."

Isaiah watched her remove her fanny pack. "What's in that thing anyway? Looks like you don't leave home without it."

Ebony placed the fanny pack on the milk-crate nightstand next to the waterbed. "My cell phone, pager, and a few other necessities. I have to be able to reach my family at all times."

"Oh, yeah? And why is that?" He appeared genuinely interested in her reply. "Is somebody seriously ill?"

Yolanda's cracks about Ebony's obsessive fretting over the

rest of the MacKenzies rang in her ears so she kept her response brief. "No, nobody's seriously ill. How much do I owe you for the bill?"

"That's okay. I got it covered tonight."

"No, I insist. I pay my own way—"

"Fine." As he raised one hand, she heard the sharp intake of breath, a sure sign of his waning patience.

When he revealed what he had slipped in Kenny-Wayne's pocket, she whipped out the tiny calculator tucked in a pocket of her garment bag. "Let's see." She punched the buttons, then put the calculator aside to rummage inside another pocket where she kept several rolls of quarters.

"What did you do? Rob a gumball machine?" He chuckled.

She split one roll and began counting the coins one by one.

"Crack a parking meter?" He continued with his teasing. "Stick up the tooth fairy? Look, just forget it. I don't like being weighed down by a lot of change, anyway."

Disregarding his request, she stuffed the rolls of quarters in a side pocket of his duffel bag, then removed a small leather-bound book from her overnight bag.

"What's that?"

"My planner," she said testily, removing red and pink felt-tip pens from her bag. "What's with all the questions? Don't you have some unpacking to do?" She opened the planner and began jotting down notes.

Isaiah moved closer, pretending to make his way toward one of his bags on the floor. Instead he sneaked a peek over her shoulder. "Damn! That thing looks like a flight-pattern chart, complete with color coding, graphs, and three-minute increments!"

She corrected him. "It's *ten*-minute increments." Then glared at him from over her shoulder for invading her personal space. "Do you mind?"

He didn't budge. "What? No Palm Pilot? No Blackberry? We're in a new millennium, you know."

"But manual is much more reliable. No techno glitches to contend with here."

"Bet you got a list for everything. It figures. I pegged you for the psychotically anal-retentive type. It's written all over you and that planner of yours."

"And I pegged you for a flaky fly-by-the-seat-of-your-pants type, Mr. No Reservations."

"Lot of good making reservations did you."

"When was the last time you made a list for anything? The one you left for Santa when you were six doesn't count."

"What were you just jotting down there?" Isaiah craned his neck to peer at her last entries.

Ebony finally shoved him away with one hand. "None of your business."

"What did you do? Scribble down 'Pick up Isaiah,' 'Give Isaiah a ride,' 'Stop at the Pac 'N' Snac' just so you could cross them off your list?"

That accusation struck too close for comfort. She wasn't guilty this time, but she had added unscheduled-but-completed tasks to her "to do" list in the past. Scratching off items was one of the few things that gave her a feeling of satisfaction and accomplishment. A pretty pitiful thing to 'fess up to. "Are you done with your interrogation? If not, you can stand there and quiz yourself until you're blue in the face. I'm getting ready for bed. I'm pooped."

Ebony gathered up her favorite Mickey Mouse–print cotton pajamas and marched toward the bathroom. When her foot caught on one of Isaiah's bags, she stumbled.

"Careful!" He lurched toward her.

"I'm fine." She braced herself against a stereo speaker.

"I know *you* are." With a grimace he scooped up the leather pouch on the floor and inspected its contents. "My camera equipment is in here. It's very expensive, so watch where you're going."

"Keep your junk out of my way," Ebony retorted before slipping inside the tiny bathroom.

A few minutes later she returned to find Isaiah on his knees, leaning over his duffel bag on the floor, so unzipped and unbuttoned, he might as well have been naked. His shirt parted, revealing a diamond-pattern dusting of hair. It fanned over those sculpted pecs and narrowed to a dark line that disappeared inside his pants. His belt buckle dangled and clinked, drawing attention to his fly. *Lordy, the man is fiiiine!* Her mouth went dry immediately. "The bathroom is all yours to change." She cleared her throat when her voice came out in a rusty little croak.

"Change? Change into what?"

"Your jammies, of course."

"I don't wear *jammies*."

"Shame on me. I know real men don't wear jammies. Correction. Pajamas."

"I don't wear pajamas, either."

"What do you sleep in, then? Long johns?"

"In this heat? Are you crazy?"

"Boxer shorts?" An odd mix of edginess and excitement heightened with Ebony's curiosity.

"Nope."

"Briefs?"

"Guess again."

"The altogether?"

"Yup. Commando, baby. Or as down-home folks say, 'buck nekkid as a jaybird,' " he added with an exaggerated cornpone drawl.

She instantly went slack-jawed. "If you think you're sleeping naked, you're out of your ever-lovin' mind."

"The dragon's got to be unleashed at night." Isaiah reclined on the waterbed, propping himself up on one elbow. "It's got to breathe. No confinements."

Ebony burst out laughing. "You're kidding, right? The dragon? And I thought I'd already heard every stupid macho euphemism in the book for that part of the male anatomy." She wiped her eyes, as she struggled to get her laughter under control. "Well, tonight the dragon stays under wraps or on lockdown, as the homeboys would say. End of discussion."

"Okay, check this," Isaiah said, pushing to his feet. Once again, her eyes were drawn to the broad expanse of his chest and the delicious ripple of his abs. Ebony swallowed. No way was it a smart idea to have all that naked hunkiness anywhere within reach. "I'm not sleeping in my slacks or jeans. Way too uncomfortable. Besides my underwear, those are all the bottoms I packed. I'm a briefs, not a boxers sort of dude, but think of them as Speedos. I'm sure your innocent eyes have seen plenty of those around the swimming pool."

She had, but they were usually on bodies unworthy of them. She glanced down at her pajamas and got an idea. "You can borrow my pajama bottoms. They're big and extra roomy. It's the perfect compromise." The pajama top which hit the middle of her thighs would pass as decent coverage.

Isaiah drew in his thick brows. "I am *not* sleeping in anything with Mickey Mouse on it."

"I won't tell," Ebony persisted, batting her lashes in a flirtatious manner she had yet to perfect. She didn't do cute-and-coy very well. "*Please*. Pretty, pretty please."

Isaiah frowned and reached for her face. "Hold still."

"What for?" Ebony asked, pulling away in a panic. Heaven help her. Would her body betray her if he touched her right now?

"I think you've got something in your eye."

Pouting, Ebony swatted his outstretched hands away.

"Aw, hell," he groaned in surrender. "All right. Hand them over."

Ebony chewed her lip and reached under her shirt, well aware that removing garments with his eyes intently focused on her would have a provocative edge. She fumbled to untie the drawstring, tugged it loose until she heard the soft swish of cotton slipping to her ankles. She stepped away from them, feeling light-headed as his leisurely gaze swept from her ankles to her thighs. She shifted nervously under his scrutiny as her toes scrunched the carpet.

An appreciative gleam danced in his eyes. Had she imagined it? She had stork legs. Everyone in her ninth-grade gym class had told her so. She handed the pants to him. Their gazes held for the longest minute. The temperature in the room soared. A corner of his mouth kicked up with a suggestive smile. He took a step closer. Her breath caught and she thought she heard her blood pounding through her veins and pooling to her tingling pelvis. She moistened her lips as if prepping for a kiss. *Bad idea.* Who was this man? More importantly, who was she? She didn't recognize these feelings or her racy thoughts. She tore her gaze away and turned, determined to put as much distance between them as the cramped room would allow. She got busy arranging the zebra-print covers and forced herself to hum a happy little ditty the whole time for a distraction. She climbed into bed, sank back on her sweatshirt-swaddled pillow, then closed her eyes, acutely aware that Isaiah's gaze lingered on her for the longest minute. Far from modest, he didn't bother to slip inside the bathroom to change. The rustling of fabric signaled when he began removing his clothes. Aware of the exact moment he was completely naked, Ebony's skin prickled with pleasure. The temptation to peek overwhelmed her, but could she handle what she saw? Could she risk him catching her?

Isaiah finally said, "I look like a damn fool."

Ebony cautiously cracked open one eye then the other. "You have them on?"

"Yeah, but not for long."

She sat up to inspect them but caught him untying the drawstring. "Don't! Remember, you promised."

Pants that were so long and roomy on Ebony resembled clamdiggers on Isaiah.

"Too short, too tight." His tone was firm. "They're coming off. Now."

"Can't you adjust them a little? You know, shift things around down there a bit." Desperation laced her suggestion.

"Wait. These things have creases in them." He looked up at Ebony. "You actually iron your pajamas?"

"So, what of it?" She hitched her chin. "They're nicer that way."

"I'll bet you iron your panties, too." Isaiah shook his head in disgust then began fiddling with the drawstring and yanked at the waistband. "What the hell . . . ?" He sniffed his hands. "Flowers?"

"My fabric softener."

"Not only am I wearing starched-to-hell Mickey Mouse high-waters, but I've got to smell April-fresh, too," Isaiah snorted in disbelief. "I can't believe I let you talk me into this."

Ebony tried to hold back an impish giggle, but failed. "It could've been worse. I left the Minnie Mouse pair at home."

"If you ever repeat any of this..." he grumbled as he tugged at the sheet and slid a long leg between it and the water mattress.

Ebony sprang off the bed so fast she could've started a tidal wave. "What are you doing?" she squawked.

Isaiah stared as if she were crazy. "I'm getting in bed."

"You can't sleep here! I thought you were going to sleep on the floor!"

"Oh, no you didn't." Amusement flickered in his eyes though his tone held no humor. "And I don't want to hear that yang about what real gentlemen do 'cause I ain't trying to hear it."

"I just assumed when I let you talk me into sharing the room, it was understood that you didn't mean sharing the *same* bed."

"I'm not sleeping on that nasty floor. Look at it."

"I thought you said you'd seen worse in San Juan."

"Okay, hold up. Check this out." Isaiah raked a hand through his short fade haircut. "We can do the head-to-toe thing if that makes you feel better."

It didn't. Ebony considered claiming the floor until a crispy critter with too many legs and antennae skittered across the carpeting.

"I'm not going to touch you," Isaiah promised.

Ebony looked at Isaiah, at the bed, then back at Isaiah. On a visceral level she believed him, but being conscious with a stranger and being asleep with one were two totally different things.

But on the other hand, if he'd had sinister intentions, surely he would've tried something long before now, she reasoned. Her gut instincts about people were usually dead-on. But then she had to admit she was wildly attracted to this man and had been operating on a gut feeling that he was harmless ever since she picked him up off the highway. She did not sense danger.

But could the fact that she clearly lusted for him skew her radar for wackos? While desperate for a comfortable place to sleep, she was nobody's fool. She considered her sleeping options then zeroed in on the giant beanbag chairs. "I'll just line these up and sleep on them." She dragged them away from the wall and arranged them like train cars then tugged the zebra-print flat sheet off the bed. Kneeling, she punched a trench in sagging vinyl that resembled giant deflated beach balls. "I'll be fine," she said unconvincingly, sinking on top of the beanbags and stretching her legs. "Just make sure you stay in that bed." Ebony cut him a warning glare. "I'm a very light sleeper, you know. In case you get any funny ideas, I have two words for you: 'pepper spray.' "

Isaiah made a sour face then watched her squirm in a futile attempt to get comfortable. After a few minutes he snatched up his pillow and hovered over her.

"So you're not even going to bother waiting for me to fall asleep?" She peered over the sheet at timberlike legs with smiling Mickeys all over them. "You planning to smother me now?"

"Woman, I repeat, I'm not going to touch you, but hey, you have a right to be antsy. We did just meet yesterday. But remember, I don't know you either—a man can be equally vulnerable in his sleep."

"I suppose . . ." She considered his point.

"And you've got weapons and you're packing enough gadgets to do MacGyver proud."

"Well, what are you doing over here then?"

"Get in the bed. I'll sleep on the beanbags."

Ebony hesitated.

"Look, I said I wasn't going to touch you, but I'll break my word if you don't cooperate. Don't make me yank you up, because I guarantee you won't enjoy it." He looked annoyed.

"But I thought—" His warning expression cut her short. "Well, if you insist." Ebony got up, plopped her pillow on the bed, then scooted so far to the opposite side that one false move during the night would mean hitting the floor—face first. She reached toward the milk-crate nightstand, but thought twice about switching off the Colt .45 shade lamp. She palmed her pepper spray in one hand. Sleeping with the Swiss Army knife in a waterbed was pushing her luck. "Do you mind if we keep the light on?"

"No. Whatever makes you feel most comfortable."

She heard the screech of vinyl and the crunch of beanbag innards as Isaiah settled in. She appreciated the unexpected yet chivalrous gesture.

A few minutes later he surprised her again by breaking the quiet. "Good night, Ebony MacKenzie."

" 'Night, Mickey," she replied as a small smile formed on her lips.

The soft patter of rain on the roof and the gentle sloshing of the waterbed were soothing as they lulled her to sleep.

CHAPTER 8

The next morning Isaiah awoke with a stiff back and a slight crick in his neck. Beanbags had to rank somewhere between a bed of nails and hot coals when it came to comfort. He sat erect and stretched, taking in his surroundings.

Drenched in sunlight their accommodations looked even tackier than they had the night before. He watched Ebony sleep, her face in angelic repose, her slender body sprawled across the waterbed. She'd kicked the covers to a heap at the edge of the bed, giving him a spectacular view of her silky legs. When she shifted, the pajama shirt skittered upward and a hint of her panties was revealed. A slip of sexy red lace. Color him about a dozen shades of surprised. Pleasantly surprised. Victoria wasn't the only one with a secret. He took Ebony for the big body-snatching-bloomers type. But these weren't your granny's panties. No way. Nohow. These were hot, hot, hot and his jimmy immediately responded. Mickey saluted *again*. He'd experienced hair-trigger erections since Ebony dropped her pajama pants the night before. She had awesome legs. Slim yet shapely and strong. Now here they were, sprawled apart before him in invitation. But instead of getting his rocks off gawking at her, he felt a need to protect her vulnerable state from his view. He got up and began to untangle the sheet to cover her up. The move baffled him. After all, he deserved a little reward for torturing his back on those beanbags last night. With one knee resting against the edge of the waterbed, he leaned to spread the sheet to a corner on the opposite side. Ebony's hand slid near his hip, mere millimeters from where Mickey Mouse saluted. She drove him crazy. Last night she obviously didn't have a clue how desirable she looked. He'd noticed her self-consciousness. Those legs of hers went on forever and he couldn't help imagining what it would feel like to have them wrapped around him. Every pleasure nerve in his body seemed to stand on end, do a little jig, and scream: *Make that move! Jump those bones!* But he couldn't let his thoughts linger there. Bad move. Bad, bad move, he reminded himself as he tugged at the sheet, trying not to wake her. He smiled. She'd have two cows if she knew she'd ventured so dangerously close to the dragon's fire. *The dragon.* His friend Butta Bean would flog him to death with his own belt collection if he got wind of that one. Isaiah chuckled lightly, recalling the look on Ebony's face when the cheese-ball term tumbled from his lips last night. He'd only used it to evoke her knee-jerk reaction. Unbeknownst to her, he'd never had any intention of sleeping naked last night. And he had only been kidding about them sharing the bed. However, he had to admit seeing her reaction had been worth it.

He tucked in the last corner of the sheet when Ebony murmured something in a sleep-husky voice. Her lashes fluttered just before she bolted upright with wild rounded eyes. "What are you doing?" she shrieked, clutching the zebra-print sheets to her breasts as if he had X-ray vision, and aiming her can of pepper spray at him.

"Whoa . . . Don't shoot!" He lifted his hands in surrender.

"What are you doing?" she repeated, still poised to spray.

"What am *I* doing?" he echoed, pointing to her empty hand. "You almost copped a feel in your sleep, lady. You were sleeping, weren't you?"

Ebony screeched in anger. "Darn right I was asleep!"

"So *you* say."

"If I . . . I touched you, I can assure you it was . . . unintentional," she sputtered, obviously mortified. "And why is your knucklehead over here anyway? You're supposed to be on the beanbags!"

"I was over there, but I came over here to put the covers back on you. You kicked them off. What were you dreaming about anyway? Tae Bo class?"

"Ha, ha. You're so funny." Ebony, whose fear had obviously dissolved, put the pepper spray on the milk crate, lunged and thwacked him with her pillow.

Isaiah stared at her in disbelief. Then he grabbed his pillow and thwacked her right back.

Ebony gasped as if she couldn't believe he had dared to defend himself. Her eyes narrowed in determination and then it was on. For serious-minded adults, they were soon whooping it up like a couple of kids. The pillow fight went on much too long until they both collapsed on the bed in a laughing heap. Ebony's top had inched up, generously exposing her curvaceous brown thighs. When the laughter tapered off, the vibe between them was charged with enough voltage to fry them both alive. Ridges from the wristband of the sweatshirt she'd wrapped around her pillow creased one side of her face. Her lips beckoned, puffy and moist. Eyes sultry and wild with what looked a lot like desire taunted him. Her braids stuck out every which way. But damn! She looked sexy as hell! Slowly they inched closer. He leaned in, desperately aching to taste her lips, until a determined person pounded on the door. They jerked apart.

"Hey, you two! Up and at 'em!" Kenny-Wayne shouted from the other side.

A couple of buttons on Ebony's pajama top had worked themselves free. She self-consciously clutched it closed with one hand while the other fussed over her braids.

The pounding continued.

"Yeah, man, what's up?" Isaiah finally responded.

"Uncle Waymon doesn't feel right about leaving you two

here all alone while we're at work. We both get off at four. You can come back around four-fifteen."

"Like they actually own something we want to steal," Isaiah grumbled to Ebony before shouting his reply to Kenny-Wayne. "Can you give us an hour to shower and get ourselves together?"

"We're already late. You've got twenty minutes."

"Uncle Waymon doesn't play, does he?" Isaiah said lightly, trying to ease her obvious awkwardness.

"It's just as well. The paintball tournament registration starts in an hour." Fun-pillow-fighting-dimpled-cheeked Ebony vanished in a heartbeat. Poof! Zip! Outta there! Evil Ebony returned—all prickly and tight-assed. "That *is* what we're both here for, remember?"

Her chilly tone hit him like a bucket of reality on ice, so he snapped back, "How could I possibly forget?"

Ebony averted her gaze then quickly scooped up her garment and overnight bags. "Mind if I go first?"

Isaiah watched her stumble to the bathroom. "No. You go right ahead."

On a muddy Grundie field surrounded by a fringe of forest, the paintballs were flying. Kinetic pieces of rainbow zigzagged and crisscrossed like M&Ms in a corn popper. Bone-tired, Ebony crouched between tangles of bramble and bush to catch her breath. "How hard could an adult version of Capture the Flag be?" The words rose in her throat mockingly like a bad case of indigestion. A paintball zinged by, barely missing her head. A sudden shift to avoid the speeding projectile caused her Reeboks to slip. As she fell backward, her butt squished into pasty earth. "Darn it!" she grumbled out loud, possibly alerting the enemy of her exact location, but she didn't give a hoot. She wasn't cut out for this mock-combat crap. Nor did she realize how seriously the other players would take their roles as "soldiers." She peeked through a bush to see folks snaking on their bellies or somersaulting on the ground to avoid paintball fire. Others brashly charged up the middle of the field like Rambos on speed. The object of the game had sounded simple enough at that morning's orientation. Capture the opposing team's flag, which hung on a pole in a makeshift fort at one end of the field. Prevent the enemy from laying their grubby hands on your flag, housed in a fort at the other end of the field. And last, but not least, avoid getting hit by a paintball in the process. A spot of paint anywhere on a player's body or rifle meant elimination from the round. Dodging the paintballs, which reminded Ebony of bath beads only not nearly as fragrant, had proven easier said than done. When her protective helmet wasn't restricting her peripheral vision, her goggles were fogging up. When her goggles weren't fogging up, her air-powered rifle was jamming.

Ebony scrambled to her feet, feeling the clammy coolness of the brown pancake clinging to the seat of her camouflage-print jumpsuit. She wanted to hoist her rifle overhead in surrender and wait for Renfro from the safety of the sidelines. But she couldn't stand the idea of letting Renfro see her, one of only a handful of women participating in the tournament, scurry away like some yellow-bellied, muddy-butted wimp. And Isaiah, he'd have a field day if she threw in the towel so quickly. Darn him! She'd been much too flustered by what almost happened between them that morning. She had craved a taste of him in the worst way. What would've been a major dumb move weighed heavily on her mind. As a result, she'd made at least half a dozen tactical errors that cost her team, the Red Squad, valuable yardage in its push toward enemy territory. While Isaiah, a member of the opposing Blue Squad, was well on his way to impressing the heck out of his team general, who happened to be none other than Reuben Renfro himself.

Ebony had studied photographs of the Ice Cream King during her research, but this was her first time seeing him in person. She managed to get close enough to note that he was a short, plump man with tawny brown skin, bow legs, and black bristle-cut hair. Newspaper clippings put his age in the mid-sixties, but he could easily pass for a decade younger. She never got within chatting distance of Renfro before the game started, but she did manage to strike up a quick conversation with Claudio, Renfro's limo driver. She considered that little maneuver a coup, but she still couldn't believe Isaiah's luck. Not only had he been chosen to participate in this particular paintball battle by special lottery, but when the group split in half to form the Red and Blue Squads, he made Renfro's team. Well, she'd show him. Down, but far from out. A rush of much-needed adrenaline surged through her bloodstream. She reached toward her sling vest to reload her air rifle but found her paintball supply dangerously low. She was under heavy fire again. The throck of CO_2 guns filled the air, followed by the splat of paintballs exploding on impact. The landscape looked like a page from a nursery-school coloring book with its kaleidoscope of greens, blues, reds, and yellows spilling outside the lines. Biodegradable paint splattered the ground, trees, tires, overturned paddleboats, sand bags, and other field props positioned to provide hiding nooks and crannies. Ebony managed to survive the shower of fire unmarked. She started for a neutral ammo reloading station when a dreaded throck rang in her ears. A stinging sensation at the small of her back followed it. "Ouch!" she howled as she reached around to rub the area. Warm, goopy green paint smeared her fingers.

"Gotcha!" roared Rocco Romalotti from the Blue Squad. During orientation the no-neck ex-marine had gotten on Ebony's last nerve with his offensive come-ons and wisecracks. The jackass actually had thought he could wheedle her phone number out of her. She'd crunch on broken glass before she'd hook up with a muscle-head like Rocco and she had told him so. Rocco hadn't taken her smart-mouth snub kindly. But she'd done a pretty good job of handling the situation without Isaiah, who had conveniently distanced himself after they had arrived at the playing field. But now here was Rocco, hellbent on avenging his bruised ego, leveling the barrel of his air rifle at her.

"I'm hit." Ebony raised her rifle overhead in surrender and prepared to walk off the field as game rules dictated. "I'm out."

Rocco squeezed the trigger, pelting her with a series of

paintballs, each stinging more than the one before. Throck. Throck. Throck. Splat. Splat. Splat.

"I said I'm out!" Ebony shrieked as her skin burned with enough pain to make her curse. "You're supposed to cease fire, you asshole!"

"Oh, am I, Sweet Cheeks? I guess I skipped over that part in the rule book." Rocco's lips formed a sadistic grin as he prepared to shoot her some more, until someone came up from behind and tapped him on the shoulder. "What the hell . . . ?" When Rocco turned around, a fist coldcocked him on the chin. He flew backward, landing spread-eagled in the mud as his attacker proceeded to squeeze off a round of paintballs at point-blank range. "Hey! You're picking off your team member!" Rocco shouted, tugging at his blue ID armband and deflecting paintballs hitting his gut. "See, I'm on the Blue Squad like you!"

Goggles and a bandanna tied bandit-style obscured the mystery man's identity. "Oh, really?" he replied glibly as he proceeded to turn Rocco into a 3-D version of a Dali painting. "I guess I didn't read that part in the rule book."

Ebony instantly recognized the voice. A referee darted over to order the three of them off the field. Ebony marched off in a daze, unsure of what had just happened. Isaiah had actually turned on one of his team members and jeopardized his good favor with Renfro to come to her rescue *again*.

As Isaiah walked toward the bleachers Ebony scampered around his heels like a puppy angling for a treat. "Thanks for helping me out back there," she said in a winded and overly excited voice.

"Don't sweat it." Isaiah sat on the bench and removed his goggles and bandanna before tipping a water bottle toward his lips for a quick drink. "Romalotti was bad news." He wiped his mouth with the back of his hand. "I heard how he was hassling you at orientation. I started to knuckle up on his ass then, but you seemed to be holding your own so I hung back."

"And here I was thinking you only had eyes for Renfro once we reached the paintball field." Ebony plopped down next to him, loosening the laces on her mud-caked Reeboks and the pink, sweat-drenched bandanna around her neck.

"A lot of macho crazies are out here today." Isaiah studied the battle action on the field. "Good thing you wore that pink bandanna or it would've been damn near impossible to recognize you in that cloud of camouflage."

"This makes the second time you've got my butt out of a scrape," Ebony said.

Isaiah considered rubbing it in. Nothing like having the competition beholden to you. Instead he replied, "We're square."

Ebony knitted her brows. "Square?"

"Yeah. You gave me a lift yesterday and I leveled Rocco for you today."

Ebony fidgeted uncomfortably and shifted the conversation back to paintball as she rubbed her thighs. "My skin is still stinging from those hits I took. Who would've thought those little bath-bead-looking things could do so much damage. They actually hurt."

"Paintballs fired from the high-pressured air rifles like the ones we were using travel at about three hundred feet per second," Isaiah explained. "And some of those guys are sadistic sickos. They actually juice up their air rifles so the paintballs hit harder."

"Rocco strikes me as the type of lowlife slime who would get his jollies from that sort of dirty trick," Ebony grumbled. "Where did he disappear to anyway?"

"One of the ammo tents. He's not too happy about getting disqualified. Truth be told, neither am I."

"I'm sorry," she said softly, looking at him with pretty brown eyes that made him want to protect her from everything.

Oh, no. Heeeellll, no! He refused to get all soft and gooey now. "You *should* be sorry," he said with a hard note of reproach. Just like that, he'd gone Jekyll and Hyde. But he had to. He wasn't about to go out like a sucker. Ebony still had that take-no-prisoners mind-set while he'd become overly preoccupied making sure she didn't get hurt. Not only had he blown another prime opportunity to get to Renfro, but he'd turned on a team member. "If you're going to play the damsel in distress, don't expect me to keep watching your back. I've got a job to do."

"And so do I!" She surged to her feet with fire in her eyes. "I'm not traipsing around Podunkville for my health, you know."

Isaiah did not budge, but stayed as cool as the refreshing water in his bottle. He helped himself to another big gulp. "I'm just saying you should steer clear of the big boys and try to stay out of trouble."

"Why, you chauvinistic Neanderthal knucklehead!" Ebony promptly upbraided him, eyes still blazing. "Why don't you try hitchhiking back to Kenny-Wayne's, then!"

Isaiah reveled in her anger, letting it fuel his own and burn away the protective feelings for her that began to surface. It made him feel better about his obvious lack of concentration where Renfro was concerned. "My transportation is no longer your responsibility. I'll get a ride from one of the fellas here and I'm taking Kenny-Wayne's uncle up on his offer to rent me his truck."

"Well, bully for you! I saw that raggedy truck. It's a foot-propelled Flintstones-mobile." She turned on her heel to leave, then pivoted. "I hope you step on a rusty old nail." She turned and marched off, putting a few yards between them, then whirled around again to shout, "And I hope you forgot to update your tetanus!"

Isaiah couldn't help but chuckle as he watched her stomp off to the opposite side of the playing field. He drained the rest of the water, thinking he'd done a pretty good job of sealing the hairline crack in his resolve.

CHAPTER 9

The world seemed to whirl around Ebony in a big crimson blur. She couldn't believe Isaiah had tossed her gratitude back in her face. She plunked herself on the bleachers at the opposite end of the playing field and glowered at him when she should've been watching for Renfro. If looks could kill, Isaiah Malone would've been zapped into a pile of smoking ash right then. Her beeping pager interrupted her vengeful thoughts. The pager's face displayed the MacKenzie code for family emergency. A wave of apprehension rolled over her. She reached for her cell phone out of habit, then cursed when she remembered that while her pager service was national, she'd opted for that superdiscount-rate cellular service that didn't extend far beyond Cincinnati city limits. Dumb penny-pitching move. She hadn't schmoozed enough to feel comfortable borrowing one from a stranger and she wasn't about to ask Isaiah for anything. She'd have to find a pay phone. She'd seen one in downtown Grundie, but maybe she'd get lucky and spot one closer. She took off toward her car, leaving Renfro to Isaiah.

At the Pac 'N' Snac Ebony phoned home. "What's going on?" she asked anxiously, sandwiching the pay-phone receiver between her head and shoulder.

"Althea botched an entire load of laundry," Jolene cried. "Several of my favorite pieces were shrunk!"

Ebony heard what sounded like a tug-of-war over the phone before the plunk of their receiver falling to the ground, then Granny Mac was on the line.

"It was an accident, a mistake, Ebony. I swear. I was just trying to help out with the chores while you're away—"

"If it was an accident, why were *my* clothes the only ones reduced to munchkin size?" Jolene commandeered the phone again.

This was the family emergency? Ebony felt the pressure of a headache mounting, as she dragged a hand down her face and slouched against the pay phone. She wanted to kick herself for leaving the playing field to arbitrate yet another silly spat between them.

"Look you two, I've got to go."

"But—" Jolene protested.

"Work it out," Ebony said firmly before ending the call. She replaced the receiver unsure whether she'd return home to find two mortally wounded bodies, but she couldn't worry about that now. She returned to the field then realized in panic that the day's paintball match had ended. Players still milled about, but Renfro and Isaiah were missing. She had to keep her wits about her and figure out where Renfro would go next. Her first hunch was to check his cabin.

Renfro's rented lodge in the woods sat just outside Grundie. Surrounded by a breathtaking realm of greens and wild flowers, the multilevel structure with an immense wraparound deck had little in common with the quaint rustic cottages and hemlock cabins Ebony had passed en route. Wedged between a thicket of trees and an enormous cloud of a shrub, the Escort was positioned several yards away. The inconspicuous parking place provided a clear view of the cabin. As Ebony reached for the binoculars on the passenger seat, the realization that she'd been reduced to celebrity-hunting tabloid tactics hit hard. She was no better than the sleazoid stalkarazzi, hiding in bushes and perched in trees, poised to raid someone's privacy.

She pitched the binoculars back on the seat. Not one of her finer journalistic moments.

Disgust swelled in her chest. She'd sold out. Her ethics were not only compromised, they'd been steamrolled. But this wasn't about winning a Pulitzer Prize or any other coveted journalist-of-the-year accolades. Financial stability for her family was her goal. She would get busy repairing whatever damage sullied her journalistic integrity later. Integrity would not pull her family out of its financial black hole. That weighed on her mind, as she anxiously fingered the frayed surface of the macramé bracelet encircling her right wrist. Guilt climbed from the pit of her darkest memory when she thought of her dad. She swallowed the knot in her throat, blinked away the sting of unshed tears, and scooped up the binoculars again. She aimed them at Renfro's stretch limousine parked in front of the lodge until movement at the largest front window caught her attention. One of Renfro's flunkies closed the curtains, but not before she got a glimpse of Renfro in the background. Confirmed. He was inside. Now what?

Ebony slumped behind the steering wheel. Knocking on the door to introduce herself as a reporter was out of the question. Renfro's minions would slam the door in her face. Pretending to be the Avon lady or a Jehovah's Witness probably wouldn't go over much better. She stepped out of the car with her binoculars in hand and surveyed the cabin. A tornado of wild ideas swirled around in her head before she rationalized them all away. Playing the stranded or lost motorist had potential, but she squelched that idea, as well. Ambushing Renfro at his lodge had been a sound plan in theory, but now that she was actually here, she couldn't think of a foolproof way to wrangle an invitation inside. She would have to finagle a meeting in a less private, more social setting. The paintball tournament was supposed to have provided the perfect opportunity to meet Renfro, but he'd been so focused on that stupid game, he was hardly in a commingling frame of mind.

A Grundie restaurant or bar was her best bet. After a few drinks and a good meal maybe he'd be in a meeting-and-greeting mood. But what were the chances he'd venture out to the Pac 'N' Snac, Pearlie Mae's Diner, or Big Bob's Buffalo Wings and Things that evening? That lodge looked as if it were stocked with all the amenities anybody could want. Probably even came with its own five-star chef, Ebony thought, groaning in frustration. She also couldn't dismiss the possibility that Renfro might go out so she would have to wait—at least until a little past suppertime.

Ebony removed the tattered green blanket she kept in her trunk and spread it over the short damp grass near the front of the car. She sat, relaxing against the grill, until she heard footsteps tramping through the weeds edging the woods. She tensed as irrational memories of every woods-stalking serial-killer and slasher movie she'd ever seen rushed to mind. She clenched her pepper spray in one hand. In the other she positioned her keys with the sharp point of one key poking between two fingers as she had seen demonstrated in a self-defense course. Poised to gouge and spray at the same time, Ebony shot to her feet in a defensive, wide-footed stance. She tried to shout for the interloper to announce himself, but fear clogged her throat like cotton. The pace of footsteps through vegetation increased with the thumpity-thump of her heart. *Fight or flight?* Recalling that she'd been the lamest student in that self-defense course, she made a break for the car door. As she groped for the keyhole, an arm coiled around her shoulder. Ebony jabbed her attacker in the ribs with a force that surprised her. Something part-English, part-grunt spewed from his lips. She managed to scramble away just enough to launch a mean roundhouse kick when a strong hand grabbed her by the calf.

"Isaiah!" She wobbled on one leg. "You scared the living daylights out of me!" she panted, practically hyperventilating. She tugged her leg away. "You idiot! I almost pepper-sprayed you!"

"And made me a soprano for life." Isaiah heaved and coughed, leaning over to brace his arms against the hood of her car.

"Why didn't you say something?"

"You didn't give me a chance." He grimaced, rubbing his ribs. "Shit! That's some jab you've got there."

"Sorry," she said reluctantly, still jittery from the adrenaline rush. "I guess I don't have to ask what you're doing here."

"Staking out Renfro's place, what else? I lost him in the paintball crowd. Before I knew it his little army of yes-men had whisked him away."

"So how much did Claudio extort from you?" Ebony asked, thinking of the bucks she'd had to give the sleazoid limo driver in exchange for directions to Renfro's lodge.

"I didn't ask Claudio. This one only cost me a wink and a compliment. Phyllistine—you know, the pretty paintball registration coordinator—told me where he was staying."

"Of course you'd stoop to flirting." Ebony would've done it herself if she thought she was Phyllistine's type. "Well? So what are you waiting for? Go on, knock on Renfro's door." She gestured toward the lodge.

"Now, you know good and damn well that won't fly. I plan to tail Renfro if he goes out tonight. It's best to try to catch him on neutral territory then strike up a friendly conversation. Though I'm really not sure what I could say after what happened on the field today. He probably holds me personally responsible for the Blue Squad's embarrassing loss."

"Yeah, you and Rocco." Ebony couldn't resist rubbing it in, but Isaiah ignored her remark.

"Looks like you plan to hang around for a while, too," Isaiah said, as if he'd just noticed Ebony's setup. "I see you've made yourself at home." He crouched and tugged at a corner of her blanket. Good vantage point. Out of sight, but with the cabin in full view. Looks like we had the same idea."

"So where is Chitty Chitty Bang Bang anyway?" Ebony sat down and relaxed against the Escort, trying to ignore how well he filled the fly of his jumpsuit. "I take it you and Kenny-Wayne's uncle worked out some sort of deal."

"Wouldn't call it a deal exactly." Isaiah rose to his full height again. "More like highway robbery. He and his nephew have no scruples when it comes to gypping folks out of their hard-earned money."

"Let me guess. For triple the usual car-rental rates—"

"I get the use of his rusty, backfiring, cracked-windshield, busted-muffler-having piece of shit. Had to park it about a block down the road to get up here as discreetly as possible."

Ebony's stomach suddenly growled loudly enough to wake every woodland creature in the thicket of trees.

"Was that you?" Isaiah quirked a brow. "Or Bigfoot?"

"I didn't hear anything," she lied. Hunger on a stakeout could be construed as a failure to plan and anticipate. Definite weaknesses.

Isaiah's gaze swept over her. "I see you didn't change out of that muddy jumpsuit or grab a bite to eat."

"You didn't bother to change, either," she parried, gesturing toward his spotless jumpsuit. He'd obviously had little trouble maneuvering around that muddy field or dodging paintballs.

"A *true* stakeout pro wouldn't go out on an empty stomach. He or she would also know it's important to pack provisions because you never know how long these things might take."

"For your information I have stakeout provisions, thank-youverymuch." Ebony unzipped the fanny pack around her waist, removed a package of Tic Tac and rattled them at him. She shook several in her palm before tossing them inside her mouth. She would have offered to share, but he'd been so smug, rambling on about how prepared a true stakeout pro would be. She wanted to make him beg. Put him in his place. "I have these *and* a bottle of water in the car."

"On that hot new supermodel diet?" He grinned, crossing his arms across his broad chest.

"Yeah, breath mints, water, and all the greens I can eat. There's plenty of vegetation around here, as you can see."

"Enough to make one of those hoity-toity nouvelle cuisine salads."

"Yes. I saw a really nice patch of poisonous mushrooms near one of those elms over there." She smiled. "Help yourself."

Isaiah watched her shove more mints inside her mouth. She reluctantly surrendered to her good manners. "Would you like some?"

Isaiah raised a hand to refuse. "Maybe later, after I've eaten my sandwiches."

"Sandwiches?" Ebony gulped. "You have sandwiches on you?"

"Back in the truck." Smiling, Isaiah crouched until they were face to face again. The sun reflected off his glossy black moustache and goatee. He was more gorgeous than the law should allow. "I figured I might be stuck out here for a while so I stopped at the Pac 'N' Snac and picked up some sandwiches and stuff. Too bad you're filling up on those Tic Tacs. I happen to have enough for two."

Ebony's traitorous stomach grumbled again. The mints exacerbated her hunger pangs. "Yup, I'm stuffed."

"All right." Isaiah turned and trekked back in the direction from which he'd come. "See ya."

"Where are you going?"

"Back to the truck."

"Oh yeah, right," she said glumly, squelching the urge to invite him and his chow back.

A few minutes later Isaiah returned without an invitation. He wouldn't allow her to hog the best stakeout position in the vicinity, at least that's what he told himself.

"Forget something?" Ebony asked, doing a piss-poor job of hiding her preoccupation with the Pac 'N' Snac bag he carried.

"You happen to have the best vantage spot for Renfro's cabin. Mind if I join you?"

"It's a free country."

Isaiah sat down. When he stretched his legs the blanket suddenly seemed too small. He began removing items from his bag. The smell of fresh-baked bread, roast beef, and hickory-smoked ham wafted on a light breeze.

"Hmmm. Let's see here. Ham or roast beef?" Isaiah made quite a production out of contemplating his options.

"Is it that overprocessed cold-cuts stuff or the kind sliced right off the bone?" Ebony asked, practically licking her lips.

"Definitely the top-quality right-off-the-bone stuff." Isaiah removed a can of soda and several bags of chips. When he removed a jumbo honey bun glistening with icing, Ebony's eyes nearly popped out of their sockets.

She gazed longingly at the gooey pastry. Isaiah tore a plug out of the roast beef sandwich with his mouth.

"Does that ham sandwich have cheese on it by any chance?" Ebony tossed another Tic Tac inside her mouth.

"I believe it does. Let me check." He opened the wrapper and peeled back the top slice of bread to reveal the thick slice of red meat lightly dabbed with gourmet mustard.

"Yeah, it does. Cheddar, I believe."

"Cheddar, huh?" Ebony swallowed again, then jerked her gaze away. She snatched her binoculars off the blanket and aimed them at Renfro's lodge.

Isaiah studied the determined set of her jaw and those succulent lips. He'd had his fun taunting her. He knew she'd starve to death before asking him for a bite. Damn, she was stubborn. But a part of him had to admire her spirit. Grudgingly, he let her off the hook. "Yo, Ebony."

"What?" She wouldn't take her eyes off the lodge.

"Why don't you do me a favor and take that ham sandwich there off my hands? I hate to let perfectly good food go to waste. I've seen people starving up close and personal in Third World countries. It ain't pretty."

"No, thank you," she replied resolutely.

"C'mon, woman. Eat the damn sandwich. Besides, you owe me one for Rocco."

"But I thought you said we were even." Ebony lowered the binoculars and leveled her gaze at him.

"Forget that. As of now, we aren't. Now take the sandwich."

"Well, if you insist." She reached for the sandwich and polished it off so fast, it was a wonder she didn't chomp off a couple of fingers in the process.

"It is beautiful out here." Isaiah admired the blue cloudless sky and the thatch of lush trees. "The photos I could take . . . Almost makes me want to run back to the truck and fetch my camera." He smiled at her. "My Nikon would love you, too."

"In this old muddy thing?" Ebony muttered through a

mouthful of ham and cheese as she looked down at her soiled jumpsuit. "Over my dead body."

To Isaiah she looked perfectly adorable with her braids in a jumble, a slash of dirt across her cheek, and dabs of mustard at the corners of her lips.

Isaiah smiled. She was no prissy eater and her appetite rivaled his. He liked that. "Help yourself to that honey bun, too."

"You were just kidding about visiting Third World countries, right?" she asked, accepting the pastry and tucking into it.

"No, I wasn't."

"And what you said last night . . ." She smacked her lips and licked her fingers. "About the hovel in San Juan."

"That's true, too."

"Really?" She seemed intrigued. "Those hardly sound like hot vacation spots." She bit off a chunk of honey bun. "Business?"

"Sometimes, sometimes it's not. I like to travel."

"You must freelance for one of the those hard-hitting weekly news magazines."

He didn't answer as he fiddled with a chip he didn't want.

"Which is it? *Time*? *Newsweek*? *U.S. News and World Report*? All three?"

"Not exactly."

"What's that supposed to mean?"

"That I don't freelance for them." Isaiah wasn't sure why he was suddenly so guarded about his tabloid gigs. Ebony was in no position to judge. The *Butler County Bee* wasn't exactly known for its groundbreaking, kiss-ass journalism.

"Why so quiet all of a sudden?" Ebony, obviously unaware that she was treading on a sensitive subject, prattled on. "One would think you wrote for *Hustler*, *Penthouse*, or one of those supermarket tabloids."

Isaiah clamped his jaw to stifle a dig about the *Butler County Bee* when something caught his eye. A cat-sized critter ambled toward the blanket. There was no mistaking that bushy tail, glossy black fur, ratlike face, and white stripes streaking along its back. "Uh, Ebony." Isaiah reached out to her.

"What?" she asked, staring at his outstretched hands as if they were attached to the Boston Strangler.

He gestured for her to look over her shoulder. "We have company. Don't make any sudden moves right now," he whispered.

Ebony turned just enough to catch a glimpse in her peripheral vision.

"Take it easy. Real easy," Isaiah instructed her. "It only ejects that foul smell when disturbed or scared. So far so good."

Ebony carefully placed the pastry on the grass for the uninvited guest. "Do skunks like honey buns?"

"Shsssh." Isaiah watched the creature sniff Ebony's offering.

Ebony and Isaiah rose and backed away from the blanket with the light-footedness of cat burglars.

"So far so good," Isaiah added in a hushed tone as they eased toward the edge of the woods and watched the skunk abandon the honey bun to polish off Isaiah's roast beef sandwich instead. The sudden activity stirring outside Renfro's lodge drew their attention away from the skunk. They saw Claudio exit the lodge and slip behind the wheel of the limo to crank the engine. A moment later Renfro and one of his lackeys emerged and climbed inside the vehicle. The car rolled into reverse then glided forward toward the paved road.

Ebony lurched to make a break for the Escort. "He's leaving!" she screamed.

Isaiah latched onto her arm. "Hey, hold up!" he reminded her in a stage whisper. "Did you forget? You can't take off now!" He gestured toward the skunk.

"The heck I can't! Watch me! Renfro's getting away!" When Ebony tried to tug out of Isaiah's grip she lost her footing and went down, taking him with her. A wide bed of bushes and weeds cushioned their landing. She found herself cradled in Isaiah's arms. In all the commotion their uninvited guest scuttled away.

Ebony watched the limo roll onto the main road. The driver steered away from Grundie to who-knew-where. "He's gone!"

Isaiah chuckled. "The skunk or Renfro?"

"Let me go." Ebony punched Isaiah's shoulder. "This isn't funny."

She tried wiggling out of his embrace, but gave up when he held on tighter. Isaiah savored the feel of her softness in his arms and his lips were a mere inch from hers.

Her expression softened and her muscles relaxed. Her silky braids caressed his cheek. Her sweet breath tickled his whiskers. "How could you just let him get away like that?" What he saw in her brown eyes made him question whether she really wanted a reply.

With their legs entwined, his sex pressed against hers. Even through fabric he savored her heat. "The skunk," he whispered. "Remember?"

"The skunk?" She seemed dazed, her eyelids heavy. "Yeah, the skunk. Right."

Every breath was amplified. Heartbeats were synchronized.

Isaiah pressed his pelvis against hers. To his surprise she thrust back, intensifying his hard-on, which surged forth the moment she landed on top of him.

"Oops, did I do that?" she teased in a surprisingly sultry tone.

Isaiah nodded with a small lusty grin. He moved his face closer to hers to brush her lips when something in the bushes rustled. Then came a plaintive yowl. Ebony stiffened and peered up toward the noise. "Who's there?"

A cat scrambled out with yet another skunk on its tail.

"What is this? Skunk central?" Ebony pinched her nostrils. "Ugh! That smell! We'd better get away from here before we get something on us that Ajax won't take off."

Isaiah released her to cup a hand over his nose and mouth. "Too late. Look what we landed on." He recognized the triad clusters of shiny green leaves with notched edges.

Ebony moaned, "Please tell me this is not what I think it is."

"Leaves of three. Let them be."

They wouldn't make it to soap and water in time, but Isaiah believed some fast damage control would lessen the severity of their reaction. He stood and helped Ebony up.

"We need to wash as soon as possible," Ebony said, flapping her hands in alarm.

"Washing's not going to be enough." Isaiah shook his head. "It only takes a few minutes for poison ivy to sink in. Even in this jumpsuit, I know it brushed my neck, hands, and ankles and only God knows where. I'll go to that Pac 'N' Snac. Maybe they have something that'll help. You go on back to Kenny-Wayne's and wait for me."

"Why don't *I* go to the Pac 'N' Snac and *you* go back to Kenny-Wayne's and wait for me?" Ebony countered, pinning him with a wary expression.

"Where the hell do you think I'm going?" Isaiah felt his nostrils flare. "To chase after Renfro? Get a grip. We just fell on a hot bed of poison ivy. We'll both be ready to jump out of our skin once the itching starts."

"Why don't we both go to the Pac 'N' Snac? I need to make sure you buy the right stuff. I have a bit of experience with this. I did a summer survival piece on conquering poison ivy, mosquito bites, and sunburn for the *Bee* once."

"Whatever." He refused to spar about it. "I'll meet you at the Pac 'N' Snac in ten minutes."

He turned and sprinted to the truck.

CHAPTER 10

At the Pac 'N' Snac Ebony and Isaiah cleared the shelves of every itch ointment and tossed in a few miscellaneous items to concoct home remedies.

Ebony arrived at their rented room first. The itching hadn't started yet, but she longed for a bath. That would have to wait because Isaiah had their itch-ointment stash and the rubber gloves she would need to remove her clothes to prevent further contamination. More than thirty minutes had passed with no sign of Isaiah. Feeling stir-crazy in the cramped room, Ebony went outside to pace the driveway. "Where the heck is he? That rat. If he took off for Renfro anyway, I'll . . . I'll . . ." Then she heard the rat-a-tat of the pickup truck and saw him chugging up the street. Once Isaiah parked she met him at the driver's side. She glowered at him. "Where the heck have you been?"

"Have you forgotten what I'm driving?" Isaiah snarled, practically vaulting out of the truck's cab. "Damn thing stalled on me."

A few minutes later Ebony was soaking in the most glorious warm oatmeal-and-baking-soda bath. She wanted to linger, but knew Isaiah needed his turn. She got dressed in a pair of baggy Bermuda shorts and a Howard University T-shirt.

After Isaiah bathed, he changed into a pair of loose-fitting jeans and a faded Reds baseball sweatshirt with the sleeves hacked off. They sat on the waterbed commiserating about their streak of whacked-out luck.

"Guess it could've been worse." Ebony made a feeble attempt to peek at the bright side. "Miraculously, we don't smell like skunk."

"Think we'll be lucky enough to avoid an itching rash?" Isaiah rubbed his strong ropy forearms.

Ebony recalled how wonderful it felt to have them wrapped around her. "I wouldn't count on it," she snorted.

"Maybe we caught it in time with the oatmeal bath, or better yet, maybe we're immune. Some people are, you know."

Ebony knew better. "True, but the onset of itching varies. Some people feel it instantly. For others it can take up to a week, but I think most break out within a few hours after exposure."

As if on cue, a hot prickly sensation skimmed the flesh on Ebony's shoulders and neck. "Uh-oh, I think I'm starting to feel something."

"Don't scratch." Isaiah got up and dashed inside the bathroom. "That'll only make it worse." He returned with two wet hand towels. "Here, try these first."

Ebony accepted the cool wads of terry and pressed them where it felt as if an army of chiggers were break-dancing on her skin. She itched in places she didn't realize had been exposed. Removing the jumpsuit had proven trickier than anticipated. The contaminated side of the fabric had brushed across her back. "Thanks."

"How's that?" he asked, with a note of concern.

"A little better." She resisted the urge to rake her nails over her flesh.

Isaiah reached inside one of the Pac 'N' Snac bags on the bed. He removed a tube of itch cream and passed it to her. She darted to the bathroom to remove her T-shirt. The silky cream brought instant relief, but she strained trying to reach the itchiest part of her back. That would require assistance. Dropping her hands to her side, she sighed. She hesitated, then straightened her shoulders in resolve. With her modesty in check she reached for a towel to cover her breasts.

Isaiah sat on the bed, rummaging through the bag of items they'd purchased. He looked up when she stepped back into the bedroom. His lips parted ever so slightly as he took her in, standing there in her shorts with a towel swaddled around her torso like an oversized tube top. His eyes gleamed and his Adam's apple dipped, making her feel much more exposed. There was nothing remotely sexy about hydrocortisone cream or the angry itch blazing across her skin, but his eyes seemed to rake over her as if it were all part of some elaborate seduction. She felt desirable. Heat cupped her in that neglected place between her thighs. "I need your help." Determined not to meet his gaze, she sat on the bed and presented her back to him as if it were the most natural thing in the world. "My back, I can't reach the itchiest part. Do you mind?"

"No, um, uh," Isaiah stuttered. "N-not at all." He eagerly reached for the rubber gloves he had placed on one of Kenny-Wayne's old stereo speakers.

"That poison ivy has already infected our skin. The gloves are useless now." Ebony gathered her braids off her shoulders with one hand and lifted them. "Unless you think the cream is too messy for your hands."

Isaiah placed the gloves back on the speaker. The telltale signs of inflammation had yet to surface so her skin was still flawless. She instructed him where to apply the cream.

Isaiah gently tugged at her towel. "Would you lower this a little more?"

Ebony obliged and let it drop an inch.

"A little more," Isaiah coaxed as she let it fall an additional inch until it draped at the small of her back. She clutched the rest of the towel closer to conceal breasts she believed were way too small and wondered how she was going to survive this.

As Isaiah squeezed the cream across his fingers he admired Ebony's long slender neck, delicately toned shoulders and the feminine V taper of her sleek back. He found the female back unexpectedly erotic. While he could appreciate plunging necklines and nice cleavage as much as the next guy, the sexy curve of a woman's spine in a halter top was highly underrated.

Ebony's dark skin glowed like burnished mahogany. A single braid escaped from her hand, accenting her neck like an ornate curlicue. Her loveliness should be captured on film and he immediately thought of his Nikon, but at that moment he was too enthralled to move. He took a mental snapshot that would surface again and again in his dreams. Simply breathtaking, Isaiah thought.

"Isaiah." Ebony squirmed. "What are you waiting for? I'm dying here!"

Isaiah started with her neck then moved to her shoulders, shoulder blades, and her back. Slowly and lightly, he rubbed the cool, thin cream, first with one hand, then with two. Her tensed muscles relaxed. He let his fingers linger on her supple, hot skin. He couldn't control the tightening between his loins and the ache of need throbbing there. "How's this?"

"Much better." Ebony sighed. When her head lolled back, the scent of her coconut-scented shampoo cut through the smell of hydrocortisone cream. "That stuff is actually working. I don't believe it. Hmmmm," she moaned. "Yes. Yes. Yes. Oh, yes. Right there. That's the spot. Hmmm. Yes. Yes."

What was she doing? Teasing him? Did she have to sound so damn orgasmic?

"Hmmm," she moaned again. "Yeah."

What the hell was in that damn cream, anyway? Isaiah quickly sniffed one hand as the Rock of Gibraltar between his legs grew harder and heavier. "So you like it like that, huh?" he heard himself ask in a husky whisper as he applied more pressure and quickened his machinations across her skin. He scooted closer and sniffed her soft braids. He wanted to bury his face in them and plant a trail of kisses along her neck. He wanted to suckle her earlobes then trace that seductive trench of her back with his tongue. Isaiah took a deep breath. If he didn't get a grip right that minute he'd flip her over, tear off her shorts, and give her a big piece of the rock. He pushed to his feet, trying to snap out of the pleasure haze clouding his judgment and weakening his self-control. He had to get the hell outta there. "You know, I hardly got to eat any of that roast beef sandwich thanks to the skunk. I'm still hungry. Your itching's better, right?"

Befuddled, Ebony turned to face him. "Yeah, thanks."

"Cool." Isaiah swiped his keys from the milk-crate nightstand and made a break for the door. "I'm running out to get us some more food. I saw a little diner in town. They're bound to have better eats than that Pac 'N' Snac."

Ebony narrowed her eyes, adjusting her towel.

"I'm coming right back," he promised before she could protest. "I can't believe you still don't trust me after everything we've been through today."

Her stubborn mask slowly cracked. "I suppose you're right. I guess you've earned the benefit of the doubt—for today at least."

CHAPTER 11

Isaiah found Pearlie Mae's Diner packed with players from the paintball tournament. Most hadn't bothered to change out of their paint-and-mud-stained jumpsuits. Cigarette smoke hovered like swamp mist. Pop music masquerading as new-style country romped from speakers hung high on the walls.

A waitress with ratted red hair that looked like a coppery wire pot scrubber met Isaiah at the door. "Gonna have to seat you at the counter. All the tables are taken."

"I want to place an order for carryout." Isaiah's voice got lost in a round of hearty laughter from the crowd.

"Excuse me? You're gonna have to speak up. They're kinda boisterous tonight," she said, trumping the noise.

"Carryout," Isaiah shouted back.

"Today's specials are chicken-fried steak, bacon mushroom burgers, smothered pork chops, turkey pot pie, salmon croquettes, pickled beets, and chipped beef."

"Does that burger include fries?"

"Yeah, fries or onion rings."

"I'll take the onion rings," Isaiah told her. "Two orders. No, make that three orders. Extra large." That should put the kibosh on any urges to turn up the heat with Ebony again.

"And I'll have two mushroom burgers, extra onions, and a couple cans of soda to go."

The waitress scribbled on her notepad. "That'll take about twenty minutes. Have a seat at the counter over there. Get a drink while you wait."

Isaiah claimed a cracked vinyl stool and ordered a soft drink. The burly guy behind the counter passed him a glass of cola. Isaiah toyed with the straw leaning against its rim, thinking he'd broken away from Ebony in the nick of time. He couldn't deny that he was hot for her, but when all was said and done, she was still the competition. This trip was about getting Renfro, not getting laid, he reminded himself. And the fact that he was so turned on by his sexy little rival made him all the more determined to handle his business. Snatched from his thoughts by a tap on the shoulder, Isaiah swiveled on his stool to find Roxanne LaRue smiling at him.

"Well, well, well, if it isn't the handsome Isaiah Malone." She licked her lips as if she could just taste him.

"Ms. LaRue. Grundie is the last place I'd expect to find you," Isaiah said, though it actually made perfect sense that Renfro's head public relations flack would be lurking about with all the others. Ol' Boy was known for traveling with an entourage. Isaiah became acquainted with Roxanne a few weeks ago when his quest for the Renfro exclusive began. He'd taken the obvious route and contacted Roxanne. Why the enigmatic multimillionaire required a media-slash-public-relations director at all was a mystery. Renfro hardly interacted with the media, or the public for that matter. When he had called on Roxanne at Ice Cream Dreams' corporate headquarters, he'd tried every trick and technique of artful persuasion he'd learned over the years to convince her to arrange a one-on-one meeting between him and her boss. The woman had been impervious, delivering her reply as if on autopilot: "Mr. Renfro doesn't do interviews." Isaiah had known it wouldn't be that simple, but he figured he had nothing to lose by giving it a shot.

Roxanne had made it clear that while she couldn't help Isaiah the reporter, she could do plenty for Isaiah the man. At the time, he had politely declined her advances. He wasn't above using a little flirtation to get the information he needed, but he knew Roxanne had a lot more in mind than a few winks and suggestive wordplay.

"Please, you're going to hurt my feelings if you don't call me Roxy," Roxanne pouted as a waitress squeezing by wedged her deeper inside the spread of Isaiah's thighs. Roxanne took her time easing away. Isaiah smelled industrial-strength perfume on her breath and wondered if she'd gargled with it. "It's packed in here, isn't it?"

Isaiah refused to gawk at the cleavage swelling out of her low-cut, painted-on top. "Don't tell me Renfro had you playing in the paintball tourney today?"

"No, I was there to cover the event. You know, take pictures and do a write-up for the corporate newsletter. Paintball ain't exactly my thing, if you know what I mean, but it's a lot more interesting than those boring annual reports I just finished." She inched closer and smiled up at him. Lipstick smudged one front tooth. "I'll bet I can guess why you're here. Still angling for that exclusive with my boss, right?"

"You know what they say. If at first you don't succeed..." Isaiah stood and gestured toward his stool. "Almost forgot my manners." Relinquishing his seat appeared to be the only way he could tactfully lure Roxanne away from his crotch.

She sat down and crossed her legs. "Have you eaten? I'd love it if you'd join me."

"Sorry. I ordered takeout."

"So? Just change it to eat in."

"Can't. I'm delivering to another starving paintballer who's waiting for me to return with the grub."

Roxanne leaned toward Isaiah as if her centerfold bosom would convince him to reconsider. She was fine. Just overdone. Her too-long-to-be-natural hair feathered around the racing stripes of blush on her cheeks. Her lips were pouty, just the way he liked them, but he found that dark Vampira lipstick she wore frightening. Her hands and neckline hinted that beautiful café-au-lait skin glowed beneath the goo-gobs of makeup. She had the kind of crazy mad curves that drove most brothers wild and sent skinnier sisters racing for a big plate of greasy pork chops. Though Roxanne's assets were obvious, she wasn't Ebony. His rival's image superseded what Roxanne thrust at him. He had yet to recover from the feel of Ebony in his arms or the sight of her delectable back and legs. He sipped his watered-down cola as he imagined those legs clamped around him as they rocked to a rhythm as old as time. He saw himself plunging into her hot, wet center with long lazy strokes until he exploded inside of her. A sensual ache throbbed beneath the zipper of his pants. He shifted his hips toward the bar so Roxanne wouldn't assume her low-cut shirt had elicited that reaction from him.

The waitress returned with Isaiah's order. "That'll be eleven ninety-eight."

Isaiah paid for the food and tipped the waitress generously. Her timing couldn't have been better. "Well, Roxanne, I mean Roxy, it was good to see you again, but I'm about to break." He started for the door, cradling his bags.

"I might be able to help you after all." Roxanne paused and studied Isaiah's reaction when he turned back around to face her. "With my boss, I mean."

With his interest sufficiently piqued he stepped closer. "Oh, yeah? That's a different tune from the one you were singing a few weeks back."

"Isn't it a woman's prerogative to change her mind?" she asked, batting her mascara-caked lashes.

"So what can you do for me now that you couldn't do when I first came calling?"

"Not much, here in Grundie, I mean." Roxanne removed a business card and pen from the small purse dangling from one shoulder. She placed it on the counter to write something. "Give me a call when you get back to Cincinnati. My home number is on the back. I'm sure we can work something out that will be mutually advantageous." She dragged a fingertip across his jawline then circled his lips. I'm talking dinner and movie." She reached and pinched his ass. "You and I can take turns being the dinner and we'll make our own dirty movie. What do you say?"

Isaiah tucked the card in his pocket, fully aware of the scandalous mess that might ensue. Is that what he really wanted? He'd had no problems having sex for the sake of sex, but it was always his choice and certainly not part of a quid pro quo or bartering arrangement. He wasn't sure how far he was willing to go to get the Renfro exclusive, but he'd find out soon enough. "I say, I just might be giving you a buzz," he replied with a roguish wink. "Real soon."

CHAPTER 12

Isaiah returned to their rented room in less than an hour.

"You came back." Ebony had replaced the towel with a T-shirt. She tucked its tail inside her khaki shorts. "And so quickly."

Isaiah closed the door behind him. "Told ya."

"Yeah, that's what you said, but—"

"But nothing. What happened to you giving me the benefit of the doubt for the rest of the day?"

Ebony's gaze locked on his bags. "It's not like I have a choice, right?"

"I'm holding the eats."

"And all the cards."

"Damn right. That makes me king of the world." His mouth kicked up in a lopsided smile.

Ebony gave him a mock salute. "Aye-aye, Captain."

"Make that 'Your Highness.'"

When Isaiah placed the aromatic bags on the milk-crate nightstand Ebony drew a deep breath. The appetizing scent of onions, mushrooms, and seasoned meat filled the small room. "What did you get?"

"Burgers, onion rings, and sodas."

"Mmmm. Smells heavenly. Any dessert?"

"They were fresh out of everything but the rhubarb pie. Passed on that. You didn't strike me as the rhubarb type."

Ebony crinkled her nose. "Good call."

Isaiah began removing items from the bags. "So how's the itching?"

"Practically gone. That hydrocortisone cream did the trick. What about you?" Ebony reached for the bill tucked inside one of the food wrappers, scanned it for the total, and reached for her fanny pack to reimburse him for the burgers and the stakeout lunch.

"So far so good. Maybe I have some type of resistance to poison ivy."

"Don't get cocky yet." Ebony plucked a warm onion ring out of its Styrofoam container, then took a bite. "You're not out of the woods yet. I told you it could take as long as a week or two for a reaction."

"You almost sound—"

"Here." Ebony shoved the neatly folded bills toward him.

Isaiah looked down at the money. "So I'm not allowed to treat you to a meal?" He sounded offended.

"Isaiah, please. Take the money."

He sighed and shook his head, then tucked the money in a back pocket. "As I was saying, you almost sound as if you want me to get a rash."

"Misery loves company. Actually, I wouldn't wish that maddening itching on anyone—not even you. I'm—" Kenny-Wayne's Lola Falana poster suddenly snapped off the wall and fell to the floor. "Shoot, I've fixed that doggone thing a dozen times already."

"So I take it Lola's down for the count now?" He laughed.

Ebony wanted to yank the old Dr. J-slam-dunking poster off the wall, too. "I'm tired of looking at him in his itsy-bitsy basketball shorts, Lola, and this room that time forgot. I could use a change of scenery."

"How about we check out the backyard? I got a glimpse of a deck. It looks empty." The eagerness in his suggestion caught Ebony off guard.

"Sounds like a plan," she said, strapping on her fanny pack.

"Think Kenny-Wayne's Uncle Waymon will mind?"

Isaiah gathered their food. "As much as they're charging us for this jacked-up room, we should have the run of the whole damn house."

Despite the chaotically baroque décor in Kenny-Wayne's garage-top bachelor pad, the house had an abundance of curb appeal. The brick ranch sat on a spacious manicured lot shaded by scads of hardy trees. Somebody had given it plenty of TLC. In the backyard voluminous shrubs, carefree vines, and vivid annuals hugged an expansive cedar deck. Water trickled melodically from a small frog fountain a few feet away and a soft breeze carried the fresh scent of lavender.

"This is nice." Ebony sank into a comfy deck chair. "Waymon has quite a green thumb."

"Or enough green to hire a professional landscaper." Isaiah retracted the umbrella looming over the deck table. "We don't need this."

As an early evening sun dipped toward the horizon, a swarm of iridescent dragonflies arrived.

Ebony had sensed a change in Isaiah when he returned from the diner. He was laid-back. Polite even. Too darn polite for comfort, actually. She should've insisted on tagging along. She had to stay on her toes with this slicker. She wondered if he'd managed to get some sort of line on Renfro when he slipped out. That would certainly account for his mood. He crackled with good-humored energy. She pushed two onion rings inside her mouth and cut him furtive glances as he worked his way through his burger. She took in the curves of his amazing lips and the occasional flick of his tongue and imagined all sorts of panty-scorching possibilities. She crossed her legs, but the move only heightened the sensitivity stirred by her lusty thoughts. She quickly uncrossed them, hoping the balmy breeze would ease the slow simmer. What the heck was wrong with her? She hadn't made so much as one phone call to track down other accommodations and she'd never had so much trouble staying focused in her life. Good thing Isaiah had bolted for the diner when he did because God only knew what would have happened had she let loose while he rubbed her back. While Yolanda and Taffi had raved about Decadent Delights Massage Oil in Piña Colada and Passion Fruit, the scent of hydrocortisone cream would be forever etched among Ebony's erotic triggers. Thanks to Isaiah and those magic fingers of his. He could make BenGay an aphrodisiac. She'd been a heartbeat from dropping the towel and demanding that he put his hands all over her. Never mind that her experience as a seductress was woefully lacking. Something about him made her fantasize. Boldly. Brazenly. In 3-D. Technicolor. Rated X.

Isaiah's voice horned in on her runaway thoughts. "Another HU shirt. Is that your alma mater?"

She squirmed in her seat, dropping the sandal that had been dangling from one toe. "No, my younger sister, Kenya, is a freshman there. She sends all kinds of stuff—caps, T-shirts, mugs—regularly."

"Good school." He stuffed the last bite of his burger inside his mouth and took a sip from his cola can. "Does she like it there?"

"Yup. Loves it."

"It would've been cool to go to a historically black college."

"So why didn't you?"

Isaiah shrugged, dabbing at his mouth with a napkin. "Followed in my father and brother's footsteps instead and went to Northwestern."

"Not too shabby. They have one of the best journalism programs in the country."

"What about you?" he asked.

"Went to the University of Cincinnati," she replied, her eyes lowered. "But I don't want Kenya following in my footsteps."

"There's nothing wrong with UC."

"I know. It's a solid school, actually. What I really mean is I don't want Kenya taking as long as I did to get a bachelor's degree."

"How long is too long?"

"About seven years going part time and working full time."

"Everybody doesn't earn a degree in four years. That's nothing to be ashamed of."

"Let me guess." Sarcasm threaded her words. "Bet you had a four-year education, plus expenses, handed to you on a silver platter. Scholarships or a full ride at Mommy and Daddy's expense?"

"Yeah, I had help," Isaiah revealed with a note of disdain. "Shoot me."

"Most of my friends graduated with outrageous student loans hovering over their heads. And I'm still paying mine off." She shook her head. "I don't want that for Kenya. She's earned scholarships and government grants that cover most of her tuition, but there are still all sorts of other expenses—books, supplies, room and board, personal necessities, and the cost of traveling from D.C. to see the family occasionally."

"There are worse things than having debt hovering over your head."

"True," Ebony agreed softly as she fingered the frayed macramé bracelet encircling her right wrist. "So what's hovering over your head, Isaiah?"

"Nothing," he replied too quickly. "What were you saying about your sister?"

Ebony hesitated, wondering at his quick denial, then decided to let it drop. "I plan to help Kenya out as much as I can financially. That's one of the reasons that *Examiner* job is so important to me. I could use the hefty raise. She deserves the best for being the best little sister."

"Proud of her, huh?"

Ebony smiled. "Yes, so much I could just pop. Kenya thinks it's kinda silly, but I still keep her school awards and honors in my bedroom. I never won that many of my own."

"Bad student?"

"Nah, just never was any good at superlatives or distinguishing myself academically. I wasn't the best or the worst, just sorta average. I got the job done. But Kenya's so smart and much more of a social butterfly than I ever was. She was president of her senior class, valedictorian, and prom queen."

Isaiah appeared genuinely impressed. "Sounds like little sister's got it going on."

"Funny how two sisters can be so different," Ebony replied wistfully.

"Big sister ain't bad," he said, smiling.

Ebony felt her cheeks warming with a blush. "I wasn't fishing for compliments."

"But it is okay to accept unsolicited ones, you know. You may thank me now."

She made a face at him and Isaiah laughed.

"Thanks." Ebony toyed with an onion ring. "What about you? You mentioned a brother. Is it just the two of you?"

"Yeah. His name's Tarik."

Ebony swallowed her bite of burger, then turned to him with wide eyes. "Wait a second. Tarik Malone is your brother?"

He nodded, then she smiled.

"You know him?" Isaiah's easy, open body language shifted. His posture snapped militantly rigid as he gazed into the distance.

"Yes," Ebony replied, wondering what had triggered that reaction. "He's a nice guy. Met him through the African-American Journalists Coalition. He's the local chapter president, but you already know that." She paused. "So George Malone is your father?"

"Yes."

"Impressive."

"More like repressive," Isaiah muttered.

"Excuse me?" Ebony asked, wondering if she'd heard him correctly.

"Never mind."

"I purchased the compilation of your dad's Pulitzer Prize–winning columns on the civil rights movement. Riveting. He did some great stuff." Ebony had already picked Tarik's brain about George Malone. She wanted to hear Isaiah's comment, but it would have to wait until she checked on her folks. "Think Waymon will mind if I use his phone for a minute?"

"Probably not. It's another opportunity to gouge his houseguests. Call collect or be prepared to surrender the equivalent of a car payment on the spot."

As Ebony moved toward the glass door to the house, she knew Isaiah was ogling her butt. She might have been short-changed in the boob department, but she'd been blessed with a nicely rounded rump. So why not put a little ha-cha-cha in her hips for his viewing pleasure?

She made her collect call and insisted on speaking to her mother and Granny Mac to insure one hadn't murdered the other and disposed of the body. She returned to the deck a few minutes later to find Isaiah stuffing food wrappers inside a bag.

"Everything all right?" he asked. "I noticed you left the field earlier today. One paintball official said you got a page and went in search of a pay phone."

"Had to call home."

"I'd think you'd have to sandblasted from Renfro after getting so close. Must have been damn important."

"Hardly. Ma and Granny Mac tend to be overly melodramatic."

"If you know that, why do you jump every time they beep?" Isaiah asked innocently enough.

Ebony still bristled. "I do not jump *every* time they beep, but I do try to keep tabs on them. Never know when a catastrophe might arise." The night of the fire came to mind.

"Now who's overly melodramatic?"

"You don't have a clue."

"Then enlighten me," he challenged, as if he actually cared.

Ebony stood and stretched. "Maybe another time. It's been a long day. I'm going to turn in so I can be fresh and rarin' to go on that paintball field tomorrow."

"Didn't mean to get all up in your business," he said, his manner instantly contrite.

"I'm just tired." She moved to climb the stairs leading to the room over the garage. "You coming?"

"Nah, I think I'll sit out here a bit longer and enjoy the view."

Isaiah kept his eyes front and center, to spare himself the

temptation of watching her sexy butt as she sashayed toward their room. If he stayed on the deck long enough he'd avoid that Mickey Mouse top that showed way too much of her legs. Despite his decision to call Roxanne when he got back home, he couldn't neutralize the seductive pull of Ebony. He had tried to concentrate on his burger, then that stupid bug-eyed frog fountain, to keep from gawking at those sweet little cupcakes she had for breasts. He had a clear view of her nipples, which instantly hardened when the first breeze brushed along her flimsy T-shirt. Spears of fire shot from his thighs to his groin. He wanted her with a ferocity even onion breath couldn't quell. And if he wasn't mistaken, Ebony was suddenly working it. Working it for all it was worth. He could've sworn she was trying to tempt him with that come-and-get-it sway of her hips. A far cry from the woman who had freaked out that morning after that near-miss kiss. Her chaste wholesomeness only intensified the honeyed sexuality she oozed whenever she dared to loosen up.

Isaiah crumpled the bag containing their trash. Ebony had to be experimenting with some sort of new angle to keep an edge. Now that he knew this job meant a lot more to her than sprucing up her résumé, he wouldn't put it past her. She'd do anything to help her little sister. He couldn't fault her for that, but empathizing too much would be the kiss of death for him. Maybe that was why she'd revealed all that stuff about her sister in the first place. Good thing she had clammed up and taken off when she did. The conversation might have circled back to the great George Malone and he definitely didn't want to go there with her. He also refused to let his mind get blown to bits now that Ebony had decided to bring out the big guns. She'd blown the dust off her feminine wiles and spun her warm-and-fuzzy tales about sibling devotion.

Isaiah stood and made his way to the vinyl garbage barrel at the far corner of the yard to discard their trash, then plopped back on his deck chair. He planned to sit right there until dusk turned to full-fledged night. At least until he was sure Ebony was safely tucked between those zebra covers and settled into the deepest sleep.

CHAPTER 13

The sound of the bathroom shower and the sun's brightness filtering through the open blinds awakened Ebony. The night before, she had fallen asleep before Isaiah returned. With a new day the race for Renfro resumed and their temporary truce abandoned. She looked over at the forlorn beanbags. Empty. Isaiah, who was singing in the shower, had already prepared to man his battle station and gear up for another day on the paintball field. Melancholia pricked her. She already missed the mushroom burgers, onion rings, and the light-and-easy vibe that had hummed between them the night before. She reached for her watch on the milk-crate nightstand. Seven-twelve A.M. Why hadn't her alarm gone off? And more importantly, why hadn't Isaiah bothered to wake her when he knew the paintball competition would start in less than an hour? She leaped from the bed, berating herself not only for oversleeping, but for even wondering why Isaiah hadn't awakened her. Despite the easy camaraderie they'd shared the day before, *they were still rivals*. She grabbed her garment bag, tossed it on the waterbed, and began removing the shorts and T-shirt she planned to wear to the paintball tournament. Her contaminated jumpsuit was no good. She'd have to rent another one once she got to the field.

A few minutes later Isaiah emerged from the bathroom, his navy blue polo shirt molded to his hard-sculpted chest and biceps while his loose faded jeans skimmed his impressive thighs. "Good morning, sleepyhead."

"So were you going to wake me or what?" Ebony asked, not bothering to hide her rancor.

"Yeah, after I got out of the shower and dressed." He smelled of deodorant soap, cologne, and mouthwash. She found him squeaky clean and scrumptious enough to lick from head to toe. "You were snoozing so peacefully I thought I'd let you catch a few extra winks." He dropped the leather toiletries pouch he was carrying inside his duffel bag on the floor.

"Yeah, right," she scoffed.

"Here we go again." Isaiah made a weird, impatient sound. "I'm not nearly as Machiavellian about this Renfro thing as you imagine me to be, Ebony. I *was* going to wake you."

"So you say." Ebony gathered clean undies, toiletries, and clothing then slipped inside the bathroom. "We don't have time to stand around quibbling over it."

Ebony removed her Mickey Mouse top to find her skin prickled with a light rash. Fortunately the itching had ceased and most of the fine bumps were confined to her back and areas well hidden by her T-shirt. After showering and dressing, she emerged from the bathroom. Isaiah sat on the waterbed frantically patting at his forearms. "What's wrong with you?" Before he could reply, she read discomfort on his face. "The poison ivy?"

"Kicked in big time. Where's that hydrocortisone cream?"

Ebony plucked the bulging bag of itch ointments from her piece of luggage. "I started to think you wouldn't need these." She passed him the tube that had brought her relief the day before.

"It's just my forearms so far." He quickly twisted off the cap and squeezed a generous glob in his palm.

"That stuff will knock it right out," she said to him just as he began patting at his neck. "Your neck now?"

Isaiah nodded. "I think I'll take one of those oatmeal baths again. Maybe that'll head off any more areas that might join the party."

"You all right?" she asked, with a note of concern creeping into her voice.

"After a bath, I'll be fine." He dashed toward the bathroom, gripping the bag of itch ointments. "I'll see you later over at the paintball field."

Ebony checked her watch. The match would start in twenty minutes. If she left now she'd get there in the nick of time. As she strapped on her fanny pack, Isaiah's muttered curses penetrated the thin walls separating the bathroom from the bedroom. She did an inventory check—pager, planner, notebook, Chap Stick, Wet-Naps, Swiss Army knife, change purse, ID, and the cell phone that was useless to her in Grundie. She fiddled with the yellow bandanna around her neck, adjusted her macramé bracelet, then kneeled to untie and retie her Reeboks securely, obviously stalling when she needed to be on her way. The rush of water from the tub's faucet drowned out Isaiah's muttering. She scooped up her keys and headed out. This was Isaiah's problem, not hers. She slipped inside the car, fitted the key in the ignition, and took off. Halfway to the paintball field, a twinge of guilt escalated into a full-blown grappling match with her bothersome conscience: *"How could you just leave him there like that?"*

"Gotta get to Renfro. This is the last day of paintball competition. I can't be late. Isaiah will be fine after a little hydrocortisone cream," Ebony told her conscience. "I was."

"But who helped put that hydrocortisone cream on the spots you couldn't reach yesterday?" Goody Two-shoes interrogated.

"Okay," Ebony huffed, ignoring the stares of the trucker in the lane next to her who surely thought she was bonkers for talking to herself. "Isaiah did."

"He might get itches in unreachable places, too, but who's going to slather hydrocortisone cream on them? Not Kenny-Wayne or his uncle, Waymon, that's for sure."

"But Isaiah was going to let me oversleep this morning, remember?" Ebony parried as she caught sight of the paintball field and the swarm of camouflage-covered combatants ahead. Reuben Renfro was among them.

"And you're so sure he wasn't going to wake you after he finished showering?"

"Yeah, because—"

"Because a man who'd intercept a flying plank, deck a creep, endure a torturous beanbag bed for you, then lovingly slather hydrocortisone cream on your flaming flesh, share his ham sandwich and honey bun when you were hungrier than a bear after a long winter hibernation, then dash out to get you mushroom burgers and onion rings later and return within an hour as he promised most certainly and positively could not be trusted. Go on, kick the dude to the curb. He deserves it. After all, this is war!" Goody Two-shoes reasoned with too-obvious-to-actually-be-effective reverse psychology. But doggone if it didn't wear Ebony down.

"Oh, mind your . . . my . . . own beeswax!" she snapped, then slammed on the brakes. Her wheels screeched a sharp U and she tore back to Kenny-Wayne's room, where she found Isaiah, face distorted with anguish, hunched over the sink in the bathroom. Heaving and struggling to breathe, he reached out to her with swollen fingers just before he lost his balance.

With a cry of dismay, she rushed to him, curling her arms around his lean torso and wedging her shoulder under his armpit. He steadied his weight using her body as a crutch. "I've got to get you to a doctor fast!"

Less than three hours later, Ebony drove away from a rambling farmhouse, the residence and office of Grundie's only physician. With the help of the clerk inside the Pac 'N' Snac she had located the doctor. He'd dispensed a steroid shot to Isaiah, who had suffered a delayed but severe allergic reaction.

"And I actually thought I had some sort of immunity to poison ivy." Isaiah chuckled dryly and secured his seatbelt. "Hmmm. That stuff got in my system and festered, just waiting to explode." The swelling of his fingers had subsided, but a rash splotched his golden skin.

"Poison ivy is very unpredictable. You just never know if

or when you're going to react after exposure." Ebony reined in her I-told-you-sos. He'd been through enough for one day. "I have a light rash myself."

Isaiah nailed her with a measuring look. "So what made you come back?"

"I... uh... forgot my pager," she lied. He didn't need to know she'd actually been worried about him.

"Well, whatever the reason, I'm glad you did. Thanks," Isaiah said with indisputable sincerity. "I don't even want to think about what would've happened if you hadn't got me to a doctor in time."

Ebony actually felt like a creep for leaving him in the first place. "I know you would've done the same for me," she said before she realized it.

Isaiah noticed the clock on the car's dash. "I made you miss the paintball tourney. Maybe if you drive over there now we can still catch some of it. They could be in overtime."

"Not on your life. You heard what Dr. Johnson said. You need to take it easy for the rest of the day, and besides, I think you're going to be persona non grata looking like Leprosy Man and all."

"This rash isn't contagious, and besides, paintball isn't a contact sport."

"I know that, you know that, and I think most folks know that... in their rational minds, but still..."

"I look like I've got... What do you call it? Cooties, right?"

Ebony grinned and nodded.

"That bad, huh?"

"It's only temporary. You'll be back to your fine Shemar Moore–looking self before you know it."

"Shemar Moore?" His eyes were bright with surprise. "That pretty-boy dude who used to be on that soap opera?"

"Yeah. I'm not a *The Young and the Restless* fan, but Granny Mac and Ma are. They talk about it and watch it religiously so I caught a glimpse of him."

"So you think I look like him?" Isaiah smiled, obviously flattered.

"Yeah, kinda, sorta." Ebony couldn't help but grin. "If I squint a little . . . When your skin's not looking like a rotisserie chicken's."

"So you think I'm fine, huh?" He would zero in on that. He rubbed his smooth shadow of a goatee and flashed her a look that always caused little tingles to play ring-around-the-rosy along her spine.

"You're sorta easy on the eyes, I guess," she said casually, declining to add that Isaiah easily outclassed that former soap star. Isaiah was taller and more fabulously buff.

"Reeeeal-ly now?" He smiled.

Ebony shook her head in mock exasperation and fixed her eyes on the road. "Are you going to make me wish I'd never given you a compliment?"

"Okay, okay. I won't get obnoxious about it. But I must say I am flattered. You ain't too bad looking yourself."

"Well, it's good to know I don't have a mug that frightens small children or cracks mirrors."

"Far from it."

His eyes were on her, so intense and unyielding, she felt flushed and dazed. The horizon before her blurred. Her fingers fumbled for the radio, but static crackled at every setting.

"Allow me." When he reached for the dial his hand grazed hers. She'd give just about anything to have those fingers dillydallying at her secret places. He finally found a station without static. Twangy vocals warbling "Get Your Biscuits in the Oven and Your Buns in the Bed" filled the car. "I think this is the best we can do in these parts unless you want to pop in a tape or CD."

"Tape player's busted, never got around to buying a CD player. Afraid we're stuck listening to this little ditty or nothing."

They listened in silence for a few minutes until she added, "Gotta hand it to country music, though, some of the songs don't get any cornier."

"You listen to country?"

"Only because I have no choice. Granny Mac does, but unfortunately it's never the cool, pop-sounding Shania Twain or Faith Hill stuff. No, sirree. Granny's favorites include oldies like 'If I'd Shot You When I Wanted To, I'd Be Out By Now.' "

Isaiah chuckled. "That's a real song?"

"Yup." Ebony loved the sound of his laughter. "And then there's 'She Got the Ring and I Got the Finger,' and 'If the Phone Don't Ring, Baby, You'll Know It's Me.' "

"And I'm thinking Sisqo's "Th-Th-Th-Thong Song" pushed the envelope."

"Hardly, you've obviously never heard 'I Hate Every Bone in Your Body Except Mine.'"

Isaiah howled, throwing his head back against the rest. "Your granny sounds like a real hoot."

"That and then some, believe me."

"So you're going to drop me off at Kenny-Wayne's and go back to the field?" Isaiah asked.

"The doctor said you should have supervision for the rest of the day." Ebony gripped the steering wheel and kept her eyes on the road, fearing he could see the truth in her eyes. She didn't want to abandon him. "You could suffer a relapse or have some weird reaction to that steroid shot."

"So you're supervising me?" He sounded surprised, but not as if he had a problem with the idea.

"Baby-sitting is more like it," she replied dryly.

"I appreciate that, but I don't care what Doc said. I, for one, am not looking forward to going back to that skuzzy room just yet. And besides, we're not allowed to return before four P.M. anyway."

"Aren't you feeling weak or something? Just a couple of hours ago you looked like death warmed over."

"What can I say? Those shots did the trick. I feel like Popeye after a spinach hit. Let's cruise for a bit."

"Cruise?"

"Yeah, I'll spot you the cash for the gas if that's what you're worried about."

"There's not a heck of a lot to see in Grundie."

"Hey, didn't Kenny-Wayne mention something about a Garlic Festival not too far from here in Potts County?"

"A Garlic Festival?" Ebony crinkled her nose. "You can't be serious."

"Hey, where is your sense of adventure?"

"After showing up at Shangri-La and the paintball tournament, I'd say my sense of adventure is just fine, thankyouverymuch."

"Oh, I get it," he teased, pretending to be offended. "You don't want to be seen in public with me. I mean, with me looking like a rotisserie chicken and all."

"I'm not that shallow, Isaiah. I just thought you might be more comfortable avoiding people for a while . . . in your condition."

"So they'll stare. Big freakin' deal."

"All right. If you insist." She gestured toward the glove compartment. "Grab that map out of there. How far up the highway is Potts County, anyway? Am I headed in the right direction?"

Ebony read a big sign ahead. "Oh, look! It's about thirty miles up the road. We're on the right track. A Garlic Festival should be pretty easy to find. I mean, how big can Potts County be, right? We just follow our noses."

"I hope you have an army's supply of Tic Tacs on you." He smiled. "We're going to need them."

"Hhhow many hhhorny hhhhamsters have heavy hippos hidden at their hhhouses?" Ebony giggled at the alcohol-induced foolishness she'd rambled during the thirty-minute drive from the Potts County Garlic Festival back to Grundie. "C'mon Isaiah, answer me. Hhhhow many horny hamsters hhave heavy hippos hidden at their houses?" She hiccuped, then flumped back in the passenger seat of her Escort.

Ebony hadn't been fit to take the wheel so Isaiah had appointed himself the designated driver. He couldn't remember the last time a day that had started on such a lousy note had ended right on key. He'd actually enjoyed himself at that goofy little Garlic Festival. He and Ebony had spent hours there and were among the last attendees to leave once night descended. Such countrified affairs usually weren't his thing.

Why had he suggested it in the first place? He suspected the company had a lot to do with his new-found appreciation for small-town Americana. When Ebony loosened up she was a lot of fun. They'd savored the Latin reggae stylings of Poncho and the Jumping Beans, the rhythm and blues riffs of Captain Cujo and the Zydeco Zing-Zangers and the folk-grass jams of the Mama's Boys trio. They'd perused the wares at tacky arts and crafts tables, peeked in at livestock shows, and watched the crowning of Li'l Miss Baby Bulb as they noshed on garlic pizza, garlic fries, garlic ice cream, and garlic rice pudding. They quenched their thirst with garlic smoothies and garlic tea. He passed on the alcoholic beverages after Ebony threw back a couple of gartinis. One of them had to keep a clear head for the drive back to their room.

Wimpy breath mints were useless. It would take a cocktail of Lysol, Pine-Sol, and Tide with bleach to lift the toe-curling stench from their garlic-infused breath, Isaiah thought, steering onto the road leading to Waymon's house.

Ebony, who obviously couldn't hold her liquor worth a damn, had a good ol' time firing her dragon breath at him as she enunciated every *h* word in her vocabulary. She playfully inched closer to Isaiah's face and sang, "The hhhappy hhhog hatched a hhalibut with hemmorhoids."

His eyes teared and the hairs in his nostrils withered after the vaporous onslaught, but he laughed anyway. "Damn, woman, how many of those gartinis did you drink?"

Ebony giggled and slurred. "What . . . are you tryin' to say?"

"That you're lit."

"Lit?" She made a silly face and slurred. "*Moi?*"

"Yeah, lit. As in zooted, blasted, bombed, pickled, schnockered, shit-faced, to' up from the flo' up." Isaiah parked the car at the curb in front of the house, cut the engine and climbed out.

On the passenger side, he opened the door and tugged Ebony out. She wobbled a bit when she came to her feet. "I only had three, maybe four. They were so small. Wonder what was in those gartini things, anyway?"

"Obviously a lot more than garlic."

Ebony slumped against him as he locked the car door. "More of what?"

"Remember, I stuck with the nonalcoholic garlic smoothies so I'm just guessing here. Vermouth, a couple jiggers of gin in each one."

"Gin?" She snickered as her eyes went wide. "You mean that's what's got me feeling all warm, tingly, and happy?"

"Yup." Isaiah coiled a supportive arm around her slim waist. "You obviously don't drink much, do you?"

"Do, too." A crease settled between her brows as if he'd offended her. "I can throw down on some wine coolers," she slurred. "I'm a wine-cooler conno...shhh...conno...shhh."

"Connoisseur?"

"Expert." She burped. "I always get them when I hang out with my girls, Yolanda and Taffi."

"What made you slug down those gartinis like you did today, anyway?"

She shrugged, hiccuped, and snuggled closer on unsteady feet. "Looking for some more of that adventure you mentioned, I guess."

Ebony had replaced her oversized Howard U T-shirt with a skimpy one she'd gotten from one of the festival vendors. It boasted two large garlic appliqués positioned directly over her boobs. "Bodacious Bulbs! I've Got 'em!" glittered across the front in big block letters. Isaiah could feel her breasts against his chest and once again his thoughts dashed where they shouldn't as a hard-on swelled in his pants. When she plastered herself to his body and he was in no hurry to pry her loose. In a swift move, Ebony's hand roamed and slid over his crotch. Isaiah gasped in surprise.

"Ooooh-la-la. I think the dragon is awake." Ebony giggled then cupped him as casually as she would a zucchini in a supermarket produce department. "Think he's too hot to handle?" He saw the naughty gleam in her heavy-lidded eyes.

Isaiah enjoyed the firm, intimate touch as her fingers dallied along the length of him before softly cradling his balls. That was nearly his undoing. He groaned, then managed to remind himself that this was obviously those gartinis acting out. He placed his hand on top of her offending one and guided it safely away from his crested zipper. He lifted her soft hand to his mouth, where he gently kissed her knuckles. "Believe me, darlin', you're in no condition to find out—not tonight anyway."

"We're home already?" Ebony slurred as if she'd just noticed they were back at Waymon and Kenny-Wayne's place. It didn't take much to divert her attention from his manly assets and Isaiah's ego deflated.

She broke free and stumbled toward the ranch house. He came after her. "Wait. Let me help you up the garage stairs."

Ebony clung to his arm again. He relished the feel of her drawing from his strength and steadiness.

Once inside Kenny-Wayne's room, Ebony flopped on the bed, out cold as soon as her mop of microbraids hit the water mattress. As he tried to move away, his Rolex snagged her macramé bracelet. He fumbled to separate them, but couldn't without damaging his watch or her bracelet. Her dime-store ornament had seen better days and could be easily replaced so he looked around for a pair of scissors or knife to snip it off her wrist, then thought better of it. Making a judgment call about her ratty little scrap of twine was unfair. Instead he slipped his hand out of the watch and slipped it over her wrist. No harm in her sleeping with it, he decided, looking down at the pretty face he'd come to adore too much. Long glossy lashes curled above perfect high cheekbones. Sinfully full lips begged to be kissed. Isaiah leaned toward her, unable to resist. Just one kiss—gentle and light. Much like a feather's caress. His mouth lingered an inch away when her lips slightly parted and a garlic-laced snort of a snore tore from them. Chuckling lightly, he planted a soft lingering kiss on her forehead instead. Her god-awful snoring—with its raspberry noise on the inhale and broken whistle hiss on the exhale—grew louder. He gently freed the renegade braid tangled in the tiny gold hoop dangling from her left earlobe. Her Reeboks came off before he covered her with a sheet then settled on his beanbag bed for the night.

CHAPTER 14

Ebony awoke to the irritating buzz and tap-tap of a fly trapped between the windowpane and blinds. She groaned and covered her throbbing head with a pillow, but Isaiah's chipper greeting broke through.

"Good morning." He appeared happier than a man with a rash scattered on his person had a right to be.

Ebony peered over the pillow. A rash had never looked so darn sexy on anyone. He stood before her with his hunkiness emphasized by a ribbed black shirt and jeans.

"What's so good about it?" She squinted, growing more fractious with the assault of sunlight that commandeered the room when Isaiah contracted the blinds and freed that blasted fly. As she stretched, the chunky watch on her wrist slid along her forearm. "Where did this come from?"

"It's mine. Got snared on your bracelet last night when I was helping you up the stairs. I didn't want to damage either so I thought it was best to keep them together until you woke up."

Ebony worked the loose threads of her macramé bracelet until she freed it then slipped the watch over her hand. "I know it's not exactly fine jewelry, but thanks for not breaking my bracelet."

"Has sentimental value?" Isaiah sat on the edge of the water bed, sliding the gold Rolex onto his wrist.

Ebony nodded, but she could tell he wanted to know more. "I'm sure you had to save up a lot of cereal-box tops for that," she replied instead, unsure how much she felt comfortable revealing about her bracelet.

"It wasn't cheap."

"I'll bet." Ebony fingered her bracelet. "I made this when I was a kid."

"Really? And you're still wearing it?"

"Yup. I fancied myself a famous jewelry designer when I was six." The memories spilled out. "I used to make things with macramé, beads, strings, Play-Doh, and Popsicle sticks all the time for my family. Ma used to tuck the stuff away in her jewelry box and say she was saving it to coordinate with the best outfit." Ebony bit her bottom lip. "Funny, she never did find just the right outfit. But Daddy, he wore everything I made him—not just around the house, but to work, to church, everywhere—then he'd brag about his little girl who was a talented jewelry designer. That was some crazy-looking stuff I made, too." She laughed. "You should've seen the hideous cuff links I made out of SweeTarts and Super Glue. And the tie clip from lime Life Savers." She felt silly as a sob caught in her throat. "He was such a wonderful, wonderful man."

"He's gone?"

Ebony nodded, blinking and refusing to let the tears fall. "He died."

"I'm sorry to hear that." He reached for her hand, but she moved it and tucked one of her microbraids behind her ear to foil contact. A part of her wanted to let go and accept the comfort he offered, but she couldn't. She still had no idea where he was really coming from and couldn't risk confusing simple kindness for anything more.

"Wanna talk about it?" Isaiah asked with a tenderness she didn't recognize.

Ebony shook her head. "Didn't mean to get all weepy on you."

Fortunately, Isaiah didn't force things. "You could probably use a sugar blast now, right? Look what I ran out and got while you were sleeping." He shoved a box of blueberry muffins toward her.

Ebony's insides roiled and a burning sensation crept up her throat when she got a whiff of a cloyingly fruity aroma. Her stomach lurched with a wave of nausea. "Thanks, but I can't even think about food right now without hurling."

"Uh-oh. Somebody's got a hangover. I figured as much after all those gartinis you slammed down." Isaiah got up and placed the box of muffins across the room on a stereo speaker.

Ebony sat up, resting her back against the headboard. Her head felt as if it were about to implode any second and her tongue felt as if it were coated with gunk. Her breath had to be humming, judging from the foul taste in her mouth. "I can't even remember exactly how many I had. I lost count after the third one."

"You don't drink much, do you?" Isaiah opened the window, but she couldn't tolerate the lavender scent on the morning air. She pushed the covers back and raced to the bathroom, clutching her stomach.

"You okay in there?" Isaiah stood just outside the door.

"Just peachy," she replied between gags.

Isaiah stepped inside the bathroom as she knelt before the toilet with her long curtain of braids obscuring her face as she retched. She felt his hands in her hair, but was too busy purging to care. He gathered her braids and gently swept them away from her face and shoulders and held them.

"You sure you're all right?" He released her hair after moving it out of the line of fire.

She coughed and gagged one last time then plopped her bottom on the floor. "All done," she sighed as her stomach muscles unclenched. She felt weak, but better. She propped her head against the wall and looked up through weary eyes. Isaiah seemed to fill the tiny room. He reached for a washcloth and dampened it with water from the sink before passing it to her.

"Thanks." She wiped her mouth. "I'm a real sight, I'll bet."

"Oh, you don't look so bad." He smiled and extended a hand to help her to stand. He appeared to be zooming in on her breasts.

Ebony looked down at the shrunken T-shirt molded to her body. Two large garlic appliqués were stitched over her breasts. She slowly read the glitter lettering above them, wincing in horror. " 'Bodacious Bulbs, I've Got 'Em.' Where did this tacky thing come from? Where's my Howard University T-shirt?"

"You bought that T-shirt at the Garlic Festival yesterday. Don't you remember?"

"I remember the festival . . . Well, most of it anyway." She went to the sink, brushed her teeth and rinsed with mouthwash, but could still taste a hint of garlic. Rubbing her temples, she squeezed past Isaiah and walked toward the water bed.

"I guess things got a little fuzzy for you after that third gartini, but *we* had a really good time," he said with bawdy mischief in his voice.

Ebony poked his chest with her finger. "Just how good of a time did *we* have?"

"You don't think that I . . . You don't think that I'd actually take advantage of a woman when she's, she's—"

"I believe 'inebriated' is the word you're searching for." She pursed her lips and crossed her arms beneath her garlic appliqués. "How did I end up with this . . . this . . . thing on?"

"You put it on yourself, but don't worry, I retrieved your HU shirt. I know how much it means to you. You'd bartered it away for that garlic number."

"I did?" Ebony searched her muddy memory.

"Yup. You did." Isaiah reached for a blueberry muffin. "The vendor only charged me twice the price of his most expensive T-shirt to get it back."

"Thanks," Ebony said with much reluctance. "I'll pay you back." She reached for her fanny pack.

"Don't worry about it." Isaiah blocked her hand. "Really, it's cool. Please accept it with my compliments."

"What else did I do? Please tell me I didn't do anything too embarrassing."

He settled on the edge of the bed. "You don't have anything to worry about."

She sighed, relieved. "I don't?"

"As a tourist, you'll never see any of those folks again. And I'm sure Mrs. Garlic has already forgiven Mr. Garlic so the happy couple and the little clovettes should be just fine."

"Mr. Garlic? Mrs. Garlic? The clovettes?" A feeling of dread welled in Ebony's empty stomach as a vague memory of the garlic-bulb-costumed characters working the festival grounds materialized. "What about them?"

The amusement in Isaiah's voice belied his poker face. "You sure you want to know?"

He was having way too much fun toying with her. In one swift motion she latched onto his thumb and mimicked a maneuver she'd seen in her self-defense class. "Tell me now or else."

"Hey, violence won't solve anything." His laughter rocketed around the room.

"Maybe not, but I'll bet I can snap your thumb like a twig." Though she had no intention of actually dislocating a joint, she applied just enough pressure to make him think she would in a heartbeat.

He laughed so hard tears misted his eyes. "Why exert all that extra effort? Just exhale. You can melt metal with your breath alone."

Ebony released his thumb, punched his shoulder, then cupped her hand over her mouth. "C'mon, Isaiah, stop clowning around. I need to know what I did."

He pulled her hand away from her mouth. "I was just having fun with you. Your breath's not *that* bad."

"Tell me what I did at the festival. Pleasssse."

"Well, if you must know. You sort of propositioned Mr. Garlic."

"Propositioned him?"

"Yeah, hit on him. You were shameless."

"Shameless?"

"You told him garlic is best stored in a cool, dark place then you tried to coax him over to one of the empty 4-H tents."

Ebony's jaw dropped. "Did not!"

"Did, too. Then you told him garlic was best crushed or pressed and then you tried to—"

"What?" She tugged at his arm.

"Demonstrate."

Ebony squealed.

"I didn't know you went for the tall cartoon-character type," he said. "But hey, whatever floats your boat."

"Oh, no, no, no. I made the biggest fool out of my—" she lamented just before detecting a devilish gleam in his eyes. "You're lying!"

He made a gotcha! face, then let his laughter rip again. "Had you going there for a minute, didn't I?"

Ebony reached for a pillow and swatted at him until a knock at the door interrupted. "Yo, Isaiah!"

Kenny-Wayne—*again*.

Ebony dropped her pillow to open the door.

"Damn, man, what happened to your mug?" Kenny-Wayne pimp-strolled inside, wearing thick polyester high-waisted slacks and a kaleidoscope-print shirt so busy it made Ebony's eyeballs hurt.

"Had a run-in with a bed of poison ivy," Isaiah told him.

Kenny-Wayne winced like a wimp. "Yuck."

"It's not that bad," Ebony piped up in Isaiah's defense. "It's a lot better than yesterday. It'll heal in no time." Kenny-Wayne ogled her garlic bulbs. She grabbed her pillow again and placed it in front of her to block his view. She began gathering some of her things to clean up.

Kenny-Wayne turned his attention back to Isaiah. "Just got a call from Elroy down at the auto shop. Says that part came in. Your car's ready, but if you want it today you'll have to get it within an hour. He's closing up early to head up to Potts for that Garlic Festival. I'm headed to town, I can give you a ride."

Ebony froze, awaiting Isaiah's reply.

Isaiah hesitated.

Ebony hoped he'd refuse Kenny-Wayne's offer. When he didn't, something blooming inside of her wilted a little.

"Thanks, just let me get my keys." Isaiah began searching through a side pocket of his duffel bag.

"You guys only paid for three nights," Kenny-Wayne reminded them. "Not to rush you or anything, but my lady Leanita's coming over in a bit. So I'm ducking out to pick up a bottle of Pink Champale and some green-apple incense. That incense always drives Leanita wild." He wiggled his brows and appeared to salivate in anticipation. "Uncle Waymon's digs ain't exactly a private player's paradise, know what I mean? He's really strict about what goes on under his roof."

"No problem," Isaiah said. "Just let me throw a few things in my bag and I'm good to go. The tournament's over so I can hit the road for Cincinnati after I get my car."

Isaiah seemed too eager to bolt. After everything they'd been through together in the past few days, Ebony had foolishly expected a more private, lingering goodbye. "I need some time to shower, dress, and pack, but I should be gone before you get back," she told Kenny-Wayne.

After giving the room a quick once-over and gathering the rest of his belongings, Isaiah turned to Ebony, obviously as an afterthought. "Hey, lady, thanks for helping me out this weekend—the rides, the trip to the doctor, the company... When you weren't being a pain, I actually enjoyed myself." When he reached out and grasped her hands, she thought she saw something more in his eyes, but it had to be wishful thinking on her part.

Ebony's lips parted. She wanted to tell Isaiah not to leave with Kenny-Wayne. She'd drive him to the auto shop. Maybe they could even grab a quick bite at Pearlie Mae's Diner for the road. Well, maybe her stomach couldn't handle a meal so soon, but a ginger ale and a couple of crackers would ease down okay. "Isaiah, I—"

"Hey, man, we gotta go." Kenny-Wayne was a disco-duds-wearing knot of impatience, with his fidgeting and interruptions. Darn him. He'd obliterated Ebony's courage. "Leanita's going to blow this way before I know it. That's my ass if she shows up and I ain't back from the store."

"Just a minute." Isaiah glanced over his shoulder at Kenny-

Wayne then faced Ebony again. "You were saying?"

"I . . . I . . . uh . . . hope you have a safe trip back," Ebony replied.

"Oh." Isaiah's gaze lingered on her a little longer. "Well, I guess this is it, then. I'm sure we'll bump into each other again."

Bump into each other? It sounded so impersonal and random, but what did she expect? Did she actually think he'd ask for her telephone number? Maybe even a date? She squelched any deluded hopes that he would. Besides, she really didn't have time for intimate entanglements anyway.

She gave him an anemic smile and freed her hands from his. "See ya around."

Isaiah hoisted the straps of his duffel bag onto one shoulder, then turned to leave with Kenny-Wayne. "Yeah, see ya around."

Isaiah rode to Elroy's auto shop half-pondering his hasty farewell to Ebony and half-listening to Kenny-Wayne's jawing about his hot date with Leanita. Feeling oddly bereft, he focused on the thatch of trees flanking the road. If he had his druthers, Ebony would've given him a lift to Elroy's, but turning down Kenny-Wayne's offer was akin to admitting he wasn't ready to say goodbye to her. No way in hell would he tip his hand like that. He dug Ebony a lot more than his comfort zone allowed and he wondered if she possibly felt the same way about him. For the briefest moment he thought he saw a flicker of regret in her eyes when they had exchanged goodbyes, but he'd quickly dismissed it. She wasn't exactly falling all over herself to counter Kenny-Wayne's offer. More likely, she couldn't wait to get Isaiah out of her hair. Sure, there'd been brief cease-fires over the weekend, but there was never any doubt that the earth-scorching battle to the death was still on. They both still wanted that Renfro exclusive and that *Examiner* job in the worst kind of way.

"Leanita really knows how to put a hurtin' on a brother," Kenny-Wayne boasted, as he guided his old but pristine green Ford Grenada along a small two-lane road leading to downtown Grundie, all four blocks of it. "A real good kinda' hurtin'. Know what I'm saying?" His overprocessed curls gleamed in the bright Sunday morning sunlight. "So is that Ebony hot or what?"

Isaiah simply shot him a none-of-your-damn-business look. "Not the kiss-and-tell type?" Kenny-Wayne smiled, showcasing his gold-capped front tooth. "That's cool. She's a little too stringy for my taste. I tend to like women with a little more junk in their trunks. Catch my drift?" He hardy-har-harred, slapping Isaiah's knee. "But she's cute, though—in a girl-next-door sort of way. Looks real intelligent and all."

Isaiah didn't reply as he quelled the urge to stuff both of the big fuzzy red dice dangling from the rearview mirror in Kenny-Wayne's mouth. They couldn't arrive at Elroy's soon enough. Isaiah would slip inside his Mustang, hit the highway, and put as many miles as he could between himself and Grundie.

Ebony's hellish hangover passed after a warm shower. She quickly dressed in a yellow T-shirt and matching Bermuda shorts, but packing proved problematic. She couldn't find her favorite Howard University T-shirt.

She'd searched everywhere, even worked up the courage to sort through Kenny-Wayne's dirty clothes exploding from his closets and beneath his bed. She came across a plain white Fruit of the Loom T-shirt instead, wedged between a stereo speaker and one of the sagging beanbags. It wasn't Kenny-Wayne's. It held the faint scent of Isaiah's cologne. She buried her nose in it. A grin tugged at her lips. If it was one of his favorite shirts—which she was sure it was—he'd want it returned immediately. So it was a plain white crew-neck Fruit of the Loom, but what if it held some great sentimental value? Certain her misplaced Howard University T-shirt would surface later among her packed things, she checked her watch. If she hurried she might make it to the auto shop before Isaiah departed.

* * *

In the parking lot of Elroy's auto shop, Isaiah removed his duffel bag from Kenny-Wayne's Grenada and placed it in the trunk of his own idling Mustang.

"Thanks for the ride," Isaiah told Kenny-Wayne, who, much to Isaiah's surprise, didn't request taxi fare.

"Ain't no thang, but chicken wang," Kenny-Wayne cheesed from the driver's seat of his car. "Well, I'm about to bounce. Pleasure doing business with you and your lady. If you're ever in these parts again, look me up. Maybe we can double-date or something."

Isaiah smiled, but remained noncommittal as he reached for his wallet to pay Elroy.

"Later, dude." Kenny-Wayne took off.

"Thanks, man." Isaiah settled his bill with Elroy. "Great job."

Elroy moved to lower the double-wide doors to his garage. "Glad I could help."

"Heard you're closing up early again today."

"Yup. Headed up to Potts for that Garlic Festival. Today's the last day."

Isaiah realized he missed Ebony already. "Yeah, I was just up there yesterday."

"Got to pick up the wife and kids first." Elroy wiped his grease-stained hands on a rag. "My wife just loves that zydeco group there."

"Have a good time, but watch out for those gartinis. They'll sneak up on you."

Isaiah ducked inside his car. The sun blazed. He couldn't wait to blast the air-conditioning. In the meantime he patted his shirt pocket for his sunglasses before he remembered that, in his rush to pack, he'd tossed them inside his duffel bag. He got out and popped the trunk. As he retrieved the sunglasses, he noticed Ebony's T-shirt wadded among his own clothing inside the duffel bag. Her favorite Howard University T-shirt from her beloved sister. He checked his watch. Ebony had to shower, change, and pack so she was probably still at Kenny-Wayne's. There were no two ways about it, he decided with a sly grin. He'd have to drive *all* the way back to Kenny-Wayne's to return it.

Parked on Shady Oak Road at the curb in front of Kenny-Wayne and Waymon's place, Ebony prepared to crank up her Escort when she looked up and saw Isaiah's Mustang turning off Weeping Willow Way onto Shady Oak. He parked at the opposite curb.

Ebony and Isaiah climbed out of their cars clutching garments as if they were spun from pure fourteen-karat gold and studded with Tiffany diamonds. They met in the middle of the quiet road.

"You forgot your—" they exclaimed in unison before breaking out into a round of anxious laughter.

Ebony's heart beat with a lickety-split cadence. "Your T-shirt!" she said breathlessly, shoving it at him.

"*Your* T-shirt." Isaiah held it up by the sleeves.

They swapped the garments with equal fervor.

Judging from the smile on Isaiah's face, she knew he was glad to see her, though they'd only been apart an hour. "Thanks," she said, peering up at him through her lashes, as she clutched her T-shirt. Suddenly self-conscious about her own obvious glee, she added, "I was just looking all over for this. You know it's my favorite."

"Yeah, you told me. Your sister Kenya bought it for you. And thank you. This T-shirt..." He inspected the clump of white fabric in his hand. "This T-shirt... Well, as you can see here on the label, it's a hundred-percent combed cotton..."

"Yes, pure combed cotton."

"Preshrunk."

"The best kind."

"Made in Jamaica."

"Yeah, Jamaica, mon," Ebony echoed, affecting a bad West Indian accent.

They stood in the middle of the street, grinning at each other like idiots.

Ebony spoke first. "So, you haven't left town yet," she

stated dumbly, marveling at how amazing his warm brown eyes looked in the sunlight.

"You neither, I see."

"So your car's all fixed and ready to go, huh?"

"Yeah, but I'm not," Isaiah blurted. "Are you in a big rush to get back to Cincinnati?"

"No!" flew out of Ebony's mouth before she had a chance to think or check her planner.

"What do you say we head back up to that festival? It's the last day so it's bound to be a bigger blast than yesterday."

"Okay, but I'm steering clear of those gartinis." Ebony turned to head for her Escort when Isaiah took her hand.

"No use burning double the gas, just ride with me. I'll drive you back to your car later."

"Okay." Carpooling appealed to Ebony's penny-pinching sensibilities, but the opportunity to spend the ride time with Isaiah appealed to her even more. "Can we stop at a pay phone on the way? I'd like to call my folks to tell them I'm going to be late."

"You can use my cell phone in the glove compartment. I'm not on any restrictive supersaver plan."

Ebony and Isaiah were turned away when they tried to sneak on the Whip-O-Whirl and the Go-Go Gator Coaster.

Giddy with anticipation Ebony climbed into a car on the Scrambler, one of the few festival rides that accommodated adults.

"This is my all-time *favoritest* ride." Ebony repeated an expression she hadn't uttered in over twenty years. She scooted across the Scrambler seat to make room for Isaiah, who followed close behind. "Actually, when I was little they were all my favoritest rides. I used to love it when my dad would take Kenya and me to fairs and carnivals. I never wanted to leave. I wanted to live in the Moon Cars."

Isaiah settled in, engaging the safety bar in front of them.

Ebony wedged her bottom in the opposite corner, putting several inches of space between them. Isaiah reached up and draped his arm along the back of their car.

"You're like a big kid, know that?"

"Are you making fun of me?" She quirked a brow.

"No, I think it's cute."

The car slowly glided ahead. The momentum jerked and snatched them in all directions. The Scrambler cars twisted and turned in a pattern similar to the beaters on a cake mixer.

With braids whipping across her face and her arms in the air, Ebony squealed in delight. The centrifugal force practically thrust her into Isaiah's lap. He laughed heartily, welcoming her in his embrace. She snuggled even closer, with her back pressed against his chest. She used the herky-jerky motion of the ride as an excuse to savor the solid strength of his body and the intoxicating scent of his cologne. As his arms curved just under her breasts, she let her fingers caress the soft silky hairs and snaking veins along his powerful forearms. Minutes later the ride came to a halt. Isaiah held on to her. But without the momentum of the ride, she couldn't think of one rational reason why she shouldn't pull away. Sure she resembled Medusa, she scooted back to her side of the seat and smoothed her wind-whipped braids. She unlatched the safety bar and hopped out.

"Man oh man, that was fun!"

"Wanna go again?" he asked, with an arm still resting on the back of the car as if he'd settled in for the duration.

Boy, was she tempted, but sitting so close to him scrambled her brain more than any amusement ride could. She had to keep her wits about her and stay focused—especially now that it was becoming more difficult to do. "Not right now. I'm feeling pretty lucky. Let's hit the midway games."

Ebony knew she should've stopped while ahead, but she was having way too much fun kicking Isaiah's butt at the Ring-a-Bottle game. When they'd moved to the dart game, she'd gotten cocky and agreed when Isaiah challenged her to up the ante.

Moving on to the dart games had been her downfall as Isaiah evened the total score four to four. The first to win five games would take possession of the prizes that had been won by the two of them during their trip down the midway. The loser would head over to the dunking booth to take the hot seat and the winner would get three chances to soak the loser. Ebony watched Isaiah, dart poised in hand, deep concentration etched on his handsome face as he surveyed the pink balloon that would seal his victory. Ebony's attempt at coughing to distract him hadn't worked. She shimmied closer, invading his personal space to throw off his aim. She forced a cough again. The dart glided from his hands and landed on the corkboard wall with the pop of its intended target.

"And we have a winner!" The man operating the dart game reached for a toddler-sized stuffed bunny and passed it to Isaiah.

"I think I've been hustled." Ebony swatted at Isaiah, who blocked the blow with the bunny.

"Hustled?"

"Yeah, I smell a rat, a big rash-covered one with tricks up his sleeve."

"Me?"

"All of a sudden you got awfully darn good at that dart game when the stakes got higher. Here." Ebony handed over the stuffed snake and garlic-bulb baseball cap she'd won at the penny- and ring-toss games.

"I'll just take the cap. Don't have much use for soft, cuddly things—at least not the ones that don't wear skirts." He deployed that blindingly sexy smile of his. "In fact, you get to adopt ol' Bugs here." He passed her the stuffed toy as they strolled along the midway.

"We can do the dunking booth now or later." Isaiah reached for the fuzzy purple snake and curled it around his neck like a winter scarf.

"You're serious?" Ebony released a jagged gasp of a laugh. "You're actually going to make me go through with it?"

"Damn straight." Isaiah was all dazzling white teeth. "A bet's a bet, babe."

"But the stuffed animals . . ."

"Toys are one thing, but seeing you dangling precariously over a giant tank of water . . . Now that's an image just too tempting to resist."

Ebony shoved his shoulder. "You're a sadist."

"But you agreed to it."

"Yeah, when I was sure it would be your butt dangling precariously over a giant tank of water."

"Let's go." Isaiah took her by the arm, leading her toward the dreaded festival attraction.

"But Isaiah . . ." Ebony groaned, trying to free her wrist.

"You can swim, can't you?"

"Yeah, but . . . my clothes. I'll catch pneumonia walking around in wet things."

"I'll buy you a brand-new garlic T-shirt and matching shorts to change into. How's that? And for being such a good sport, you get to keep them."

"But . . ." Ebony fumbled for something—anything—to change his mind.

"But nothing. It's just water, H_2O, not a bubbling cauldron of hot oil."

At the dunking booth Isaiah had to pay the operator extra bucks to bend the rules and allow Ebony to sit on the hot seat for his round.

Ebony relaxed when she noticed the dunkee she would temporarily replace was bone-dry.

"Good luck," the rangy, freckle-faced young man said as he scrabbled down the ladder leaning against the giant Plexiglas unit.

"So is that target very easy to hit?" Ebony asked.

"I've made out all right for my set. Maybe you'll get a bunch of bad arms, too. But the woman before me . . . Got dipped so much, she was all pruned up by the time her break rolled around."

Ebony settled on the cool metal bench with her feet dangling a few inches above the huge water tank, about seven feet deep.

"Ready?" Isaiah had the nerve to ask.

Ebony gave him a plastic smile then the finger.

That only broadened Isaiah's devilish smile. "Ahhh, motivation."

Ebony wasn't half as agitated as she pretended, but Isaiah

seemed to get such a kick out of teasing her so she played along. Before this weekend excursion, she couldn't remember when she'd ever had so much fun.

Isaiah kept his eyes trained on the metal bull's-eye he had no intention of actually hitting. As a joke, he'd let Ebony believe he couldn't wait to dunk her. She looked so cute when she bunched those lips of hers in a stubborn pout.

He made a show of winding up with a long arm, lifting one leg in an exaggerated motion before releasing the ball, which soared way off course toward East Mississippi someplace.

"Damn, man, you throw like a girl," one of the guys in line behind him shouted. Isaiah's male pride kicked in, but he refused to let the heckler alter his plan. Isaiah lobbed ball number two, which hit the wall of the garlic french fry stand several feet to his right before ricocheting off the chalk portrait artist's easel. He had one more turn.

Ebony stopped squirming and waved her arms in a victorious gesture. "Strike three and you're out, bud!"

Isaiah did that stupid windup again, but just before he could release the ball someone plucked it out of his hand.

"Let me show you how it's done." It was that jerk from the line.

Before Isaiah could retrieve his ball, the guy pitched it toward the booth. It hit the bull's-eye with a ping, triggering the bench release. With a yelp of surprise and a tidal-wave splash, Ebony plummeted into the tank.

Isaiah shoved the jerk hard enough to send him tumbling to the ground. He drew back to slug him, then turned away from him and rushed toward the tank instead.

Isaiah met a drenched Ebony at the bottom of the ladder. "Are you all right?"

"Yeah!" She smiled up at him, skin, braids, eyelashes, and delicately arched brows glistening with water. "It was actually fun! I've got to do it again!"

Not the reaction Isaiah expected, but he should know by now. Ebony MacKenzie was full of surprises. "You're sure?"

"Yeah, it was great! Refreshing! Exhilarating, even!"

He grinned. "You sound like you just took the Nestea plunge or something."

"Yeah! It was exactly like those old commercials!" As she scaled back up the ladder, Isaiah did a drop-jawed double take at her wet shorts. The imprint of skimpy black panties hugged the seductive curves of her rump. What was it with this ultra-conservative woman and sexpot underwear? He liked it. A lot!

"What are you staring at?" As she twisted on the ladder to peer down at him he also noticed that her yellow T-shirt plastered the swells of her breasts. The intricate pattern of a lace underwire bra swirled around the twin chocolate areolas and pebbled nipples. An erection quickly filled his pants.

"Ebony... uh... I think you'd better come back down here." She obviously didn't have a clue that her wet duds were sheer as Saran Wrap. He could just imagine the ogling and wolf calls she'd generate from the testosterone troop standing in line.

"*What?* This was *your* idea, remember?" She'd already plopped back down on the metal bench.

Isaiah quickly ripped his shirt over his head and started up the steps to cover her. Too late.

"Oh, baby! Hubba-hubba!" someone from the line yelled with exaggerated smooching sounds. "What a rack!"

"OOO-weeee! Nice knockers!" another guy bellowed amid a chorus of whistles.

Isaiah reached the top of the ladder, just as it dawned on Ebony what the hoots and howls were about. "Oh, my goodness!" she shrieked, crisscrossing her arms over her chest. Isaiah drew her into his arms, covering her with his shirt. Wildly, she tugged at the shirt and clutched his arms. The ladder screeched and teetered. Isaiah lost his footing. Both went tumbling into the tank.

Ebony stood inside a sun-steamed portable restroom, where she'd sought refuge while awaiting Isaiah's return with her change of clothes. It felt like a sauna inside. The borrowed polo shirt had to go, she decided, pulling it over her head, careful to keep her own wet shirt in place.

"It's me." Isaiah tapped on the door. "Are you decent?"

"That depends on your definition of decent," Ebony grumbled, unlocking the door.

"I got you a festival T-shirt and shorts." Stepping inside, Isaiah passed the Day-Glo orange and green garments to her. "That's all that was left in your size."

As the tight compartment became tighter, Ebony's breath caught and a zingy, tingly sensation danced between her thighs. All she could see was his bare chest, damp and glistening from their dip. He had the most enticing pecs she'd ever admired in her life—full, hard, and golden brown, with that diamond pattern of hair so neatly plastered against his skin, it appeared as if someone had taken a comb to it. She longed to let her fingers trace the trenches of his defined abs and explore the pipelike crest in his wet jeans. She managed to tear her gaze away from his body, but looking him in the eye couldn't cool her body temperature or calm her racing heartbeat. Not when he had a face that should be splashed across Cineplex screens and magazine covers. She didn't even think she could be attracted to men with facial hair. Until Isaiah, she'd preferred the smooth, clean-shaven type, equating beards, moustaches, and such with the sinister. But Isaiah's thick brows, dark glistening moustache, and goatee were dangerously alluring and mysterious in a way that made her want to be buck-wild with him. What was she thinking anyway, inviting him inside the tiny compartment that only allowed a few inches between them?

"I'm getting quite a reputation as the festival floozy." Ebony chuckled nervously as Isaiah pulled the door closed behind him. "One minute I'm treating guys at the dunking-booth line to a wet T-shirt show. And the next . . . well, I'm sure everybody thinks I'm treating you and the Ty-D-Bol Man to Porta Potti lap dances."

"Hmmm, now there's an idea . . ." Isaiah wiggled a brow.

"You don't have enough money on you to even entertain the thought," Ebony retorted, knowing full well she'd do it in a heartbeat if she weren't so worried about what he'd think of her afterward. She was much too principled to do anything so ... so ... brazen. Impulsiveness wasn't exactly her strong suit, either, but who said she couldn't change? The transformation had already begun. Sure he could see right through her wet T-shirt and bra, she hadn't bothered to cover herself. In fact, she rather enjoyed the smoldering look he gave her right then and the way he didn't bother to sneak peeks at her breasts. He admired them outright. All doubts that he could actually be physically attracted to her drifted away. She'd never felt so sexy and desirable. She inched closer, close enough to feel heat radiating from his chest. Her flesh tightened and goosebumped with pleasure in response.

"I'm sure we could come up with something that would be satisfactory to both parties," he whispered against her cheek, as his hand stole to one of her breasts, cupping it firmly.

Ebony sighed in response. "To both parties?" Her lips parted and grazed his chest enough to feel the rumble of his reply. If she had the nerve, it would be so easy to let the tip of her tongue taste the moist skin there.

"Uh-huh." He blew softly into her ear, enveloping her waist and pulling her close enough to feel his arousal. "You dance for me and I'll—"

"Hey, you two! This ain't the Motel Six!" somebody bellowed with an angry rap on the door. "Move it along! There's a line of folks desperate to do their business!"

"Damn!" Isaiah released Ebony and jumped back, inadvertently banging his head against the wall. "Ow! One more interruption . . . just one more interruption."

"Just a minute!" Ebony called out to the person pounding on the door. "You've got to step out so I can get dressed. There's not enough room for both of us to move around comfortably or safely."

Isaiah rubbed the back of his head. "I'd say we were doing just fine a minute ago."

"Go." Ebony pointed to the door. "Now. Before they storm this thing."

As Isaiah stepped out of the portable restroom, Ebony couldn't help but wonder if the interruptions were some divine sign that what almost happened between them wasn't supposed to be.

Ebony and Isaiah changed out of their wet clothes into matching Garlic Festival Day-Glo souvenir gear. She found the drive from Potts back to Grundie uncomfortably quiet. After Isaiah pulled his car behind her Escort parked in front of Waymon and Kenny-Wayne's place, he cut his ignition.

Ebony climbed out, tugging up shorts too loose in the waist.

"I hope I never lay eyes on those festival folks again. What must they think?"

"Who cares?" Isaiah walked her to the driver's side of the Escort.

"I do," she replied, slightly chagrined. "It's different for a guy."

"Only if you let it be. You really ought to loosen up and stop worrying about what strangers think all the time."

"I suppose you're right." Ebony searched her fanny pack for her keys. "But it's not that easy. I'm not looking forward to the long drive home."

Isaiah sighed. "Tell me about it. But I have to admit, the little detour was worth it. I can't remember the last time I've had so much fun. Today was nearly perfect—even the impromptu dip in that tank and especially the Porta Potti part. If I recall, we were negotiating the terms of a lap dance when we were so rudely interrupted."

"Oh, that." Ebony halted her search for her keys.

"Yeah, that." Isaiah let his killer grin loose. "You didn't think I'd forget, did you? We can start again. Negotiating the terms, I mean." He wrapped one arm around her waist and used a finger to trace her lips as he moistened his own. "You have the sexiest mouth I've ever seen so let's start with something simple, shall we?" He caressed her cheek, then slipped both arms around Ebony's waist. He drew her closer and nipped at her hypersensitive earlobe with his teeth. His warm breath against her skin and his spicy masculine scent caused white-hot waves of yearning to ripple through her body.

"Simple?" She'd relinquished all control, clutching the round hardness of his broad shoulders to brace herself while he dallied at the shell of her ear. She shuddered with a dizzying rush of delight. All rational thought was impossible.

"Yeah, simple. Like this." Isaiah captured her lips and let his tongue explore the warm cavern of her mouth. As his tongue stroked hers, he made her a believer in the existence of the mythical knee-weakening kiss. A kiss with so much power, magic, and fire, she should've slithered along the side of her Escort and pooled onto the gravel in a hot, sticky gob of goo. He tasted and felt better than she'd dreamed. His erection pressed against the soft curve just above her belly button like a heat-seeking missile. His husky moan of pleasure and deep breathing reverberated in her ears as his eager hand stroked one of her breasts. His thumb brushed a hard nipple as he drew his lips away just long enough to say, "You don't know how bad I've wanted to do this." Keeping her body pressed against his, he pinned her against the Escort. He slipped a knee between her legs and slowly ground his pelvis into hers with a rhythm as hot and sultry as a Latin dance. Sensation mounted as she savored the hard, thick length of him at the most sensitive tip of her sex. The heat, the motion, the delicious pleasure, his closeness, stripped away the last of her defenses and inhibitions. She didn't care that they were on a public road. An avalanche of repressed desire, want, and need crushed her. She quickly reached back with one hand to open a back door. They tumbled inside on the back seat, pushing away the faded green blanket, a pair of broken sunglasses, and faded *Essence* magazines. Ebony curled her arms around his neck and held on to him. This was about as wild and impulsive as it could get for her. If Isaiah kept touching and kissing her that way, she'd let him take her right there in the back seat of her car.

CHAPTER 15

The unflinching beam of headlights shocked Ebony and Isaiah apart.

Ebony recognized the busy paisley print of Kenny-Wayne's shirt through the Escort's steamed-up windows. He tapped the glass.

Isaiah lowered the window.

"What's up! Boy-ee! I see you getting a little somethin'-somethin' going back here." Kenny-Wayne lifted his hand to pound fists with Isaiah, who was clearly in no mood for exchanging jovial brother-man greetings. "So you two decided to stick around town a little longer."

Somebody honked the horn in the Grenada he had double-parked next to the Escort. "That's Leanita," Kenny-Wayne told them. "I was about to get into a little somethin'-somethin' myself, but hey, since the gang's all here, we should hang out and kick it like we talked about this morning." Kenny-Wayne soon had the door open and Leanita by his side. "This is Isaiah and his lady, Ebony, the folks who rented my crib for a few days."

"Hey." Leanita offered a shake. Her hands and wrists were heavy with assorted gold baubles and bracelets. "Nice to meet y'all." She had gel-molded and freeze-dried her hair in one of those sistah-girl styles that resembled an abstract postmodern sculpture. She wore baggy cargo pants that emphasized a pear shape and a tiny T-shirt revealed a flat tummy with an outtie navel.

"I was just trying to get Ebony and Isaiah to hang out with us," Kenny-Wayne told Leanita.

Isaiah opened his mouth to decline, but Kenny-Wayne continued. "They're two of the coolest people you'd ever want to meet, Leanita. You know how some city people are all stuck-up, treating small-town folks like something they scraped off their shoes? Well, Ebony and Isaiah here are realer than real—good people, way down-to-earth. Know what I'm saying?"

"That's all Kenny-Wayne's been talking about since you two came to town," Leanita added with a sugary smile. "How nice you were. I'm so glad I got a chance to meet you before you left."

"So how 'bout we play a few hands of spades for the road?" Kenny-Wayne persisted.

"Oh, yeah, that'll be the bomb!" Leanita said. "That'll give Ebony here a chance to tell me about her braids. I've been thinking about getting some myself, but I'm not sure. You know, I've heard the stories about sitting in the chair for ten to twelve hours at a time to get them. I don't think I can sit still that long."

Kenny-Wayne slapped her bottom. "Girl, you got enough roast in the meat house back there to cushion you till Christmas. You wouldn't have to move for food or water for days—sorta like a camel with its hump." Kenny-Wayne yukked it up.

Leanita shot back, "This camel and her hump will have you begging for it later tonight. Believe that."

Kenny-Wayne, who turned his attention back to Isaiah, obviously decided he'd worry about that later. "Say, man, you and your honey going to come play some spades with us in Uncle Waymon's den or what?"

Isaiah looked at Ebony as if he expected her to play bad cop and decline, but she simply shrugged in surrender.

Kenny-Wayne's spiel about what nice city folks they were had obviously gotten to Isaiah, because it had gotten to her as well.

Isaiah caved much faster than expected. "All right, but just a few hands. How about you, Ebony?"

Ebony checked her watch. "All right, but we still have to drive back to Cincinnati tonight and I need to use your phone to call my folks to tell them I'm going to be later than I thought—again."

"Cool!" Kenny-Wayne and Leanita enthused at once.

Five hands of spades later, Ebony and Isaiah, who had paired up, lost miserably. Kenny-Wayne and Leanita believed in winning at all costs and the cheating at the card table was shameless. Their overly animated gestures and coughing spells were anything but subtle.

It didn't take long for Ebony to crack their code.

An earlobe tug: Don't play hearts.

Two fake coughs: Cutting diamonds.

An exaggerated clearing of the throat: Hold on to your clubs.

A scratch on the left nostril: Trump tight.

A big ol' Kool-Aid smile: Holding the big joker.

But winning a card game was far from Ebony's mind as she and Isaiah exchanged heated glances.

Kenny-Wayne's uncle, Waymon, had played the perfect host, supplying his guests with an assortment of soft drinks and snacks, but Ebony couldn't forget how the two men had bilked them out of beaucoup bucks for the smallest amenities during their stay. She almost declined his offerings, believing the older man would present them with another outrageous bill, like ten bucks for a can of cola, before the evening ended. She'd only sipped a Seven-Up and dug into the guacamole dip with a rippled potato chip after Waymon assured them the refreshments were on the house.

After losing their seventh hand, Isaiah stacked the cards in front of him and shoved them to the table's center, ready to call it a night. "I think I'd better hit the road."

"Yeah." Ebony stifled a yawn. "Me, too."

"Wait, it's kinda late." Kenny-Wayne pointed to the clock on the paneled den wall which read 11:13 P.M. "Sure you two don't want to stay another night?"

Isaiah's brows hitched up. "What? So you can overcharge us for one more night?"

"No, man." Kenny-Wayne chuckled. "I wouldn't play you like that. And besides, I was the one who talked you into hanging around." He looked at his uncle. "You don't mind if they stay one more night for free, right?"

"Mi casa, su casa," said Waymon, a balding little gnome of a man with a tendency to make grand gestures with his hands.

Skeptical about the pair's sudden generosity, Isaiah concluded Waymon must've already squeezed the month's mortgage payment out of them.

"What about me?" Leanita stretched in exhaustion, exposing even more of her brown belly. "You know the handyman was at my apartment painting my bedroom. The fumes are awful."

"You can stay, too!" Kenny-Wayne's lips kicked up in a wolf's grin.

Leanita added, "It could be like one big coed pajama party!"

"Actually, I was kinda thinking we'd split up into pairs," Kenny-Wayne countered.

Now Kenny-Wayne was talking, Isaiah thought with satisfaction. One more night with Ebony in Kenny-Wayne's tacky room wouldn't be so bad after all if he wasn't banished to those damn beanbags. He and Ebony could pick up where they left off in the back seat of her car.

"Ain't gonna be no pajama parties in my place tonight," Waymon decreed. "I plan to get a good night's sleep."

"Uncle has spoken," Kenny-Wayne announced, far from regretful. "Looks like we're splitting up. You and me, Leanita."

"Not so fast, Mr. Hot Pants," Waymon said. "What you do

in your place over the garage is your business, but there'll be no mattress mambo in this house."

Kenny-Wayne groaned.

"And since we have guests, the ladies get Kenny-Wayne's room. You hard-legs sleep here in the den. You can share the sofa bed or flip each other for it. The loser gets to choose between a sleeping bag on the floor or my Barcalounger. You two dudes work it out."

Damn. Isaiah looked over at Ebony, but couldn't tell if she was equally disappointed by the sleeping arrangements.

As Kenny-Wayne and Leanita swapped sloppy good-night kisses, Isaiah made his way to Ebony. "Meet me out back on the deck in half an hour," he whispered in her ear.

Waymon let Ebony make what she hoped would be the last call to her folks to let them know she would stay another night in Grundie after all. Much to her surprise the call was free, but Waymon stood close by to make sure she didn't talk longer than the four courtesy minutes he'd allotted to her.

When she stepped out to fetch her bag from her car, she had hoped Isaiah would accompany her, but Waymon, playing the role of the eagle-eyed chaperon, beat him to the punch. Waymon also made sure Ebony and Leanita were safely tucked away in Kenny-Wayne's garage room before he turned in for the night.

As Ebony changed into her Mickey Mouse pj's she reminisced about how Isaiah had filled out the bottoms the previous nights. Leanita chattered away as she slipped into one of Kenny-Wayne's ribbed tank tees and a pair of his athletic shorts. In less than fifteen minutes Ebony was privy to all the details of Leanita's sex life—from the freaky curve in Kenny-Wayne's ding-a-ling to how he had a tendency to be quick on the draw in the nookie department. Way too much information for Ebony, who kept trying to steer the conversation back to more innocuous topics. "So, you lived in Grundie long?"

"All my life." Leanita climbed into the waterbed, positioning her pillow at the foot as they had agreed. "So, what do you think?"

"About you living in Grundie all your life?"

"No, silly." Leanita clucked with impatience. "For the third time, what do you think about Kenny-Wayne kissing my armpits during foreplay?"

"Armpits?" Ebony scrunched her nose, but wasn't surprised Kenny-Wayne would have such a fetish.

"That's what I thought at first, but hey, I'm a modern sorta girl. I'll go with the flow."

Ebony yawned and checked her watch before reaching to turn off the Colt .45 lamp. She had planned to slip out and meet Isaiah out back, but Leanita was nowhere near drifting off. She doubted she could leave without Leanita asking her a dozen questions and maybe even trying to tag along. Ebony would have to wait a little longer before she could make her move.

She had just enough time to ponder whether meeting Isaiah was really a good idea. The smoldering looks he'd given her during the card game left little doubt what he had in mind. They'd pick up where they left off before Kenny-Wayne and Leanita interrupted them, but was she really ready to take things to that level? He was still her main competition for Renfro, but now that there'd been some kissing and groping in the back seat of her car, she'd almost forgotten why she'd come to Grundie in the first place. Isaiah had that effect on her and she wasn't sure she liked it. Feeling out of control of her thoughts was too foreign. She needed to slow things down. As she yawned into her sweatshirt-swaddled pillow, Ebony's eyelids grew heavier as Leanita's yammering faded out.

Isaiah won the coin toss and got the sofa.

"This Barcalounger ain't cutting it." Kenny-Wayne had been bumping his gums nonstop and had no plans to visit Snoozeville anytime soon.

Isaiah checked his watch. He had ten minutes to get out to that deck. He said the first thing that popped in his head as he got up to leave. "Gotta take a leak."

"Hey, man, the bathroom is the other way." Kenny-Wayne

pointed in the direction that would take Isaiah deeper inside the house.

"My bad." Isaiah headed down the hall and waited in the bathroom for ten minutes. He returned to find Kenny-Wayne dozing in the recliner with a blanket tossed across his body. As Isaiah tipped toward the back door, he noisily stubbed his toe on the leg of a chair. He cursed under his breath, stopping briefly to rub his big toe and check a sleeping Kenny-Wayne. In the kitchen Isaiah unlocked the back door.

"Going someplace?" Waymon stood framed in the doorway between the kitchen and the hall.

"Just stepping out for some fresh night air, usually helps me sleep better."

"Whatever it is, make sure you keep it outside. I'll have no hanky-panky in my house," Waymon warned.

Twenty-five minutes passed with no sign of Ebony. Isaiah paced the deck then scooped up a few pebbles and tossed them at one of the garage-apartment's darkened windows. The curtains fluttered. When Ebony waved he waved back. He smiled in anticipation, then stretched out on a vinyl deck chair. He looked up at the bright stars piercing the perfect night sky until soft hands covered his eyes.

Isaiah's grin broadened as he moved the soft hands to his mouth and pressed kisses on each palm.

"What took you so lo—" Isaiah turned on the lounger then froze. "Leanita?"

"I knew you were feeling me in there, baby." Leanita hitched one leg up and straddled his thighs and massaged his bare chest.

"But—"

She pressed a finger to his lips. "Don't worry, I was feeling you, too."

Isaiah grabbed both of her hands with one of his. "There's been a misunderstanding."

"No misunderstanding, sugar. I know you want me. I want you, too. Chemistry's a bitch, ain't it? Sometimes you just can't fight it." She leaned forward, puckering at him. Big wet lips came at him, about as appealing as those on the day's fresh catch.

He pushed her shoulders and held her in place. "Look, I thought you were Ebony."

Leanita snickered. "Oh, so that's how you want to play it. I'm game. It'll help us both deal with the guilt we might feel later. I thought you were Kenny-Wayne." She began puckering her fish lips again. "We both just sleep-walked out here and ended up in each other's arms."

"Leanita... I was trying to get Ebony's attention when I threw the pebbles at the window." Isaiah would never manhandle a woman, but Leanita was buck-strong. That made it difficult to pry her off without using some force.

"I waved and you waved back. Girlfriend ain't thinking about you. I could tell she wasn't taking care of business judging from all those nature bumps on your face. It's obvious you need it and you need it bad!"

"Nature bumps? I've got poison ivy!"

"Yeah, whatever you say. Anyway, your girl's been calling the hogs since her head hit the damn pillow. She's a sound sleeper, too, so we don't have to worry about her hearing us. We can get as loud as we want out here. I like it loud, rough ... and nasty." Her tongue flicked out like a snake's. "Talk dirty to me."

When Leanita reached for the fly of his festival shorts he bolted upright, sending her catapulting across the deck where she landed on a vinyl lawn chair. Lights snapped on and Isaiah attempted to inch as far away from the crime scene as possible without looking guilty. Kenny-Wayne stepped out onto the deck. "What the hell are you two doing out here—*alone*?"

Leanita adjusted her T-shirt. "Just came out to get some fresh air, Pookie Bear, and uh... just bumped into Isaiah here."

A long tension-infused minute passed among Isaiah's thundering heartbeat and rapid breathing mingled with the chirp of crickets and the rustle of a night breeze through the trees.

"I suppose Isaiah just wanted some fresh air, too?" Kenny-

Wayne gave them both long, searching looks as suspicion gleamed in his eyes. The silence stretched a minute too long for comfort as he sized up Isaiah and obviously concluded jumping in his face would've been hazardous to his health. "Guess everybody's having trouble sleeping tonight," he finally said.

Relieved he wouldn't have to mix it up with Kenny-Wayne, Isaiah faked a yawn and stretched. "I think the sandman's about to roll around here after all." He strolled past Kenny-Wayne and his freak of a girlfriend.

The next morning, Isaiah awoke in the funkiest funk. He still couldn't believe Ebony had stood him up the night before and left him a sitting duck for lusty Leanita. After a quick shower and gathering the few items he'd brought inside, he thanked Waymon for his hospitality and swapped goodbyes with Kenny-Wayne, who didn't seem nearly as chummy as before. Isaiah stalked to his car, determined not to look back. To hell with Ebony.

He'd started the engine when Ebony came running toward his car, her garment bag flying behind her like a superhero's cape. "Isaiah, wait! Wait!"

He lowered the driver's window though he felt like burning rubber on her Reeboks. "What?"

"You're leaving? Without saying goodbye first?"

"What happened to you last night?"

"I'm sorry. I was more tired than I thought. I guess I fell asleep." She caught her breath and lowered her bag. "But—"

"The anticipation was just too much, eh?"

"I . . . I . . . don't know." Ebony stared at her sneakers, as she pushed rocks off the curb with her foot. "I'm not sure it's a good idea for us to . . . you know . . . I—"

He lifted his hand in a peremptory wave. "Say no more. You're absolutely right. It wasn't a good idea. Well, anyway, gotta hit the road. See ya around." He revved the engine, then pushed the gearshift from park to drive.

"See me around?" Ebony had the gall to give him attitude. "Maybe I will, maybe I won't. And if our paths do cross again it'll be too soon!"

"Better get home to *your mama*, before she puts out an APB on you." The way he said "your mama" could've been construed as stooping to play the dozens, but he didn't care. He'd felt like a fool waiting around for her the previous night and that wrestling match he'd endured with Leanita only added insult to injury.

Ebony couldn't believe this was the same man she'd allowed to touch her so intimately the day before. "What's *that* supposed to mean?" she asked through clenched teeth, taking the remark as the insult clearly intended.

"It means..." He paused, then plowed ahead. "Forget it. Later, babe." The Mustang took off.

"And I am *not* your babe!" Ebony shouted at the departing vehicle, then kicked at another rock, wishing it were his knucklehead instead.

CHAPTER 16

Ebony had barely slipped her key into the front door of the MacKenzies' brick colonial when the commotion exploded.

"Drop the broom or the guppies are goners!" Granny Mac dangled a giant white button over Jolene's cherished fishbowl. "I'm warning you!"

Jolene, wielding a broom like a pitchfork, jabbed at Black Gal. The dog barked so frantically that her scrawny jet body seemed to vibrate.

"What's going on here?" Ebony dropped her bag on the floor.

Granny Mac and Jolene shouted at once. Black Gal's incessant, high-pitched yelps added to the racket.

Ebony shrugged out of her jacket. "Please! One at a time!"

Jolene, a short wisp of a woman with vivid red hair, ranted, "That pop-eyed little rat of hers has got to go!"

"If Black Gal goes, I go!" Granny Mac's gray eyes burned with intensity.

"That can be arranged," Jolene spat.

"You can't throw us out!" Granny Mac waved the white disc. "This isn't *your* house! It's Ebony's. Black Gal stays. Right, Ebony?"

All eyes, including Black Gal's bulging marblelike orbs,

were fixed on Ebony. Like her mother, she wasn't thrilled when Granny Mac brought the mischievous Chihuahua to live with them. But her grandmother had bonded with the creature. Ebony didn't have the heart to demand that she find it another home.

The fiercely protective little scrap of a dog worshipped Granny Mac. It nipped and yipped at anyone who got within a three-foot radius of her. Black Gal insisted on an all-access pass inside the house to stay on Granny Mac's heels. The dog would howl until all doors sat ajar just enough for her to slip in and out of every room. Ebony had tried keeping her own bedroom door shut. But Black Gal wasn't having that. She would toss her six-and-a-half-pound body against the door until granted entry. Then as if on some Napoleonic power trip, she'd simply trot inside and trot right back out, showing little interest in Ebony or her belongings.

The dog had done quite a bit of damage around the rest of the house because of its penchant to chew. The legs of furniture, the edges of rugs, stray shoes, dirty laundry and just about everything else within paw's reach. Black Gal had broken Jolene's favorite vase and unfurled so many rolls of toilet paper that the family took to using Kleenex instead. The move and a sudden shift in the dog's routine had also caused too many lapses in its housebreaking, but Ebony needed all the facts before she would say another word. "Okay, what's Black Gal done now?"

"That little rat has pooped and piddled on my belongings for the last time!" Jolene told Ebony. "I was about to swat her flea-bitten behind when Granny Mac started threatening my fish!"

"An eye for an eye!" Granny Mac lifted the big white button over the fishbowl again. "And Black Gal doesn't have fleas. If she does, you gave them to her!"

Ebony still hadn't identified Granny Mac's weapon of choice. "What is that thing, anyway?"

"A Two Thousand Flushes Drop-In!" Granny Mac taunted.

"Toilet-bowl cleaner?" Ebony approached her grandmother, whose white hair seemed to glow above her dark skin.

Granny Mac cackled. "Yup. Two Thousand Flushes, two thousand dead fishes."

"Give me that," Ebony demanded, extending her hand.

"Not until she drops her broom or flies away on it first. Her choice."

Ebony turned to Jolene. "Please drop the broom, Ma."

Jolene narrowed her eyes at Granny Mac then Black Gal, who returned her glare with the audacity of a Doberman, growling and baring tiny sharp teeth as if to say, "Dammit, I'll bite cha!" Reluctantly, Jolene released the broom, which hit the hardwood floor with a clatter.

Ebony then faced Granny Mac. "Okay, your turn."

Granny Mac teased as if she were going to plop the tablet into the fish tank anyway, but the stricken look on Jolene's face was reward enough. When she too relinquished her weapon, Jolene appeared to release the breath she'd been holding.

"You have got to stop this." Ebony dropped on the sofa. "You're two grown women, adults, for crying out loud, behaving like bratty children."

"That pop-eyed little rat of hers is making my life a living hell. Why should I have to put up with this in my home?"

"It's Ebony's home," Granny Mac countered.

"It's *our* home," Ebony corrected both of them. "And you two have to try to get along better."

"It would've never gotten to this point if you had been back here when you promised." Jolene moved to inspect the fishbowl.

"Ma, you know I was chasing a story in Grundie." Ebony tried to get comfortable on the sofa by wedging pillows between it and the small of her back.

Granny Mac sat beside Ebony and scooped up Black Gal, who nestled on her lap. "Did you get your man?"

Ebony knew her grandmother referred to Renfro, but an image of Isaiah Malone flashed in her mind instead. "No, but I'm not giving up yet," she replied, unsure whether she meant Renfro or Isaiah.

"You just missed a good one." Granny Mac scratched Black

Gal's tentlike ears. "I just finished *Fist of Fear, Touch of Death*, a Bruce Lee classic. Rented it from the public library. Got to return it first thing tomorrow, though."

Ebony sounded more disappointed than she actually felt. "Sorry I missed it."

Granny Mac shot off the sofa, clutching Black Gal. "I can pop it back in the VCR—"

"Oh, no, that's all right," Ebony said. "I'll catch it another time."

"Nobody but you likes that kung fu mess anyway," Jolene carped as she sprinkled food resembling pencil shavings into the fish tank. "Tell her, Ebony. Tell Althea how much you hate watching those karate movies."

"Shut up, Jolene!" Granny Mac warned. "I've got another Two Thousand Flushes where that other one came from."

"Please." Ebony got off the sofa. "You two are giving me a headache and I haven't been home five minutes."

She pecked kisses on their cheeks, though she wanted to slap them silly. She longed for the serenity of her bedroom. They were going to drive her crazy before they worked out their differences.

Just before Ebony stepped inside her room Granny Mac told her, "Taffi called about a dozen times while you were gone."

Ebony stretched across her chenille-covered bed, determined to get her mind off squabbling—theirs and the round she'd had with Isaiah. She'd phone Taffi later.

It didn't take long before more pleasant thoughts of Isaiah drained the tension from her body. She squirmed and grabbed a pillow to hug. They'd been apart approximately four hours. She mooned over him even though he'd behaved like a jerk before they departed.

"Isaiah," she whispered dreamily as she fantasized about his rock-hard abs, shoulders, buns, and the heat he packed in those Levi's of his. She wondered what it would be like to be filled with all that Isaiah. She sighed, lowering the pillow, pressing it at the juncture of her legs until she caught herself. "No. No. No." Such silliness did not bode well for her plan to forget about him and file away their weekend together as a harmless diversion. In a sudden fit of frustration she sent the pillow soaring across the room where it bounced off an old wicker chair before landing on the floor. When she went to pick it up, she caught sight of Kenya's award certificates and honor roll ribbons on the wall. She let her fingers run over the soft satin ribbons and remembered the reason she'd wanted the Renfro story in the first place. Ebony went back to her bed to sit. She reached for the phone on the nightstand and a minute later her sister was on the line.

"How ya doing, kiddo?" Ebony asked, grateful she'd caught Kenya in her dorm room.

"Everything's great, but organic chem was kicking my keister," Kenya told her. "I have a handle on it now that I have a new study partner. It wasn't working out with Jeleel."

"Wait a minute." Ebony tucked her legs beneath her and rested against the headboard. "I thought you liked this Jeleel."

"That was the problem. I liked him too much and whenever we got together to study there was never enough studying going on—"

"And just what were you two doing instead of studying?" Ebony went into protective-big-sister overdrive.

"Don't worry. I've taken everything you've told me about the birds and the bees, books and boys, to heart, which is why I had to fire Jeleel as my study partner. We can't hit the books together, but we take in a movie or get pizza here and there."

"So you're seeing each other?" Ebony felt some apprehension about her baby sister dating so far away from home, away from her watchful eye. But she reminded herself that Kenya was not only book-smart, but extremely levelheaded about boys. The way she'd handled that study situation with Jeleel, whom she was obviously very attracted to, proved that.

"Yeah, I guess you could say we're dating, but only after the homework and studying are done."

"That's my girl." Ebony felt a warmth and pride in her sister that seeped deep in her bones. The phone call was just what she needed.

When the doorbell rang she didn't have time to tell her

mother or Granny Mac that she wasn't receiving company. She wanted to chat with Kenya a little longer then take a nap, but seconds later she heard Taffi Wilcox's rapid-fire chatter.

"Gotta go, sweetie. Taffi just came by," Ebony told Kenya just before ending the call.

Ebony pasted on a smile as her friend and neighbor from two doors down swept inside her bedroom wrapped in a rose-print sundress and trailing the potent scent of an expensive floral perfume. Taffi had used her deep décolletage, deliberate sweetness, and overcharged femininity as weapons in the mating-and-dating game. The twenty-seven-year-old had been planning her wedding since the age of twelve, when she began stuffing a three-ringed Cinderella binder with potential gowns and bouquets ripped from magazines. With the big day fast approaching, Taffi had morphed into Bridezilla, fitfully fussing over every detail as if Martha Stewart herself were attending the backyard gala. At first Taffi's parents, who were footing the bill for the ceremony, had insisted that the entire wedding party be comprised of close members of the family, much to Taffi's chagrin. Ebony and Yolanda were quickly plugged in as replacements after Taffi had a big falling-out with not one but two of her first cousins. Ebony wasn't a first-round draft pick, but a close and convenient sounding board when the bride-to-be needed an opinion on something. Vera Wang or Badgley Mischka? Vendella roses or calla lilies?

Ebony refused to hurt Taffi's feelings by letting on just how completely bored she'd become with the constant jabbering about nuptial niceties. She loved Taffi and wished her a picture-perfect wedding. Not only had she recorded all her bridesmaids' obligations in her planner, but she'd highlighted each with a top-priority gold star.

"Oh, Ebony, I need your help again! Decisions, decisions, and more decisions." Taffi eased down on Ebony's bed, tucking her shiny auburn curls behind her ears. She removed a stack of fabric swatches and paper squares from her floral tote bag. "I simply cannot decide what color to go with for the tablecloths. Ecru, sand, mother-of-pearl, off-white . . . ? And about the thank-you cards... What do you think of this ink with this lettering?"

Ebony had never fantasized about boutonnieres and poufy white dresses, but Taffi's wedding, filtered through her weekend in Grundie with Isaiah, made her think. Would she ever fall so crazy in love that she just had to announce it to the world via handmade invitations fashioned with gold-threaded Japanese paper letter-pressed in silver ink and tied with organdy ribbon?

Ebony nodded her approval of Taffi's card choice, but was less help on the fabric swatches that appeared identical.

"You didn't forget we've got a fitting this afternoon, did you?" Taffi held one swatch of fabric toward the sunlight spilling through the window. "Did Granny Mac tell you I called? I was afraid you weren't going to make it back from Grundie in time."

"No, I didn't forget, but... Well, I was kinda hoping I could catch a quick nap before we left for the shop. That drive from Grundie..." Not to mention her distracting thoughts of Isaiah which wouldn't make her the best company. "Kinda tuckered me out."

"You'll be fine once I get a nice cappuccino in you." Taffi stood erect as a drill sergeant and yanked Ebony from her comfy spot on the bed. "We'll stop at that quaint little gourmet eatery across from the bridal shop and have a nice lunch—on me, of course. We'll phone Yolanda and have her meet us there, then the three of us will walk over for our fitting. How does that sound?"

Ebony gazed longingly at her pillow. "Well—"

"Please," Taffi pleaded. "We haven't spent much time together since you helped me set up for my last Mary Kay party. That was weeks ago. I live right down the block and I hardly see you anymore. I've missed you."

"I've missed you, too." Ebony gave her friend a small smile. Taffi didn't harp on Ebony's family obligations as much as Yolanda, but she knew her schedule often made Taffi feel low priority. "Okay, lunch sounds good."

* * *

A couple of hours later, Taffi stood before the bridal shop's three-way mirror. Perched on a carpeted block that elevated her several inches off the floor, she scrutinized her reflection as the shop's head seamstress fiddled with the hem. "What was I thinking, eating all those tortilla chips before my fitting? I look like the Pillsbury dough girl."

"Taffi, you look beautiful as usual, like a fairy-tale princess." Ebony's eyes teared a little, her voice became breathy with emotion as she admired her friend in the lace-and-silk confection for the first time. The dress featured a full skirt, short train, and a low portrait neckline. Ebony had peeked at it when Taffi ordered it from the shop's bridal-gown catalog. On that anorexic model with the vacuous grin, the gown had looked unexceptional. Plucked from the flat, static pages and filled with Taffi's warm, womanly curves, the gown took on new life. Its fine beads and crystals winked under the shop's lighting. When the gray-haired seamstress disappeared in the back of the shop to hunt for pins, Ebony reached out and caressed the hem. For the first time she wondered what it would be like to walk down the aisle with the man of her dreams in a church filled with guests and the scent of fresh roses. She imagined a handsome tuxedoed groom awaiting her at the altar. That man looked a lot like Isaiah. She sighed dreamily and purred, "Absolutely beautiful."

"Bloated is more like it," Taffi whined, interrupting Ebony's daydream. "All those chips went straight to my poosh here." Taffi patted the curve of her abdomen then tried to suck it in. "Like yeast in a soufflé. That's sodium and me. My face looks puffy, too, doesn't it?" She sucked in the roundish cheeks that gave her face a pretty doll-like quality.

"Cut it out, Taffi," Ebony told her. "You're turning blue."

"That's easy for you to say." Taffi exhaled the breath she had been holding. "You don't have a gut or cheeks like a Cabbage Patch doll."

Prewedding jitters struck her friend with a vengeance. Taffi was usually one of the most confident women Ebony knew. Admirably comfortable in her own skin without being as vainglorious as Yolanda. "You look wonderful and the dress is wonderful," Ebony countered. Unfortunately, she could not say the same about the burgundy bridesmaid dress swishing around her own limbs.

Ebony peered around the bridal gown's full skirt and viewed her own image in the mirror and decided Taffi had definitely taken fashion cues from *Gunsmoke* reruns. Toning down the Miss Kitty look of her tulle-and-satin gown with the giant bustle of a butt bow would be next to impossible. But far be it from Ebony to complain. Yolanda, however, the glamour-puss among them, had no qualms voicing her disapproval of Taffi's choice. Since the trio had walked over from the restaurant, Yolanda had hidden away in one of the private dressing rooms and refused to come out. Only one person, the shop attendant doing the alterations, could see her in the ugly bridesmaid dress. With the ceremony a few weeks away, Yolanda still had time to buoy her courage. Ebony supposed she had to give her a few brownie points for not backing out of bridesmaid duty altogether when she'd seen their dresses.

"Now *this* is what I'm talking 'bout." Yolanda had quickly stripped off the bridesmaid gown and sashayed out of the dressing room in a shimmering, body-skimming floor-length thing. The hot pink number had the vampiest slit Ebony had ever seen.

Petite, but impossibly curvy, Yolanda believed in advertising her goods. The slit started at the hem, zipped up Yolanda's left leg to her hip, then continued a diagonal path up the middle of her back. From hip to back the slit was laced loosely together with a satin tie where a long strip of Yolanda's brown flesh peeked through. "Taffi, how come you couldn't hook a sistah up in something yummy like this?"

"Yolanda." Ebony rolled her eyes then gave her a reprimanding look.

"Just kidding, Taffi." Yolanda moved in front of Ebony and Taffi, to admire herself in the three-way mirror. "I saw this on the rack over there and I just had to try it on. So Ebony, I forgot to ask, how was Grundie?"

"Yeah, you hardly said anything about your trip over lunch," Taffi chimed in. "How did it go?"

"Fine," Ebony replied cryptically, as she moved to the glass counter filled with ornate jewelry, tiaras, and hair ornaments.

"So you made progress with Reuben Renfro?" Yolanda asked, turning her body this- and thataway in front of the mirror to dazzle herself from every angle.

"Nope," Ebony replied too quickly. "Hey, Taffi, did you see these pretty beaded combs over here?" She lifted a satin barrette for closer inspection.

"How was that paintball thing?" Yolanda lifted her bobbed hair off her neck and fashioned it in a twist.

Taffi stepped from her perch. She couldn't see much of her gown anyway with Yolanda hogging the mirror. "Yeah, how was that?"

Ebony, who stank at subterfuge, dropped the barrette on the floor.

Yolanda always seemed to know when Ebony was hiding something. "Okay, give it up." She let her hair fall back around her neck and got in Ebony's face.

"Give what up?" Ebony feigned ignorance and crouched to retrieve the barrette.

"You're acting really jumpy all of a sudden. What happened in Grundie?"

Ebony came to her full height and swished over to the long silk chaise near the shop's glass front to sit. The butt bow made it a challenge, but she managed.

"Careful," Taffi warned. "You don't want to get too wrinkly."

Yolanda sat beside her, showing off enough of her gams to warrant an R rating.

Taffi, fearing she'd pop a seam if she joined them on the chaise, chose to stand.

Ebony gave them a rundown of her Grundie weekend with Isaiah—the good, the bad, and the head-bangingly bewildering.

"So when are you two getting together again?" Yolanda asked, with one brow peaking with interest.

"Getting together?" Ebony asked stupidly. "Didn't you hear what I just said? Isaiah and I didn't part on the best terms."

"So you two had a little lovers' spat." Yolanda dismissed Ebony's response with a wave of her hand.

"We are *not* lovers!" Ebony popped to her feet. "I don't even know if I *like* the man. One minute he seems nice enough, but then the next . . . And let's not forget he is one of my rivals for Renfro."

"So?" Yolanda nudged her. "Use his obvious attraction to you to your advantage. Distract him off his game."

"That's your specialty, not mine. Isaiah strikes me as the type who's had a lot of experience with women. And how do I know he's not just pretending to be attracted to me to distract *me* off my game?"

"Girl, what are you talking about?" Taffi took Ebony by the hand and led her to a mirror. "Look at yourself. He'd have to be blind to have to pretend to be attracted to you. You're gorgeous."

Ebony turned away from her reflection to face Taffi and Yolanda. "Look, you guys, I think you're really sweet and all, but the bottom line is, Isaiah didn't even bother to ask for my phone number before we left Grundie. I'd say that's a darn good indication what he's thinking and it ain't about me. And that's like . . ." She paused. "Totally okay, actually." Ebony forced a good-riddance note into her voice. "And besides, it's probably best that we leave what happened in Grundie in Grundie. I have an exclusive to bag, ladies."

Yolanda and Taffi exchanged skeptical glances before Ebony sought refuge in one of the dressing rooms.

CHAPTER 17

Last New Year's Eve Ebony had vowed to cut back on sweets, drink more water, and avoid frittering away Saturday mornings at long, boring meetings. Five months later, she had broken the last of her resolutions by boarding an elevator to the top floor of a downtown office building.

An overwhelming urge to check on the happenings at the African-American Journalists Coalition monthly confab wouldn't let her go. At least that's what she told herself when she phoned an acquaintance and fellow AAJC member to get the particulars on the meeting time and place. She'd been AWOL for so long, she wasn't sure where the group held its meetings these days. But that morning, returning to the AAJC fold when she had a long list of chores to tackle had more to do with the need to gaze into a particular freelance journalist's dreamy long-lashed eyes than anything else, despite what she'd told Yolanda and Taffi. It had been nearly a week since she'd left Grundie and Isaiah Malone behind. And as hard as she tried to get him off her mind, she couldn't. Though miffed about the way they'd parted, she still hoped Isaiah was an active member of the AAJC these days and that he might show at the meeting that morning. Ebony's emotions had zigzagged all over the place like a pinball the past few days. She stepped off the elevator when it reached the tenth floor, thinking maybe she was too hard on herself. She hadn't sat around twiddling her thumbs, mooning over Isaiah. For the *Bee*, she'd pounded out a decent feature piece on the woman who'd broken a world's record for crocheting ten thousand lace doilies for charity. Ebony had also scheduled an interview with Renfro's nephew, aspiring fitness guru Diesel Raheem. She would befriend him to get to his uncle. Unsure how she felt about the slightly underhanded tactic, she forged ahead out of desperation. Diesel simply could not turn down free publicity—even a column in the lifestyle section of the *Bee*. She rounded a corner in the plush foyer leading to a conference room, perking up with the prospect of meeting Diesel at his fitness center in a few days.

In an expansive, air-conditioned room at the end of a long hall, young professionals in the newspaper, TV, and radio industry milled about helping themselves to breakfast goodies.

Tarik Malone, AAJC chapter president, met Ebony at the parted double doors. "Ebony, it's so good to see you again." She noted Tarik's strong resemblance to Isaiah. They both had the same honey-brown eyes, golden skin, and tall, sleekly muscular build. Tarik was good-looking, but tweedy and clean-cut. Brooks Brothers, polished wing tips, and executive uniformity to Isaiah's Pelle Pelle, black broken-in jeans, and any-way-the-wind-blows autonomy. Tarik was the comfortably constant type who hung banal Successories posters on his office wall and grilled on Sundays while his brother was an enormous question mark, who prided himself on keeping folks guessing. Isaiah could be arrogant, contentious, capricious, and downright maddening. But also sexier, edgier, than Tarik could ever hope to be as far as Ebony was concerned. Between the two, Isaiah was the Malone brother she simply could not purge from her thoughts for long.

"Sorry I haven't been able to attend these meetings in a while." Ebony's motives for showing up were suspect so she rushed in with an unsolicited excuse to compensate. "My weekends have been so crazy lately."

Tarik gently shoved her toward the table of muffins, bagels, and scones. "All that matters is you've returned. Hey, grab something to eat and drink. We'll start the meeting in a few minutes."

Ebony reached for two jumbo sugar-topped cranberry-walnut muffins and poured a cup of coffee before claiming one of the high-backed leather chairs at a grand cherrywood table. She knew most of the faces surrounding it, but one was conspicuously missing. Momentary disappointment gave way to relief. Showing up at the meeting just to see Isaiah again was not only dumb, but pathetic. Thankfully, fate had granted a reprieve until she snapped to her senses.

"First order of business, Beverly needs someone to fill in for her at the journalism workshop at the college next weekend. It coincides with a professional reporting seminar she's been accepted to attend. Any volunteers?"

WLZF reporter and *Good Day Cincinnati* cohost Camille Davenport raised an impeccably manicured hand. "I'll do it."

Camille's coordinated ensemble boasted the work of at least a dozen designers. Tasteful diamond studs winked on her earlobes. According to chapter gossip, Camille was a well-bred, trust-fund baby, who didn't have to work like the rest of the AAJC crowd. She only dabbled in TV journalism as a hobby.

"Thanks, Camille, but we're a little heavy with TV personalities right now. We need another newspaper journalist." Tarik scanned the faces as he leaned against the lectern at the front of the room.

Ebony seized the opportunity to redeem herself. "I'll do it. Sounds like fun," she piped up, feeling darn proud to turn the blunder of seeking out Isaiah into something constructive.

"Great." Tarik shuffled his papers. "Now that that's settled, on to the next item on the agenda, the chapter scholarship fund. We need to get that balance up, people."

All eyes shifted to the parted glass doors as Isaiah entered with his trademark swagger and claimed a place at the table. Ebony's heart did a little flip.

Every woman in the room ogled Isaiah's denimed derriere as he turned to hook his lightweight jacket on the back of a chair. *Show-off.* Ebony frowned, sure he'd intentionally shifted his sexy backside to his audience.

Tarik cut his scholarship spiel. "Isaiah, Beverly won't be able to do that workshop with you, but Ebony here just volunteered to help."

When Isaiah nodded in Ebony's direction she imagined his head swelling in cartoonish proportions though his expression remained unreadable. But if she ventured a guess, he probably assumed she'd volunteered to participate in the workshop to spend time with him. *Ha!* She snatched her attention away from Isaiah back to Tarik, then decided to set Isaiah straight at the first opportunity. She felt his eyes on her throughout the proceedings, but stubbornly refused to look back in his direction. Why had he behaved so badly that morning they left Grundie? Okay, so they didn't part on the most pleasant note, but why hadn't he tracked her down when he got back to Cincinnati? Between the *Butler County Bee* and her listed phone number, it wouldn't have taken much effort at all. They had shared poison ivy, skunk, greasy onion rings, garlic rice pudding, and voracious tongue-twisting kisses, for crying out loud. But that obviously meant nothing to him.

When the meeting ended, Isaiah made a beeline for Camille, a stunning Vanessa L. Williams look-alike. *Figures.*

Ebony had planned to work the room with a few smiles and drive-by farewells to Tarik and other members of AAJC then get the heck out of Dodge, but she couldn't peel her gaze off the excruciatingly photogenic pair. Isaiah just couldn't seem to turn off his industrial-strength charisma whenever he picked up a gorgeous woman on his radar. The *Good Day Cincinnati* hostess beamed, deploying an arsenal of time-tested mating maneuvers—coy laughter, frequent brushes against his muscular forearm, the batting of her ridiculously long lashes. As Camille gushed and blushed in response to Isaiah's private jokes, her sun-kissed sienna curls bounced, punctuating her graceful movements.

Gag. Gag. Gag. Ebony had seen entirely enough. She spun away from the pair and plowed inside her fanny pack for her car keys.

"Leaving so soon and without a goodbye?" Suddenly the clean, masculine scent of cologne and something distinctly Isaiah wrapped around her like a taut embrace. His stealth approach rattled her, as did the caress of his warm breath against the back of her neck.

"You had no problem attempting just that a week ago." Ebony whirled around to face him with a forced smile, pretending their parting spat in Grundie hadn't really mattered at all. Up close, she noticed only faint traces of the rash that had marred his golden skin before. "What do you care anyway? Run along and play with Bousgie Black Barbie. I've heard she comes with a dream house and pink convertible, batteries included."

"If I didn't know any better I'd say you were jealous," Isaiah noted with an assessing look.

If Ebony got any greener, Tiger Woods could putt golf balls off her, but she refused to admit it. "If *I* knew any better, I wouldn't be standing here listening to this nonsense." She tried to keep her devil-may-care demeanor intact. "Gotta go. See ya around."

"Wait." When Isaiah reached out and touched her arm, hot currents of need shot through her and she realized just how much she missed being close to him.

Ebony plucked at her lightweight cotton top. Rooms suddenly turned to saunas and her brain to Cream of Wheat whenever he was around. "What?" A long awkward silence followed the question.

"I'm sorry. I behaved like a jackass that morning we left Kenny-Wayne's. It's just that . . . well . . ." Isaiah rocked back on his heels and buried his hands in his pockets as if he hoped to pull out a script with just the right words to say. "Anyway, I'm sorry. So we're doing that journalism workshop together, huh?"

Pi-ti-ful. Ebony sighed, disappointed. *That was the best he could do? What about "I've missed you!" "Wanted to see you!" "Can't get you and Grundie off my mind!"* "Yeah." She would not cut him any slack.

"I'm a little surprised, that's all, after the way we left things in Grundie. But I'm glad you volunteered." Then there it was. What she'd yearned to see all week. That smile—warm, wide, and oh-so-delicious—aimed at her.

Her heart fluttered, though she still smarted from the way he'd departed from Grundie. She refused to act swoony. "I volunteered before I knew you were part of the deal." She couldn't get it out fast enough.

"Oh." He blinked, paused, then recovered. "Well, it might be a good idea if we went somewhere to talk. You know, coordinate our plans for the workshop. Maybe we can grab a bite while we're at it."

As Isaiah stepped closer to Ebony, all activity and chatter of their fellow AAJC members ceased to register. He had a knack for invading her personal space. And it annoyed her to no end that she wasn't annoyed whenever he did it. Instead a tingle skittered through her body and nestled as a warm silkiness between her legs. What was this man doing to her? How she wanted to accept his invitation, and that in itself was enough to shake some sense into her. Besides, she had a good excuse. "Can't. Plans."

"Anything that can be rescheduled?" He took a step closer.

"I don't like breaking promises to my family. Tops on today's to-do list is taking care of Black Gal."

"Black girl?" Isaiah arched one brow. "An odd way to refer to a relative, don't you think?"

"I said Black Gal. That's my grandmother's Chihuahua. Granny Mac's not feeling well today. I promised to take Black Gal to her vet appointment. Heartworms." She checked her watch. "Well, I'd better get going."

"Wouldn't want to make you late for that." He actually sounded disappointed.

Awkwardness settled between them, then Camille slinked over and linked a possessive arm with Isaiah's. "You're joining me and the gang for brunch at Costello's, right?" she asked, snottily ignoring Ebony, who fumed when she realized how strikingly perfect Isaiah and Camille looked together. With the right dapper duds he could easily be the Moët to her Chandon, the crème to her brûlée. And Isaiah appeared to be in no hurry to extricate himself from Camille's clench.

"Just a sec," Isaiah said to Camille before turning back to Ebony. "How can I reach you so we can coordinate workshop ideas?"

"E-mail." Ebony removed a business card from her fanny pack. "I'll look over your ideas then e-mail mine." She marched toward the door without sparing Camille or Isaiah a second glance.

Isaiah ditched Camille and her crew. Instead he headed to the Zodiac bar for a stiff drink to take the edge off that disappointing encounter with Ebony. And to think, he'd actually been happy to see her at the meeting and thought maybe he'd willed her to appear. He'd even extended himself to her, only to get shot down. He supposed he deserved it, but it didn't make him feel any better to acknowledge it. She'd refused to make much eye contact with him during the meeting so he went out of his way to get her attention. His little flirtation with Camille Davenport had backfired and he'd had just about enough of exasperating females for one day. He settled on a stool at the Zodiac counter.

Zodiac owner Clyde "Butta Bean" Walker rolled up, eased his wheelchair next to Isaiah and slapped him on the back. "Whatcha know good, dude?" he asked in a raspy voice scorched by decades of chain-smoking.

"Bean, hey." Isaiah came off his stool to wrap Butta Bean in a manly-man hug.

"Haven't seen you around here in days." Bean wore his trademark Braves baseball cap over his salt-and-pepper hair gathered in a rocker-dude ponytail. His robust chest and beefy arms, honed with religious weight lifting, underscored the frailness of legs that had atrophied after five years in a wheelchair.

Years ago the pair had met at a neighborhood recreation center. Butta Bean, a former Cincinnati narcotics cop, had coached there. A teenage Isaiah often hung out at the center on weekends shooting hoops and talking trash. Butta Bean had become somewhat of a father figure because Isaiah's relationship with his own was so strained. Butta Bean had purchased the watering hole when his law-enforcement career came to an end after he took a drug dealer's bullet in his spine.

"Been up in Grundie," Isaiah told him.

"Grundie? What for?"

"Renfro."

Isaiah sat on his stool again as Butta Bean wheeled up a ramp and maneuvered behind the bar where he parked on a raised platform that brought him to Isaiah's eye level. "I don't even know why I asked."

B. B. King, Bobbie Blue Bland, and Gatemouth Brown in all their rich but forlorn glory blared from bar speakers. The blues was the last thing Isaiah needed to hear. "Hey, Bean, you're going to scare away your younger, hipper crowd if you don't stick with Lauryn Hill, Jill Scott, and D'Angelo."

"Like I want to attract the kind of folks who can't appreciate good old-fashioned blues every now and then." Butta Bean began polishing a row of shot glasses, then restocked a tray with cherries, lemon wedges, and olives. "Most of that mess the kids are listening to these days is gutless, studio-engineered, hibbity-ahibbity-hip-hop crap with no heart and soul. It's all about sampling a beat and squeezing in as many gyrating damn-near-naked booties in a music video as they can get."

Isaiah speared an olive with a drink stirrer. "Hit me. Courvoisier. Make that a double."

"Trouble? How's the old man? I take it he wasn't too pleased with your 'Space Baby Found in Iowa Cornfield' scoop."

"I haven't seen Dad in days, but it's the giant hairball piece that's got his knickers in a knot now, according to Tarik."

"That one was a real doozy." Butta Bean chuckled. "Your old man's got no sense of humor. It's gonna take dynamite to dislodge that stick in his ass."

"Tell me about it."

"This one's on the house." Butta Bean filled a glass for him as a police scanner, a remnant from his days on the force, crackled and spewed static over the music. He reached where it sat on a shelf under the bar and lowered the volume.

For reasons Isaiah didn't completely understand, keeping that scanner on like a favorite R & B radio station made Bean feel as if he still possessed some part of a career that ended before he had been ready to let go.

Isaiah's babe radar homed in on a trio of attractive females a few tables away. His lips arced up in a smile as he lifted his glass in a toast. The most attractive of the three was a toffee-hued sister wearing a red knit dress that clung to her curves like a condiment. She sent him the most blatant ready-and-willing vibes with a flirtatious wave and an air kiss.

Butta Bean took note, shaking his head. "Look at that. The ladies do love them some Isaiah, don't they? For you, it's like shooting fish in a barrel. What I'd do to have your youth and good looks."

Any other time, Isaiah would've been hot to score, way beyond the intros and slipping that babe's phone number inside his pocket by now, but he couldn't muster the enthusiasm for it.

"Well?" Butta Bean prodded.

"Well what?"

"Aren't you going to bust a move? The one in the red dress is primed and plenty ready to be plucked."

"Nah." Isaiah shook his head. With a finger he absently traced the rim of his glass and stared down at its rich amber liquid. "Not feeling it."

"Don't tell me that mess with your father's still got you distracted."

"Nah, I was just thinking about something else . . . I mean, someone. Her name's Ebony."

"Ebony, huh? Somebody you're trying to get next to?" Bean wiped the bar top with a damp sponge.

"I've managed to get next to her last nerve. We're going after the same exclusive."

"She's in the tabloid business, too?"

"No, but just so happens she wants that same reporting job that I'm going after at the *Examiner*."

Butta Bean whistled and nodded. "Oh, I get it now, and

she's going after the Renfro piece. So you can't court the lady 'cause you're competing with her."

"Court?" Isaiah scoffed. "Hardly. Besides, I'm not looking for a serious relationship. I just want to kick it, you know, have some fun."

"This lady must have you thinking about revising that plan. I mean, the fact that you're obviously all deep in thought tells me there's more to this thing with... What's her name again?"

"Ebony."

"Than you're willing to admit to me or yourself right now."

"I don't know about all that, but... This one intrigues me though."

"Just make sure it's not the type of intrigue that leaves your body the moment you nail her."

Isaiah grimaced and groaned. Butta Bean's crude candor could be too much even for him sometimes.

Butta Bean ribbed Isaiah in a tinny feminine voice. "What? Did I offend your delicate sensibilities?"

"You're crazy, man." Isaiah laughed with his friend.

"Yeah, like a fox, dude, and don't you forget it."

"You won't let me."

Butta Bean sobered. "Hey, I almost forgot. You still fiddling with that fancy camera of yours?"

"Yeah, what do you need?"

"Can you snap a roll of shots of my van? I'm getting a new one, and selling the old one using one of those on-line sites, but I need some really good, clear shots to scan. The service offered to send somebody out, but I ain't paying extra for that."

"No problem. I'll shoot them first thing tomorrow," Isaiah replied, glad he could do something for his friend, who was always eager to lend an ear and advice when he needed it.

CHAPTER 18

The *Butler County Bee*'s small newsroom was crammed with used office furniture and outdated computer equipment. Situated in the basement of a suburban office building, its lack of windows gave it a dreary ambience. Ebony sat at her corner desk typing an installment of her three-day series on the hottest new products for fighting fleas and ticks. It had become more difficult to crank out such drivel when her Renfro leads were much more interesting. She couldn't wait to get to the interview she had scheduled with Diesel Raheem later that day. She tried to push it to the back of her mind. After all, the *Bee* still paid the bills and the publisher hadn't balked about her taking on freelance assignments—as long as she met her *Bee* story quota.

The *Bee*, a family-owned community newspaper, never aspired to much beyond providing recipes, gardening tips, practical how-to features, the fanciest local weather maps, and the longest, most impressive listing of area garage sales. The front page was heavy on wire stories lifted from the Associated Press and slight on locally generated hard news or in-depth personality profiles. When Ebony initially pitched the Renfro piece to the *Bee* publisher and editor-in-chief, the response had been less than enthusiastic, but she'd told them early on she intended to pursue the story whether they chose to publish it or not. Ultimately they decided a big blow-out profile on a business tycoon was not what *Bee* readers wanted or expected so Ebony could do the story for the *Examiner*—on her own time—without repercussions from her present employer. While the *Bee* did not consider the *Examiner* direct competition, they would change that tune if they knew landing the Renfro story came with an *Examiner* staff position attached. And of course, Ebony was nobody's fool. She had been careful to omit that part of the freelancing arrangement.

"So how did it go at Shangri-La?" Stella Ellis seemed to swoop in out of nowhere. She dropped at her desk next to Ebony's. The fifty-something socialite and her wealthy husband had relocated from the Northeast about five years ago after he retired. Stella had become bored with a life of leisure and local charity balls so she penned the *Bee*'s Deep Dish gossip column for fun. She was a sweet spirit—on Zoloft days. When she stopped taking the popular antidepressant she'd all but sprout horns and a pointed tail.

Stella had just returned from a trip to St. Bart's tanned and rested, but had yet to hear the lowdown on Ebony's foray into the world of nudism.

"I got inside, but I didn't connect with Renfro," Ebony told her.

"He showed up, didn't he?" Stella asked in her rapid-fire "Noo Yawk" sorta way as she fiddled with the expensive onyx and diamond baubles on her lobes. "My sources rarely steer me wrong."

"Yes, he showed up all right, but there was a little misunderstanding and I . . . uh . . . had to leave before he actually arrived." Ebony omitted the more interesting details of her nudist-retreat adventure. Stella didn't need to know she got booted out because the Shangri-La's manager had jumped to all the wrong conclusions about Ebony and Isaiah. "Those are lovely earrings. Did you get them in St. Bart's?"

"Yeah, a gift from the hubby," Stella said quickly. "That's too bad about Shangri-La, but there are more leads where that one came from. The hubby wrangled an invite to Renfro's annual Ice Cream Dreams Ball."

"The Ice Cream Dreams Ball?" Ebony swiveled around to face Stella and scooted to the edge of her seat. "Renfro's always there, isn't he?"

"Yes." Stella picked at her brightly painted nails. "And it would be perfect if you could tag along . . ."

"Yeah?" Ebony leaned forward, clutching the arms of her seat.

Stella sighed. "But the invitation is just for two and the security is so tight at that thing. I'm sorry."

"Oh." Ebony slumped back and sighed. "I understand. Keep your ears open for me." Though disappointed that she couldn't crash the festivities, she was glad Stella was on her side and had no interest in going after Renfro's story herself. With "the hubby" 's choice connections and strategically placed moles, Stella would've had the coveted scoop by now and drop-kicked Ebony *and* Isaiah's butts six ways to Sunday in the process. "I really appreciate what you've done. I realize you don't have to help me."

"Glad to, dear." Stella waved a hand glittering with diamonds. "And besides, you're always such a sweetie. No one rolls with my mood swings better."

"Mood swings? What mood swings?" Ebony teased. "Why, I'm sure Harry Freemont hardly missed that carton of Marlboros you swiped from his clutches and stuffed down the paper shredder."

"He was pissed, but he'll thank me later," Stella reasoned. "I'm sure I added months to his life expectancy."

They shared a laugh, then peeked over at their chain-smoking colleague's empty desk. "Oops, looks like he's missing in action again," Ebony noted. Then they chanted in unison: "Cigarette break!"

Ebony reached for her ringing phone as Stella came to her feet. "I'm going for a cup of joe—decaf, of course. Want some?"

Ebony declined, then addressed Kenya, who greeted her from the other end of the line. "Hey, kiddo, what's shakin'?"

"Got the info on the student loan programs available for next year."

"Kenya." Ebony drew out her sister's name with a warning note. "I thought we already discussed this. I don't want you accruing too much debt right now. It's just your freshman year for crying out loud. We'll think about going the loan route only as a last resort."

"I know, but I feel really weird about dumping everything on you right now. Lots of students take on more than half of the expense for their college education. I want to do my share, too."

"You are doing your share. You study hard and make excellent grades."

"You've got to let me shoulder some of the financial responsibility," Kenya pleaded. "I can get a loan and sign up for a work-study program."

"No, you hear me!" Ebony realized her tone was more emphatic than she intended. She took a deep breath before she continued on a calmer note. "You should be concentrating on studying. That's the way Dad would've wanted it."

"At least look at the information I'm going to send you on the loan I'm considering, okay? The interest rate is fixed and extra low and I don't have to start paying it back until six months after I graduate. And you know I *will* have a great job, so paying it back will not be a problem."

"I know all about student loans. I also know how difficult it is trying to hold a job and study, which is why I don't want you going that route either if you don't have to."

"I think you're being too pigheaded about this. You're not rich."

Ebony felt the pressure of a headache coming on. "Can we just drop this? How are classes coming along?"

"Fine. I know you're at work, but this is not the end of this discussion, not by a long shot."

When Ebony ended the phone call five minutes later, she realized Kenya was worried because she believed Ebony had no prospects for a better-paying reporting job. Ebony, of course, knew better. She hadn't told Kenya yet, preferring to surprise her once the job offer was official. Then Ebony immediately thought of Isaiah. It had been a couple of days since that AAJC meeting. They had exchanged a few polite but strictly-to-the-point e-mails about their ideas for the workshop they'd lead in a few days, but she really wanted him to call. She stared at the phone on her desk, willing it to ring. It startled her when it did. "*Butler County Bee*, Ebony MacKenzie speaking," she answered in her most lilting voice, then sagged against her seat upon discovering it wasn't Isaiah.

"Are you free for lunch today?" Yolanda asked. "We need to discuss plans for Taffi's bachelorette party."

"Things are kind of tight for me today." Ebony flipped through her planner. "I've got a bunch of loose ends to tie up here so I'll probably work through lunch. I need to check out earlier than usual today. I'm working another angle on the Renfro piece."

"And who knows? You just might run into that sexy Isaiah again."

Ebony refused to go there again with Yolanda so she quickly changed the subject. "About Taffi's party. She wants something classy and tasteful."

"Tired and boring, you mean. Knowing Taffi, that's a flutist, four-string quartet, and Vivaldi."

"She doesn't want you getting carried away with the booze and the . . . adult entertainment."

"Don't tell me I have to cancel the guys from Hunky Hot Chocolate's All-Male Revue?"

"It may be at your condo, but it's her party, remember? We give her exactly what she wants. I know Taffi. Now that she's *betrothed* to Frank, she doesn't dare ogle other half-naked guys."

"Taffi flaunts way too much cleavage to be so damn prudish all of a sudden," Yolanda countered. "Did she specifically say no male strippers?"

"Well, no, but—"

"But nothing. I say Hunky Hot Chocolate's still on!"

"Oh, brother," Ebony droned. Once Yolanda set her mind to something, there was no stopping her.

* * *

A few hours later Ebony was a couple of blocks away from Diesel Raheem's fitness center. Party planning with Yolanda and poring over the research about Diesel left little time for obsessing about Isaiah. She obviously had a silly crush and would get over it sooner or later—as long as she stayed busy.

She drove her Escort to the driveway leading to Diesel's Sweat Factory, parked and went inside. The glitzy, neon-lighted fifty-thousand-square-foot facility boasted megabucks' worth of gleaming high-end exercise equipment and physiques that looked as if they'd been chiseled by Rodin and cast in bronze. At Spunky's Funky Gym, the little hole-in-the-wall facility where she huffed and puffed through a moderate regimen of treadmill running and light weight training, she could count the superbuffed bodies on one hand. But Diesel's Sweat Factory was overrun with folks whose idea of a perfect three-course meal was obviously Gatorade, a protein bar, and a hefty helping of steroids. With so many who looked as if they'd flexed right off the cover of *Pecs and Pump* magazine, Ebony suddenly felt like Olive Oyl on a grapefruit diet. She approached the purple-Lycra-clad Amazon at the reception desk. The woman's muscles were so lean and defined they appeared sliced and diced.

"Hello, I have an appointment to see Diesel Raheem. I'm Ebony MacKenzie from the *Butler County Bee*."

"Okay, let me check with him. I'll be right back." She left her station and disappeared between rows of weight machines.

Ebony used the time to remove a reporter's notebook from her fanny pack to peruse her preinterview notes. Renfro had raised Diesel as a son after Diesel's mother died. Diesel had been an angry, troublesome fourteen-year-old when he went to live with his rich uncle ten years ago. Renfro had been the ever-patient, but stern guardian to his only sibling's child according to most reports. Diesel had been headed down the wrong path, latching on to gang members and other unsavory characters, when Renfro stepped in. As an adult with a popular fitness facility, a large local following, and a new exercise contraption he'd developed and dubbed the Butt Bomber, Diesel had dreams of building a fitness empire that would make him a household name like Richard Simmons, then an action-flick superstar like Ar-nuld. Ebony wasn't particularly proud of trying to use Diesel to get to Renfro, but she took consolation in the fact that Diesel's story would've made good column fodder regardless of his family ties.

The Amazon returned. "You can join Diesel and the others at the bench press racks near the back." She pointed.

"Diesel and the others?" Ebony asked. "What others?"

"The other reporters. He got so many requests for interviews he decided to meet everybody at once."

"So it's a press conference?"

"Yeah . . . I guess you could call it a '*bench press* press conference.' " Bewildered, the Amazon scrunched up her face. "Or would it be a 'bench press conference'?"

Great. Ebony grumbled as she made her way across the floor toward the group clustered around a bench press rack. She counted five, but five too many. All of her get-to-Renfro ideas had obviously been hand-me-downs. She recognized Diesel immediately. She'd read that he dabbled in competitive bodybuilding, but the photos she'd seen of him didn't capture his sheer awesomeness. His shaved head gleamed like a gigantic Milk Dud under the fluorescent lighting. Everything about the man was super-sized. His biceps appeared as hard as frozen turkeys. A black tank top strained to cover his barrel chest and matching bicycle shorts stretched over his boulder-like butt cheeks. A familiar voice caught her attention. "Well, if it isn't Ms. Ebony MacKenzie."

She pivoted and came nose to sculpted chest with Isaiah.

CHAPTER 19

"Looks like Diesel is very popular these days," Isaiah said as if he were actually pleased to see her.

Ebony looked up. "Let me guess," she said, sighing wearily. "You're participating in the press conference, too."

Isaiah's assets were displayed in a brown tank top and shorts. He smelled like cologne and soap so he obviously hadn't worked out yet. While Isaiah wasn't as freakishly muscular as Diesel, he clearly had the more aesthetically pleasing physique. Diesel was a massive mountain range. Isaiah's lines were sweeping and sleek, but he looked strong enough to take any one of the males in the gym—including Diesel. When one of Isaiah's flat brown nipples peeked around his tank top, Ebony suppressed the urge to kiss it. She'd become accustomed to the decadent thoughts that sprinted through her consciousness whenever he was around.

"You're not dressed for a workout," he told her, taking in the conservative blazer and skirt she wore, accessorized with her fanny pack.

"I wasn't aware that working out was part of the deal and I didn't know this was a group shebang, either." Ebony didn't hide her agitation. "I thought I had an exclusive."

"Me, too," Isaiah confessed. "When I called to make an

appointment, Diesel's assistant failed to mention anything about a press conference. But as you can see there are at least five other reporters hovering around. Diesel probably has no idea why everybody is so damn interested in his Butt Blaster—"

"Butt Bomber," Ebony corrected him.

"Blast, bomb, beat, batter, whatever that contraption is supposed to do to all those rear ends puffed up with too much of his uncle's Mega Mocha Chip. But hey, he's certainly not one to turn down free publicity—especially now that he's trying to get investors to expand his business."

"He's got a rich uncle. Why bother?"

"The rich uncle helped him get this place and everything in it," Isaiah relayed in a glib manner. "The rich uncle has squandered a boatload of money on some of Diesel's other harebrained fitness flops that never saw the light of day so the rich uncle has refused to give him another dime."

"Oh, yeah. I think I read something about a protein-drink idea of his that never quite took off."

In a swift, too-familiar maneuver, Isaiah drew Ebony closer by her blazer lapels. A hot, but distinctly pleasurable sensation rippled down her neck as his forearms brushed across her breasts. "You better get out of those clothes."

"I beg your pardon," Ebony managed, though she felt as though all the wind had been sucked out of her. Desire burned at her loins.

His lips grazed her earlobe. "You'll need to change into your exercise gear. Didn't Xena Warrior Princess over there tell you?"

Ebony shook her head. Isaiah released her, but she found breathing and thinking at the same time challenging. "Well, I'm certainly not going to take your word for it." She approached the group clustered around the bench press rack. "Mr. Raheem, I'm Ebony MacKenzie from the *Butler County Bee*." When she extended her hand Diesel's hand swallowed it.

"Nice to meet you, Ms. MacKenzie. Please call me Diesel." Ebony was unprepared for Diesel's plummy voice, tinged with what was obviously a faux British accent, similar to the one Madonna occasionally affected ever since she got hitched to her English movie director. "We'll be starting the press conference soon so you'll want to change out of what you're wearing into something more suitable for working out."

Ebony avoided making eye contact with Isaiah, but she could just feel him smirking. "You must forgive me, but I was under the impression this was an interview. I didn't bring any workout clothes with me."

"No problem. Natasha at the front desk will get you something from our pro shop."

"But, but—" Ebony faltered.

"Hurry along, now. You've got five minutes," Diesel said as he lifted dumbbells off a rack and began performing a series of bicep curls.

In a dressing stall in the locker room Ebony removed her clothing, wondering what the heck she'd gotten herself into this time. Did anybody do anything the usual way anymore? Everything and everyone attached to this Renfro piece had been off the wall and way over the top. She shouldn't have assumed her encounter with the nephew would be any different. As she neatly folded her skirt Natasha shoved two bright red pieces of cloth and a sock wad over the door of her stall. "Here you go. I believe these will fit."

"Who? The Gerber baby?" Ebony inspected the itsy-bitsy shorts and matching top.

"They stretch. Get a move on, hon. Hey, what size shoe do you wear?"

"An eight." Ebony released a long-suffering sigh and quickly squeezed into the pieces. The shorts fit like panties and the top . . . Well, she'd seen headbands that provided more coverage. Not only was she overexposed, but the skin on her legs was dry as the Mojave. "I am *not* going out in this."

"Suit yourself, but the bench press press conference er . . . I mean, the bench press conference has just started." Natasha tossed the shoes over the stall and barely missed bonking Ebony on the head.

Ebony imagined herself poolside. Yeah. Or at a sun-steamed

beach, wearing a bathing suit. That could possibly get her through this ordeal. While the one-piece tank-style bathing suits she generally favored weren't nearly as skimpy as the getup she wore, this was no time for modesty. She searched through her fanny pack for a mini travel-sized container of lotion to apply to her ashy legs, but found the container empty. Her only options: a lemon-scented Wet-Nap packet from Red Lobster and a Strawberry Twist Chap Stick. Improvise, she decided, dragging the waxy tip of the lip balm across her brown thighs then rubbing it in with her fingers.

"I'll take care of locking up your personal belongings. You'd better go. They've started already," Natasha informed Ebony, who bolted out of the stall sufficiently moisturized, but smelling like a cheap car deodorizer.

Diesel hovered over a scrawny guy lying on a bench with a weighted bar wobbling a few scant inches above his chest. Cheeks puffed out. Face brick-red.

"Breathe, inhale, exhale," Diesel instructed him until he caught sight of Ebony. "Glad you could join us. I see Natasha fixed you right up. Not bad." He nodded toward her darn-near-illegal shorts.

Isaiah and the other male reporters were staring. Ebony felt flushed beneath their intense scrutiny. She nervously tugged at her shorts and shifted her weight from one foot to the other. Her feet rattled around inside gym shoes that were at least two sizes too large. Her shorts crept where they shouldn't and gave her one colossal wedgie. She wanted to jump and run, duck and hide, but refused to get intimidated into retreating. She had to fight fire with fire. She not only stared at Isaiah and his fellow gawkers, but she brazenly zeroed in on their crotches to give them a dose of their own medicine. Okay, so she looked like someone who trolled for customers on Eighth and Vine streets, but she would not stand for their rude leering. They soon got the hint, stopped focusing on her itsy-bitsy outfit, and did a little fidgeting of their own.

"This is how it works," Diesel piped up. "Every time you complete a set of repetitions on the old bench press here, you get to ask me a question. And of course, the weight has to get progressively heavier with each set. Thought this challenge might give you guys a nice twist to add to your stories about me. I think your readers will particularly enjoy the novelty of this approach. Ebony, you're up."

Isaiah couldn't believe Ebony came strutting over to the group in those do-me shorts and top. *Damn! She looked hot!* It wasn't as if he hadn't noticed before, especially when she was soaking wet at the Garlic Festival, but the other clothing only whispered about the treasures underneath. These shouted with a megaphone: "Dangerous curves ahead!" He drooled like a hound with its head poked out the window of a fast-moving car. Fortunately, his own shorts were baggy enough to conceal his instant reaction to her.

When he arrived and discovered his exclusive interview with Diesel had been turned into a free-for-all, he had a hunch that Ebony would be somewhere in the mix. But he hadn't been prepared for the mishmash of emotions that raced through him. He was comfortable with annoyance. She treaded on his territory once again. Competitiveness was a piece of cake. He'd beat her to that Renfro exclusive if it was the last thing he did. He could handle lust and the combustible chemistry he felt whenever they shared the same space. What man wouldn't want to jump her bones and lick her up and down—especially when that hot body of hers was half-wrapped and smelling like a strawberry Jolly Rancher? What stumped Isaiah was he couldn't deny how good he felt being near her and that had absolutely nothing to with sex. Or did it? He watched Ebony perform ten clean reps before placing the naked barbell back on its rack. She'd have to add plates on the bar for her next round. No doubt she'd go for the unchallenging saucer-sized ones. She sat upright and lobbed her first softball question. "So Diesel, where did you get the idea for the Butt Bomber?"

Isaiah recognized her approach. She'd feign interest in Diesel until he lowered his guard, then she'd hit him with questions about his uncle. Isaiah had planned to do that himself. But now that Ebony was distracted and locked into Lois Lane mode he could thoroughly check her out. Man, she had killer legs and they looked damned flexible, too. He smiled as he imagined the erotic acrobatics they could perform together. He'd never wanted any woman so badly and not been able to have her. That was it! The reason he'd been obsessing about her ever since they left Grundie. Butta Bean was on to something. Isaiah probably wouldn't be so intrigued after he bedded her. She held this witchy-woman spell on him because the unknown drove him nuts. He wanted to taste her all over. He wanted to know if she'd scream, moan, or just whimper when he found his rhythm and hit his stride stroking her just the right way. Once the shroud of mystery lifted he could get her off his mind and concentrate on what was important again.

"You're up, Isaiah." Diesel broke his reverie.

Isaiah and the other male reporters had the option of starting with an empty bar just like the female reporters, but machismo wouldn't let them. The first two had started with thirty-five-pound plates on each end. Isaiah was bigger and obviously more fit than the other three so he grabbed two forty-five-pound plates and slid them on each end of the bar. He reclined on the bench and pumped a set of reps effortlessly. "Is there any truth to your plans to do an infomercial for the Butt Bomber?" Isaiah asked, though his mind wandered during Diesel's reply. Isaiah watched Ebony as he lifted his arms to perform a quick chest-stretching exercise. If she only knew what he had in store for her. He would go all out with a plan to seduce her.

An hour and a half later, the press conference had dwindled to a one-on-one exchange between Isaiah and Diesel. One look at Diesel and Isaiah had assumed the fitness freak was dumb as a box of hammers. But he'd actually turned out to be fairly articulate. As the weights grew progressively heavier, the other reporters, including Ebony, couldn't complete the requisite full set of repetitions, which afforded them the opportunity to question Diesel. One by one they collapsed on the gym floor in defeat, but managed to dredge up just enough strength to take notes as Isaiah continued to pump the weights and Diesel for information. Whenever Isaiah slipped in a query about Diesel's rich uncle, he saw Ebony's ears hitch up like a canine's, but Diesel didn't reveal much.

Actually Diesel annoyed Isaiah big time. Not just because he'd clam up when questioned about his uncle, but because Isaiah noticed the way Diesel looked—no, leered—at Ebony. Diesel had taken a big shine to Ebony. She obviously had just the right fuel to make ol' Diesel's motor hum. When Ebony maxed out lifting a pathetic forty pounds, she had plopped on the carpeted floor. The edges of her shorts curled and rolled, exposing even more of those hot legs.

While Ebony was obviously not pleased when the rest of the guys ogled her, she didn't seem to mind special attention from Diesel one bit. Her little coquettish act had to be all about Renfro. She couldn't possibly be romantically interested in the nephew. Or could she? Ebony chuckled louder than the other reporters at Diesel's lame-ass jokes and Isaiah knew he had to distract Diesel the only way he knew how. "Yo, Deez, what's your personal best on the bench?"

"My bench max?" Diesel asked in that prissy little voice that would ordinarily come from a man a third his size.

"Yeah, your max."

"Why don't I show you?" Diesel lifted his gargantuan physique from the spot on the floor next to Ebony and began sliding plate after plate on both ends of the barbell resting on the bench press rack. He straddled, then reclined on the bench. "This is just a warm-up set, mind you."

Warm-up set? Isaiah couldn't believe it. Diesel zipped through five repetitions—pow! pow! pow! pow! pow! His pecs pumped like pistons under weight equivalent to a VW Beetle.

Diesel slammed the weight back in the rack, then stood and swaggered toward Isaiah. "You look like you're in pretty good shape. You should give it a go, ol' chap." Diesel slapped him on the back.

The blood in Isaiah's veins iced as all eyes locked on him.

"You're nice and warmed up from your previous sets. This should be a cinch." Diesel's tone held a challenge.

Ebony and the other reporters were watching Isaiah. He'd

look like a weenie if he backed down. "Yeah, a cinch," Isaiah echoed in a cocky voice that belied how he really felt.

"Don't worry. I'll spot you," Diesel offered. "Just say the word. If you get stuck, I'll grab the bar and help you out."

Yeah, right. Isaiah would look like an even bigger weenie if Diesel had to come to his rescue. He wasn't worried about what the other reporters thought. To hell with them, but he did care what Ebony thought. He couldn't succeed at seducing her if she saw him as a weakling. Her neatly arched brows and those pretty pillowy lips of hers drew tight with concern.

Isaiah settled on the padded bench, reached for the bar and slowly brought it toward the middle of his chest. As he suspected, it was heavy as hell. The most weight he'd ever handled in his life, but his blasted ego egged him on. His blood thawed and rushed to his head. As promised Diesel stood close to assist if needed.

The bar went up and down—slowly—for the first rep. Diesel had done five. Isaiah had to do at least that.

Up and down. Slower for the second, third, and fourth reps.

Isaiah's pecs were burning. The veins snaking along his forearms expanded. Sweat beaded and tickled his skin as it rolled onto the bench. His right eye twitched.

With unsteady arms, Isaiah hoisted the weight up and down in an excruciatingly deliberate fashion for the fifth rep. But did he stop there? No way.

A determination to do one more gnawed at him. He didn't care that it felt as if he were going to purge his breakfast— from both ends. He held on to the bar to push it up, down, and back up again. At the midway point of that last trip up his muscles stalled. His elbows and wrists threatened to buckle. He had to cover just a few more inches to put the bar back in the weight rack, but his arms and chest would not cooperate.

"You can do it, Isaiah!" Ebony's encouragement seemed to lighten the load, but not nearly enough. "C'mon, you've got it! You're almost there!"

The other reporters joined in a chorus to urge him on.

"C'mon, Isaiah! You can do it!"

"Light weight! Light weight!"

"It's all you! It's all you!"

"Mind over matter!"

Diesel did not join the cheerleading. "Just say the word. I've got you. I'll lighten that load."

With clenched teeth, Isaiah glanced toward Diesel, whose smirk was unmistakable.

Then the stubborn bar wouldn't budge. Isaiah's arms wobbled and the bar began descending toward his neck. Diesel reached out to grab it.

"No!" Isaiah managed in a winded growl as he felt every muscle in his upper body rebel in pain. "I've ... got—"

"I can't heeeeear youuuu," Diesel replied in an annoying singsongy voice.

Isaiah ground out, "I–said–I've–got–it!"

"Suit yourself." Diesel retreated.

"C'mon, Isaiah, you can do it!" Ebony shouted over the other reporters. Isaiah knew she had moved closer when he smelled strawberries.

"Idiot, that bar is going to snap his freaking neck off." Diesel chuckled cavalierly.

Isaiah heard that and sucked in his second wind. Then came the adrenaline surge. He gut-powered the bar up and back into its resting place with a loud clank.

"Yeeeaaahhhh! BOO-YOW!" Isaiah shouted, bolting upright and pumping his fist in the air to cheers from the onlookers. He felt like gliding into the electric slide.

"You did it!" Ebony shouted. And if Isaiah's eyes weren't deceiving him, she was beaming.

"Yeah, I did." Isaiah drank from the water bottle that somebody had passed to him. He had drawn a crowd beyond the press group.

"Way to go!"

"All right!"

"You da man!"

Diesel clearly didn't like all the attention Isaiah got and proclaimed that the bench press conference had officially ended. Then he wasted no time shifting his attention to Ebony, whom he quickly escorted back to his private office.

"Damn," Isaiah hissed to himself as Natasha ushered him and the rest of the press group toward the locker rooms to change.

Isaiah lingered in the shower and took twice as long as the other reporters to slip back into his clothes, in an effort to stall and wait for Ebony to emerge from Diesel's office. When he stepped out of the locker room Natasha escorted him to the exit—on Diesel's orders. Impatience and anger got the best of him. He waited in the parking area a little over an hour before taking off.

Inside Diesel's office the jaunty classical music from a portable CD player did little to mask the rhythmic clinks and clangs of the weights in motion just outside the door. With its gleaming chromes, stainless steels, white glass wall, and lustrous black leather, the room had the upscale techno-deco ambience one would expect to find in a swanky New York loft, not a Midwestern gym. No tattered posters of oiled beefcake ripped from the pages of *Flex* and *Muscle & Fitness* here. Instead the subtle beauty of Ansel Adams nature photos and reproductions of famous Impressionist paintings in sleek metal frames adorned the walls. Sandwiched between two abstract Lucite sculptures on a metal bookshelf were pristine copies of *The Complete Exercise Book for Butts and Guts* and dog-eared copies of *Man's Search for Meaning*, *The Essential Guide to User Interface*, and *Design Architecture from Prehistory to Post-Modernism*.

Ebony took a chair and accepted a glass of a pink concoction that looked like lumpy Pepto-Bismol. Diesel had whipped it up with ice cubes, water, and pouches of mystery ingredients.

Diesel flicked off the buzzing blender on his glass and metal desk. He poured the goopy contents into his own glass, then sprinkled a golden powder on top. "I like mine with extra wheat germ."

"What is this exactly?" Ebony asked, restraining an upchuck reflex.

"Diesel's Beet-flavored Protein Powder Drink, what else?" He shelved his beefy rear on the desk's edge.

The beet might have been the featured ingredient, but the unmistakable funk of rotten eggs emanated from Ebony's glass. "Yum." She smiled stiffly, moving the cool drink from one hand to the other. "I heard something about you trying to take it national, but it didn't quite catch on."

"It didn't catch on because I didn't have the money to do the kind of advertising and promotion it needed," Diesel spat. "I mean, you'd think my uncle could help with the financing instead of dropping everything he has pushing that bovine slime of his."

"Bovine slime?"

"Yeah, that's all ice cream is, you know. Cheers." Diesel turned up his glass and quaffed until it was empty. He licked away the hint of a liquid moustache with the tip of his tongue, then smacked his lips as if he'd never tasted anything so deliciously refreshing. "Go ahead, drink up. It's good for you and you could definitely use the protein. You're cute as the dickens, but your upper-body strength is pathetic, love. We'll have to work on that."

Ebony gave him what she hoped was a smile, but it was more like a glimpse of her front teeth. "I prefer mine at room temperature so I'm waiting for it to warm up a bit."

"Suit yourself." Diesel had been quite charming to Ebony actually, though she'd caught glimpses of his mean streak when he taunted Isaiah at the bench press rack. That spectacle obviously had been a clashing of titan egos. But she had been worried when it looked as if that weighted bar would behead Isaiah.

"Tell me, when can I expect to see my story in the *Butler County Bee*?" Diesel asked.

"Soon."

"Might that be before or after the Ice Cream Dreams Ball this weekend?"

"Why do you ask?"

"Because I'd be honored to have you as my guest for the evening."

"Your guest?" Ebony couldn't believe it. This was perfect and much more than she had hoped to accomplish by interviewing Diesel. She'd definitely underestimated the power of a little flirting and wearing hoochie-mama shorts. That annual ball, which benefited several noteworthy charities, was among the hottest annual social events in town. Guests paid handsomely for coveted spots among the revelers. After brief hopes of tagging along with Stella and "the hubby" were dashed, she hadn't considered the possibility of actually attending though she knew that as the founder and CEO of Ice Cream Dreams, Renfro would most definitely show.

"Well?" Diesel prompted as he refilled his glass with the beet drink. "Will you attend as my special guest for the evening?"

"Yes. I'd like that a lot." An understatement, but Ebony kept her cool.

"Very well, then. It's settled." Diesel lifted his glass to clink with Ebony's. "To your health."

A potent whiff of rotten eggs flitted beneath Ebony's nose and rocked her stomach, but she refused to offend Diesel by not sharing a friendly drink with him—especially now that she basked in the glow of his good graces.

"Salud!" Ebony raised her glass, lowered it, then raised it again. "Bottoms up!"

Diesel nodded. "Here's to you, love."

Ebony brought the glass halfway to her mouth, paused, and smiled weakly. "Down the hatch!"

Diesel's gaze was unrelenting.

"Here's to mud in your eye." Ebony held her breath, clutched the glass with both hands, and chugalugged as if the disgusting goop were the tasty nectar of youth and vitality.

Diesel smiled.

"All gone," Ebony declared triumphantly as she plunked her empty glass on his desk. Her insides instantly churned and gurgled in revolt. She shuddered a bit, but managed not to gag. She was unstoppable now. "Well, I'd better get going," she told Diesel as she manipulated a wince into a feeble smile.

"Leave your phone number and I'll give you a ring about

the particulars for our date. I'll probably send my uncle's car for you." Diesel reached for that blasted pitcher again. "But before you go, why don't you have another protein drink for the road?"

"Oh, goody," Ebony replied limply.

CHAPTER 20

The next morning the ringing phone beside Isaiah's bed jolted him out of a deep sleep. Bone-deep pain ripped through his chest and down his arms as he reached to answer it. From waist to neck he felt as if he'd been leveled by an eighteen-wheeler.

"Speak," he groaned, pressing the receiver to his ear and blinking in the sunlight blanketing his bedroom.

"Isaiah? Is that you?"

"Yeah," he answered in a deep, creaky voice.

"It's Ebony."

Isaiah glanced at the digital clock on the floor, instantly wondering how long she'd been glued to Diesel the day before. He considered asking, but wasn't about to let her know it mattered to him. "What's up?"

"About the workshop on Saturday. Maybe you're right. We probably should get together to discuss our game plan. I want our presentation to be informative and entertaining for the kids."

Isaiah winced as he eased up to rest his naked body against the headboard. The tenderness in his chest, back, and arms was so severe, his eyes watered from the effort.

"Damn," he moaned to himself.

"Are you all right?" Ebony asked. "You sound awful."

"Just a bad case of the doms."

"The doms?"

"Yeah, gym-speak for what's officially known as delayed onset muscle soreness."

"From that bench press press conference yesterday, huh?"

"Afraid so."

"Ahhh, the price of showing off," she chirped with zero sympathy.

Isaiah should've known she'd try to rub it in.

She went on. "Nobody forced you to accept that idiotic challenge, you know. I wouldn't be surprised if Diesel was taking steroids or some other performance-enhancing drugs for an edge. And there you were, with only your pumped-up ego and big mouth to back you up."

"I didn't do too badly. I outlifted him by one rep—one full rep."

"Guess that calls for a parade," she retorted.

"A win is a win is a win, whether it's by one extra rep or a dozen."

"Maybe, but for a minute there things looked pretty hairy. I thought that bar would drop like a guillotine." She sounded like a mom scolding her child.

"How sweet. You were worried about me," Isaiah teased.

She didn't deny it, but quickly changed the subject. "Whatever. That's not what I called to discuss. Back to the workshop. Do you have some spare time so we can meet?"

Isaiah eased from the bed. Sandwiching the receiver between his ear and shoulder, he tried stretching his throbbing triceps, but stiffness limited his range of motion. He groaned again.

"Hurts that bad, huh?" Ebony asked with a little more sympathy.

"I'll be all right. It's nothing that a little BenGay, ibuprofen, and ice won't heal."

"Why not try a little hair of the dog that bit you? I talked to some fitness experts once for a piece titled 'Coaching the Couch Potato'—"

"I am *not* a couch potato. I work out five days a week religiously."

"Geez, will you let me finish? I wasn't trying to imply that you were a couch potato. The article was actually about inspiring a nonexerciser to exercise. The sidebar was on how beginners sometimes push themselves too hard and how to cope with the pain that follows. One tip was to do more of the exercise that made you ache in the first place. Seems working out will circulate blood to the sore area, help carry nutrients to the muscles, and transport any leftover toxins that cause the pain right out of there."

Isaiah opened a dresser drawer, removed a pair of threadbare sweatpants, and stepped into them. "My toxins are staying just where they are. I've more than earned a break from the weights today."

"Suit yourself. I was just trying to help."

"I'll bet."

"So what's your schedule like? I was thinking we could meet at Java Jubilee, that little coffee bar on Seventh and Delta. I'm assuming, with your pain and all, today's out."

"It doesn't have to be. Why don't you come over here?" The extended silence on the phone line made him wonder if she'd hung up. "Ebony, are you there?"

She cleared her throat. "Yeah."

"So how about you coming over here?"

"Well . . . I don't know—"

"Don't trust yourself, eh?"

"You might as well wipe that cat-who-ate-the-canary grin I know you're wearing off your face. There will be no repeats of what happened between us in Grundie, you hear?"

"Trying to convince me or yourself?"

Ebony made an exasperated sound. "What's your address? I'm on my way," she quipped as if she had something to prove—just as Isaiah figured she would.

He gave her the address and directions. "I'll be waiting."

Isaiah hung up and went to the bathroom where the motion of lifting his arms to brush his teeth and wash his face was excruciating. A hot shower brought little relief. He slipped into a less ratty pair of sweatpants, but skipped the shirt, then took a minute to check his e-mail for revision messages from his *Inquisitor* editor. After finding none, he signed off his computer and pushed away from the rickety kitchen table, which served as a makeshift desk.

Though sparsely furnished, his place was a mess. A bunch of pillows and cushions were strewn across the carpeted living room floor. Stacks of *Inquisitor*s lined the walls. A large box with half a sausage-and-mushroom pizza, opened bags of Cool Ranch Doritos and Heineken bottles from dinner the night before crowded the kitchen counter. His gym clothes, still damp with sweat, were clumped—practically molding—in a corner. He tidied up as quickly as his screaming muscles would allow, stuffing three shirts and two pairs of running shorts under sofa cushions and kicking a pair of mismatched footies under a chair. He chomped on a slice of petrified pizza before discarding the rest. The walls had no photos or personal bric-a-brac to straighten or arrange. He'd never signed a lease anywhere that extended beyond six months in his life. Anything that had held the telltale reek of permanence made him claustrophobic.

When the doorbell rang, Isaiah opened the door without checking the peephole. Ebony stood on the other side, wearing a lime T-shirt and one of those ugly jumper things that should be illegal for anybody over the age of ten. She obviously refused to hew to what those slick women's magazines deemed fashionable. "Well, good morning," he said, moving aside so she could enter. He considered executing a showy bow, but couldn't manage any sudden exaggerated movements.

"Good morning to you, too." She stepped inside clutching a stack of folders and a large brown paper bag. "I bought coffee and lots of Ding Dongs for you. They were on sale. Two packages for the price of one, so I loaded up."

He still found her incredibly sexy though her alluring hips were obscured by that baggy jumper. "Good call. I'm afraid my cupboards and fridge are bare."

"Why am I not surprised?"

"Make yourself at home." He gestured toward the sofa.

Ebony sat, resting her folders and bag on the coffee table cluttered with bills, junk mail, and the last four issues of *National Geographic*. She lifted the one featuring a cover story about grizzly bears and arched a brow. "What? No *Playboy*?"

"I keep those next to the bed with my *Penthouse*, *Player*, and *Bodacious Black Booty* magazines, Kenny-Wayne's personal favorite." He winked to let her know he was only kidding, but her sense of humor was on hiatus *again*.

She replaced the magazine and got right down to business. Isaiah took a seat on an adjacent chair. For the next hour and a half they swapped ideas and honed strategy for the workshop.

Ebony found it difficult concentrating on their presentation. Isaiah sat there shirtless with the waistband of his sweats slung low on his lean hips. He obviously knew he had a body that wouldn't quit because he simply couldn't quit showing it off. "So I think we've got a pretty good plan here." She stuffed papers back inside her folder. "You sure you don't mind my leading?"

"No. I'll just jump in here and there. Public speaking isn't my thing. There's definitely an art to doing it without boring people."

Ebony noticed the large vinyl-covered photo album on his coffee table. "What's this?"

"Travel photos."

"Mind if I take a look?" she asked, though she already had the book in her lap.

"Sure, go ahead."

She flipped through the pages, commenting on the beauty and quality of each shot, as he provided the requisite travelogue details.

Isaiah cared what she thought and the fact that her compliments sounded sincere warmed him in an unexpected way.

"These are wonderful," she said.

"You really think so?" Isaiah felt his cheeks flush with a bashful pride.

"Yeah, you know me. If they sucked—"

"You wouldn't have told me they sucked. Not your style."

She smiled. "True, but if I didn't like them I wouldn't ask for copies. Can you do reprints of the Africa shots? I'd love to have them. I'll pay you."

"I'm flattered that you want copies. I'm more than happy to oblige, free of charge. I'll have them ready in time for the symposium. How's that?"

"Great."

They sat in awkward silence for a few moments until Ebony stood and began removing her keys out of her fanny pack. "Well, I'd better go. I've taken up enough of your time."

"What's the rush?" Wincing, Isaiah slowly came to his feet.

"You sure you're all right?"

"Whenever I sit still for longer than a few minutes at a time my muscles stiffen up more."

"Have you tried any stretching at all? That's supposed to help."

"Massage is supposed to work better." He stepped closer, wiggling his brows. So close she had to tip her head back to look at him or bury her nose in the deep indentation separating his pecs.

"You're anything but subtle and I'm afraid I have to go," Ebony said, stepping back.

"I promise I'll keep my hands to myself."

"Can't stay."

"Oh, c'mon, after all we've been through together—the skunk, the poison ivy . . ."

Before she could counter with reasons why she shouldn't, Isaiah dropped to his knees, then stretched across the carpet, face up. "Would you pass me those pillows, please?" He twisted his face in pain as he attempted to reach for them himself.

Ebony knew he was juicing his agony for all it was worth, but she unbuckled her fanny pack and placed it on the coffee table along with her folders, then grabbed a throw pillow and kneeled to tuck it beneath his head.

"Now what?" She felt awkward and unsure what to do next.

"I want you to put your hands on me, of course." Features twisted in discomfort moments before relaxed in a come-hither look. She'd been hoodwinked. "Let's start here." He stroked the firm swells of his pecs.

"I'm not a professional masseuse, you know." She cracked her knuckles to stress that there would be no fooling around. "I could end up doing you more harm than good."

"Let me worry about that. Just start off with a light touch." He reached for her hands and placed them on his bare chest. "Because I'm on the floor, it might be best if you were on top of me, uh—for ergonomics' sake, of course, you know, less strain on your wrists."

"I thought you were so sore." She pursed her lips with suspicion. "The extra weight on you might be too uncomfortable."

"Extra weight? Why, you're light as a feather."

She hesitated for a minute, then relented, carefully straddling his hips.

"Yeah. There, that's it," he said, unabashed contentment on his face. "Isn't this cozy?"

She rolled her eyes.

"What? A brother can't want a therapeutic massage for what ails him?" He rested his large hands on both of her thighs, just below where the fabric of her jumper began. "Comfortable?"

She couldn't reply as the heat of a blush crept up her neck to spread to her cheeks.

"I don't know why you're acting so shy all of a sudden," he said as his voice went low. "It's not like we haven't been this close before."

"I told you there would be no repeats of what happened in Grundie," Ebony replied, refusing to get lost in honey-brown eyes that darkened with sensual mischief.

"All right. All right. Can we just get on with it?" He placed his hands on top of hers and guided them in the slow circling motion he preferred over his chest. She absorbed the heat from his taut golden-brown skin. The thick dusting of silky black hair tickled her fingertips. "Yeah, that's it." He sighed as his eyelids closed in rapture. "Hmmm. Yes."

Ebony's mouth went dry as she skimmed over the muscle-thick blocks of flesh. *Omigod!* He was simply magnificent. And way too enticing. That now familiar ache of longing overtook her.

"You can use more pressure now," Isaiah instructed her.

"Won't that hurt?"

"Yeah, but it hurts so good."

She went from a feathery touch to a deeper kneading motion using her thumbs to exert more localized pressure. He moaned his gratitude. As she leaned forward to work his shoulders, her crotch inadvertently brushed against the thick ridge expanding inside his worn sweatpants. The contact at such intimate places on their bodies was brief, but electrifying. She couldn't deny the pleasure it brought. Now slick with yearning, she drew in short choppy breaths then bumped against him again, but that time was no accident. She chewed her lip and stared into his eyes, where she saw the green light needed to have her way with his beautiful body. His hands slipped under her jumper until he cupped her rear, sliding her on top of his erection. For a few dizzying minutes, he pushed her hips back and forth for a deliberate grind heightened by the friction of the moist cotton fabric between them. Ebony's own moan of pleasure startled her. Suddenly frozen with embarrassment at how easily she could be manipulated by Isaiah, she looked everywhere but at him.

"What's wrong?" He massaged her thighs.

"I have to go, that's all." She got up, adjusting her outfit.

Isaiah rose up on his elbows, cringing again as if the pain had inconveniently returned. "This thing between us . . ." He sighed with impatience. "I can feel it and I know you can, too. The sexual pull, I mean. It's too strong. It's inevitable. All the dancing around it and the interruptions are only adding fuel to the fire. Sooner or later it's going to explode. Why not just go with it? Why keep fighting?"

"I don't know about you, but I can't just go around acting on every impulse and scratching every itch simply because it feels good, Isaiah," she said in a tight voice. "There's something to be said for self-control. You lured me over here to seduce me and it didn't work. Well, not all the way at least. I know what you're up to."

Isaiah flopped back on the pillow. "Why can't I just want to give and receive pleasure from a woman I'm extremely attracted to?"

"If only it were that simple." Ebony strapped on her fanny pack. "And you and I both know it's not. I've got to hand it to you, though. You're good, damn good. Almost had me going there for a minute."

"What are you talking about?" Isaiah sat upright again. She didn't buy his clueless act.

"I know you're trying to mess with my head and get me all sidetracked. Maybe I'll forget all about Renfro. You're probably thinking, 'If I sleep with her, maybe she'll get all goofy.'"

"You mean goofier than you already are?" He released a dry chuckle. "Is that even possible? You're one schizo babe, you know that? Running hot and cold at the drop of a hat."

"Say what you want." She scooped up her folders and headed for the door, briskly dismissing him. "I'm outta here. See you at the workshop next Saturday."

Isaiah struggled to stand. "Wait!"

She turned and watched him walk toward her. A part of Ebony hoped he would try to come up with the right reasons and words to convince her that his interest in her wasn't just a strategic maneuver.

Instead he snatched up the brown bag and shoved it at her. "You forgot your Ding Dongs."

"How tacky of you to return a gift from a guest," she chided.

"And how tacky of you to try to foist something you obviously didn't want on me." Hard lines bracketed his mouth.

"Huh? You know I love Ding Dongs."

"*Hel-lo*, Queen of the Two-for-One Deal." He plunged a hand inside the bag, removed a Ding-Dong, reached across her shoulder and tapped the cake against the door three times. "In case you hadn't noticed, they're stale and hard as hockey pucks. I don't want them."

Balancing her folders in one arm, Ebony snatched the Ding Dong from his hand, ripped the wrapper open with her teeth, and stuffed the chocolate cake inside her mouth. "Fine! More for me!" she muttered, then marched off to her car with the bag of discount Ding Dongs in tow.

CHAPTER 21

The journalism symposium at DeWalt College went well, much to Isaiah's surprise. After the little Ding Dongs debacle, he and Ebony did the rest of their collaborating via e-mail, which made his plans for seduction difficult.

Still, positive energy crackled throughout the classroom as they worked together with tag-team precision, offering tips on selecting a solid journalism study program. While most of the symposium attendees were college juniors and seniors, Ebony and Isaiah led the only session geared to high school students. Ebony had more reverence and enthusiasm for the industry than Isaiah. When their session wrapped, his father wasted little time pointing that out.

"I'm surprised you even volunteered," George said to Isaiah when DeWalt College faculty and AAJC members gathered in a room for a postsymposium reception.

"I didn't exactly volunteer. Tarik asked me to do it and I agreed, as a favor to him," Isaiah replied, trying not to read anything negative into the comment.

George was erudite and elegant, in his small wire-rimmed glasses, crisp shirt, slacks, and camel jacket. "So exactly what type of courses might a young aspiring tabloid reporter want to consider? Science fiction writing 101? Intro to *Ripley's Believe It Or Not?*"

Every journalist within earshot chuckled at the jab, except Ebony.

Isaiah was tempted to snipe back, but didn't. Now wasn't the time or place. In spite of everything, this man was still his father. He would show him the respect in front of others that his father never afforded him. George always seemed to take such wicked glee in putting Isaiah on the spot.

Tarik wrapped a warm arm around Isaiah's shoulder. "Hey, bro, good job. The kids told me how much they enjoyed your session."

"I had help. Ebony really clicked with the students. She deserves most of the credit." Isaiah reached for Ebony's hand and pulled her closer.

Tarik turned to her. "Thanks for helping out, Ebony."

"I had a good time," she replied. "If you ever need me for something like this again, don't hesitate to sign me up."

"Will do."

"I don't believe we've been officially introduced." At arm's length, George offered a hand. "George Malone. I'm Tarik and Isaiah's father."

"Nice to meet you, Mr. Malone." Ebony shook his hand. "I've read and loved all of your work, particularly on the civil rights movement."

"So you write for the *Butler County Bee*, I take it."

"Yes."

"Well, we've all got to start some place." George adjusted his silk necktie. "I was the editor of the *Jefferson High Bulldog* at one time."

Isaiah noticed that Ebony's warm expression chilled. He could take his father's jabs, but he refused to let his unprovoked swipes against Ebony go unchallenged. He wanted to shake him until his porcelain veneers rattled. "I wouldn't exactly compare the *Bee* to a high school publication, Dad."

"This from a man who once penned a piece on a man-eating grasshopper," George quipped with a condescending laugh.

"Where are those damn man-eating grasshoppers when you

need one?" Isaiah retorted, glaring at his father in such a way that left no doubt who he'd use as grasshopper bait.

Titters rippled around the room. So much for Isaiah letting his father's digs roll off him. Fortunately, Tarik rushed in to diffuse the escalating tension between them.

"Hey, folks, dinner is starting in a minute in the George Washington Carver room down the hall. We'd better start heading that way."

"I'm going to pass." Isaiah watched his father as he joined a group as they made their way down the hall toward the food.

"You're not staying for dinner?" Tarik asked.

"Nah." Isaiah patted his brother's shoulder. "Now that the students are gone, it's gotten a little too stuffy in here for me. Need some fresh air."

"I'm not staying, either," Ebony said.

"Sure I can't convince you two to stay?" As usual Tarik appeared let down that Isaiah was running away from his problem—again. "The menu is quite good. We actually landed a pretty good caterer for a bargain. They're famous for their lip-smacking desserts."

"No, I really have got to go," Isaiah said.

"Me, too," Ebony added.

Isaiah stared at her. "*You're* passing up all the free dessert you can eat? I don't believe it."

"Yup. What of it?" she challenged with a lift of her chin.

Tarik turned to join the group in the George Washington Carver room. "Bye, you two, and again, thanks for your help today."

Isaiah only half-listened to his brother. He wondered what could come between Ebony's sweet tooth and sweet potato pie. Was she rushing home to check in on her loopy relatives . . . Or did she have a hot date? With Diesel?

"I'll walk you to your car," Isaiah offered, hoping he could get an explanation out of her before they reached her Escort. When she didn't refuse, he considered it a small victory.

In the parking lot, he searched for just the right thing to say. He was touched that—unlike some of the others—Ebony hadn't found his father's verbal swipes at him the least bit amusing. He wanted to show his gratitude. And he wasn't quite ready to let her go. "I'm buying you dinner," he said when they reached her car. "And I won't take no for an answer."

"I don't think that's a good idea, especially after what almost happened in Grundie and at your apartment." She averted her gaze as her voice quavered with uncertainty.

"It's a public place, Ebony. C'mon. Besides, the only way you're going to get those reprints you wanted is if you come with me."

"You actually have the prints?" she asked, obviously surprised. "When you agreed to do that, I thought—"

"I promised, didn't I?"

Ebony looked away from him as if to conceal her inner conflict. "I just don't know—"

He curled a finger under her chin and gently turned her face toward his. "Here's what I know. I need to spend some time with you tonight. I'd like to make it up to you for the Ding Dongs thing. It was a nice gesture and I was so rude."

Something smoldered in her eyes, something that told him she was no more ready to part than he was. He upped the ante by moving closer. She didn't step away. His gaze roamed to her lips. The moment was thick with intimate possibilities. "Got a hot date?" he asked.

"That's really none of your business, but no, I don't have a date."

"Does the Black Girl need to be whisked off to the vet again?"

"No." Ebony chuckled. "I don't have to take *Black Gal* to the vet."

"Then let me hook you up with some slammin' fried catfish, collard greens, and sweet potato pie. Forget what Tarik said about that caterer. The sweet potato pie I'm talking about is so deliciously sinful your toes will curl."

"That good, huh?" Her brows arched.

He almost had her.

"There's this little restaurant on the east side. You're going to love it."

"I don't know." Uncertainty crept into her voice again.

"C'mon now, I've missed..." Isaiah paused and took a deep breath before plunging into the deep end. "I've really missed hanging out with you."

Skepticism flitted across Ebony's pretty features, then a small smile soon settled on her lips. "Really?"

"Really."

Dusk quickly faded to night as Ebony's car trailed Isaiah's Mustang through the east side's oldest neighborhood to a parking lot. At a small storefront building Isaiah parked, then met Ebony at her car and placed an arm around her waist as they walked toward the restaurant.

"Catchy name." Ebony looked up at the Fit to Be Fried sign blinking in violet neon from the largest window.

"I take it you've never been here before," he said.

"No."

To the left of the small structure sat a boarded-up building that had been a record store in a former life. A dilapidated movie theater with an angular, jutting marquee flanked it. Isaiah didn't strike her as the type to frequent restaurants with valet parking, maître d's, and boot-licking amenities, but she'd never peg him as a regular at this little dive.

"The buildings are old and most of the businesses are long gone, but a lot of good folks still live around here." He opened the large metal door so she could enter first. It clanked closed behind them.

An older woman whom Ebony guessed to be in her sixties greeted them. She wiped her hands on her grease-smeared, white apron before she reached out to Isaiah, who had to bend to accommodate her short, plump arms. "There's my boy. How you doing, baby?"

"Good." Isaiah pecked her cheek.

With curiosity lighting her eyes, the woman immediately turned to Ebony. "Well, well, well. And who have we here? Got a new woman on the hook?" she asked Isaiah.

Isaiah's woman? Ebony's insides went aflutter with the thought. So Isaiah usually brought dates to Fit to Be Fried?

Did that mean this was an official date? Her body hummed at the possibility.

Isaiah started the intros. "Lucille, this is Ebony. Ebony, Lucille."

"Hello, nice to meet you." Ebony offered her hand and a warm smile to the older woman.

"And nice to meet you." She gave Ebony's hand a meaningful squeeze. "I have a good feeling about her." She nudged Isaiah. "Forget those other siddity heifers. Bring this one around more than once, will you? I'm a whiz at reading people and I get a real good vibe here."

"Damn, Lucille, will you stop spewing my business. Are you trying to kill my groove or what?" Isaiah chuckled then turned to Ebony with a stage whisper, "Lucille here is the owner of this fine establishment and the big dipper."

"The big dipper?" Ebony asked.

Lucille and Isaiah laughed at their private joke.

"Is somebody going to fill me in or what?" Ebony looked to Isaiah.

Lucille explained. "He calls me the 'big dipper' because he says I'm always dipping all in other folks' mustard trying to ketchup. His way of calling me nosy." Lucille slapped Ebony's arm and yukked it up with a laugh that sounded as if she were having a mild asthma attack. "Ketchup as in 'catch up.' Get it?"

It was too corny, but Ebony laughed because she liked Lucille. The woman's warmth and unabashed earthiness made her feel instantly at ease.

"Yeah, I'm afraid she did get it." Isaiah smiled. "Now, I'll complete the intros if that's okay." He described Ebony as a friend and colleague.

They most certainly were not an item, but Ebony kinda liked pretending that they were for just a night. Though unspoken, another cease-fire was obviously in effect. His hand brushed up and caressed her shoulder in an intimate fashion, but she wouldn't read too much into this extra attentiveness.

"Friends? Colleagues?" Lucille made a face. "That's no fun. My advice is you'd better do something about that, mister man. She's such a pretty thing. Look at her." She reached out and lifted one of Ebony's silky braids. "I don't usually care for braids too much, but they look real nice on you."

"Thanks." Ebony felt her cheeks flush.

"Yes, she is fine, a real Nubian beauty," Isaiah agreed, looking into Ebony's eyes as if he actually meant it. Lucille had put him on the spot. What else could he say? That Ebony looked as if someone had beat her face with an ugly stick—as one of Granny Mac's homespunisms went? "I can't wait for Ebony to try the food. Lucille can throw down on some catfish, too," Isaiah continued.

The pair followed Lucille as she guided them through a cluster of tables to an empty one near the front.

"I'll be right back with the menus," Lucille said before departing.

"I'm sure you noticed Lucille can be a little nosy," Isaiah said in a hushed tone.

"A *little* nosy?" Ebony grinned, settling on the seat Isaiah pulled out for her.

"Correction, very nosy, but she's good people." Isaiah took their lightweight jackets to the coat rack in the corner then returned as Lucille approached their table.

"The catfish special, right?" Lucille asked Isaiah, who declined a menu.

"You know it," he replied.

"I'll have the same," Ebony said. "How can I pass up this catfish he's been raving about?"

"Good choice. Coming right up." Lucille turned and slipped inside the kitchen.

Ebony propped her elbows on the clean white linen tablecloth and fussed with the centerpiece of assorted silk flowers. "I like Lucille and I like this place." The nicked hardwood floors, mismatched silverware and kitschy black velvet portraits of Motown greats added to its charm. Pool and foos ball tables beckoned those in a competitive mood.

"Told ya."

Ebony perused the menu left behind. "But if Lucille could fry water I'm sure she would." The menu was a veritable homage to lard and Crisco, boasting deep-fried everything from okra to apples. You name it, Lucille had slapped some batter on it and dipped it in hot oil.

"The smothered oxtails, bread pudding, and sweet potato pie aren't fried," Isaiah pointed out.

"Oh, yeah, I see." Ebony paused then garnered the courage to reveal what had been on her mind since the workshop. She placed the menu back on the table. "Isaiah, why do you do it? Write for the tabloids, I mean."

His expression changed from playful and open to stony and closed. "I do it because I can. I'm good at it and it frees me up to travel."

Sensing that she'd ventured into forbidden territory, Ebony tried to lighten the mood again. "Favorite locale? Judging from your photo album I'd say Africa, right?"

His face softened again with a disarming smile. "Got several actually. Chile, Morocco, Australia. But I must admit Africa really takes my breath away. I've seen the great pyramids of Giza, floated along the Nile in a small felucca. In Luxor I visited the temples of Karnak."

"I've always wanted to visit Africa, China, and Europe."

"Been to Europe, too."

"Where?"

"England, France, Italy, Czechoslovakia. The architecture in Prague is simply fantastic. The colors of the buildings... Awesome. I wanted to take photographs of everything. I've included some reprints of those places, too." He paused. "They're yours if you want them."

"Of course I want them. All of your photographs are fabulous," Ebony replied softly. An awkward minute stretched into another before she spoke again. "All that traveling must cost a fortune."

"Not necessarily, you'd be surprised at the great bargains you can get when you're willing to travel at the spur of the moment and get creative with your accommodations."

"So most of that globe-trotting is not just for work. You don't have to travel to write all those tabloid stories, right?

Isn't most of that stuff made up? You can pen that from anywhere."

"Exactly, which is one of the reasons I've done it all these years. That kind of freedom is hard to walk away from. It's like writing fiction—actually it is fiction writing, but every now and then there's a grain of truth—"

"That's embellished," Ebony completed his thought. "So why not just write fiction and call it that? You know, write a novel or short stories."

"The money's not as good or quick. Scoring the big-money book advance that you read about is like winning the lottery."

"Do you enjoy it? The tabloid writing, I mean?"

Isaiah took a pensive minute. "I enjoy the photography part."

"Your photography is so wonderful. Ever considered pursuing that full time?"

He shook his head. "I've always thought I had to be a writer, any kind of writer, because that's what we Malones do. The photography has been more of a hobby, though I do take photos for some of my pieces. Of course, there's all kinds of computerized manipulation involved to get the picture to actually *match* the story."

Ebony was fascinated. "Like enlarging that flesh-eating grasshopper until he's the size of the Incredible Hulk."

"Yup."

She laughed.

"You know, you're full of surprises," he said, eyes shining with appreciation. "I expected you to hop on your high horse and give me a hard time or poke fun when you found out what I write for a living."

"Hey, I can't knock you. I mean, I slave away for the *Butler County Bee,* remember? I've done an eighty-inch personality profile on a local man who makes cow sculptures out of Gouda."

"And it doesn't get any cheesier than that. Bad pun intended."

Ebony laughed again and fiddled with her silverware. "But

I do have bigger aspirations. You do too or you wouldn't be going after that *Examiner* job, right?"

Isaiah paused. "When I graduated from college I saw the tabloids as a way to stick it to my Pulitzer-obsessed father. After today, I'm sure you know what a journalistic snob he is."

"He said some pretty harsh things to you."

"He didn't exactly go easy on you either, comparing the *Bee* to the *Bulldog*. Sorry about that."

Ebony shrugged. "I'm used to the snarky put-downs from those who think writing for a weekly community paper is tantamount to not writing at all, but coming from him, yeah, his comment stung a little because I admired him and his work for so long. I didn't expect him to . . ." Her words trailed off.

"Go ahead. Say it. You didn't expect him to be such a colossal asshole." Isaiah chuckled despite the tinge of bitterness that crept into his voice. "Yeah, he's a real trip. I don't know if I'd fully grasp what stellar examples of journalistic excellence he and my brother Tarik are if my father didn't point out what a complete and total screwup I am."

"Does this have anything to do with why you're going after the *Examiner* job?" When Isaiah didn't reply she had her answer. "But is it what you really want?"

He visibly stiffened as that wall between them went up again. "Whoa, is this a career counseling session or what?"

"Sorry. Didn't mean to . . ."

"It's all right." Isaiah sighed, but continued with some reluctance. "My relationship with my father is very strained and . . . complicated. But in all fairness I have to add I did more than my share to tick him off. I was a real pain in the ass in elementary and junior high school."

For the first time since they met, Ebony got a glimpse of Isaiah's vulnerable side. "Elementary and junior high? You were just a kid." She reached for her glass to take a drink of water.

"Yeah, a kid with a hard head, piss-poor grades, and undiagnosed dyslexia."

She nearly choked mid-swallow. "You're dyslexic? I never would've guessed."

"It's not like we all walk around with the big letter *D* stamped on our foreheads."

"I know, it's just that . . . well, you're a writer. That must be challenging."

"It's not one of the more severe cases—especially after my diagnosis and training. I just have to be more creative with how I approach certain written material, that's all."

"I'm impressed." And she really meant that. She began to get a clearer picture of what that *Examiner* job meant to him. After meeting his blowhard of a father, she could empathize with Isaiah. Their motivations were hauntingly similar. Both had something to prove and felt a need for redemption. Isaiah needed his father to see his worth. Ebony needed to believe her own worth. "What about your mother? Has she been very supportive?"

"She divorced my father when Tarik and I were boys." His voice was barely audible. "Started a new life and a new family for herself in California. Save for major holidays, we didn't see her much."

"Oh. I'm sorry." When Ebony rested her water glass she almost reached for his hand. Instead she fussed with her place setting, pushing a butter knife to the left of her fork.

"It's all right," he said, eyes lowered. "With enough time you can learn to adjust to just about anything."

Ebony felt compelled to circle back to his father. She wondered if he had hopes that they could be closer someday. "Is landing that *Examiner* job the way you hope to get through to your father? He must be pleased that you're going after a . . ."—she made quote marks in the air with her fingers—"*real* journalism job."

"He has no idea what I'm doing."

"So you two have never discussed this?"

"What's to discuss? You see how he jumps all over my case about my tabloid work. My landing a job at a *real* paper should shut him up once and for all and . . ." Isaiah faltered as if something had ripped inside of him and all his fondest dreams dangled out to be judged. Obviously feeling too exposed, he used the Temptations classic "My Girl" the band played to change the subject. "Listen to that. That's the jam right there." He smiled, came to his feet, and reached for her hand. "May I have this dance?"

Though disconcerted by the abrupt gesture, she let him guide her to the small parquet dance floor where their bodies came together and swayed to lyrics floating on a mellow beat. Her lids drifted closed as he hummed the melody and pressed a soft kiss against her ear. She could almost believe she was indeed *his girl*. Almost. She knew better. When the song ended he held on to her, but Ebony drew away to check her watch, then remove her cell phone from her fanny pack. "I didn't realize what time it was. I need to find a quiet spot, maybe the restroom. Have to check on my folks to let them know I'm going to be late."

"Do what you have to do." He smiled. "But hurry back."

She glanced over her shoulder to see Isaiah watching her depart.

Distracted, Ebony returned to their table a few minutes later.

"Is everything all right?" Isaiah asked.

"I guess I just started to feel a little guilty about staying out later than usual and so soon after that trip to Grundie. Ma and Granny Mac don't get along at all. I worry about them."

His brow furrowed with curiosity. "These are grown-ups, not children, you're talking about?"

Ebony bristled a bit. "Yes. And your point is?"

"Nothing. You must be extremely close."

"We are. Some people think it's weird, but..." Isaiah struck her as the type who would side with Yolanda on the subject of how close is too close. "They were expecting me to get home earlier, as usual. We have certain nights when we do things together. There's a Scrabble night, a bid whist night—"

"So what did you and your family have planned this evening?"

"Promise you won't laugh."

Isaiah raised a hand. "Scout's honor."

"Okay. Well, it's Bruce Lee video night. Granny Mac loves him."

"Bruce Lee video night?" Isaiah erupted in laughter.

Ebony wadded a napkin and pelted his head with it. "What happened to Scout's honor?"

"I wasn't a Scout." He made a silly face. "Bruce Lee videos, Scrabble, bid whist... Damn, you MacKenzies really know how to party. But I'm sure your mom and granny are just fine as long as you're having a good time. You *are* having a good time, right?"

Ebony hesitated. "Yes," she admitted in a near whisper. "Maybe that's why I started to feel a little guilty."

"Sweet and sensitive." He leaned toward the table, propping his chin in his hand. His eyes went soft and dreamy. "Can't beat that combo."

Ebony felt the heat of blushing slash across her cheeks. "But don't take that for weakness."

"Believe me, I know better than anyone. Ebony MacKenzie is *not* to be messed with. But maybe, just maybe, if I play my cards right, the evening won't end with you stomping away from me in a snit for once. I'm looking forward to that."

Lucille reappeared, carrying trays with plates of food and Mason jars of iced tea. The catfish looked as good as promised and tasted even better. Tender filets coated with hot crispy breading danced on Ebony's tongue. "Oh... this is heavenly," she moaned, savoring the medley of spices as her eyes drifted closed. "Mmmm."

"Hmmp, hmmp, hmmp. I do love the way you enjoy your food," Isaiah crooned.

She felt his unwavering gaze and snapped out of her private fried-catfish heaven. "Staring is rude, you know."

"I didn't mean to make you uncomfortable." His eyes darkened with desire. "It's just that I'm here, you're here—"

"And all is right with the world," Ebony replied with more sarcasm than necessary just to reclaim control of the situation. She had to remember who she was dealing with.

"What's with the attitude?"

"It's just that I've gotten so used to our verbal jousting most of the time," she replied, instantly contrite.

"I know, but tuck away your little snide grenades for the rest of the night."

Though Ebony questioned his sincerity, she truly enjoyed this side of him. "All right, I'm disarmed. No more cracks or cutting remarks for the rest of the evening."

"You can't blame me for checking you out." Flattery was obviously his weapon to keep her off balance. "You're very easy on the eyes, but you have to know that already. It's like . . . Well, I can't stop looking at you."

"Like you couldn't stop looking at Camille Davenport at the last AAJC meeting?" Ebony asked, quickly forgetting her promise.

His sexy smile flattened into a severe line. "Camille Davenport?"

"I couldn't help but notice how you two were . . . How does Stella say it in her *Butler Bee* Deep Dish gossip columns? Canoodling? Yes, that's it. You two were canoodling at the AAJC meeting."

"Canoodling?" Isaiah laughed. "Sounds like some obscure pasta-making technique from the Old Country."

Isaiah tried to change the subject, but she would not let him off the hook so easily regarding Camille. She'd probably chink his too-cool exterior, but a determination to find out just how close Isaiah and Camille were wouldn't let her go. "Camille's really attractive *and* loaded, I hear."

Isaiah didn't rise to the bait, but smirked like a man with a juicy secret. Instead he reached for his glass of iced tea, indulged in a leisurely swallow first. "If you're so curious about my sex life, at least be woman enough to ask me— straight-out. I'm not sleeping with Camille nor am I interested in sleeping with Camille. And it's really none of your business, but we can make it your business if you like." Isaiah winked, tossing the ball in her court, where it landed with a resounding thud.

Ebony longed for a way with saucy repartee, but her mind went blank as a shaken Etch A Sketch. Instead she cleared her throat, summoned a waitress, and ordered a slice of sweet potato pie with a tennis-ball-sized dollop of whipped cream.

"It's none of my business, either, but since all bets are off tonight, what about you and the Diester?"

"You mean Diesel?"

"Who else? I noticed how he was checking you out and you were holed up in his office a mighty long time."

"There's nothing going on between me and Diesel." Ebony didn't know where the truth ended and a lie began. She had accepted a date with Diesel, but that was strictly business as far as she was concerned though Diesel obviously had other ideas. No need to get into the particulars with Isaiah. They'd decided another cease-fire was in effect, which meant any talk about strategy to land the Renfro exclusive would surely rouse the fierce competitive tension lingering just beneath the surface.

Isaiah's scoff was percussive. "Nothing at all?"

"Nope. Nothing at all. Zip."

With that Isaiah was all toothy grin again. She wondered why it mattered. He couldn't possibly be . . . jealous? Or did he merely want to know how close she was getting to Renfro?

They enjoyed their desserts and blitzed through discussions about everything from politics to the nosedive of tech stocks.

When the conversation boomeranged back to the personal, Isaiah revealed that his love life had been a series of short, hot bursts of passion without purpose. He considered himself the classic commitmentphobe. He'd guarded his independence with unyielding determination. Ebony didn't know what to make of his candor. She had pegged him from the get-go. Player. But she was in no position to judge. She actually felt an odd kinship of sorts. She'd had her share of superficial relationships as well. Though it had been a while since she'd actually dated anyone longer than a few weeks. And of those guys, none had been deemed worthy enough to take home to meet the family. Having a man in her life would require reassessing her priorities and opening up, not only to reveal, but to give more of herself. Too busy working, finishing school, jump-starting her writing career, and tending to one family crisis after another, she never gave relationships the time and nurturing required to flourish. She would have the time someday—just not right now.

Ebony overdosed on sweet potato pie and the undivided attention of an incredibly good-looking man who was just as sweet—when he wanted to be. She was on a buzzy sugar high when Isaiah walked her to the Escort shortly after ten P.M.

"Just a second. I almost forgot." He quickly went to his car, grabbed a manila envelope, and passed it to her as she stopped at the driver's side of her car. "The reprints you wanted. If you'd like any of them enlarged, just let me know."

"Thank you . . ." She accepted the envelope and quickly looked inside then back up at him. "For the photos and the excellent dinner."

Isaiah tugged the envelope away from her, placed it on top of her car, then reached for her hands. "And the company?"

"Nice. Very nice." She smiled.

Isaiah lifted her hands to his mouth and kissed her knuckles. His warm breath and the brush of his soft, moist lips sent languorous shivers up her spine. Before she realized it, he held each side of her face and tilted her head back. He brushed her lips with his own. Soon his tongue slipped inside her mouth—stoking the flames deep inside of her. She didn't fight it, but went with the smooth and silky flow as he pulled her closer. Moans of pleasure drifted on the night air as they melted against one another. The intensity and pressure of their kiss heightened until it felt as if they were fighting to draw precious breath from one another. At her core she expanded and ached with a desperate need to be filled. Her breasts blossomed, hot and full. She wanted him. Had to have him. *Tonight.*

She was not the one-night-stand type, but after their little tête-à-tête about relationships, she knew that was all Isaiah was prepared to offer, and then again, that's all she needed at this point in her life anyway. *Right?*

Isaiah slowly drew back, but just enough to say in a thick whisper, "Come home with me." He flicked the tip of his tongue across her lips. "Say you'll come home with me now."

"I . . . uh." Her senses scrambled, but she quickly nodded her reply.

Giving in to her lustful obsession would mean she could purge it once and for all. While Isaiah's kisses didn't guarantee that he wasn't lousy in bed, she got weak in the knees just thinking he could be half as good as his kisses suggested. She couldn't wait to find out. If he wasn't, well, that knowledge would certainly neutralize the ever-increasing hold he had over her thoughts. "Yes, I'll go home with you."

CHAPTER 22

Isaiah maneuvered through the thick postconcert traffic along I-75, careful to check his rearview mirror often to see if Ebony's Escort trailed him. He still couldn't believe she had agreed to follow him home. He was damn happy about it as long as he didn't think too hard. He'd been honest and was doubtful she'd harbor any false expectations about what it all would mean later. He eased into an idling stop behind a silver Taurus halted by a bottleneck of cars loaded with concertgoers departing from the coliseum. He chided himself for not taking an alternate, less traveled route, but he hadn't known one of those teenybopper boy bands had played to a packed venue that night. He reached to adjust his rearview mirror. Glancing at the reflection, he couldn't make out Ebony's features, but he felt her smile. He imagined it all cute and dimply. He liked her cute and dimply. The driver in the black Ford Explorer in an adjacent lane laid on his horn as if that would alleviate the jam of creeping vehicles.

Inside Ebony's car second thoughts haunted her. The heat of desire and anxious curiosity that had had her stomach flip-flopping since she locked lips with Isaiah were subsiding and her better judgment surfaced. Was going home with him really a good idea? She held the steering wheel with a white-knuckled grip, and watched Isaiah adjust his rearview mirror. She smiled, unsure whether he could see her. She was actually headed to his place to make out and make nookie. Then what?

As if trapped in an altered state of consciousness since she'd first tasted his lips in Grundie, her view of the world had grown increasingly narrow with each passing day. The yearning to feel him pressing deep inside of her grew to an all-consuming preoccupation. She'd even gone so far as to purchase a box of condoms. If he happened to be lousy in bed, she could get over the unrelenting longing that had made her downright scatty as of late. She could write him off once and for all. He'd no longer commandeer her daydreams and night fantasies. He'd be relegated to the ol' what-was-I-thinking? purgatory of former crushes. Like college classmate Duane Jackson, who happened to be a world-class kisser, but tarnished his sexy-as-hell mystique the night he chugalugged too much malt liquor then proceeded to burp the national anthem. Then there was Harry Boltwright, who always had enough dirt embedded under his nails to grow turnips. And who could forget Clifford Stevens? His magnetism evaporated after Ebony saw him wipe pizza dribblings from his mouth with his shirtsleeve one time too many. One false move and a guy got demoted from fantasy fodder. Why would Isaiah be any different? Once she got to know him intimately, he was sure to reveal another unflattering side, besides the cocky, competitive opportunist she'd pegged early on.

But what if he were an amazing lover? What if his technique rocked her world? She'd be helpless. Hopelessly hooked. And all the bad manners and poor hygiene in the world wouldn't set her free. She'd be addicted because she simply could not ever get enough Isaiah. Is that where she really wanted to be? Heck, no! The traffic crawled ahead and Ebony tapped on the brakes as the asphalt between her Escort and Isaiah's Mustang extended. That pesky Explorer driver in the adjacent lane who had been laying on his horn crammed between them, followed by a Volvo, Camry, minivan, and an old Cadillac.

* * *

The traffic sped up, but when Isaiah peered at his rearview mirror again, he saw no sign of an Escort. He eased off the gas and let vehicles whiz around him. Still no sign of Ebony's car. He pulled over to the shoulder and watched several makes and models pass. She'd obviously gotten lost, maybe experienced some sort of car trouble and was forced to pull out. Or maybe she'd just played him for a fool—*again*. He didn't want to think the latter, but she had agreed to go home with him so quickly, it not only thrilled, but surprised the hell out of him.

As far as he knew, she didn't have his cell phone number. He reached for the phone in his glove compartment then tossed it on the passenger seat to dig for her business card in his wallet. He flipped on a car interior light and read it. No cell phone number. He got her home phone number from an operator. At a little before eleven P.M, he'd probably waken her mother and grandmother if he called this time of night. But he had to be sure she'd made it home safely and wasn't stranded on some dark lonely exit with a flat tire or worse. He had to be absolutely sure those overly aggressive drivers hadn't separated them by horning in and intimidating her into submission. Then he would decide whether to wring her pretty little neck or not.

Fickle didn't begin to describe what Ebony felt as she neared the exit for her subdivision. She'd purposely let those cars come between them, then she'd veered off at the nearest exit. Isaiah deserved an explanation, she decided as she steered her car toward his apartment again.

He met her at the door with a welcoming look of surprise. "What happened to you back there? I thought you'd wimped out on me again." He leaned against the doorframe with his arms crossed over his chest, leaving just enough room so she could enter.

"The thing is . . . uh . . ." She wrung her hands. Once ensnared by his steady gaze, it was impossible to think straight. "I did change my mind, but I didn't want to—"

"Leave me hanging like you did in Grundie," he finished her sentence and closed the door. The click of the lock reverberated throughout the room. The lights were already low, then by degrees he turned a dimmer until the shadows on the carpeted floor softened and vanished.

"Yeah," she replied softly.

His lips eased into a knowing smile as he stepped closer to her. "You could've phoned, you know. You have my home number."

"I . . . I suppose . . ."

His teeth tugged at his bottom lip as his finger trailed along her mouth for a moment heavy with anticipation. "Know what I think?" he whispered.

She could only shake her head and focus on his next move.

Isaiah dropped his hands, then drew her into his snug embrace, where she instantly became intoxicated by the masculine scent and solid feel of him. "I think you came here to tell me you changed your mind . . . so I can change it right back for you."

Ebony's eyes slid closed and her arms circled his trim, muscular torso. That familiar hot and hollow feeling at her core dispersed. He slipped both hands under her blouse to cup her breasts. She sucked in her breath and shivered in need as he deftly circled and plucked at both nipples until they peaked into taut points.

He was right. She had driven all the way over there in hopes that he wouldn't take no for an answer. His lips came down hard over hers—so brash and sure—like everything else about him. God, how she wanted him. She slid her hands downward to grab his rear. She pressed her pelvis against his to savor how much he obviously wanted her, too. Isaiah ended the deep kiss first, but only long enough to utter in a husky voice, "Bedroom's this way."

Tearing at each other's clothes between zealous kisses, they stumbled their way to Isaiah's unmade bed. He disappeared into the adjacent bathroom, but promptly returned with a small packet that he tossed to Ebony. Soon her naked body was wedged between him and the mattress as she slipped the condom over his arousal. His hands and lips traveled over her skin as she moaned. She spread her thighs, urging him to nestle between them. He eased inside, giving her body a chance to adjust. She moaned as she felt the tightness give way to delicious stretch as she accepted all of him. His strokes were long and steady until her own desperate tilts and thrusts of her hips let him know she would not break. After so many close calls and too much second-guessing, their coupling was fast, frantic—as if both feared slowing down would invite interruptions. Isaiah managed to stop kissing her long enough to whisper, "Am I hurting you?"

She clutched his rear to draw him deeper inside of her. "Yes," she managed in a small, breathy voice as they maintained strong eye contact. She enjoyed the raw, uninhibited pleasure on his face. That moment held an intensity more intimate than the joining of their flesh. "Yes, you're hurting me, but only in the most exquisitely sublime sorta way." The coiling tension inside of her escalated with each smooth and powerful stroke until it gave way with a strong, spiraling release that felt as if she were slowly melting away.

A couple of hours later, Ebony lay awake beside a snoozing Isaiah, his arm draped across her torso, pinning her down. Her body hummed with satisfaction while regrets seized her thoughts.

She and Isaiah had been wonderful together, but it wasn't just sex that had complicated things. She couldn't get that conversation they'd had about his father out of her head. Isaiah's determination to win the respect of a man who clearly didn't deserve it touched her more deeply than expected. No longer just a rival blocking her way to getting what she wanted, he'd become more with each discovery. He was a man desperate to reach his father the only way he knew how. Why couldn't there be two *Examiner* jobs? Because that was the game. Somebody had to lose. She hadn't planned on being that somebody. And she really didn't want that for Isaiah, either, she decided with clarity, admiring his handsome face. She imagined him as a little boy, crushed by the weight of his mother and father's rejection.

What a mess. *Doggone it!* What had she done? The more time she spent with Isaiah the more she wanted to spend with him. As she found her heart softening, daring to entertain thoughts of having a real relationship, a million tomorrows didn't seem like enough time to spend with him. The vulnerability that came along with such feelings was simply too much to bear. Her heart swelled almost painfully in her chest. She sighed, contemplating how awkward things would be between them now. When she lifted the dead weight of his arm, he stirred a little, but didn't awaken. Ebony eased off the bed, tipped out of the room in search of her discarded clothing. She quickly dressed in the living room, then searched her fanny pack for a pad and pen to leave a note. Hard-pressed to come up with the right words, she left nothing but the scent of her body on his sheets. They would talk later, when she had had time to think about the ramifications of what had happened between them that night.

She pulled into the driveway of her darkened house, dimming her headlights. She bunched her keys in her palm so the jingle wouldn't wake her mother, Granny Mac, or the pesky brat-dog. She eased out of her shoes and dropped her fanny pack on the sofa, then tiptoed to the kitchen guided by a trail of night-lights. On the way home, she remembered how miffed she'd been when Isaiah tried to leave Grundie without saying goodbye. She really should've left him a note at least. Her ping-ponging back and forth was indisputable proof she'd gone flaky. Her indecisiveness was getting to her so she could only imagine how crazy her mixed messages were making Isaiah. She dialed his number and listened to his mellow recorded voice, which kicked on after the fourth ring. *Thank goodness!* She sighed with a coward's relief. After the beep, she spewed her apologies for stealing away without a proper goodbye. He was sleeping so peacefully she didn't want to wake him, then she cited her need to check on her family immediately. She left her message then cut off the ringer. He couldn't tear into her until later. Much later.

CHAPTER 23

The next night, Ebony squirmed on the sumptuous leather seats of the stretch limousine that Diesel had sent. She tugged at her shimmering indigo evening gown as the scary high heels on her feet pinched her toes. A rhinestone clip snatched her braids into a tight ropy chignon.

In less than fifteen minutes she would arrive at the Ice Cream Dreams Ball as the special guest of the host's nephew, who obviously had no qualms about taking full advantage of his rich uncle's trappings. Renfro's driver, Claudio, sat behind the wheel.

Ebony should have been ecstatic, jittery with anticipation. Her goal seemed within her reach. Instead her thoughts zipped back and forth between her uncomfortably provocative dress and her sneaky escape from Isaiah's place the night before. She nipped at her Mango-Tango-glossed lips and lacquered fingernails, wondering how he had reacted when he heard her message. He hadn't bothered to return her phone call. Typical Isaiah. Keep folks guessing. Ebony adjusted the crocheted antique wrap she'd borrowed from Granny Mac then secured the tie of her gown's halter-style bodice. *Secured*. What a joke. When Yolanda dropped off the frock at Ebony's house earlier that evening, she'd passed along a tiny roll of toupee tape with instructions to apply it wherever Ebony felt a breeze.

Ebony's hand stole to the beaded gown's depth-defying neckline, which plunged to a couple of inches above her belly button. For the first time in her life, she was grateful for her small breasts.

She let her fingers press the postage-stamp-sized squares of toupee tape she'd strategically placed between her nipples and the fabric to keep the dress from shifting out of place. The tape guaranteed that her high beams wouldn't poke out somebody's eye in a chilled ballroom. She had no inner Li'l Kim who reveled in flaunting skin, but her options had been limited. She wasn't about to blow a bundle on a gown she'd only wear once. In her own closet the formal-wear choices were a couple of ill-fitting, sorbet-hued bridesmaid dresses.

It was Yolanda's J. Lo number or nothing. Out of habit, Ebony's hands dropped to where her fanny pack would rest had Yolanda not pointed out that the bulky thing would look silly encircling Ebony's waist that night.

Ebony only acquiesced and left it behind because Granny Mac and her mother were out of cell phone range on a four-day Mall of America excursion arranged by their church, Greater New Hope Missionary Baptist. Initially Ebony wasn't convinced that the two were ready to travel together without her supervision. But the bachelor pastor, the Reverend Jeb Munser, a Harry Belafonte look-alike with twinkling brown eyes and a caressing deep voice, convinced Ebony he could handle the pair. He promised to phone her at the first sign of trouble. Granny Mac worshipped Reverend Munser and Jolene obviously had a crush on him so the two were likely to keep their squabbling to a minimum, if only to win his favor.

A glass barrier separated Ebony from Claudio. "Ms. MacKenzie, feel free to help yourself to the fully stocked wet bar," his gravel-voice came through a speaker. Though she had benefited from his obvious disloyalty when she paid him for directions to Renfro's Grundie lodge, he made Ebony uneasy. He had a too-familiar way of holding her hand when she'd first introduced herself to him. His Windex-blue eyes gave his pallid face an eerie *Children of the Damned* appearance.

"No, thank you." Ebony felt a chill as her eyes met the reflection of his in the rearview mirror. She drew her shawl snugly over her shoulders and breasts.

"You sure?" As he looked back at the road, his lips slid up in an unctuous smile.

"I'm sure," she replied, grateful when the limo pulled into the driveway of ball central, the Wellington Estates Hotel, a dome-shaped architectural mishmash. Water cascaded from two ornate fountains and a caravan of limos and European luxury vehicles were lined near the entrance. People dressed in their finest milled inside. Claudio got out and opened a door to assist Ebony. Again, he clasped her hand a little too long for comfort. Ebony had never been in a chauffeur-driven limo before and was unsure of the tipping protocol. She reached inside her impractical beaded clutch bag and removed a couple of bills. Claudio turned up his nose as if he expected much more. She dug inside the bag again, doubling the tip.

Inside the lobby, a tuxedo-clad Diesel soon approached her. He kissed her cheek and tickled her nostrils with the scent of his woodsy cologne. "You're here. And you look absolutely smashing, love."

A gaggle of Cincinnati's elite swirled around them.

"Wow, this place is packed," Ebony said, peeking around his massive frame.

"This thing gets bigger and bigger every year. Pretty soon we're going to have to move it to the coliseum." He cupped her elbow. "Come, let me show you to our table."

She wasted little time getting to business. "Is your uncle here?"

"Why, of course the ol' fart's around here someplace. He lives for this thing and he makes sure he personally greets all of the guests to thank them for their contributions."

"He meets everybody?"

"Everybody, at some point during the evening."

With that information, Ebony's aching feet, too-tight chignon, and too-provocative dress no longer mattered. This was the night!

Ebony and Diesel swept up a grand stairwell leading to the ballroom. Inside, a celestial motif twinkled on the ceiling. The décor screamed gaudy Vegas-inspired glitz—leather banquettes, stained-glass tables, brothel-red lighting. The servers were dressed as sequined chorus girls or top-hatted magicians with sparkly wands. The band had too many members to count and a Liberace look-alike warbling classic lounge crooner tunes. Just the kind of extravaganza Ebony imagined an eccentric like Renfro would stage.

"Shall I get drinks?" Diesel asked.

So caught up in the festive atmosphere and the prospect of finally meeting Renfro, Ebony almost accepted his offer. Almost, that is, until she remembered Diesel was liable to return wheeling an industrial drum of that nasty beet-flavored protein drink. Just thinking about it made her stomach roil. "No, thank you. I'm fine."

"Well, all right then. I'll show you to our table."

The circular table for twelve was nearly filled except for the two chairs clearly reserved for them.

"One of your colleagues is here," Diesel said when they reached their chairs.

Ebony quickly scanned the faces and froze when her gaze landed on Isaiah. Her insides fluttered with pleasure, then dread. To his right sat an aggressively painted lady.

"I see you've found your date," the woman said to Diesel. Isaiah had an unreadable expression on his face.

"She was never lost," Diesel quipped, pulling out Ebony's chair.

Ebony sat and avoided staring at Isaiah, who looked even more droolworthy than usual in his black tuxedo.

"This is Ebony MacKenzie." Diesel started the introductions. "That's Roxanne LaRue and you already know her date, Isaiah Malone, from the bench press conference."

The other names Diesel rattled off seemed to fade in the distance. Ebony clenched her jaw in irritation. So Isaiah was Miss Maybelline's date. When he'd interrogated her about

Diesel over fried catfish and sweet potato pie the previous night, he'd failed to mention he was dating Renfro's public relations director. Obviously a strategic move, much like her date with Diesel, but jealousy rippled through her anyway. Despite her showgirl makeup and pounds of flowing faux hair, Roxanne was attractive and who knew how far Isaiah was willing to go for the Renfro scoop?

"What bench press conference?" Roxanne asked, clutching Isaiah's arm tightly enough to leave claw marks.

"Never mind," Diesel cut in before Isaiah could answer. "No talking business tonight. I forbid it." He turned his attention to Ebony. "How was the limo ride, love?"

There Diesel sat, like a life-sized action figure stuffed in a penguin suit, with his arm draped behind Ebony's chair in a territorial maneuver while he whispered sweet nothings in her ear. If Diesel called Ebony "love" one more time, just one more time, Isaiah would jump up and snap Diesel's beefy arms like pretzel sticks.

Isaiah gritted his teeth as Diesel's thumb brushed across Ebony's silky bare shoulder. His gaze followed Diesel's thumb—up and down, up and down, and up and down, then skimmed the rest of Ebony's perfect parts accentuated by the sexiest freakin' halter dress he'd ever seen. Isaiah swallowed as his sex hardened. He remembered pressing her against him last night, how hopeful he'd been when she'd agreed to come to his place to finish what they'd started in Fit to Be Fried's parking lot then how utterly duped he'd felt when he thought she'd stood him up again. That had only heightened the elation he felt when she actually showed up at his door. They finally made lo—No. Love had nothing to do with it. They'd had sex, fantastic sex, but he'd awakened to discover she'd dipped out on him and he didn't like that one bit. He wasn't sure why he was so aggravated. He'd had sex without the cuddling and conversation afterward. But this time, it just felt different. Had he expected, maybe even *wanted,* more from her? No way! He definitely didn't roll like that. It was an ego thing. Most definitely an ego thing. If anyone was going to do a postcoital vanishing act without the goodbyes, it was going to be him! Sure she'd phoned later and left a lame-ass excuse about having to rush home to her folks, but Isaiah was convinced she was toying with him now and rubbing Diesel in his face. Last night he'd asked her point-blank if the two had anything going on and she'd denied it. But there Ebony sat. And if she smiled any wider he was sure her jaw would unhinge. Diesel whispered something in Ebony's ear again.

"Oh, Diesel, behave." Ebony giggled and slapped Diesel's knee.

Isaiah's blood went from a slow simmer to a raging boil, but he wouldn't let on. No, he had a better idea. He curled a possessive arm around his date. "Foxy Roxy, would you like to dance?"

"I'd love to," Roxanne replied in a raspy coo, as she stood and let Isaiah guide her toward the dance floor, but not too far away on the dance floor. Ebony needed an unobstructed view. He'd show her! He didn't need Ebony. He didn't want Ebony. He curled his arms around Roxanne's waist. Her dress dipped low enough to expose most of her back. His fingers played leisurely along her spine, then came to rest just below the small of her back. They swayed as the band performed an instrumental rendition of a popular Brian McKnight ballad. He caressed the nape of her neck and let his fingers inch upward to the edge of her hair to massage that sensitive area. One of his power passion moves. Women usually loved when he did that, but he quickly removed them when his fingertips tangled in bumpy weave tracks.

"I'd rather have your hands here." Roxanne took the lead and guided Isaiah's hands toward the full unbridled curves of her hips. "I'm not wearing panties, you know."

Isaiah swallowed as he fought to keep his expression from showing what he *really* felt about that little revelation. She shimmied closer, plastering her breasts and hips against him. "I'm finally in your arms," she said in a breathless swoon. As she gazed into Isaiah's eyes, he counted her cakey mascara spikes and wondered just what the hell he had gotten himself into.

Ebony fumed. Last night obviously had meant nothing to Isaiah. He groped Miss Maybelline right on the dance floor for everybody to see! They danced so closely a switchblade couldn't wedge between them.

Ebony jumped to her feet. "C'mon, Diesel, let's dance!" She stalked to the dance floor, practically dragging him to a spot next to Isaiah and Roxanne, but her timing couldn't have been worse. The mellow Brian Knight ballad faded to an up-tempo Ricky Martin tune. The frenetic Latin-flavored number was more than Ebony could handle in her sky-high heels, but she couldn't wimp out now. She began swiveling her hips in perfect sync with Diesel, who was surprisingly spry for a man of hulking size. Ebony shot Isaiah a haughty look. *Take that, you womanizing weasel!*

Isaiah, who had put a little distance between himself and Roxanne when the music changed, reached out and clutched his date and thrust his hips toward her. "Ahh sukie, sukie now!" he coaxed an obviously enamored Roxanne, whose long fake hair snapped to the beat with a whiplash action.

Ebony shimmied closer to Diesel. With seduction in her smile, she wrapped her arms around his thick neck. Her dress clung in places it hadn't before she began perspiring. "Shake it, don't break it!" she chanted to Diesel. Isaiah couldn't keep his eyes off Ebony and she knew it. A smug smile curved her lips. *Ha! How ya like me now?*

Isaiah removed a handkerchief from his tuxedo pocket and patted sweat from his face. Ebony's bump and grind with Diesel made Isaiah hot. Something besides anger bubbled beneath the surface. He wanted to snatch her up and show her a few more moves of his own. Images of their limbs entwined on his rumpled sheets from the night before flashed through his mind.

Hyped up on the liberating vibes that came with taking control of the situation, Ebony broke away from Diesel and became Isaiah's private dancer, working him into a frenzy with every lascivious swivel of her hips—to the left, to the right, big circles, little circles, then the snaking pelvis move. Swivel. Swivel. Turn, turn, for full a 360-degree view.

Isaiah's gulp was audible. Distracted, he had slowed to a slack-jawed, no-rhythm, side-to-side shuffle.

Not to be outdone, Roxanne pivoted and pressed her back against Isaiah's chest and crowed, "Now I'm gonna back my thing up, baby!" She leaned forward, anchored her hands on her knees, and nudged her bottom against Isaiah's groin and gyrated wildly.

Aghast, Ebony tried to compete by mimicking an intricate little maneuver she'd seen in the latest Janet Jackson video. She didn't quite nail it. The hem on her gown snared the tiny buckle of her shoe. Her legs wobbled on the sky-high heels, the dress tangled around her ankles, and the floor came rushing toward her. She heard the distinct ripping of fabric and tiny beads scattering on the floor.

Diesel had reached out, but failed to break her fall. The band didn't miss a beat, but people close by stopped dancing to stare at her. Ebony, who'd landed flat on her rear, had never felt so humiliated in her life. She'd made a spectacle of herself, dirty-dancing to get Isaiah's attention. And for what?

As Ebony tried to lift herself up, one heel slid on the beads, sending her back on her tender bottom.

A snort followed by snickers ripped from Roxanne. Ebony glared at the woman, who quickly covered her mouth with her hand, but couldn't restrain the unmistakable satisfaction of witnessing Ebony's tumble.

Isaiah lurched toward Ebony, taking her arm. "Are you all right?"

"I'm fine!" She jerked out of his grip. "No thanks to you!"

"She's my date." Diesel wedged between them, puffing up his chest. "I'll help her up."

"I can help myself up, thankyouverymuch." Ebony managed to stand. "All of you, just get away from me."

Roxanne couldn't resist pointing out the obvious. "Miss Thang, your dress is torn in the back. Looks like you're ass out—literally." She snickered again.

"I know I have a hole in my dress, Weave-punzel." Ebony's fingers gathered in lobsterlike pincers. "But unless you want me to strangle the life out of you with that yard of doll hair you've got stitched in, I suggest you get the hell out of my face—now."

An irate blush spread under the severe rouge of Roxanne's cheeks. The wench flipped her long fake locks off her shoulder and wisely stepped out of Ebony's reach.

Ebony clutched the tear, grateful that it was much lower than the air-conditioned breeze whipping around her legs suggested. The crowd only got a flash of her legs, not her panties, thank goodness. When Isaiah held out the shoe that had catapulted from her foot and the handbag she'd dropped, she snatched them out of his hands. She couldn't stay at the ball in a ripped gown—even for Renfro. "I'm leaving, good night."

"I'll have Claudio drive you, love," Diesel offered.

"No, thank you. I'll take one of the taxis stationed in front of the hotel," Ebony insisted, wanting to get away from everything and everyone associated with this horrendous evening as quickly as possible.

Isaiah left Roxanne's side and stepped in front of Ebony. "I'll take you home."

"Isaiah," Roxanne whined, clearly offended.

"I'd rather crawl home through shards of poison-dipped glass. So I suggest you get back to your date," Ebony snarled at Isaiah then hobbled toward the door on one high-heeled shoe.

CHAPTER 24

Less than an hour later Ebony collapsed on her sofa, grateful she had the house all to herself. Black Gal nipped at the big toe poking through her hosiery, then a run streaked its way up her leg. The evening had been a disaster. In record time, she'd managed to make a complete fool of herself shimmying like a lap dancer desperate for lunch money, ruined her friend's pricey designer gown, broken the strap on a pair of shoes she'd expected to return for a refund, and missed out on yet another opportunity to meet Renfro. The grandfather clock in the corner read 9:14 P.M. She had time to drive back to the hotel to hook up with Diesel again, but she still didn't have anything to wear, and that embarrassing fall on the dance floor had sapped all the get-up-and-go right out of her. Besides, she'd had just about enough of watching Isaiah and that Roxanne chick paw at each other.

"Black Gal! No!" Ebony swatted at the dog's dome head as it gnawed on her broken shoe. Ebony lifted it and began removing the masking tape she'd attached to the sole. She'd done a pretty good job. It showed no sign of wear, but little good that did now that the darn strap was broken. It was one thing to return them in good condition, but her conscience wouldn't let her try to wheedle a refund with damaged merchandise. She had dropped the shoe, then removed its match from her foot when the doorbell rang.

Black Gal trotted at her side as she moved across the hardwood floor to look through the peephole. Her knees went wobbly again at the sight of Isaiah on the other side of the oak door. "What do you want?"

"I'm returning your wrap." Isaiah had her grandmother's crocheted antique shawl in his hands.

She'd left in such a huff, she'd forgotten all about it. Losing the shawl that had been in their family for four generations would have added to her misery. Ebony opened the oak door, but kept the screen sealed. Black Gal stood on hind legs, yapping at Isaiah.

"Thank you." Though grateful for the shawl's return, her tone was clipped. She opened the screen door just enough to reach for the neatly folded square of fabric without allowing Black Gal to bolt outside. "How did you find my house?"

"I followed your taxi."

"So you left the biggest soiree of the year, the arms of your red-hot mama, and a chance to meet Renfro just to return my wrap?" Ebony was mystified, but there he was—in the flesh.

"I didn't want you to worry when you discovered it was missing."

"Well, that was nice of you," she managed.

Silence ensued as he stood there, looking more gorgeous in his tuxedo than any man had a right to. But she would not invite him in. "Well, what do you want? A biscuit?"

Black Gal barked louder.

"Not you," Ebony scolded the dog. "You've had all the cheddar and bacon treats you're going to get in one night."

"I want to know where you get off with all this attitude?" Isaiah lashed out, catching her off guard. "You're the one who dipped out on me last night, remember? Why did you tip away like that? Didn't want daylight to catch you in my bed? Was the shame of it too much to handle?"

"Didn't you get the message I left on your answering machine? I told you I was sorry. I . . . I . . . had to get home to check on my folks. I hadn't told them that I was staying out all night." Ebony took a step back and prepared to close the door. "I think you should leave now."

The screen door screeched as he yanked it open and stalked inside. "Not until I have my say, lady. Then I'll leave."

The swift, startling maneuver caused Ebony to stumble back. "I didn't invite you in!"

"Tough. I invited myself." His eyes were dark and wild with anger. Black Gal clamped onto the edge of his pant leg with her teeth and growled. "You'd better get this neurotic little dog or it'll be gumming its Kibbles 'n Bits from now on," Isaiah warned.

"Black Gal, down, girl!" Ebony commanded, but Black Gal had a mouthful of soft summer wool and wasn't about to let go.

Ebony quickly placed the shawl on the coffee table, then kneeled to pry the dog's jaws apart without damaging his pants, when her dress ripped a few more inches. "Darn it!" She scooped up Black Gal with one hand and reached to clutch her tear with the other.

"Looks like you're busting right out of that thing." Isaiah's voice dipped. There was no mistaking the gleam in his eyes. Desire. It might as well have flashed in neon lights. "Are we alone?"

"Yeah, so what?" Ebony's breath came out in ragged little puffs. All nerve endings electrified. Heat simmered between her thighs. Black Gal squirmed and scratched Ebony's forearms.

Ebony released the dog then tossed a wiener-shaped squeak toy across the room. Black Gal scrambled after it, claws clattering across the hardwood floor.

"Come here," Isaiah commanded in a low rumble as his eyes burned with intensity.

Ebony's stomach flip-flopped. "Talking to me or Black Gal?" she asked.

A lopsided smile tilted Isaiah's moustache, but he didn't bother to dignify the silly question with an answer. "I *said* come here."

Ebony wanted to fling herself into his arms. "No," she

stated like a bratty child instead. "Who do you think you are? You certainly don't waste any time, do you? Weren't you just groping Roxanne, oh what? Like, say, a little less than an hour ago?"

Isaiah stepped toward her. "Only because you were gushing all over Diesel."

Ebony took a step backward. "I wasn't gushing." She had difficulty pulling air in and out of her lungs.

Then there was that roguish smile of his. "Was, too."

"Was not."

"Was, too."

"Nuh-uh."

"Uh-huh."

Juvenile, but articulating became more difficult the closer he got. "Nuh-uh."

She thought she wanted to step back again, but curiosity and anticipation anchored her feet. "I was just . . . uh, um . . . what do you call it . . ." Hypnotized by the predatory look in his eyes and the perceptible quickening of his breathing, she stammered. "Sociable . . . Yeah, sociable with Diesel to soften him up," she shrilled and swallowed so hard her ears wiggled. "You know . . . to get to Renfro."

"So you lied about having a date with him."

"I don't recall you giving me a rundown of your plans with . . . What did you call her? Foxy Roxy."

Obviously stumped for a comeback, Isaiah took another step forward instead, but this time he removed his tuxedo jacket and tossed it on the chair. "Are your folks away for a while?"

She nodded. "They're out of town."

"Good." All the while, he kept his eyes locked on hers. The hard muscles along his angular jaw and beneath his shirt and vest flexed when he took yet another step. "It's a shame you left so quickly last night, because I hadn't done nearly all I'd planned to do with you."

He stroked her with a look so hot she thought she'd spontaneously combust, but she managed to babble on anyway. "Back to Roxanne, I suppose you're going to say you were just being sociable with Roxanne to soften her up to get to Renfro." Isaiah moved so close she felt heat radiating from his body, or was it hers? The tip of his nose brushed her forehead, his breath fanned across her skin. She heard and felt the pounding of his heart near her cheek. "But if you were any more sociable somebody would've . . . uh, had to toss you two a condom."

Her body felt like a big tingle and darn if she didn't hear bells, too, until she realized it was just the tinkling of the chimes outside a living room window. "I mean, it was a—"

She felt his hands around her waist, drawing her closer. The bulge in his pants pressed against her pubic bone. Every drop of blood in her body pooled between her trembling legs. "Shameless display of—"

"Know what?" His voice was a thick whisper as he nudged the tip of his nose against hers.

"What?"

"You talk way too much." With that Isaiah reached up and slowly untied the halter knot resting at the back of her neck and pulled the thin beaded fabric away from her body. It dropped to her waist, exposing her breasts.

Slight amusement and curiosity settled on Isaiah's face. "And what have we here?" he said, fingering stamp-sized brown squares over her nipples.

"Toupee tape . . . To keep my dress in place."

"We have no use for these now, do we?"

Her nipples puckered and peaked instantly beneath the tape.

Isaiah covered her mouth with his. His kiss was hard and persuasive. She held nothing back, grinding her hips against his. He tasted like champagne and sweet temptation. Ablaze, she moaned of deprivation when their lips parted. Isaiah cupped the smooth curves of her breasts then dipped to remove the tape with his teeth. Slowly. The tug of the adhesive as it reluctantly released her skin was stimulating. After he blew the tabs on the floor, he took one nipple in his mouth, circling it with his tongue. She savored the contrast of textures—soft lips, wet tongue, the stubbly scratch of his moustache and goatee. A rasp of pleasure escaped as she wrapped her arms around his neck and traced slow circles in his hair. When he shifted his attention to her second breast with the same manipulation, she thought she would dissolve into the hardwood floor.

Isaiah felt her go limp in his arms. He swept her up and carried her toward the sofa. He placed her on her feet in front of it, then removed the rhinestone clip corralling her braids and peeled off the dress. The nylons were next, but he left the garter belt in place. "Sexy, hmmp, hmmp," he whispered as he kissed his way down her taut torso. Hooking his teeth in the band of her silk panties, he slid them down her smooth thighs toward her ankles so she could step out of them. "You won't be needing these, either." He kissed the panties, damp and fragrant with her essence, then stuffed them inside his pants pocket.

Ebony tugged his shirt out of his trousers and released the buttons securing his vest. Her hands slid down to undo his fly. As her fingers fumbled against his stiffened sex, she thought ripping the trousers off would be faster.

"Careful, this tux is a rental," he teased. Her impatience was such a turn-on. "Allow me." In seconds flat he'd shed his underwear and the borrowed threads. He wanted to pace himself, go slowly, but he already quaked with need. He had wanted this woman in the worst kind of way and he was hellbent on giving her pleasure like she'd never experienced before. She was so beautiful, so perfect, so damn sexy, as his eyes took in the flawless dark cocoa skin. When he lowered her onto the sofa it squeaked like a whoopee cushion.

"Sorry. Black Gal's things." Ebony chuckled softly as she admired the muscle-sculpted perfection that had enchanted her since that first encounter at Shangri-La. They freed half a dozen pieces of vinyl and rubber shaped like T-bone steaks lying underneath the cushions and tossed them at the dog, who thankfully found a rawhide bone to amuse herself.

Ebony sat with throw pillows at her back. Isaiah kneeled between her thighs, then cushioned his knees with pillows. When he placed her legs over his shoulders, she met his wicked smile with one of her own.

"I have a bit of a sweet tooth of my own, you know," he said.

"Is that right?" she asked, practically panting as he reached to tease her breasts.

He pressed wet kisses along her soft inner thighs. "That's right, and I'll bet you taste better than all fifty of Ice Cream Dreams' fabulous flavors."

"You think?" she murmured.

"I know. And I'll bet you're familiar with them all, am I right?"

"Them all?" Her question floated on a sigh.

"I'm tracing the first letter of one of the top ten flavors right now. What is it?" He licked a vertical, then a horizontal line on her left inner thigh.

"What?" Ebony fell deeper into a haze of pleasure.

"What letter is it?" he asked.

"What is this, *Sesame Street*?"

"No." Isaiah's low chuckle rumbled from his chest. "C'mon, be a good girl. Tell me what letter this is." This time repeating the move on her right inner thigh.

"Uh, was it a *T*?" Ebony cooed.

"Right. *T* for Triple Truffle Treat." He went to work again—deftly tracing a neat wet trail closer to the apex of her thighs. "What was that?"

She squirmed. "Uh, um. I don't know. You're driving me nuts."

"That's the point, but stay with me." He did it again.

"Um, was it a *P*?"

"Wrong. Guess again." He retraced the letter again.

"*B*?"

"No, *R* for Raspberry Razzle Dazzle." When he nuzzled his nose between her legs, she bucked her hips. "Hold on, game's not over yet, darling."

"You're torturing me," she whined.

"Yes, but isn't it the sweetest torture?" He quickly flicked his tongue over the nub of her throbbing center. Ebony moaned.

"Now what letter is this?" he asked, tracing an alphabet

symbol on the delicate skin on her right inner thigh.

"*V?*"

"Nope, guess again.

"*N?*"

"Nope, *M*."

"For Mega Mocha Chubby Chip?"

"Uh-uh, for Marshmallow Macadamia Madness."

He kissed her thigh. "Last one."

"Promise?" Her breathing grew more strained and shallow.

"Promise." He traced the final letter.

"*F*? For Fudge Fantasy?"

"Nope. Wrong again. *E* for the newest flavor. I'd like to call it Ebony's Erotic Elation," he whispered just before dipping to stroke the tight wet curls at her center. The circling of his tongue soon followed a gentle suction that had her moaning his name in reverence as her passion mounted. The velvet gem he gently manipulated swelled and quivered in response. When she thought she couldn't soar any higher, he took her further still, reaching up occasionally to stroke her tummy and tease pebbled nipples as if the activity below wasn't enough. He plunged his tongue deep inside of her, then in and out again. Deliriously limp, she spread her knees wider. Her heels tapped against his back. Tangling her fingers in his hair, she pressed him deeper into her damp heat. No one had ever made her feel such pleasure with total abandon. Ebony watched his expert maneuvering—relentless and rhythmic. When her hips bucked from the cushions again, he slipped his hands underneath to cup the soft curves of her bottom as he feasted with hungrier lashes. Moments later, she was hurled into orgasmic orbit, as a delicious mounting pressure rippled into a release that left her flushed and dewy all over. Breathless and limp with satisfaction, she managed a strangled, "Omigosh."

"Just the appetizer, baby," he promised, looking up at her with sultry, glazed eyes. "Just the appetizer."

When Isaiah stood and kissed her temple, his arousal loomed in front of her. Evidence that there was still work to be done. Her hands traveled over his firm pecs to the ridges of his muscle-rippled torso. With his sex in her hand, she fueled the erection with long, polishing strokes, then prepared to nip and lick its plump head. Isaiah felt like a hand grenade sure to detonate with one touch of her lush mouth, so he lifted her chin, then pressed her back against the sofa. "No, this all about you right now," he whispered, then reached for his pants splayed on the floor. He removed a condom from his wallet. When she stretched across the sofa, he covered her body with his. As he slipped on their protection he knew he wanted to pay proper tribute to all of her honeyed delights. It took indomitable restraint not to burrow and piston inside of her like a turbocharged madman. But he managed to take his time, kissing and caressing her until she was ready and open to him again. When she was, he entered heaven—one long and steady thrust at a time. They found their own gliding rhythm, the perfect duet of give-and-take. And the soft sound of colliding flesh coupled with her whimpers of pleasure made the sweetest music. He'd never been so sexually in tune with anyone before. Moments later he savored the decadent clenching and squeezing of her walls as she climaxed. Sure she was with him, he sailed back to earth with a convulsing release of his own, so powerful his teeth rattled. "Oh, yes," he ground out as a shock wave of pure bliss raced through his system. When her name sprang from his lips, he knew this was no run-of-the-mill romp in the sack.

And man, was he in trouble.

CHAPTER 25

The next morning, Isaiah awoke to the squawking of crows just outside the window. If he believed in omens, that would've signaled that some bad mojo was afoot.

Black Gal raced to the window with high-pitched barks. Isaiah wondered how the dog got in the room until he noticed the bedroom door sat ajar.

"Damn, dog, do you ever shut up?" Isaiah eased up on his elbows and frowned at the scrappy pooch, who quickly forgot the birds to growl at him instead.

"Oh, yeah?" Isaiah made a sour face. "Well, back at ya, flea magnet, back at ya."

The sheets flapped under a ceiling-fan breeze and sunlight seeped through the blinds in the bedroom, where he had spent the better part of the night engaging in a mind-blowing sex-athon with Ebony. He shifted under the covers and admired the tranquil prettiness of her features as she slept next to him, soft snores drifting from her lips.

Okay, dude, you've done the deed. Not just once or twice, but several times. Mystery solved, mission accomplished. Now what? Sleeping with her was supposed to take the edge off. No more obsessing about what it would actually be like to have her. But if anything, getting a taste of her made him want her more. And he wasn't so sure he could just walk away. And the fact that he questioned whether he could, made him all the more determined to do just that. The other night at Fit to Be Fried he'd gone out of his way to convince her he was a certified stud with no use for long-term relationships. With all her talk about obligations and not wanting a romantic relationship to muck up the works, she'd made it blatantly obvious her loopy family came first. And he wasn't about to stick his neck out for sloppy seconds. He'd come second with his mother, who ran off to start a new life in California with her chiropractor. And he'd always come second and even third with his father. Isaiah wasn't about to line up behind anybody else if he had anything to say about it.

When Ebony stirred in her sleep, a single braid drifted across her face. He lifted a hand to brush it away, but decided to let it be. He ached to touch her, hold her, but he reminded himself that he wasn't the snuggling-cuddling type. He had slipped up not once, but twice, and fallen asleep with Ebony in his arms. It was nice, but something he didn't want to get used to. He could tick off plenty of reasons why a real relationship with her would be too much of a hassle. He sank back on his pillow and sighed, then swung his legs to the side of the bed, scooped up the barking dog and deposited it outside the room before closing the door. He ignored Black Gal's whimpering and scratching. Somebody had to discipline that damn dog and teach it that the two-legged species ruled. Isaiah made his way across the cool floor to search for his underwear.

Photos of various people he presumed to be kin and close friends captured his attention. He lifted one frame from the mahogany dresser. In the enlarged snapshot Ebony beamed as she stood beside a younger woman in full graduation regalia. Kenya had to be the young graduate. When Ebony had first spoken of her younger sister, her face lit up and her voice took on a musical quality. To him Kenya was this nebulous being hundreds of miles away. Now she had a face, much like Ebony's, he noted. Her many accomplishments were laid out before him—dozens of honor roll ribbons and outstanding scholastic achievement certificates were tacked to the wall. A homecoming queen trophy, also Kenya's, sat next to a World's Greatest Sister carnival loving cup. The engraving read, "For always having my back, you know I'll always have yours. Your loving little sis, Kenya." The two obviously had a special bond. No wonder Ebony was willing to dog Renfro's trail for her. At least she was motivated by her love for someone who truly appreciated her. Isaiah could not say the same. That fact alone made Ebony more deserving of that exclusive and the *Examiner* job, but he shook off the thought.

He reached for an older studio-posed family portrait of a teenaged Ebony, an adolescent Kenya, an attractive woman, and a handsome man. Isaiah took in the details of the photo—Ebony's fuchsia angora sweater, glassy lip gloss, pastel-tinted eyelids, and overplucked brows. Makeover? More like she'd undergone a make*under* since that photo was snapped. The mustachioed man with his arm around Ebony had black wavy hair and placid brown eyes. He wore a blue cotton sweater and coordinating necktie.

Isaiah looked over at the door when the scratching and whining on the other side ebbed. Black Gal had finally accepted defeat. The bedcovers rustled as Ebony awakened with a stretch.

"That's my family," Ebony told him in a sleep-thickened voice. "Kenya, my mom and dad. It was one of the last photos we took before he died."

"You never did say how he passed away." Isaiah turned to face her. "An illness?"

She yawned and sat up amid the pillows. "He died in a fire."

"No shit?"

"A house fire."

"Damn, that's messed up. Were you there? Were you hurt?"

"Unfortunately, no," she replied, almost convincingly, scooting off the bed to stand. She wrapped herself in the top sheet—as if he hadn't already seen every delightful inch of her, including the tiny daisy-shaped birthmark near her left big toe. At his side, she reached for the family portrait.

"What kind of foolish thing is that to say?"

"I didn't get hurt, but I started the fire."

"Whoa." He reeled with the revelation. "You? How?"

She paused as if gauging whether she wanted to continue. "I was constantly burning candles. You know, those little scented votive things." She took the photo from Isaiah's hand and placed it back on the dresser, but continued to stare at it as if looking into some window to the past. "Well, one day I left for a school dance and forgot to blow one out. It happened to be the one that was sitting too close to my stereo and the heat or spark from the open flame must have shorted some wires or something. That's what the fire inspector said. Anyway, the stereo exploded, causing the fire. Kenya and Ma got out all right, but Dad... He died from smoke inhalation, trapped in his basement workshop."

Ebony put on quite a front, despite the torturous subject. "Oh, baby." He quickly abandoned his no-touching mandate and closed comforting arms around her shoulders and pressed a lingering kiss on her forehead. An urgency to find the right words to comfort her consumed him. He whispered, "Don't. Please don't do that to yourself. It wasn't your fault." He tightened his embrace. "It sounds like an accident to me."

"It was my fault and my father died because of me." She wriggled out of his arms and needlessly adjusted the knot above her breasts where the sheet was securely cinched. "Are you hungry? I'll make omelets."

Isaiah studied her and in that moment it all clicked for him—the deranged penchant for checking on her family, logging their whereabouts, and the obsession to provide for them. It wasn't just about control-freak tendencies as he had initially suspected. Ebony was obviously trying to fill the void left by her father's death, all fueled by misplaced guilt of monster proportions.

"Forget about breakfast for a minute. Come here," Isaiah said in a gentle voice as he extended a hand toward her. He knew he should opt for the omelets instead of digging too deeply into her personal problems. Besides, her revelation only confirmed what he'd suspected. She had major baggage to unpack before she'd have room in her life for anyone else.

But damn if he still didn't want to take all the festering pain away. "I'm sure nobody blames you." When she took his hand, he drew her into his arms again and led her to the bed. This time he sat and eased her down onto his lap to rock her gently.

"Let's just drop this subject, okay?" she sniffled, holding back the tears.

Clearly reluctant to let him see how vulnerable she was right then, she made a feeble attempt to break away again, but he wouldn't let her go. Shoot, he felt vulnerable himself, completely stripped of his cocksure, devil-may-care veneer. He needed her near.

"All right," he whispered against her cheek as he caressed the satiny length of her braids. "We don't have to talk about that or anything else, just let me hold you."

Ebony relaxed against the wall of his chest. He wasn't sure how long they sat there. He would've held her all day had the bumpity-bump-bump against the door not startled him. "What the hell?" Isaiah eased Ebony off his lap and got up to investigate.

Ebony chuckled softly, reaching for his hand to stop him. "That's just Black Gal using her body as a canine cannonball to break the door down."

Isaiah shook his head in disbelief. "That dog is psychotic."

"She likes to have the run of the place. Once I open the door, chances are she'll peek inside and go away. Or she'll come in and plop down for a nap that would be much more comfortable on the plush doggy bed in Granny Mac's room."

"She just likes keeping all of her options—as well as all the doors—open, is what you're saying?" Isaiah couldn't help but smile. "I guess I can relate to that."

"Exactly." Ebony went to open the door.

The dog pranced inside, quickly snarled at Isaiah for locking her out in the first place, then relaxed on a nubby rug, resting her muzzle on her front paws. A minute later Black Gal left.

"Told ya." Ebony grinned, as her mood rallied.

Isaiah went to Ebony and laced his fingers with hers. "Oh,

I get it. So the dog is running things around here now?" He kissed the tip of her nose.

"The key to peace around this house is to know when to take the path of least resistance, my friend." Her lips formed a seductive smile. "I know I said I would make breakfast, but—"

Isaiah's arousal was instant when he focused on the body beneath the sheet. "But what's the rush? With the exception of the devil dog, don't we have the house all to ourselves?"

Ebony nodded, easing up on tiptoe to trail the tip of her tongue over his lips. "Uh-huh."

Isaiah growled and removed the sheet wrapped around her body. It pooled around her ankles and she stood before him proudly like an exquisite Nubian goddess. He took in the gentle swells of her breasts, mocha nipples, flat tummy, softly flaring hips, and her long, long legs. "Just looking at you can make me come." He wrapped one hand around his hardened sex and stroked it. "Touch yourself..."

"What?" Her eyes widened.

"Go on. Don't be shy."

"But that's so ... so ..."

"So what? Don't tell me you've never done it. When you're all alone in the quiet darkness of your bedroom, when everyone else is asleep..." Isaiah said in a low voice. He continued stroking himself as his gaze scorched her from head to toe.

"No! I haven't!" she blurted as if appalled by the very idea.

"Liar." Isaiah gave her a scoundrel's grin, before falling deeper into a sensual haze as he increased the motion of his hand.

Her hands remained at her side, but her fingers flexed. "But..."

He knew he had her. "Do it, baby," he coaxed with a husky whisper. "It's just you and me."

Ebony's breathing deepened as she fell under his spell. Watching him pleasure himself so boldly had her inner walls quivering with the need to be filled by him. Before she realized it, one hand slipped to her breast, first caressing the full undercurve then plucking gently at the nipple.

"Yes," he moaned as every sculpted muscle in his magnificent body flexed. "That's it. Now lick your finger and touch the other one."

Following his command, she felt wild, free, but most of all—safe. Her breasts tightened as liquid fire coursed through her. Her breathing grew more ragged as she watched his face twist in a grimace of pleasure.

"Now take it lower, much lower." Isaiah's strokes grew fast and forceful.

She dropped her hand to her dark thatch, teasing and probing, surprised how wickedly delicious it felt with him watching. A moan escaped her lips.

"Yeah, that's it, that's it."

The flush of passion enveloped her from head to toe. She gasped from the intensity of it. Her legs trembled.

Before she got lost in her own private paradise Isaiah released his sex and grabbed her waist. "Oh, no you don't. Not just yet." His fingers dug into her hips. "Little quick on the draw, aren't you?" he rasped with a rumbling chuckle against her neck. Roughly he turned her to face the mirror attached to the dresser. "My pants are still in the living room. Way too far to walk away from you right now. Do you have protection?"

She gave him a lazy smile and reached inside a drawer and removed an unopened box of Trojan Magnum. "A gift for you."

Isaiah was flattered that she considered his manly proportions larger than average, but as usual she kept his ego in check. "There were only two boxes left at the Cozy Corner Convenience store. It was either these or the Snuggy Fits for the little fella who knows it's not the size of the ship . . ." she teased with a little chuckle as her words trailed off.

Isaiah ripped open the box, removed a foil square then quickly covered himself with latex. "Ha, ha. Let's see who'll be laughing in a moment when I get my luxury liner out of dry dock."

He swept her mass of braids over one of her shoulders. On the opposite shoulder she felt the coarse hair of his goatee where he anchored his chin. He filled his hands with her hips again as his rock-hard erection nudged against the small of her back.

She braced herself, locking her elbows and latching her hands along the edge of the dresser. Through a passionate fog, she made out the image of their flesh pressed together. He reached for her breasts, cupping and squeezing them, then brushing the pebbled nipples with his thumbs. He slid his hands down her tummy to caress where she ached the most. She arched, pushing her bottom against his hips. She spread her legs and savored the sweet stretch of him entering her. His fingers softly stroked the peak nestled in her tight curls. Once tucked deep inside, he crushed her body closer to his chest for the deepest body hug and a torturously slow circling grind of his pelvis. The scratch of his goatee against her sweat-dampened skin, the raw whispers of carnal need in her ear nudged her closer to the brink. Stroke by stroke. The dresser slid and banged across the wall, thumping a steady erotic beat as she held on. The force toppled the framed portraits and a tall bottle of coconut-scented lotion. Ebony inched up on her toes as she clenched around him, then pulsated with a scorching rush of pleasure.

Through passion-glazed eyes Isaiah relished her reflection. Supple, glistening brown skin. Swaying braids. Undulating hips. "Damn, you feel so damn good," he hissed and pumped harder, faster—holding nothing back. He wanted to crawl inside of her, curl up and never come back out as his fingers covered the soft curves of her breasts. Her face contorted as she climaxed with a whimper. His own body soon jerked with his own aggressive release.

Moments later, Isaiah collapsed on the bed, listening to the whir of the ceiling fan and their heavy breathing. Despite his better judgment, he moved closer to Ebony and spooned her. "That was . . ." He paused, careful to choose the right words. What he said now would set the tone for how they would proceed. "We have—"

"*Sexual* chemistry." Ebony inched away from the curve of his body.

"Yeah, that's what I was going to say," he lied, still unsure what would've emerged had she not cut him off. He kissed her earlobe, thinking how odd and empty it felt to hear her characterize what happened between them with little emotion. "I'll make breakfast while you shower. I'll shower when you're done."

"I was kinda hoping we could save time and water and shower together." He threw his leg across hers to hinder her escape.

"I don't think that's a good idea." She scooted off the bed. "Besides I have to feed Black Gal." Her tone was a little too sharp.

He released her. "Sorry."

She expelled a heavy breath and turned to face him. "Isaiah, I didn't mean to—"

He raised a hand. "It's cool. I understand." At this point most women were trying to pin down his intentions, get them down on paper if possible—notarized and signed in blood. Most had expected something beyond a fuck-buddy type of arrangement. He ventured to clear the air first and find out what expectations there were—if any. "Ebony, about what's happened between us—"

"No need for a disclaimer, Isaiah." Ebony went to the dresser and removed a pair of pink sweatpants and pulled them over her hips. "I remember our little talk at Fit to Be Fried. No strings." She tugged the matching sweatshirt over her head.

Isaiah sat up, resting his back against the headboard. "Yeah, no strings," he echoed, not feeling half as relieved as he should have.

Ebony became so aloof, his gut twisted in knots. Suddenly, she yelled, "Black Gal! No!"

Isaiah looked down just in time to catch Black Gal squatting over his most expensive pair of leather dress shoes.

CHAPTER 26

While Isaiah showered, Ebony went to the kitchen where she filled Black Gal's bowl with Dog Chow then began slicing and dicing mushrooms, onions, and broccoli for the veggie omelets. Though she had the day off from the *Bee*, she considered using work as an excuse to get rid of Isaiah. Offering to make breakfast only prolonged the awkwardness both obviously felt. She'd lusted for him for so long, but hadn't considered that giving him her body would lead to deeper feelings. Could she dare admit it to herself? He'd been so sweet when she opened up to him about her father. His sensitivity to her pain had pushed her over the edge. Now she had to admit that she'd fallen in love with him. The shock of the admission jolted her so the knife in her right hand slipped and nicked her left one. "Ouch!" She brought the tiny wound to her lips and sucked. This was not good. Not good at all. Isaiah wasn't the relationship kind and neither was she right now. They'd both made that clear just the other night. She couldn't get mushy now. Besides, falling in love meant losing control. It meant compromise. It meant rearranging priorities. She wasn't in a position to do that. And if she had the guts to surrender to her feelings, would he return them? She had been determined to reiterate the rule first. No strings. She couldn't help but notice how his tightened features had slackened with relief when she reminded him she had no expectations. Her voice had been devoid of emotion as her heart coiled painfully in her chest.

Isaiah had been everything she could've hoped for in a lover—giving, tender, passionate, and uninhibited. Her mind spun with erotic images of the two of them on the sofa, on the floor, in her bed. She'd never look in that dresser mirror again without imagining his hands all over her body. The memories played in a nonstop loop. Her skin still sizzled everywhere he'd touched and stroked her. She even relished the faint abrasions his whiskers had left. She sighed, fighting the urge to join him in the shower. "Stop it, Ebony. Get a grip." They had awesome sex, but she obviously couldn't handle a casual relationship. She'd flipped out, thinking it might be love. Black Gal toppled the garbage can, tearing her from her musing.

"Do you have a death wish, brat-dog?" Ebony crouched to clean up the mess. "Because you're really working my nerves."

"I can see it now. Headline: 'Demons Exorcised from Devil Dog Zapped in Microwave.'" Isaiah's voice suddenly came from behind.

Ebony spun around and saw him leaning against the doorframe between the kitchen and living room. His shoes dangled from his fingers. He looked disheveled but utterly irresistible in his tux. His hair was shiny from his shower. "I tried cleaning my shoes so the linings are still damp."

"Sorry about that," Ebony said.

"Black Gal's the star of my next tabloid piece." When Isaiah smiled she wanted to march him back to her bed and wrinkle that tux some more.

Ebony put the last of the smashed milk cartons and wilted lettuce back inside the garbage can and sealed the lid. "You're serious."

"Hell, yeah." He dropped the shoes near his sock-covered feet.

"Fortunately for Black Gal you don't actually have to put her in the microwave to write the piece."

"Maybe this time I'll try a different approach and go with fact rather than fiction." Isaiah narrowed his eyes at Black Gal.

Black Gal growled, showing her teeth, her satellite-dish ears flattened against her head.

"Ah, I'm just kidding, of course, devil dog." Isaiah chuckled.

"Do you ever wonder about the people who buy the *International Inquisitor*? You know, wonder if they think those stories are true?"

"The *International Inquisitor* is meant to be pure, outlandish entertainment, not the *Wall Street Journal*. Anybody who actually believes there are man-eating grasshoppers is too stupid to live." Isaiah straddled a chair with his chest resting against its back. "But you won't find me hiding in a tree trying to snap a photo of Brad Pitt's naked butt or trying to out some closeted gay movie star. I don't do the celebrity stalkerazzi thing. That's where I've drawn the line."

Ebony washed her hands then began whipping eggs in a bowl. "Except when it comes to Renfro." There. She'd done it. Dragged the conversation back to reality. The reality that guaranteed there would be no instant replays of last night or earlier that morning, because she still yearned to put her hands all over him. Bickering about Renfro and the *Examiner* job made it easier to maintain emotional distance. But even that had become more difficult now that she knew what drove him.

"The Renfro piece is different," he replied in an even tone.

"How do you figure?"

"It just is."

"Renfro obviously doesn't want to be interviewed, just like most of the movie stars who suddenly find themselves splashed across the centerfold of a tabloid. Yet you're going after him anyway."

"And so are you."

"It just seems, you know, a little hypocritical. That's all."

"Hypocritical? You're one to talk," Isaiah parried with a scornful chuckle, then left it at that.

Tense silence fell between them when Isaiah didn't take the bait.

"Well?" she prodded.

"What's for breakfast?" he asked instead.

"Veggie omelets, remember?" Ebony went to the stove and poured the egg mixture over the vegetables now simmering in the skillet. "The glasses are over there in the top left cabinet. Help yourself to anything in the fridge."

Isaiah did, pouring himself a glass of orange juice. "Where are your folks?"

"Away on a church trip. They'll be back in a couple of days."

"Surprised you let them off their leashes for that long," Isaiah muttered.

Ebony whipped around, still spoiling for an argument. "What's that supposed to mean?"

"Just that I've never seen someone cluck like a mother hen over grown folks quite the way you do. You've got to stop micromanaging the hell out of the people you love."

Ebony bristled. "Well, some people actually care about their families and want to be involved in their lives."

"Involved and running their lives are two different things. Can't you see? It sounds like they've fallen into this lazy pattern. They make little effort to handle any crisis—big or small—on their own because Ebony's always going to swoop in and take care of everything. Fix all the fights, the boo-boos, and make them all better. Is that how you want to spend the rest of your life? Baby-sitting grownups?"

"What's it to you, huh?" She got in his face.

"Sacrificing or suppressing every dream you've ever had is not going to bring your father back. Are you expressing love or doing penance?"

"And what would you know about it?" She thrust her chin up and waved her spatula at him. "You've been traipsing around the globe the last few years without a care or thought for anyone besides yourself!"

His jaw clenched and the biggest vein in his neck bulged. Finally, she'd gotten a rise out him and she immediately regretted it. He did care about earning his father's respect and approval. Her own blood roared in her ears. The eggs burned, the toast was charred, but all she wanted to do was latch on to his lips. "Isaiah, I didn't mean . . ."

He stood and gripped her arms, his eyes dark with some intense emotion, battling between anger and desire. He was about to kiss her when they heard muffled conversation and jingling keys at the front door. She freed herself from Isaiah's clench and dashed toward the living room then back to the kitchen. She returned flapping her hands. "I'm sorry. You've got to go."

"But we were just in the middle of—"

"Rain check, okay?" Ebony scooped up his shoes and shoved them at him along with his glass of juice. He'd run out of hands so she tucked a slice of burnt toast in his tuxedo pocket. "You have to take the back way."

"Who's at the door?"

"Granny Mac and Ma. They're back early."

"They are? Well, I'd love to meet them."

"No!" Ebony dismantled the second table setting. "You can't. Not now. Not yet."

"But why? I'm dressed, you're dressed," he reasoned. "There's nothing wrong with having company over for breakfast, is there? You're a grown woman."

"Isaiah, please," she pleaded, as the front screen door screeched open. "You're wearing a *rumpled* tuxedo, for crying out loud."

"Ebony," her mother called out. "We're home."

"I really don't understand you," Isaiah snapped as he stalked toward the back door.

"Call you later," Ebony said in a whisper then quickly sealed it behind him. Pressing her back against the door, she sighed just as her mother and Granny Mac stepped into the kitchen.

"You're back so soon." Ebony removed the smoking skillet

with the burnt eggs from the stove just as the smoke detector kicked on.

"Althea's acid reflux was acting up so she couldn't have any fun." Jolene dropped onto a kitchen chair. "And if she's not having fun, you know no one around her is going to have fun, either."

Ebony opened the windows to let fresh air inside then darted to the hallway and fanned a magazine to silence the smoke detector mounted on the ceiling there.

"But the reverend was supposed to call me if there were any problems," she said, when she returned to the kitchen.

"I told him not to bother and that I'd just take another bus back home," Granny Mac said. "We took a cab from the bus station because we didn't want to wake you. Anyway, because Reverend Munser insisted that I not travel alone—"

"I came back with her," Jolene said with a pinched expression.

"It's not like somebody held a gun to your head." Granny Mac plopped into a chair as a hyper Black Gal danced and pawed at her shins.

"Now you two, do not get started," Ebony warned. "I am not having it this morning. I'm not in the mood."

"Does that mood have anything to do with the tuxedoed man I saw tipping through my begonias in the backyard to the red Mustang parked out front?" Jolene asked.

"Ebony, you had a young man over? Well, it's about damn time. I was starting to worry about you." Granny Mac's smile was wide as she cuddled Black Gal in her arms. "Did he spend the night? Did you lay it on him good, girl?"

Before Ebony could reply Jolene rounded on Granny Mac, "Nobody wants to hear your gutter talk this early in the morning."

"Gutter talk?" Granny Mac placed Black Gal on the floor and removed her brown Easy Spirits from her feet. "Chile, we're all grown folks here. And sex is a part of life. Was it gutter talk when Buster used to have you screaming, calling his name in the wee hours of the night?"

Jolene gasped and clutched her chest in that prissy way she

did when the conversation turned to s-e-x. After all these years her mother still acted as if admitting to having or enjoying sex was something to be ashamed of. Her father and Granny Mac finally had to explain that Ebony and Kenya had not been culled from a cabbage patch after all.

"Yeah, that's right." Granny Mac was relentless. "I used to hear you all going at it like bunnies on Viagra all those times I spent the night."

"That was different. Buster and I were man and wife. And we were in love."

"Maybe Ebony and her fella are in love, too!" Granny Mac slowly rose—a concession to her arthritic hips that must have been acting up that day.

"Nonsense, Ebony's not in love." Jolene said it with such certainty, that Ebony took offense. "She's never even spoken of dating anyone special, and besides, when would she have the time?"

Granny Mac geared up to go a few rounds. "And where is it written she has to tell you all of her business?"

Clearly detecting the edge in Granny Mac's voice, Black Gal growled at Jolene.

Ebony slipped two fingers in her mouth and whistled. "Hey, you two? Can I get a word in here? The guy you saw leaving is Isaiah Malone. He's ah . . . a friend and a colleague. We were going to have breakfast, but he had to leave suddenly to take care of something," Ebony fibbed, unsure why it was crucial that they not meet him. Maybe introducing Isaiah to her family was akin to admitting that he actually meant something to her. Maybe it was the circumstances or the guilt of knowing she and Isaiah had had hot, sticky sex on the family sofa just hours before. *The sofa!* She hadn't bothered to check the cushions. She'd have to flip them over at the first opportunity.

"Have you spent much time with this young man?" Granny Mac sounded hopeful.

Ebony commenced filling the sink with water to scour the scorched skillet. "Yeah, some."

"Just keep your guard up, honey," Jolene added. "Most young men are up to no good these days. They only want one thing. And once they get it . . . They're outta there. On to the next conquest. You're a smart girl. This . . . What's his name again?"

"Isaiah," Ebony replied, trying to keep all emotion out of her tone. "Isaiah Malone."

"This Isaiah Malone is probably that slick and shifty type anyway. Why else would a grown man want to sneak out the back way of a young lady's home? I wouldn't be surprised if he was married or something."

"He's not married." But Ebony didn't bother to explain that Isaiah had departed that way because she'd insisted on it. What would she say if her mother asked why? She had a right to a personal life. And this was her house. She'd moved her mother and Kenya in while they'd searched for a new apartment, after their old one was converted to a pricey condo. The arrangement was supposed to be temporary. Five years later, her mother had never got around to getting her own place and Ebony had never pressed the issue. When Kenya went away to college Granny Mac had moved in. There was always family around. While she relished the company and closeness, sometimes she found the setup stifling.

"Watch out, baby, that one will end up breaking your heart. Mark my words." Jolene began searching for the pot to make coffee. "Feel it in my gut. You're too smart to fall for whatever lines he's tossed your way."

Jolene's assumptions and cold assessment were like whiplashes. Her mother didn't know zip about Isaiah or their relationship yet she was too doggone sure he couldn't possibly have any genuine feelings for Ebony. As if Ebony were so obviously unlovable. But then maybe her mother was onto something. Ebony had given him her most precious possession—her body. Yet he'd acted as if nothing of significance had passed between them. True, she'd done the same, but only out of self-preservation.

"Now wait one cotton-pickin' minute here," Granny Mac piped up. "Ebony *is* a smart girl. Smart enough to know you're full of it, Jolene."

"Full of it? Why, you . . ." With nostrils flaring Jolene took a menacing step toward Granny Mac when Black Gal lunged toward her. "If that dog comes any closer, she's going to get real close and personal with my size sixes." Jolene lifted one of her Payless pumps.

"Oh, yeah? Well, just try it. Don't think I'm too old. I'll lodge my foot up your butt so deep you'll be puking brown leather for months!"

"Granny Mac!" Ebony shouted.

"I've held my tongue for too long on this, baby. And I'm not going to do it anymore—especially now that there's a young man in your life." Granny Mac reached for Ebony's hands and squeezed them. Alcohol warmed her breath. Her grandmother took what she called "a few pick-me-up nips" during the day. "I know you care for him, baby."

Ebony opened her mouth to protest, but Granny Mac interrupted. "Don't try to deny it. I can see it in your eyes and hear it in your voice. When you say his name. It's like a song on your lips." Her grandmother smiled sweetly. "And I'm so happy for you. Finally, a young man has caught my Ebony's fancy. This Isaiah must be something else."

Besides her father, Granny Mac knew her better than anyone. Tears filled Ebony's eyes.

"Are you in love with him?" Granny Mac asked in a soothingly low voice. "Is he in love with you?"

Ebony blinked to keep the tears from falling. "I really don't know the answer to either question yet. I know I feel something strong for Isaiah, but love? I don't know for sure. But whatever it is . . . It's scary. I feel so vulnerable."

"Because he hasn't told you that he loves you," Jolene stated with a definite but unspoken I-told-you-so in her tone.

Ebony shook her head glumly. "No, he's not in love with me. Things are still so new and complicated right now."

"And that's just fine with you, isn't it, Jolene?" Granny Mac released Ebony's hands and stood before her daughter-in-law. "You don't want her in a serious relationship. If she falls in love, you're afraid you'll get squeezed out. Then who will care for you? And take care of everything?"

"That's ridiculous." Jolene punched the buttons on the coffeemaker. "And I don't have to stand here and take these insults from you."

Granny Mac turned back to Ebony. "Baby, why did your young man leave out the back way?"

Ebony averted her gaze. "What does that have to do with anything?"

"C'mon, baby," Granny Mac prompted. "You can say it. You didn't want him to meet us."

"If you're trying to imply that I'm ashamed of you two, you're wrong." Ebony hugged her grandmother. "I could never, ever be ashamed of the people I love most in the world."

"I think you didn't want us to meet your fella because you were afraid—afraid how we'd feel, knowing that you were trying to have more of a social life for yourself. Afraid we'd disapprove or feel threatened."

She'd never considered that, but at that moment something about her grandmother's statements rang true. She had always downplayed romantic entanglements, reasoning that she simply never had the time to get to know someone. She had little patience for tearing down the walls required to nurture a soulmate connection. And no courage to allow any man to delve past her tightly wound layers. Few got a glimpse beyond the rigid, anal-retentive control freak. The fear of exposure always loomed. Had she allowed anyone to strip away the carefully constructed façade, they would have surely discovered just how unworthy of love she was.

Guided by the notion that repaying the debt owed to family members who'd survived the fire, she had set out to redeem herself. Then and only then could she purge feelings of guilt so overwhelming they siphoned away all desire to connect with a man in a deeply emotional way. But that was before Isaiah. Meeting him forced her to feel things she had planned to keep safely tucked away until she got her family affairs in order. Now she did silly, frivolous, and irresponsible things that women who went gaga over men were prone to do.

Jolene stopped puttering around the kitchen. "Pay no attention to her, Ebony. That's the Johnnie Walker Red talking."

She rolled her eyes at Granny Mac. "Don't think I didn't see you taking a few too many sips from that flask on the bus ride home, and with your so-called acid reflux, too," Jolene tsk-tsked her. "If I lit a match near your mouth, your head would go up in flames."

"Don't try to get off the subject by fighting with me. For once in your life, Jolene, you need to own up to what you've done to your child." Granny Mac looked at Jolene with empathy for once. "What we've all done. I'm not blameless, either. All the fighting with you, I haven't exactly behaved like an adult who could manage without Ebony."

Jolene recoiled when Granny Mac tried to reach for her hands. "What in the world are you babbling about, old bag?"

"We've all leaned on Ebony so since Buster died. It wasn't fair to put her in such a difficult position. We've all fed, albeit unwittingly—at least on my part—her guilt."

"Guilt? I don't know what you're talking about," Jolene scoffed, skirting Granny Mac and the Molotov cocktail of a confession. Instead she pulled Ebony into her arms. "But I truly am sorry about all the fighting with Althea. I promise to do better, baby."

Granny Mac shook her head and sighed, but came closer anyway. The trio stood in a huddle swaying, embracing. Even Black Gal curled near their feet.

Jolene deftly skirted the weightier issue regarding guilt and blame, but Ebony would take consolation in the image of her grandmother and mother sharing a moment. One that didn't involve hurling insults or plates across the room. She would hold it in her heart forever.

With a cheek pressed to Ebony's, Granny Mac muttered, "Jolene, you're on my foot."

"Sorry. It's tricky dodging those boats of yours at close range," Jolene shot back.

They must've felt Ebony stiffen.

"Oops. You know what they say about old habits. We'll try harder. Won't we, Althea?" Jolene replied, giving Granny Mac an artificial smile.

"Yes, we will," Granny Mac agreed with an equally dubious promise and a robust slap on Jolene's back that had to sting.

This time Ebony didn't balk. That truce was tenuous, but at least it was a start.

CHAPTER 27

Isaiah slipped on his shoes, but now his socks were wet after he tracked through thick grass and flowers moist with morning dew. He'd skulked away like some horny teenager busted making out with his girlfriend! Incensed, he climbed inside his Mustang and barreled toward the highway—unsure where to go next. Much too keyed up to head home, he drove until he could make some sense of his situation. His foot pressed the accelerator as he approached the highway ramp, swerving just enough to miss the mutt trotting across. Maybe he'd vent to Butta Bean. From day one, Ebony had dredged up all sorts of emotional stuff Isaiah wasn't prepared to deal with, but maybe he should stop turning tail and running. Maybe it was time he explored what it was like to allow a relationship to unfold to see where it might lead. Ebony had told him the no-strings setup was fine, but he wasn't so sure that was enough. What if he were actually interested in more than sex? He couldn't say with any certainty how she'd react. Hell, he wasn't even sure what he had to offer or how to define the foreign emotions tugging at him like a relentless undertow. He and Ebony needed to talk. Face to face. Isaiah reached for the cell phone in his glove compartment and quickly dialed her number. Obviously distracted, Ebony answered the phone.

"We need to talk," Isaiah told her.

"But—" Ebony was interrupted by voices and Black Gal's barking in the background.

"Are you mediating yet another stupid fight between your mother and grandmother?"

"Isaiah . . ." Ebony became distracted once again by whatever was going on at her place. He heard Black Gal's barks and a crashing noise. "Can you hold on just a minute?"

"No, I won't hold on." Isaiah wanted to be reasonable, but his temper snapped. "Damn it, Ebony, I'm in a rumpled rented tuxedo that's due back in less than an hour. I'm wearing dew-damp socks, pissy shoes and burnt toast, but am I headed home for a fresh change of clothes? No! I'm driving like a bat out of hell. Came this close to flat-lining a mutt that darted in my path! And I'm raving like a lunatic into a cell phone because I don't know what the hell is going on between us!"

"Now, calm down," Ebony said in that cool, patronizing voice used to coax the suicidal from high ledges. "I'm just as confused as you are."

"I'm headed to the Zodiac bar on Jackson Street downtown," Isaiah ground out. "Meet me there in half an hour."

Before she could respond, he clicked off his cell phone. His behavior was irrational and juvenile, but he'd had enough of their cat-and-mouse and one-up-you games. They had to hash this thing out for once.

Ebony replaced the receiver in its cradle, taken aback by Isaiah's volatility. Obviously still smarting from the heave-ho she'd just given him, he probably just wanted to chew her out in person. She couldn't blame him. Her behavior this morning had been beyond rude. She owed him an apology. A big one. And once she got that out of the way, she planned to feel him out about a few other things. Sure, he'd told her he wasn't the settling-down kind, but she still had to tell him what was in her heart.

"Who was that, baby?" Granny Mac asked.

"Isaiah. Look, I have to step out for a little bit to take care of something."

"He's missing you already. Girl, you must have that whip appeal." Granny Mac began shimmying her hips, snapping her fingers, and belting out the rest of the Babyface tune off-key.

Ebony left the kitchen for the living room where her fanny pack sat on the table. "What am I going to do with you?"

"Not nearly as much as you're gonna do with that Isaiah fella." Granny Mac winked. "I know what's up. Don't sell your ol' granny short now. There might be snow on the roof, but the fire's still burning in the hearth."

Ebony strapped her fanny pack around her waist and checked her watch to estimate the time of her return. "I'll see you guys—"

"When you get back." Granny Mac shoved Ebony out the front door. "Go meet your fella."

Ebony had driven by the Zodiac Bar often. But she'd never ventured inside, certain it was one of those hoochie-coochie joints with half-naked women flinging themselves around firemen's poles. What type of bar would open so early on a Monday morning? And why had Isaiah picked it of all places to meet? Her cell phone jangled. Sure her mother or grandmother were spatting again, Ebony grumbled her greeting.

It was Stella. "So who tweaked your Twinkie so early in the morning?"

"I thought you were—"

"Never mind, dear. Have I got a tip for you."

"About Renfro?"

"Who else? Saw you at the Ice Cream Dreams Ball last night with Renfro's hunky nephew. Glad to see you managed to wangle an invitation after all. I was coming over to chat with you. But you know I have to do my share of grinning and glad-handing at those things. Work, work, work. I got around to your side of the room eventually, but I couldn't find you."

Stella had either missed Ebony's humiliating tumble or was too kind to bring it up. Bless her. "Sorry we didn't get to chat."

"I take it you missed Renfro, too?"

"Yeah." Ebony sighed.

"Well, you looked fabulous, dear. That dress. Wow. And the little extras like that gorgeous pin in your hair and your—"

"Uh, Stella, didn't you say you had another tip for me?" Ebony often benefited from Stella's keen sense of observation, but felt awkward when Stella aimed the magnifying glass at her.

"Yes. I managed to get in eavesdropping distance of Renfro when he was holding court with a few of his favorite party guests last night. Heard him say he was going skydiving this morning. So what color is your parachute, dear?" Stella chuckled.

"Are you nuts?" Ebony blurted. "I took a chance on the nudist retreat and the paintball tournament, but even I'm not stupid enough to jump from a plane and risk becoming a big brown splotch on somebody's lawn."

"Even for a shot at Renfro?"

"Even for a shot at Renfro. That's where I draw the line. Ebony MacKenzie keeps her feet planted on terra firma. Besides, I'm afraid of heights."

"But, dear, you don't have to go up in the plane with him. You just want to get close enough to finagle an introduction or something before he takes off. We're talking icebreaker. What happened to that adventuresome and resourceful journalist champing at the bit for this exclusive?"

"Her champers got paintballed to oblivion."

"Oh, pshaw. I don't believe that for one minute. Anyway, here's the deal. Renfro said he was leaving for the airfield at ten A.M."

"This morning? That's only twenty-five minutes from now and his estate is at least a thirty-minute drive away from where I am."

"Which is why you have to put the pedal to the metal and hightail it over there now so you can trail him when he leaves. He didn't happen to reveal which airfield he intended to use."

"Great," Ebony snorted.

"Toodles, dear."

Ebony clicked off her cell phone as Stella's tip buzzed

around in her head like an ensnared bee. It hadn't been easy pinning down Renfro's whereabouts and she'd wasted her best opportunity yet last night at the Ice Cream Dreams Ball. Could she really just ignore another shot at him? She'd never been a quitter. So she'd have to postpone the meeting with Isaiah until later that afternoon. He'd do the same given the same set of circumstances. Wouldn't he? Suddenly she wasn't so sure, then an utterly ridiculous thought came to her. What if she let Isaiah in on this tip? Maybe they could work on the exclusive together. *Double byline!* With Ebony's name first, of course. After all, it was *her* lead.

She chewed her bottom lip, considering what such a move would mean for her coveted lock on that staff writing position. Maybe she and Isaiah would do such a great job that the *Examiner* editor would find a way to get them *both* on staff. Maybe they could insist on getting hired as a tag team. Her thoughts were like a runaway train as she dreamed the foolish and highly improbable. Maybe she'd kick herself later, but the decision had been made. She would count Isaiah in and deal with the consequences later. It was the kind of selfless thing those crazy in love did and irrefutable proof that she was indeed a goner. God help her. She was hopelessly in love with the man. Ebony lifted her cell phone to call directory assistance for the Zodiac's number. She dialed, but got the bar's answering service. She left a message for Isaiah anyway. "I know you wanted me to meet you at the Zodiac, but I just got a hot line on Renfro. I'm on my way to his estate. Meet me there."

Soon parked in front of Renfro's mansion, she waited and watched. The house, a formidable 1940s Mediterranean-style, two-story structure with a peachy stucco shell, was surrounded by a wide smooth lawn. According to her research the opulent interior boasted high ceilings, towering doors, porticos, marble tiles, and an indoor lap pool. The wide spacing between the bars of the wrought-iron security gate and short tangle of bushes edging the property's perimeter made it possible to get a pretty good view of the exterior with binoculars. She tried the Zodiac's number again. "Come on, somebody pick up," she pleaded, but the answering service clicked on again. She turned off the phone, stuffed it back inside her fanny pack, and reached for the binoculars when she saw activity at the front of the mansion. Claudio emerged first, then Renfro. No entourage. Odd. The man rarely traveled anywhere without his army of flunkies. The limo rolled around the circular driveway, past the gates guarded by two stone griffins, then onto the street. Trailing the limo, Ebony stayed at least four to five car lengths behind. Twenty miles later, they neared the abandoned Ice Cream Dreams warehouse just outside of town. It was situated on acres of undeveloped land, which provided more than enough space for a private airport and strip.

The limo turned onto the gravelly tree-lined road. Ebony hung farther behind. Only an idiot could lose them at this point. She parked her car at the side of the deserted road and waited. Through binoculars she watched Claudio emerge from the car first then walk to one of the passenger doors in the back. Renfro stumbled out, hands bound and mouth gagged. Another man, whom Ebony didn't recall entering the limo earlier, also emerged. The second man had a gun. He pressed it against Renfro's back, coaxing him forward. That firearm looked awfully authentic from where she stood. If this were anyone else she'd conclude that a crime was in progress, but when it came to Renfro and his infamous hijinks, she couldn't be so sure. Once Claudio, Renfro, and the man she didn't recognize went inside the warehouse, Ebony got out of her car and stole toward the building for a closer look. The next logical step was to confirm that a kidnapping was actually taking place and not some outlandish adult role-playing game like Renfro's paintball tournament. She crept across the rocks and peeked in a window. At least two additional thick-necked goons surrounded the Ice Cream King. One struck Renfro across the face hard enough to draw blood. Gut-certain even Renfro wouldn't take a game that far, Ebony reached for her phone to dial 911 when something hard poked the small of her back.

"Hands up, Nancy Drew, and turn around slowly. Very slowly," a gruff voice from behind commanded.

Ebony did as instructed and found herself face to face with the gleaming black barrel of a handgun.

CHAPTER 28

At Butta Bean's sun-splashed loft apartment over the Zodiac Isaiah couldn't relax on the slice of teal sectional sofa. "Where the hell is she?" He shot up to pace the floor in the vinyl house slippers and cotton socks he had borrowed from Butta Bean. Isaiah wriggled his toes. The slippers felt a little snug around the instep, but were an improvement over his own soiled shoes.

The portable TV, perched on the island dividing the kitchen from the living room area, was tuned to one of those home-shopping cable channels. The volume was low, but the yammering woman on the screen stroked a pair of ugly brown loafers as if they were spoiled pets.

Crime reports spewed from the police scanner Butta Bean had moved from the bar to a nearby bookshelf. Isaiah managed to decode a bit of the dispatcher's verbal shorthand though most of it came out as static-laced gibberish.

Butta Bean had rolled his wheelchair to the kitchen table, where he was experimenting with various ingredients to create his signature alcoholic concoctions. "From what you've just told me, it sounds as if you didn't actually give her a chance to say whether she planned to meet you or not."

"But I think I made it very clear that it would behoove her to show or else."

"Or else what? You'll huff and puff and blow her house down?"

"She knew I meant business. We need to talk. Now."

"Playing the boneheaded caveman and ordering most women around like that only makes them dig their high heels in deeper." Butta Bean mixed brown sugar and three kinds of rum with apricot brandy in a glass pitcher and stirred. He sipped, smacked his lips then added pineapple, lime, and orange juices. "I thought you of all people knew that you'd have to finesse it. You're losing your cool, man. This lady must be some firecracker."

Isaiah tugged at the collar of the shirt he'd already unbuttoned down to his pecs. "She just made me so damn mad."

Butta Bean chuckled and poured half a cup of tequila in his pitcher. " 'Cause she booted you out of her house without your Wheaties?"

"Like I was some pimply prom reject." Clenching his hands into fists, Isaiah quickened his pace. "But it's not just that . . ."

"School me."

"It's everything." Isaiah stopped and massaged his brow. He was getting dizzy walking in circles and he felt a headache coming on. "This . . . this thing with her. It's driving me crazy." He checked his watch again. "She's not going to show. She's going to stand me up. Damn her." Isaiah crossed his arms across his chest in resolve. "Fine, if she wants to play it like that. Cool. Cool. I'm done with her. Gone. Forgotten. She's over. Out. Next! I have a little black book full of honeys just waiting for my call." The words rattled about the loft like the last two pennies in a jar.

Isaiah's threats must have sounded empty to Butta Bean as well. "I don't believe it."

"You'd better because I've had it up to here." He jerked a flat hand over his head.

"I do declare." Butta Bean stared at Isaiah as if he'd just been bashed on the head with a blunt instrument. "Look at you. All antsy and outraged like the jilted groom at a church altar..." Butta Bean's eyes widened with wonder. "Well, I'll be."

"What?" Isaiah began pacing again.

"You're in love, dude."

Distracted, Isaiah moved to the window and looked out at the Zodiac parking lot like he'd done at least a dozen times since he arrived. Still no sign of the Escort. "What did you say?"

"Just that ol' Cupid's nailed you. That's all. Another one bites the dust." Butta Bean smiled like a proud papa. "Didn't think I'd live to see the day. Old slick, slippery-hearted Isaiah's in love."

"Love?" Isaiah frowned. "I think you've been sampling too much of the stuff in that pitcher. It's pickled your brain cells."

"I know it's early, but this calls for a *big* drink in the good glasses." Butta Bean started for his cabinets then stopped. "Ah, what the hell." He turned up the pitcher and gulped, then extended the pitcher to Isaiah so he could do the same.

Isaiah declined, as if drinking to his friend's nonsense would dignify it. "I never said anything about love."

"You didn't have to. I know you. And I've seen a lot of your women come and go, but I've *never* seen you act like this over one."

"Nobody's ever pushed my buttons quite like her," Isaiah huffed.

"Uh-huh. And I recognize a love thang when I see it, too. My question to you is, what are you going to do about it? Besides get a handle on that huge ego of yours." A smile spread across his old friend's face, but Isaiah refused to return it. Bean had wigged out—big time.

CHAPTER 29

Ebony's breath stalled, then gushed out of her lungs as the man nudged her forward, pressing the tip of his gun at the small of her back. Her mind fast-forwarded through every maneuver she'd observed and mimicked in that self-defense course, but none seemed adequate when a gun was cocked at a vertebra. There was a heck of a difference between a classroom setting and real life. Nothing beat the security of knowing if you didn't nail a move, your spleen wouldn't get splattered to kingdom come as a result.

"Move it, Nancy Drew. We don't have all day." The gun moved up a couple of bumps along her spine.

Ebony had managed to complete her call to 911 just before this stranger startled her. The cell phone was still on and secured in her fanny pack when she turned to face him. Fortunately, the goon with the gun hadn't noticed. It was conceivable that a police dispatcher could hear them. She'd have to make use of this opportunity.

"But . . . But . . . I don't understand. What's with *the gun*? And why are you pointing *that gun* at me?" Ebony's lips quivered, as she questioned whether putting an emphasis on buzzwords was a smart move. Her captor couldn't know what she was up to, but she rattled on, nearly hyperventilating her veiled

SOS out. "I was driving. I got lost. Silly me. I'm always getting lost. I have no sense of direction. When God was handing out senses of direction, I was probably somewhere lost, trying to get the right directions, but I don't think I deserve to get shot because of it." In spite of her knee-numbing fear she forced a laugh that sounded as if she were choking on a phlegm ball. "Anyway, so I took *Exit 17* and got off *I-74* and the next thing I knew I was in the boonies. Didn't even know there was an old, abandoned *Ice Cream Dreams warehouse* here. I pulled off on that road there, hoping I could find a home or business with someone who could get me back on track. So if you'll just give me directions I'll be on my way. I really didn't expect to stumble upon someone sticking a big ol' gun in my face. What type of gun did you say that was, anyway?"

"You can knock off the clueless-lost-motorist act 'cause I ain't buying it," he told her. "We noticed you tailing the limo about ten miles back and Claudio recognized you and your car."

Still, Ebony rattled on. "Well, uh, what type of gun is that, anyway? A Glock nine-millimeter by chance?" She wouldn't know a Glock nine-millimeter from a Super Soaker, but it sounded dangerously cool when Sipowitz mentioned one on *NYPD Blue*. Besides, she had to provide as many details to the dispatcher as possible. "So it's a Glock, am I right?"

"Shut up," he said in a calm, but foreboding tone, as he jammed the gun against her back to show he meant business. "And move it."

Ebony kept her hands high, even when her toe caught on a large stone on the gravel ground. It was critical that the dispatcher knew this was no prank and that lives were at stake. Her lost motorist act was a bust, but she *had* to keep talking. It was their only chance for rescue. "Okay, so you already have Reuben Renfro, the founder and CEO of Ice Cream Dreams. Now you have another hostage with exactly seventeen dollars and twenty-two cents in her checking account. You're really in deep doo-doo now. The more hostages you have, the more cumbersome a kidnapping scheme becomes. Murphy's Law kicks in, full throttle."

"I *said* shut up. Or I'm going to be forced to shut you up for good." He reached for one of Ebony's arms and twisted it behind her back. He yanked her close with a force that sent a sharp pain up her forearm to her strained elbow. Hot breath that smelled of stale Fritos singed her ear. "You don't want to call my bluff."

He didn't have to tell her again. Her throat constricted with fear. When the front door of the warehouse clanked open, he shoved Ebony inside with enough force to make her stumble. "I got her, as you instructed. Found her snooping around outside as you said she would be," Frito Breath said to Claudio, who stood next to his two burly accomplices.

All of the kidnappers were huddled with their backs to Ebony, with the exception of the one who kept his gun aimed at her. The scumbags spoke in hushed tones, then Claudio peered over his shoulder and smirked.

As he stepped toward Ebony those spooky blue eyes of his swept her from head to toe. "Why, if it isn't Miss Ebony MacKenzie, the lousy tipper." He was still wearing his crisp black driver's uniform and matching cap, but none of the oily obsequiousness that had made her instantly suspicious of him. In its place was an angry arrogance. He lifted his wallet from a jacket pocket, removed a bill and tossed it in her face. "Your milk money back."

They watched the bill flutter to the worn tile floor.

What a pompous ingrate Claudio was. Ebony gave him a scornful look. She'd slaved for every cent she made, but still made a habit of squeezing out the best tips her meager budget would allow because certain service workers relied on them to make ends meet. She bit off a retort. She'd already pressed her luck with Frito Breath. Now was not the time to get sassy or overly plucky. "Claudio, what's going on?"

"Isn't it obvious? And by the way, that's Mr. Hackett to you," Claudio barked. "Put her with the asshole over there." Claudio pointed to a corner where a bound-and-gagged Reuben Renfro sat on the floor, his back propped against a cracked plaster wall. Frito Breath latched onto Ebony's upper arm.

"Wait." When Claudio reached for Ebony's fanny pack, unbuckled it and let it drop to the floor, she gasped and waited for the cell phone to clatter out. When it didn't, she hung on to hope that a 911 operator was listening in.

"What are you going to do with us?" Ebony asked Claudio before Frito Breath sealed her mouth with duct tape and bound her wrists. He pushed her toward the spot on the floor next to Renfro. For a moment, she'd forgotten that she was practically seated in the lap of the man she'd been chasing for weeks. Dressed in an old Ice Cream Dreams T-shirt, tan and brown camouflage-print pants, he hardly looked like the founder and CEO of a major Fortune 500 company. This was multimillionaire attire Renfro-style. A small paunch swelled over his pants. Evidence that he'd eaten his share of Mega Mocha Chubby Chip. Hairy toes jutted past the straps of his Birkenstocks. Just a few details about his personal style that she'd hoped to capture when she profiled him.

Renfro made eye contact with her. A tear suddenly slipped down her cheek. Her heart raced double time. He nodded slightly as if to assure her that everything would be all right. She never wanted to believe something more in her life.

Claudio hovered over them, full of evil and self-importance. "Looks like you finally got your chance to get up close and personal with Mr. Renfro. Is it all you've ever hoped and dreamed?" he asked with a mockingly moony expression. "I hope it was worth it because it just might cost you your life. Instead of writing the news, you'll be making the news." He shifted to a well-modulated newscaster's voice. "Local reporter and mogul found murdered at the old Ice Cream Dreams warehouse. Details at eleven." He crouched to her level and ran a finger softly along her tear-streaked cheeks. Ebony drew back so enraged, she could've gnawed through the duct tape to clamp onto one of his fingers with her teeth. "Such a shame to have to destroy such a thing of beauty. But you know what curiosity did to the cat." Claudio then turned his attention to Renfro and scowled. "And as for you . . . All these years of hauling your ass around . . . What did it get me? You wouldn't even consider me for one of those fancy suit-and-tie jobs in your corporation. Would it have killed you to give me a break? To let me do something with that college degree that I paid good money for on the Internet? To recognize that I had a brain that might have been useful to you and your firm? Naaaah. What does dumb limo-driving Claudio know? More than you ever imagined, obviously. So you forced me to come up with my own executive fast-track plan." He roared with a brittle laugh, came to his full height then kicked Renfro on the left thigh, eliciting a guttural groan from the older man and a gasp from Ebony. "My part of the ransom is going to make a mighty nice severance package."

"Hey, Claudio, the boss is on the line," the heftiest of his accomplices called out.

The boss? Ebony looked at the man extending a cell phone to Claudio. Somebody else was not only in on the caper, but had possibly masterminded the thing. Her brain spun to piece it all together.

"What did you say?" Claudio slowly turned his head to look over his shoulder. He stomped over and got in the face of the guy so huge he looked as if he could blow Claudio away with a good burp.

Still, Claudio's eyes gleamed with rage as he snatched the phone and covered the mouthpiece with his hand.

"You-know-who is on the line." The goon, realizing he'd made a faux pas, quickly edited his response, but it was too late.

"No, that's not what you said a moment ago. You said the *boss* was on the line." With his free hand Claudio snatched the gun out of the man's hand and pressed the end of the barrel against the man's nostrils. "But how can that be? How could I possibly phone myself? It's not possible."

Frito Breath, who had held his gun against Ebony earlier, tried to intervene. "Claudio, he didn't mean—"

"I *know* what he meant!" Claudio snapped. "He said I'm not in charge here. I'm not the boss because I couldn't have come up with a plan as clever as this, right? That's what you're saying? Huh? Speak up!"

"Aren't you going to answer the phone, *boss*?" Frito Breath tried reassuring Claudio. "You-know-who is still waiting on the line."

"*I'm* running this show now and we move ahead when I say we move ahead!" Claudio was in the midst of one of those foot-stomping-gun-waving-Yosemite-Sam fits.

"Yes, *you* are running things now," Frito Breath reiterated in a calm, placating tone.

Claudio was the worst sort of disgruntled employee—a kidnapping psycho with simmering megalomaniacal tendencies. Dumbstruck, Ebony and Renfro exchanged looks. She was hopeful again. Having these numskulls fighting among themselves might just buy enough time for help to arrive. Ebony looked heavenward and prayed that they'd make it out of this mess alive.

"You answer the phone and tell *him* who's in charge now," Frito Breath coaxed Claudio.

Claudio pitched the cell phone to Frito Breath, then poised the gun at the man's nose. "*You* tell that coward who was too big of a wuss to show his face or get his hands dirty—I'm the man! I've got his uncle so that means *I'm* calling the goddamn shots from here on out!"

His uncle? The words echoed in Ebony's head. The heartbreaking truth was also apparent to Renfro, who sagged against the wall as his eyes squeezed closed in despair. Diesel had a hand in this deadly plot against him.

CHAPTER 30

"Did you hear that?" Butta Bean asked Isaiah, who stood before a window monitoring the parking lot. "Sounds like something's going down at the old Ice Cream Dreams warehouse off Old Winmark Road." Butta Bean increased the volume on the police scanner. "Kidnapping. Two captives. That's a guess. But one's Reuben Renfro and the other is a woman, who made a 911 call. Squad cars are already on the way."

A woman? Isaiah turned that bit of information over in his mind. One of Renfro's flunkies? Female? Roxanne, Renfro's ever-present public relations director? He searched his pocket and removed his wallet, where he'd stashed her business card. He raced to the phone on the coffee table and tapped in her home phone number. Someone answered immediately. "Roxanne, is that you?" he asked. "Are you all right?"

"Isaiah?" she replied. "Yes, I'm fine. If you're calling to apologize for ditching me at the Ice Cream Dreams Ball last night, I accept. Now get your sexy behind over here right away and knock yourself out making it up to me."

"Just wanted to make sure you were all right. Your boss has been kidnapped." He quickly relayed what he had heard over the police scanner, then ended the call. He dialed Ebony's phone number, but her grandmother told him she wasn't home and that she'd left to meet him. Isaiah got Ebony's cell phone number, but couldn't get through to her. She'd had more than enough time to make it to the Zodiac. If she'd been delayed in some way, it's possible she would've phoned. He pivoted toward his friend. "Hey, Bean, where are the bar's calls routed after hours?"

"To an answering service. Why?"

"Check it for me," Isaiah told him. That woman with Renfro could be anybody—Renfro's wife even. But Isaiah couldn't explain why his heart contracted and his gut jerked.

"If you head out to that warehouse now, you'll be the first reporter on the scene." Butta Bean rolled up to Isaiah and took the phone to punch in the numbers to his answering service to check for messages. "This could be the scoop of a lifetime."

"This isn't about getting a scoop." Isaiah wiped beads of anxious perspiration from his forehead with a cocktail napkin he found on the coffee table. "I think...I think..." His words trailed off as if vocalizing his terrifying hunch would make it true.

"Damn, I got twenty-three messages. I'm a popular dude," Butta Bean boasted with a cocky grin as he sandwiched the receiver between his shoulder and an ear.

"Hurry it up, man. This is an emergency." Isaiah's lips twitched with annoyance. "Skip through them to see if there's one for me from Ebony." His voice caught. "I think she might be in trouble."

Butta Bean and everything around Isaiah—from the second hand on the Smirnoff wall clock to the home-shopping-channel lady now hawking a gaudy rhinestone brooch—moved in an eerie, surrealistic slow motion.

"No problem." A few minutes later Butta Bean announced with astonishment, "The lady you're waiting for called. Said she got a lead on Renfro. She's staking out his estate. Wants you to meet her there."

Isaiah was already backing his way out the door. "When did she leave the message?"

Butta Bean glanced at the clock. "Way over an hour ago."

Isaiah drove so fast, his tires squealed and skidded at every turn. He headed straight for the old Ice Cream Dreams warehouse instead of wasting time swinging by Renfro's place. If his hunch was wrong and it turned out Ebony was still staking out the estate and was not the woman held hostage at the warehouse, he'd take consolation in the fact that she was safe.

When he arrived, the warehouse was surrounded by flashing lights, squad cars, vans, cops, and an ambulance. The double front doors of the building were dangling from their hinges, where a SWAT team had obviously stormed the place. He watched Claudio, Renfro's limo driver, and four other men being led away from the building in cuffs.

"Better grab Diesel quick," Claudio ranted. "He's probably halfway to Mexico by now on the private plane chartered for the getaway. We're not the only ones taking the fall. Diesel was the mastermind! He planned the whole thing! We were just poor schmucks tricked into doing his dirty work!"

Propelled by raw fury, Isaiah lunged toward Claudio, determined to pummel more information out of him, only to be blocked by two officers.

"The woman! Where's the woman who made the 911 call?" Isaiah asked one of the officers instead.

"This area is restricted," the cop told him as two additional law enforcement officers led Claudio to a squad car.

"Just tell me, who are the hostages? Was anybody hurt?" Isaiah raced to the ambulance and grabbed the driver. A cop pried the driver's collar out of Isaiah's grip.

"The two hostages have been freed. Now calm down." The cop shoved Isaiah, who restrained the impulse to slug him. Assaulting a cop was a good way to get arrested and carted away with Claudio and his gang.

"But are they all right?" Isaiah pleaded. "I need to know something."

Before the cop could respond, a visibly shaken Ebony emerged from the warehouse arm in arm with Reuben Renfro.

Relief weakened Isaiah's knees. He could breathe again. Somehow he had known she was in danger. He wanted to bear-hug the cop standing before him. During his race from the Zodiac to the warehouse, his bargaining with God to spare her from harm had bordered on the absurd. Besides promising to give more to the needy and attend church regularly, he had vowed to give up all guilty pleasures—everything from Heinekens to pork rinds. Isaiah tried to muscle his way through a cluster of uniforms.

"Didn't I tell you to get back?" The cop shot Isaiah a don't-screw-with-me look, but Isaiah didn't give a damn. What was he gonna do? Shoot him? He felt high with joy. So high he was bound to come crashing down. He'd scooted out on a long limb emotionally. And Ebony, braced, buckled, and bolted to noncommitment, wielded the biggest freaking chain saw.

He watched Renfro wrap a shielding arm around Ebony, who leaned closer into the older man's embrace. The two had been through quite an ordeal together. Some bonding was to be expected and as a result Ebony was sure to finally get that exclusive.

Game over.

Clearly the best journalist had won and much to his surprise he really did not give a damn. Instead of anger and defeat, Isaiah felt liberated. And relieved.

"Isaiah!" Ebony's voice rang out and the overly vigilant cop finally let him pass.

Ebony left Renfro and closed her arms around Isaiah's neck. "I'm sorry about not meeting you at the Zodiac. But I got this call from Stella. This lead. I tried to phone you, but there was that darn answering service. I thought we could, maybe, uh, you'd consider . . ." she stammered. "Working together on this one."

Isaiah buried his nose in her braids and inhaled the uniquely sweet fragrance of her perspiration mingled with coconut-scented shampoo. "What matters now is you're safe."

She looked up at him, squeezing him closer. "But if I had just met you as you asked, I wouldn't have been caught up in the middle of this mess."

"Or saved my life." They both turned to see Reuben Renfro standing there. "I owe this young woman my life." He dabbed at his split lip and winced.

"The cops got us out of there," Ebony said, easing out of Isaiah's embrace. She reached inside the fanny pack to get a Wet-Nap for Renfro.

"But if it weren't for you and your cell phone . . . I don't even want to think about how this all would've ended," Renfro said, taking the moist napkin. "Thank you."

"Can you believe it?" Renfro told Isaiah what the police had managed to piece together. "Claudio started squealing before they could read his Mirandas."

"He changed his tune so fast, passing the blame like a big ol' hot potato," Ebony muttered. "Now he swears Diesel was the mastermind behind the whole scheme. That's still so hard to believe, after all you've done for him."

"It's not that hard to believe." Renfro's eyes were sad and weary as he pressed the small wound on his lip with the Wet-Nap to stop the bleeding. "I knew how enraged he was when I refused to bankroll any more of his get-rich-quick ideas. He was determined to get more money out of me—even if it killed him or me."

"I'm so sorry." Ebony touched his arm in a consoling gesture. "I know you don't know me, but if there's anything I can do—"

Renfro shook his head. "What a way to finally meet one of the pesky reporters who has been stalking me for months."

"You knew about me?" Ebony asked, cocking her head to one side in surprise.

"Yes, you and your friend here, among others." Renfro nodded at Isaiah. "I saw you two at the paintball tournament in Grundie. My assistants are up on everything," the older man stated before his voice grew vibrant with laughter. "Everything except kidnap plots against me, of course."

Renfro explained that his people generally kept him abreast of which journalists were particularly worrisome in their pursuit, popping up in the most unexpected places. They'd advised him to stay on his toes to avoid unwanted personal contact. He recognized most of the faces and had names attached to them.

"I don't know if I'll ever be able to thank you enough for

your persistence, but I know how to start," Renfro said. "I've been such a clam all these years and I swear my mortality flashed before my eyes when those thugs had their guns pointed at me. I think it's about time I told my own story, how I took my grandfather's two-truck milk delivery service and turned it into a multimillion-dollar empire. You can have access to all my friends, relatives, and colleagues. Anyone you want to interview—just name them. I'll give them the green light to speak to you. Once my authorized story is out there for the world to read, maybe the rest of your colleagues will take this blasted bounty off my head."

"Are you serious?" Ebony's smile was brilliant. "Omigosh! Omigosh!"

"You can spend some time at my estate, at the Ice Cream Dreams corporate offices downtown, and even get into the nitty-gritty about some of my hobbies and favorite pastimes. My skydiving plans, which were so rudely interrupted by Diesel and his hoods, will be rescheduled for tomorrow. You're welcome to join me."

"Only if I don't have to jump out of a plane," Ebony replied.

"Deal." Renfro reached for her hand and the pair shook on it. "You've got an all-access pass, young lady."

For a reporter, it didn't get any better than that. "Way to go, Ebony." Isaiah smiled and raised his hand to high-five her. "You did it!"

Ebony stepped closer to Isaiah. "I was wondering if . . ."

"No. It's *your* exclusive," Isaiah interrupted her. "You've earned it."

"Hey, Mr. Renfro, Ms. MacKenzie, we need you two downtown at the station to get your statements." An officer approached and ushered Ebony and the Ice Cream Dreams founder and CEO toward a squad car.

Despair settled in Isaiah's gut like a lump of burning coal as he watched her walk away.

Before ducking inside the car Ebony peered over her shoulder toward Isaiah and called out in a tentative voice, "Call me later?"

Isaiah gave a perfunctory nod and lifted a hand for a limp wave. She peered out of the back windshield. They watched each other until the car turned off the gravel road and vanished on the highway. Now that he was sure she was safe, he had a chance to process everything. For the first time Isaiah realized the depth of emotion he felt for Ebony. The fact that she'd been willing to share her last Renfro tip meant she must feel something more than lust for him, too. Things had moved beyond a simple competition and hot romps in bed to something else. Ebony had been willing to meet him halfway. Maybe they could figure this thing out together. *Together.* Suddenly dread welled and churned inside of him. Together would mean his every dream and desire was open to revision, negotiation, and compromise. Admitting he needed her had a web of constricting strings attached. Obligation. Responsibility. Expectation. He shuddered. Something he could not control was closing in on him. That claustrophobic feeling that surfaced whenever he considered slowing down with one woman wrapped its icy fingers around his throat. A voice in his head screamed: *Run like hell! Before it's too late!*

Later that night Ebony was relishing the quiet of her kitchen and reflecting on her ordeal with a cup of herbal tea when Jolene entered.

Upon Ebony's return from the police station her mother had been uncharacteristically quiet. Ebony had relayed the terrifying details about her captivity. Granny Mac cried with relief that Ebony had been unharmed. Jolene's reaction had been different. There were no tears, but she'd sat next to Ebony, reached for her hand and squeezed. Hard. Ebony knew her mother sometimes had difficulty openly expressing emotion. She'd never been one of those kissy-kissy, don't-forget-your-mittens moms. She had accepted that.

Jolene hadn't shed a single tear at her husband's funeral, either. But Ebony had heard her mother's muffled sobs late that night, when she thought everyone was sleeping.

"Is everything all right, Ma?" She motioned for her mother

to take the chair next to hers, then she took her hand. "Would you like a cup of tea?"

Jolene declined with a shake of her head, then her eyes welled up. That took Ebony by surprise.

"Oh, Ma, I know it's been a horrible day, but I'm fine. Really I am." Ebony drew her into a hug.

"I'm just so glad, baby. When I heard—"

"I know, but it's all right. I'm all right."

"But can you ever forgive me?" Jolene blurted. "That's what I need to know."

Befuddled, Ebony held on to her. "Forgive you? For what?"

"Oh, baby, it's true."

"What's true?"

"What Althea said this morning?" Jolene cried in earnest. "Inside in some deep, dark, ugly place that I didn't want to acknowledge, I have held you responsible for that terrible night your father died."

Stunned that the words were finally spoken after years beneath a cloak of silence, Ebony couldn't respond immediately, sensing that a long overdue round of emotional letting was on tap. Her limbs went rubbery, her arms dropped from Jolene's shoulders.

Jolene paused, looking exhausted, as if the weight of her confession were too much. "I've stood by and watched you devote most of your waking hours to us, while denying yourself—as if it were punishment or retribution for Buster. I'm so sorry. Can you forgive me?"

"It wasn't just my imagination all these years," Ebony said in a soft, quavering voice. She looked at her mother as if seeing her for the first time in a long while.

"But I was wrong, so wrong to blame you. It was just a terrible accident, a mistake."

"What brought all this on? Don't tell me it's because of Granny Mac. You've never taken much she said to heart."

"When I heard about you, Reuben Renfro, and those terrible men, I realized how close we came to losing you. God only knows what they would've done to you two had the police not shown up. I realized how I'd been treating you and I prayed for the strength to not only do right by you, but to confess what I've done. I just hope you can forgive me."

"Oh, Ma." Ebony pressed her cheek against Jolene's wet one. Her mother was trying to free her. Ebony could stop living her life as one big apology, but would she? It was time she gave it a good try. "I love you, Ma, and Granny Mac and Kenya. We're family and nothing's ever going to change that. And there's still nothing in the world I wouldn't do for you."

"I know that. We all do, but what about you?" Jolene sniffled. "It's time you started loving and living for Ebony, too."

Ebony managed a small smile though her throat burned to release an all-out bawl. "You know, Ma. You're right. Absolutely right."

CHAPTER 31

When the first full day passed without so much as a peep from Isaiah, Ebony simply chalked it up to his giving her space to recover from her kidnapping ordeal. By the second, third, and fourth days she realized something was terribly wrong. Isaiah was not going to call and her feelings careened between anger and sadness. There was nothing more pitiful than falling in love with someone who obviously didn't love you back, Ebony thought, crouching to fill Black Gal's small bowl with Dog Chow.

"So you piddled in Isaiah's shoes." Ebony watched the dog greedily chomp into the crunchy brown nuggets. "You should've taken a dump in them, too."

She couldn't remember ever feeling grumpier when most of the pieces in her life were finally falling into place. Kenya had won another academic scholarship. Though modest, it would cover her textbook expenses for the next three years. Ebony had also given serious consideration to the student loan paperwork Kenya sent.

She had been deluding herself about how much of her sister's expenses she could realistically take on—especially when she still grappled with a loan of her own, one minimum payment at a time. Ebony realized she had cast herself in an impossible role. She'd been too thickheaded to yield to reason. She relented and ultimately agreed that loans and a limited work-study program could be part of a diversified effort. But she was far from keen on the idea of her baby sister going into debt or squeezing work into an already jammed class-and-study schedule. She'd come to realize why it was so important for Kenya's sense of self-worth to take on more responsibility for her own education.

Her mother and Granny Mac were also pitching in. They'd taken on part-time jobs at the church to help out with the family's expenses. And their tentative truce was still intact. Strained on some occasions, but intact nonetheless. More and more Ebony felt comfortable leaving them alone without worry.

On the career front, her editor at the *Butler County Bee* would allow her to stretch her writing muscles with more ambitious projects. Between the sewing-circle and fund-raising bake-sale fluff, she'd have an opportunity to tackle deeper human-interest stories that could make a difference. She'd also received a modest raise—not as much as she needed, but it was something, at least until she started that *Examiner* job. She'd already had her first interview with Renfro just before he jumped out of a plane on a skydiving excursion. He had even agreed to let her use anecdotes from the kidnapping that none of the other journalists covering the story had. The first installment of her Renfro series would be ready for *Examiner* editor John Hogan in less than a week. As promised, he would probably offer her that staff writing job soon. Things were moving right along, but she still felt lousy. A big bolt of lightning was bound to streak from the sky and zap her to oblivion for her obvious lack of gratitude. She should be singing and dancing. Overjoyed. But she missed Isaiah too doggone much.

Ebony scratched the fur between Black Gal's ears. She had to do something. Her fingers were practically itching to dial Isaiah's number, but she couldn't bring herself to do it. Pride. After all, he had her phone number. She had asked him to call, but he obviously did not want to speak to her. She couldn't think of one good reason why Isaiah hadn't phoned.

He probably couldn't stand the fact that she'd landed the Renfro exclusive. "Sore loser." She pouted. Maybe she should call him up and rub it in. "Nanny, nanny, na, na. I got him. You didn't," she sang spitefully before vanquishing the silly thought. She might as well tool over to his apartment then launch a spitball attack, too, while she was at it.

If he genuinely cared about her, would he let professional jealousy or ego get in the way? He would if he'd only turned on that megawatt charm and seduced her as a distraction, which was obviously what he had done.

Besides, adventuresome, free-spirited guys like Isaiah didn't usually fall for militantly bland women like Ebony, who couldn't shave their legs without checking their planners first. Deep down inside she always knew this, but she couldn't stop thinking about him and craving his touch. Coming so close to danger, she'd been forced to rethink a lot of things. A part of her now longed to start living life, having more fun. Taking care of family responsibilities and nurturing a healthy social life didn't have to be mutually exclusive. Ebony had foolishly hoped to test-run this new outlook with Isaiah, but that was out of the question now.

"Jerk," she muttered as the threat of tears stung her eyes. She sniffled, wiped her nose with a paper towel, but refused to cry as she slumped in a chair and prepared for heartache to settle in for the long haul.

CHAPTER 32

Isaiah spent the last hour putting the finishing touches on what was to be his last story for the *International Inquisitor*: "Scientists Create Killer Cockroaches as Secret Weapon to Give U.S. Edge in Warfare." A part of him would miss churning out the truth-mangling nonsense and shoveling in the easy money.

But it was time to move on to a real professional challenge, something he could really put his heart and soul into. He'd even gone out on a limb and sent sample prints and photo-essay ideas to editors at *National Geographic* and *Condé Nast Traveler* magazines. Long shots, but hell, what did he have to lose? He didn't have an impressive résumé or tearsheets of his photos published in slick national magazines. He'd simply let his work speak for itself.

It now seemed inconceivable that just a few weeks ago he'd been willing to settle in Cincinnati for a while to work at the *Examiner*. For what? So he could finally earn a pat on the head and "Way to go!" from his father, which he now realized would never come? Not just because Ebony was sure to get tapped for the *Examiner* job, but because he had accepted that his father would never change. He was damn tired of jumping through hoops for his approval. He'd never really wanted that job in the first place and would've been miserable once he signed on for the monotony of a regular nine-to-five job.

Isaiah stepped inside his bedroom and began throwing clothing into garment bags. It was time to fly and he couldn't think of a better place to land than the Napa Valley. When his old college buddy Kincaid Moore had called to ask if Isaiah was interested in snapping shots of his family's vineyard for a promotional campaign, he jumped at the opportunity. When he was done with the vineyard, he'd turn his lens to the landscapes. Rolling green hills, perfect weather, and all the damn wine he could drink would get his mind off Ebony.

It had been six days since that botched kidnapping scheme. Though he wanted to call her, he couldn't bring himself to do it. What was the point? He just couldn't be tied down. He still had a whole lotta world to see. He needed to purge her from his system as soon as possible. And that wasn't going to happen if he heard her voice or saw her pretty dimpled smile. Cutting things off—nice and neat—was the way to go. He made a mental note to look up Diandra Hopewell when he hit the West Coast. Good ol' Diandra. His ever-ready-and-willing-no-hassles distraction.

Over the next three days, Isaiah had donated what little furniture he had to a homeless shelter and returned the keys to the apartment manager. He had had his mail rerouted to a post office box and his phone service and utilities disconnected. With four hours before his plane's scheduled departure for San Francisco, he had more than enough time to drive his car to Tarik's house, where it would stay parked in his brother's triple-car garage indefinitely. He would've canceled that little pit stop and paid a fortune at the airport's long-term parking facility had he known his father was lurking at Tarik's.

"I told Dad you were on your way out of town again," Tarik said when Isaiah arrived. "I know you're pissed at me for interfering again, but you two really need to talk."

Isaiah ground his teeth when he saw their father lounging on the sofa.

"Just give it another shot." Tarik slapped Isaiah on the back, then slipped inside the kitchen.

"So I hear you're taking off again?" the eldest Malone said, sucking on his pipe as smoke curled from its bowl and dispersed. "Why?"

"Didn't you hear?" Isaiah didn't budge from his spot near the front door. "Your screwup son didn't get that *Examiner* gig."

George sat up straighter and seemed to take interest in Isaiah for the first time since he'd returned to town. "I had no idea you were trying to get on there."

"Surprise, surprise," Isaiah said flatly.

"But did you actually think they'd hire you with your tabloid background without some serious strings getting pulled?" George kept his pipe, with its deep plum surface polished to a high gloss, clamped between his teeth as he spoke. He gestured for Isaiah to take a seat on the sofa next to him.

Isaiah refused, preferring to stand. He had a plane to catch.

"You should've told me you wanted that job." George maneuvered the pipe from the left corner of his mouth to the right. "I still golf with Blake Conrad, the publisher, you know. He owes me a favor. It's not too late to see what I can do."

"That won't be necessary." Isaiah's voice was even and firm. "The point was to land the job on my own—without Daddy's help."

"What difference does it make? Son, I'm just glad you finally got your act together enough to start taking your writing career seriously. It's about time. Go on and cancel that flight of yours. I'll give Blake a call first thing tomorrow."

"I said no," Isaiah replied, sounding more than a little unhinged by his father's insistence.

"But I thought you said you wanted that job. Who cares how you got it? Just go in there and show them what a true Malone man can do."

"Ahhh, so I'm a *true* Malone man now, am I?" Isaiah chuckled mirthlessly. "What was I before?"

George scooted to the edge of his seat as his obvious annoyance kicked in. "If you didn't want the goddamn job, why were you going after it in the first place?"

"For all the wrong reasons. These highfalutin journalism

dreams were always yours and Tarik's—not mine. And it's too cold and dark standing in your shadows." Isaiah decided that for once he wouldn't hold anything back. "And before you say it, yeah, I knew the *International Inquisitor* wasn't *real* journalism, but more like a way to stick it to you."

"And stick it to me you did," George echoed in a rueful tone. "And showed contempt for all that I held sacred."

"Yeah." Isaiah's jaw unclenched, his shoulders squared. He finally felt free. Invincible. There wasn't anything his father could say to hurt him anymore because he could honestly admit for the first time in his entire life that he simply did not give a damn anymore. "First I wanted to punish you then I thought I wanted that *Examiner* job to show you that I was just as good as you and Tarik. But you know what? I don't need to be validated by you anymore. No matter what I do, it'll never be good enough for you. I'd bust my butt and get a legitimate reporting job only to have you right back on my case again, hassling me about why I don't have my own syndicated column or why I haven't been promoted to an editor."

George's chin dipped, he removed his pipe from his mouth and studied it. "It was just about love, tough love, son. You have so much potential. I needed you to realize there are consequences for making the wrong choices."

"But wrong for whom, Dad?" Isaiah didn't give him a chance to respond. "Know what I've come to realize? It was never really about me, but you."

George lifted the remote control off the coffee table, zapped the TV on and stuffed the stem of his pipe back in his mouth as if to signal that this discussion was over.

But Isaiah quickly closed the space between them, plucked the remote out of his father's hand and zapped the TV off again. "You had a hard time handling the fact that you had a troubled child, a child with a learning disability, but instead of showing patience and understanding, you punished me for it, for being different from you and Tarik. And for being less than . . . well, perfect. Hell, you're not perfect, far from it, and neither is Tarik." Making this admission brought Isaiah more satisfaction. He was tired of feeling *less than,* steeped in resentiment and the pressure of trying to be something he wasn't. "Anyway, I've got to go." He tossed the remote back at his father and called toward the kitchen. "Yo, Tarik. I'm out, man."

Tarik emerged and met him at the door. "You're leaving already?"

"Yeah, I'll call once I get settled in Napa to give you my phone number there. I'm expecting responses regarding some photography gigs I'm trying to line up. You take care." Isaiah gave his brother a hug and turned toward the door.

"There you go again," George sneered. "Running away instead of trying to straighten out your life. Once a screwup, always a screwup."

Isaiah stopped, released a sigh of pity before looking over his shoulder at his dad. "You would know all about that now, wouldn't you?"

Speechless for once, George looked stunned as he reached to steady the pipe drooping at his lips.

Tarik offered Isaiah a lift to the airport, but he declined. He'd use his cell phone to call a taxi. Time alone to absorb everything was what he needed most. A little less than half an hour later, Isaiah climbed in the back of a taxi, eager to put a continent between himself and Cincinnati.

CHAPTER 33

Ebony sat in the sun-dappled Wilcox kitchen, poking her fork at a small glistening mound of peach cobbler.

"You hardly touched your broccoli-and-cheddar quiche." Concern shadowed Taffi's face as she scooped a second helping onto Yolanda's plate, then her own. "I know something must be wrong if you're not eating dessert, either. What gives?"

"Just don't have much of an appetite today, that's all," Ebony said grimly, shoving a plump peach wedge through a puddle of syrup and a patch of sugar-sprinkled crust with no intention of bringing it anywhere near her mouth.

Taffi's mom had whipped up the dessert that usually had Ebony's mouth watering as soon she stepped inside the Wilcox house. But treats such as the cobbler, the fragrant topiary herbs lining the garden window, and the cheery sunflower wallpaper that always made her smile had lost their appeal.

"Are you ill?" Taffi, abloom again in one of her ultrafeminine floral sundresses, propped the serving spoon along the rim of the cobbler dish, then pressed the back of her hand against Ebony's forehead to check her temperature. "Do you need to go home and take it easy?"

"Quick, make a break for it while you have a chance."

Yolanda dug into her cobbler as a dozen or so spaghetti-thin bangles jangled around her wrist. The low-riding Levi's and one-shouldered tank top she wore that day was one of her tamer ensembles. "Save yourself."

"I'm fine." Ebony drew back from Taffi's hand and forced a smile. "I came over to help you with wedding decorations and that's what I intend to do." An afternoon moping in the company of friends was better than moping at home. She hadn't seen or heard from Isaiah in two weeks, one day, five hours... She glanced at her wristwatch. And seventeen minutes. But even with company, she felt lonely. Her mind kept straying to the fact that she missed him desperately. She knew it was unhealthy to obsess over what was obviously a fling, but everything was still a blur. And she couldn't help wondering what he was doing and wishing she were the one he was doing it with.

"You don't seem like yourself at all." Taffi gathered up her treasured new Persian cat. He began mewling for her attention when his frequent butts and body brushes against her legs failed. "Yes, you're Mommy's sweet little boy," Taffi cooed at the silver fur puff with huge, round emerald eyes as she plopped him on her lap. After enduring the onslaught of obligatory kisses and hugs, the cat deftly maneuvered to face the table and its intended target—Taffi's plate of warm cobbler.

"I'll eat my dessert later. If you don't mind, I'd like to start on the decorations." Ebony shoved her plate away and reached for one of six neat stacks of colored paper. "What are we making?"

"Origami cranes for the reception." Taffi stamped a kiss on the cat's head while he eyed her cobbler, sitting less than three inches from his flat face. "Cranes are an important symbol in Japanese wedding tradition."

"Uh, Taffi," Ebony tried warning her. "Grenadine—"

"His name is Grendel," Taffi snapped. "He doesn't like it when people don't get it right. Anyway, as I was saying, cranes are part of Japanese—"

"News flash, Taffi, you're not Japanese," Yolanda interrupted her.

"So? It doesn't hurt to incorporate a bit of other cultures for a little international flair," Taffi explained, as the cat stretched his neck and began licking cobbler juice from her plate.

"But Taffi, Gremlin, I mean Grenade is . . ."

"*Gren*-del. G-r-e-n-d-e-l."

"But why scraggly-looking cranes?" Yolanda was still on the bird thing. "Doves are much cuter and more romantic."

"Because cranes mate for life. According to legend we must fold one thousand and one origami cranes so Frank and I will enjoy a long, long married life together, good luck and happiness a thousand times over."

"Shouldn't we be folding them into bunnies, then?" Yolanda winked at Ebony. "You know what they say about rabbits and their libidos."

"This isn't about sex, silly," Taffi told Yolanda. "The key to a successful marriage is mutual respect and keeping the lines of communication open."

"Wishing for cosmos-shaking, nirvana-quaking nookie and lots of it over the years can't hurt, either," Yolanda pointed out between bites. "After all, isn't that how you hooked Frank in the first place? If I recall correctly it was your cleavage—not your conversation—on display at Club Mirage the night you two met. Remember, I was there."

"I don't care what you say, Yolanda, there's much more to my relationship with Frank than sex. And speaking of which, I'm going to be a married woman soon and I don't want you turning my bachelorette party into some bacchanalian bender."

"English translation please." Yolanda played dumb to be more annoying than she already was.

"*No* drunken raunch-o-rama. *No* male strippers and no drinks stronger than white wine and coolers," Taffi decreed, waving her fork at Yolanda. "I mean it."

"All right. All right already," Yolanda replied with little conviction.

Ebony, who had finally given up on warning Taffi about her cobbler-craving cat, gave Yolanda an I-told-you-so look. "So Taffi, should I start with the maroon or the gold sheet?"

As members of the bridal party it was Ebony and Yolanda's duty to calm Taffi, not work her into a conniption by ignoring her wishes.

Grendel raised his sticky whiskers from the plate, rimming his mouth with his prickly pink tongue just before Taffi dug into what was left with her fork.

"Ick!" Yolanda made a face. "That cat was just licking itself *downtown*."

"As freaky as you are, if it were anatomically possible, you'd lick yourself *downtown*, too." Taffi pushed a forkful of the peach in her mouth. The same peach the cat had licked clean of sugar sprinkles and cinnamon.

Yolanda made a gagging sound. "You're gross. You know that? Real disgusting."

"The maroon or the gold paper?" Ebony rolled her eyes, lifting a piece of each.

"Let's start with maroon." Taffi eased Grendel back on the tiled floor then began demonstrating the proper origami technique. "Take one sheet and fold it diagonally in half, lining up the corners to form a triangle."

Ebony did as instructed. Yolanda improvised and fashioned a paper airplane with her piece instead, then launched it into the air.

Taffi grabbed the plane mid-glide and crumpled it into a ball, which she used to pelt Yolanda's head. "Stop being a pain in the butt or I'll relieve you of bridesmaid duty."

"Oooh, promise?" Yolanda replied gleefully.

"Yolanda." Ebony nailed her friend with a reproachful glare.

"Taffi knows I'm not exactly looking forward to wearing that maroon monstrosity of a bridesmaid's dress she chose. Not only is it ugly, but we'll roast alive in all that satin and tulle this time of year."

Ebony had thought the same thing, but would never be so gauche as to degrade Taffi's vision. It was her dream wedding after all and if she wanted them to wear Kroger sacks and carry collard-green bouquets, so be it.

"It's not maroon, it's orchard wine," Taffi countered.

"Yolanda, tell Taffi you're sorry and that you're only spouting off because you're a wee bit jealous that she's walking down the aisle with her dream guy."

Yolanda turned on Ebony instead. "Speaking of dream guys, have you heard from that superfine Isaiah Malone of yours?" she taunted, knowing full well Ebony hadn't.

"Nope, why would I?" Ebony replied breezily.

"Oh, don't try to dumb down now," Yolanda said.

"So you two finally started dating? When?" Taffi turned to Ebony.

A flicker of a glance passed between Yolanda and Ebony before Ebony continued. "Yes, no, uh." She focused on her paper-folding and -creasing. "We weren't actually seeing each other . . . or dating—officially, that is."

Yolanda reached over and plucked a peach from Ebony's saucer and popped it inside her mouth. "No, they just boinked each other's brains out a couple of weeks ago, that's all. I mean, had a real buck-wild nastyfest. Tell her about it, Eb."

"Ebony?" Taffi's voice hitched an octave as if her feelings were hurt. "Is that true? And if so, why didn't I know about it?"

"You've been so busy with your wedding and all. And it really isn't that big of a deal," Ebony told her, though it was the biggest deal. She'd fallen in love for the first time in her life. "It was a little fling, that's all, over before it ever really began."

Taffi arched a brow as if she weren't buying it. "You never struck me as a one-night-stand sorta woman."

"Correction. Make that all-night-and-all-morning-long stand," Yolanda chirped, getting on Ebony's last nerve.

Ebony had been so overwhelmed by it all, she had to share it with someone. She hadn't suspected Yolanda would be so quick to blab.

Ebony concentrated on folding her triangle paper into an even smaller triangle of paper, following Taffi's lead. "Hey, I guess there's a first time for everything." She bent one corner of the triangle, then bent another, playing unflappable on the outside while her heart was breaking inside. The edge of the sheet sliced across her finger. Blood dribbled out, staining the square of gold paper in her hands. The disillusionment and frustration welling up inside the past couple of weeks overflowed as tears slipped down her cheeks.

"Are you all right?" Taffi dropped the paper bird she'd just completed to hug Ebony. Taffi was the best kind of friend to have when a body had the blues. She was always so good at the Mother Earth nurturing thing. Regardless of what Yolanda thought, she was sure that was the quality that had made Frank fall madly in love with Taffi.

"I'm sorry, Ebony." Yolanda reached for her hand. "I didn't mean . . ."

"I'm fine, really." Ebony wiped her tears away with her knuckles.

"You really fell for that guy, didn't you?" Yolanda said as if the idea hadn't occurred to her. "You never told me how you really felt. I thought you two were just kickin' it a little. I wouldn't have been so insensitive if I thought . . ."

"That I would get all mushy?" Ebony sobbed and watched her teardrops stain a sheet of gold paper on the table. "I feel like a sniveling lovesick fool."

"So you actually love this guy, huh?" Yolanda's jaw dropped.

Ebony nodded slowly.

"Well, where do things stand?" Taffi asked.

"I haven't seen or talked to him in two weeks, since that botched kidnapping plot," Ebony replied. "He hasn't called me."

"Well, have you called him?" Yolanda grabbed a paper towel from the counter.

"No, I can't."

"Why not?" Taffi rubbed Ebony's shoulder.

"Because I know he was only pretending to be interested in me to distract me. You know, get my mind off that exclusive. Once Renfro agreed to let me interview him, Isaiah just disappeared—poof—into thin air. No reason to hang around playing the sexy lothario to the plain-Jane control freak now." Ebony accepted the paper towel Yolanda passed to her.

"What?" Taffi was incredulous. "It must've been really hard for this guy to spend time with someone as beautiful as you are."

"A beautiful sistah with a heart so big she always puts the needs of her loved ones before her own," Yolanda added.

"And haven't you always given me a hard time about that very thing?" Ebony withdrew from Yolanda with a sidelong look, chafing against her attempt to comfort. Taffi, who was close to her own family, had been the more understanding one of the two. But then Yolanda had her own baggage, stemming from her teenaged mother, who had abandoned her when she was a toddler, leaving her to be reared by overly strict grandparents.

"You're right," Yolanda said. "It's not that I didn't admire your generosity where your family was concerned. I just wanted to see you carve out a little niche of happiness of your own. Happiness that wasn't always a direct offshoot of someone else's happiness. Does that make any sense?"

"I guess." Ebony leaned against her friends again, pressing the paper towel against her cut.

"Did Isaiah make you happy?" Taffi used her hand to smooth Ebony's braids.

Ebony took a reflective minute. "Yes, he did ... When we weren't bickering about something or other. But you know what? Even the bickering was sort of fun, if that makes any sense."

"So there you go," Yolanda said. "Now that the whole Renfro race is over, there's nothing standing in your way."

"Haven't you heard a word I've said? Isaiah doesn't want me. It was always about the competition, and besides, he's not a one-woman man. And the way I feel about him now, I don't think I could settle for being just another number in his little black book."

"How can you be so sure when you haven't even told him how you feel?" Taffi asked.

"It's just like the soap operas." Yolanda shook her head. "Two people madly in love waste a whole helluva lot of time apart because both assume the other feels one way, when he or she actually feels another. One decent adult powwow could clear the whole thing up. What could've been accomplished in a one-hour episode stretches into four months of misunderstandings. And oh, how they juice those dramatic near-misses and close calls."

"But that's part of the fun," Taffi noted.

"Sometimes it can be as annoying as hell though, but I guess they're on to something. I keep going back to *Guiding Light* again and again for more," Yolanda said.

"You watch *Guiding Light*, too?" Taffi asked with wide eyes. "Honey, can you believe Scarface pulled a knife on Reva?"

"And she was half naked, too!" Yolanda tossed in.

"But what about Reva's undercover ploy?" Taffi clucked. "Can you believe she tried a boneheaded thing like that?"

"She was really tripping, thinking she could get away with that blind bag lady getup. I mean, puuuh-leeaase. Ray Charles could see through that disguise."

"And wouldn't you know Cassie's not pregnant after all."

"But what about Buzz Cooper—"

Feeling neglected, Ebony cleared her throat with an exaggerated hacking sound.

"Sorry, girl, got a little carried away there for a minute." Yolanda began patting Ebony's shoulders again. "About your problem, you're miserable now, right? Then what have you got to lose? Talking to him will do one of two things—(a) confirm what you already believe to be true, or (b) prove that you've been wrong and Isaiah has fallen for you, too."

"If it's (b), why haven't I heard from him?"

"The same reason he hasn't heard from you." Taffi flapped her hands, then pressed her fingertips against her temples. "Haven't you been listening to anything we've said? It could be a simple case of the ol' soap supposition syndrome keeping you two apart. Like Harley and Phillip on *Guiding Light*."

"Or Barbara and Hal on *As the World Turns*." Yolanda pitched in.

"Marah and Tony on *The Bold and the Beautiful*!" Taffi added.

"Like . . . maybe," Ebony mumbled, "Cricket and Paul on *The Young and the Restless*?"

"By George, I think she's got it!" Taffi raised her hand to slap Yolanda a high five.

Three hours and 232 origami cranes later, Ebony left Taffi's practically hopping with manic anticipation. She had to hear Isaiah's voice again. Pulling out her cell phone, she covered the few yards of lawn, concrete driveways, and colorful, sun-loving perennials separating her house from the Wilcoxes' brick colonial. With trembling fingers, she punched in Isaiah's number. It was no longer in service. She stopped in her tracks and dialed again, slowly this time, but got the same operator's message. Inside her bedroom, she reached for her planner, where she kept phone numbers of various AAJC members, including Tarik's. He answered his phone after the third ring.

Ebony's anxiety nearly brimmed over, but she managed to keep it in check. "I was trying to reach your brother, but his phone—"

"It's disconnected."

"Disconnected? Oh, I get it. He forgot to pay the phone bill, right?"

"Sounds like you know my brother pretty well." Tarik's laugh was deep and musical. "But no, he had the phone cut off because he left town. Went to Napa to work on a photography ad campaign for an old college buddy of his who owns a vineyard out there."

Ebony flumped on her bed and fought to keep the panic out of her voice. "He left town? When will he be back?"

"Didn't say exactly, but I'm guessing he'll be traveling for a while as usual since he had his phone disconnected. Left a couple of weeks ago. Hard to pin that one down so we stopped trying. My brother lives for racking up frequent flier miles. I've got his number in Napa if you want."

Ebony couldn't believe Isaiah actually took off without so much as a goodbye. Her heart squeezed, as she gripped the receiver. His actions only confirmed what she suspected. He really didn't give a damn and now she felt like Boo-Boo the fool again for letting Taffi and Yolanda persuade her to think otherwise, with all their crap about soap syndromes and star-crossed lovers.

"You can call where he's staying in Napa or I can pass along a message when I talk to him again."

Ebony had a message for him all right. Isaiah Malone could kiss the darkest part of her brown bottom, but Tarik didn't need to hear all that. She'd tell Isaiah herself. "Yes, I'd like his number, please, if you don't mind."

Tarik left the line for a minute, then returned to give her the West Coast phone number.

"And oh, Tarik, if you speak to Isaiah before I do, don't tell him you talked to me," Ebony said. She wanted to make sure Isaiah wouldn't have an opportunity to dodge her attack.

"So you want to surprise him? He'll love that. Don't worry. My lips are sealed."

Ebony hung up, poised to dial when second thoughts surfaced. She'd come off as a delusional harpy, tongue-lashing Isaiah long distance for leaving town. What right did she have to be so furious? He'd made no promises. They'd agreed that their relationship was strictly no-strings. He could come and go as he saw fit—without explanation.

The other option was to call and make nice. Chat about the weather and wine in Napa, then as casually as she pleased, toss in, "Oh, by the way, I love you like crazy."

She picked up the phone and dialed the first three digits when her fingers stalled and fear gripped her gut. After such blatant exposure, could she really handle that awkward hemming and hawing on his end if he didn't feel the same way. Sure the rejection would crush her beyond the point of return, she replaced the receiver. There had to be some consolation in holding on to a little pride.

CHAPTER 34

Caffeine. Ebony had to have it. Hot. Strong. Black. Pumped intravenously. A vicious throbbing ache clamped around her temples as she walked across the expansive *Cincinnati Examiner* newsroom. Struggling to deal with her heartache, she hadn't gotten much sleep the night before. Bouts of insomnia were catching up with her. She needed something big—like that much-coveted *Examiner* job offer—to force her out of her funk.

While the newsroom was easily five times larger than the *Bee*'s, it boasted none of the shining, antiseptic modernism she had imagined. Curtains yellowed by age barred morning sunlight. Scraggly gray berber skimmed the floors like a five o'clock shadow. Rows of books, newspapers, used notepads, and assortments of junk towered precariously on a grid of old desks. Chatter, trilling phones, tapping printers, and a police scanner echoed wall to wall.

The perky news aide, who greeted her at the reception desk, had directed her to a coffee alley where she could get a cup of java while she awaited John Hogan's return from an early-morning planning meeting.

Popping in without an appointment to see the assistant editor meant no grousing about the wait. The fifth and final installment of her Reuben Renfro profile was due that day, but rather than send it via e-mail attachment like the previous installments, she decided to deliver this one in person. Sure it was the day Mr. Hogan would extend an official offer to join the *Examiner* staff, she'd donned her best suit, a cranberry sheath and matching jacket, and Granny Mac's heirloom pearl necklace and earrings. Her braids were secured in an all-business bun; her feet tucked comfortably inside her ready-to-pound-the-pavement pumps. With her typed resignation for the *Bee* inside her briefcase, nothing was stopping her from starting the new *Examiner* job as early as next week if they wanted. Nothing like a new job and new routine to get her mind off old woes.

In the brightly lit break alley Ebony poured coffee into a paper cup and helped herself to one of the waxy-looking pastries stacked near the coffee machine. She weaved her way through the maze of desks, wondering which of the three empty cubicles in the metro reporters' pool would be hers. She returned to the chair just outside Mr. Hogan's office to wait and scan the first edition of the morning newspaper. She had taken a bite out of the bear claw and homed in on the landfill piece at the bottom of the front page when a voice startled her.

"Ms. MacKenzie." Mr. Hogan appeared from nowhere. A bespectacled and balding man with an extreme comb-over and skin so pale it appeared gray. "I'm sorry. I hope we didn't have an appointment that I forgot all about."

"No, sir. Excuse me." She turned away, discreetly spitting the disgusting glob of sweet dough into a napkin then pitched it in a nearby trash can. "I'm sorry. As I was saying, I was downtown and thought I'd drop off the last installment of my series."

He ushered her inside his neat, golf-themed office. "You didn't have to come all the way down here. You could've sent it by e-mail."

"Yeah, I know, but I was running some errands downtown anyway and I thought with this being the last part of the series and all, it'd give us a chance to talk."

"You received your check for freelancing for us, right?"

"Yes, thank you. It came in the mail yesterday. It was extremely generous, but I've been meaning to ask you about that. You doubled the amount that we agreed upon. Was there some accounting mistake?"

Tilting his seat back, he cradled his head in linked fingers. "No, it wasn't an accounting error. You did such a fantastic job on the series so far, I thought you deserved something extra."

She smiled with pride. "Thanks, but getting that job we discussed several weeks ago would be more than enough to show your gratitude."

"Oh, yes, about that opening..." He removed his glasses and cleaned the lenses with a wadded tissue from his shirt pocket. "There have been some changes since we first discussed that. There's a hiring freeze in effect now."

"A hiring freeze?" she asked with a wary edge. "For how long?"

"Can't really say. Came down from corporate." He pushed his glasses back on his nose.

Her shoulders slumped. "When?"

"Uh... Sorry. There is no opening now and I'm not sure when we will have another one."

"I see." Ebony got that queasy moving-elevator feeling in her stomach that usually surfaced when she'd been duped. Something about the sudden inconvenience of the hiring freeze didn't add up, but she was determined to keep a professional demeanor. Though he'd practically handed her a blowtorch, it wasn't smart to burn bridges.

"Don't read anything into this now. It's just one of those things that drops out of the sky from the powers that be and the bean counters at corporate headquarters. We have no control over it at this level."

"So what you're saying is it has nothing to do with the quality of my writing?" Ebony asked.

"No—not at all. Your work on this series has been excellent. This is about budget constraints. The timing's off. That's all."

"Speaking of timing, exactly *when* did this hiring freeze begin?" She repeated the question he'd pointedly ignored the first time she asked.

"Well, uh..." he faltered, avoiding her direct gaze. His cheeks flushed. When the phone on his desk rang, he grounded his chair and snatched up the receiver. "Hello, yeah. Yes... Sure... No, I'll take care of it right away."

He hung up, still avoiding eye contact. "That was Blake Conrad, the publisher. He needs to see me right now. Sorry, I can't chat with you longer." He stood and opened his office door, a not-too-subtle indication that their meeting had ended. "Need extra copies of the paper with your series?" he asked. Before she could reply, he continued. "I'll have them bundled up and couriered to you. How's that?" He escorted Ebony out of the newsroom toward a bank of elevators in the foyer. One set of doors slid open immediately and he all but shoved her inside. "We'll be in touch."

Once tucked inside her car in the *Examiner* parking lot Ebony released tears of crushing disappointment.

That night Isaiah's date with Diandra was supposed to take his mind off Ebony, but he couldn't help making comparisons. Diandra's voluptuousness only made him daydream of Ebony's long, lean lines. Diandra's light caramel complexion appeared jaundiced when Ebony's was rich, dark, and sweet as the finest gourmet chocolate. At that moment he'd kill for a taste of her again.

Diandra wore that sexy black dress she knew he loved. A little tube-style number made of a soft silk fabric that kissed her curves. After dinner and a show, she had invited him back to her place for a nightcap of strawberry daiquiris. Code words for lots and lots of heart-pumping aerobic sex, of course. Hooking up with Diandra was supposed to act as an exorcism of sorts. He needed something to shake him out of that disconnected feeling that had overcome him as soon as he stepped on the plane to San Francisco.

The week shooting photos in Napa hadn't been enough of a distraction and he just wasn't feeling like himself. He'd been short-tempered with his friend Kincaid and the vineyard employees. He'd chalked it up to too many sleepless nights and merciless heartburn. After an apology and long commiserating conversations with Kincaid, who had just been dumped by his wife of eight years, Isaiah concluded Ebony was the problem. Two thousand miles had not quelled his longing for her, but maybe another woman would. At his wit's end, he decided to give it a try, but as he trailed Diandra on the slate walkway leading to her front door, he wasn't so sure going inside was a good idea, after all. He couldn't work up his usual enthusiasm for what lay ahead. After Ebony, Diandra had been downgraded to the sexual equivalent of mac 'n' cheese—filling but oh-so-very-blah because his heart wasn't in it.

"Thanks again for inviting me to the show," Isaiah said, attempting to prepare her for his immediate departure. "I enjoyed it, but I'm exhausted."

Diandra worked as a publicity specialist at one of those chichi-poopoo art galleries in downtown San Francisco. Used to dating highly cultured, fancy-cuff-link types, she had made an exception when it came to Isaiah, who couldn't tell a Jackson Pollock from an oil spill.

"You know, I think I'd better call it a night." Isaiah forced a yawn, then patted his pockets for car keys.

"But you promised you'd come in for a nightcap. What's the rush? I hardly see you anymore," Diandra pouted.

One drink wouldn't kill him, Isaiah decided. "All right, I'll come in for that drink, but I can't stay the night."

She slid her key in the knob and opened the front door. She switched on the lights then lost four solid inches in stature after kicking off her strappy heels. Her long ponytail swayed then dangled from one shoulder. She gestured toward her artsy-fartsy red velvet couch in the living room. "Make yourself comfortable."

Isaiah relaxed on an end cushion and draped one arm across the back. An ornate marble bar separated the kitchen from the living room. He watched her reach for glasses in a cabinet and wondered what Ebony was doing and what he'd like to be doing to her.

She opened the refrigerator and removed a package of frozen strawberries.

"Nice room. I like what you've done with it. Your souvenirs are so cool." Isaiah took in the international decorating touches, which included Grecian sconces, Chinese Buddha candelabras, and replicas of Italian frescoes on painted burlap. One of the African baskets reminded him of something he'd seen filled with towels in Ebony's bathroom. There he went again. *Ebony. Ebony. Ebony. Damn!* His thoughts were zipping back to her more frequently with each passing day and the triggers were getting more ridiculous. He couldn't even enjoy a damn doughnut without thinking of her. He raised his voice over the buzz of the blender. "So how's everything at the gallery?"

"Fine, we just got this new oil painting collection by an up-and-coming artist that I'm very excited about."

"Oh, yeah?"

"It's called *Ebony Twilight*."

That bashed him on the head like a two-by-four. "You're kidding me, right? *Ebony Twilight*, you say?"

If that wasn't a divine message and a half from above, he didn't know what was. He shouldn't be there, but hightailing it back to Cincinnati—to Ebony's arms.

"Yeah, *Ebony Twilight* by Hugo Langer. Are you familiar with his work?" Diandra returned to the living room with the daiquiris and tried to pass one to Isaiah.

"Diandra, I'm sorry." He stood. "I have to go, really."

"But we haven't had our drinks yet." She had a puzzled expression, then her lacquered lips stretched into a seductive smile. "Oh, I get it. You want to play games. Want me to beg?" She rested their drinks on the coffee table, then reached up to undo the buttons of his shirt, but he took a step away from her.

"What's with you?" she asked, her annoyance escalating. "You've been distant all night."

Isaiah sat on the couch, pinching the bridge of his nose where tension had centered. He owed her the truth. "I think I should get this out." He sighed. "I know we had a little arrangement. No strings and all. Some things have changed. I've been doing some thinking." He paused. "You sure you want to hear this?"

"Yes, go ahead." Diandra sat beside him, resting a hand on his upper thigh.

"The thing is . . ." His heartbeat quickened. His mouth went dry, but he had to say it. "I think . . . I think I'm in love . . ."

"In love?" Diandra paused as if she were waiting for the punch line. "With who or should I say what? Your reflection?"

He looked her dead in the eye then replied with solemn sincerity. "With a woman—*one* woman."

Diandra looked stunned for a long minute, then burst out laughing as if she'd never heard anything so ridiculous. "Hit-'em-and-quit-'em Isaiah? In love?"

She yukked it up so long and hard that Isaiah began to wonder if he should take umbrage.

Sex was so simple and easy. And he'd been the master of the chase. But when it came to opening himself up to true, go-the-distance intimacy, he had to admit he'd been a women's-magazine cliché. His womanizing ways were roaring back to bite him on the butt and he supposed Diandra's incredulous reaction was understandable. The face of every woman he'd promised to call, knowing full well he wouldn't, and every woman he'd sexed then promptly Xed flashed through his mind. Sure, it took two to tango, but he'd been a selfish SOB to them all—including the woman he now knew he deeply loved. What a fool he'd been to run off and leave Ebony behind like he did.

Dabbing tears away from her eyes, Diandra finally sobered enough to speak. "Okay, okay. So who is this lucky girl anyway?"

"Her name is Ebony." Isaiah dragged his hands down his face, as if still awed by the realization that he could feel so deeply. "It took a while for it to sink into my thick head and I've probably screwed things up beyond repair, but I do love her. Damn it. And believe me, I had no choice in the matter."

"I'll just bet you didn't." Diandra erupted in peals of laughter again.

There! He'd said it! Out loud even. He'd actually admitted he'd fallen in love. The planet didn't tilt on its axis. His pancreas didn't explode and he wasn't bleeding from his eyeballs. He would be fine—just fine. In fact, he felt good as the spoken words sank deep into his consciousness and his heart—like rain saturating parched, barren earth. For the first time in weeks he felt good. He didn't care if Diandra believed him or not. All that mattered was Ebony. She had to believe him. He finally knew what was in his own heart. He was in love, love, l-o-v-e, love! And he was going home to claim his woman . . . *If* she'd have him.

"Well, for what it's worth . . ." Diandra's voice still quavered from her laughing jag. "Good luck. But once you snap out of this . . . this . . . beautiful delusion, don't come sniffing around here anymore." She wagged a finger at him. "I'm not playing the rebound good-time chick anymore."

As Isaiah walked to the door, he felt the deepest smile settle on his face. "No, you deserve much better. Take care, Diandra."

CHAPTER 35

Ebony studied her image in a bedroom mirror. The Miss Kitty bridesmaid dress didn't look any better with dangling pearl drop earrings and a matching choker necklace. The humongous butt bow was not to be restrained even with a chain of jumbo safety pins. She stopped fussing with the dress long enough to check her hair, where weaving in the requisite baby's breath proved to be the biggest challenge. It circled her braids like a crown of dandelion fuzz.

She reached inside the bodice made for someone more endowed, then lifted her boobs and emptied a box of Kleenex, plumping them up. Somewhere along the way, the seamstress or one of her trusty helpers had flubbed the order. Ebony had ended up with the wrong dress, but she'd vowed to soldier on. This was Taffi's big day and she'd do anything to insure its success—even if it meant dressing like a saloon trollop having a bad hair day. She dabbed a bit of concealer over the crescent-shaped puffs under her eyes, mementos from Taffi's bachelorette party held the previous night.

Ebony had been hard-pressed to rally her mood, but she'd refused to miss Taffi's prewedding celebration. She'd only planned to stay long enough for the wine cooler toast to the bride-to-be and oversee the opening of the lingerie gifts, then she was supposed to get the heck out of there. Thanks to Yolanda, Ebony was thrust into the referee role again to prevent Taffi from ripping Yolanda's hair out. Despite Taffi's protests, Yolanda had hired those strippers anyway.

There had actually been a good reason Taffi wanted to keep the entertainment clean. She'd had an inkling her mother and grandmother just might crash the festivities, which is exactly what they did—about five minutes before showtime and about five minutes too late for Yolanda to cancel the show.

Yolanda's living room had been overrun with shimmying thong-clad brown beefcake, bumping, grinding, and behinding to "Who Let the Dogs Out." Taffi's granny nearly had a coronary.

Taffi, hell-bent on retribution, made Yolanda promise to host two dozen Mary Kay skin-care classes—including a catered buffet of Taffi's choice—every week for the next six months. At the time Ebony hadn't dared to crack a smile though in hindsight the fiasco was nothing short of a hoot. How she longed to pick up the phone and share the story with Isaiah. But like most of her thoughts about him, she soon snapped to her senses, realizing that that exchange was not to be.

Ebony surveyed her teeth for lipstick smudges then dabbed more Mango-Tango color on her lips. Lifting her hands, she checked her Mango-Tango-slicked nails for nicks. If she crammed her brain with enough tiny details, she could almost stave off the sadness that threatened to engulf her. She always got weepy at weddings, but that day she'd awakened on the verge of tears, wondering if someone would ever love her as much as Frank obviously loved Taffi. Would she ever feel so goofily giddy with the need to touch someone—besides Isaiah—ever again? Blinking back the tears brimming in her eyes, Ebony scolded herself. *Get over it! Get over him! It wasn't meant to be!*

The puffies were bad enough; the last thing she wanted was to show up for the ceremony all red-and-raccoon-eyed, too. She tugged a tissue out of her bra and carefully dabbed her tears to prevent smearing. *You can do this. Just take it one minute, one hour and one day at time*. Maybe she'd even nab another man. Yeah, that's what she'd have to do. What better way to get over one, than to replace him with another? Squaring her shoulders with forced confidence and hope for her future, she stuffed the damp Kleenex back inside her bra, then opened the top drawer of her dresser and removed tube socks. Separating the pair, she stuffed one inside each cup of her bra to create the illusion of more cleavage, then added an additional coat of Mango-Tango to her lips. She would need all the help she could get now that she was putting herself back on the dating market. Taffi's wedding was the perfect place to start man-hunting. There were at least three unattached groomsmen in the bridal party—including Taffi's cousin Corky, who had made googly eyes at her during the rehearsal dinner two nights ago.

Corky was a tall fuzzy fella with hawkish features. He wasn't cover-model handsome or nearly as intriguing as Isaiah, but Ebony was sure she could discover the joys of his hobbies—fountain-pen collecting and fly fishing—given half a chance. And as for Corky's little fur problem . . . Well, she'd simply keep her fanny pack stocked with ear- and nose-hair clippers. And she heard there were some totally awesome laser hair-removal techniques available these days.

"You ready, hon?" Jolene poked her head inside Ebony's bedroom.

Ebony smoothed the front of her dress and took one last look in the mirror.

"Althea's acid reflux is acting up again, she won't be coming with us." Jolene nudged Ebony away from the mirror to study her own reflection.

"Poor thing. She was really looking forward to this, too." Ebony transferred her little necessities from her fanny pack to a small satin drawstring bag that matched her dress.

"Yeah, I even offered to stay here and keep her company." Jolene adjusted the tilt of the faux-gardenia-covered hat perched on her head.

Ebony turned to face her mother with a skeptical expression. "You did?"

"Only because I knew she wouldn't hear of it." Jolene

turned and peeked from beneath the wide brim of her hat. "She says she'll be just fine."

In the living room Ebony found Granny Mac relaxing on the couch, huddled in one of Ebony's oversized sweatsuits.

"My, don't you look pretty," Granny Mac said with a dozing Black Gal tucked in her arms.

With massive satin and tulle billowing and swishing around her, Ebony went to her grandmother. "I heard you're not feeling up to the wedding."

"No, baby, Granny Mac's insides are churning and burning like a furious volcano." She took Ebony's hand. "But it's nothing that a little prescription medicine, this couch, and a Bruce Lee videothon can't cure. The VCR is set and all ready to go. And look at my haul over there." She nodded toward the stack of videos on the coffee table. "Finally got my hands on *The Wrecking Crew* and *Circle of Iron*." Granny Mac released Ebony's hand to karate-chop a sofa cushion. The sudden movement awakened Black Gal, who growled at Ebony.

"Don't get snippy with me. I didn't wake you up," Ebony said to the dog before looking up at her grandmother. "You sure you're going to be all right?"

"I'll be just fine, baby," Granny Mac assured her.

"I'll bring you a slice of wedding cake that you can eat when you're feeling better," Jolene said, pulling immaculate short white gloves over her dainty, manicured hands.

"Thank you, dear." Granny Mac teased with a bogus smile. "But of course, I'll expect you to taste-test it before I'll eat a bite."

"Just in case I'm tempted to slip a little arsenic in the frosting?" Jolene went to the door.

"Exactly," Granny Mac replied sweetly.

Flying wisecracks and veiled digs between Jolene and Granny Mac hadn't stopped, but the murderous tone was replaced with a playfully mischievous one. Ebony could live with that.

"I really hate that you won't be coming with us," Ebony said to Granny Mac then joined her mother at the door.

"Will you two get on out of here? Besides, you're just two doors down. I'll be fine."

"Well, all right, but as soon as I finish my bridesmaid's duty, I'm coming back," Ebony said.

"Oh, no you won't. You will stay at that wedding, young lady, and have a good time with no worries. No calling or tipping over here checking up on me. And you'd better be the last one to leave that reception. Eat, drink, and turn that sucker out. Don't come back here until you have a lampshade on your head, you hear?"

"Yes, ma'am." Ebony waved goodbye.

They'd been blessed with the kind of clear, sunny day perfect for an outdoor wedding. The Wilcox backyard, transformed into a garden paradise, popped with white and red roses. The laughter and chatter of guests filled the air.

The ceremony took place under a lattice arch with a diaphanous swagged canopy. Corky, who escorted Ebony down the aisle, whispered, "Love is in the air," but she would just as soon hold her breath until Corky popped a breath mint.

Yolanda, whose sense of humor bordered on the twisted, had obviously decided to play the saloon trollop to the hilt by twisting her hair into sausage-sized ringlets, and donning black fishnet stockings and happy hooker heels. Her makeup, applied with a drag queen's hand, included a garish faux beauty mark that hovered near the right corner of her black-cherry-glossed lips. Judging from Taffi's horrified reaction when she first saw her, Yolanda had just added six additional months of Mary Kay duty to her sentence.

But Taffi refused to let Yolanda sour her mood for long. She looked serene and positively luminous in her satin and lace Cinderella-style gown while her groom, Frank, was dapper in white tux tails. Taffi's father, wearing his proudest smile, gave her away, as Taffi's mother watched and wept.

With the look of love shining in Taffi and Frank's eyes, no one would ever suspect the coosome twosome had fought for weeks over Taffi's choice for ring bearer. Grendel wore the two gold wedding bands dangling from his glittering rhinestone collar. He padded down the white felt runner covering the grassy aisle—only stopping momentarily to scratch his left ear, then bat at a wayward butterfly.

With the Reverend Jeb Munser officiating, it took all of fifteen minutes between the "dearly beloved" and "I now pronounce you man and wife."

Corky, who sent flirty glances Ebony's way during the ceremony, made sure he nabbed a spot next to her for the bridal party photos and the receiving line.

"Please let me take you out to dinner sometime," he said during the reception as they headed for the bridal-party table. "We could go to that little fondue place on Briarwood then maybe we could swing by my place to check out my mounted trout."

"Mounted trout?" Ebony tried her best to flirt. "Would that be a new twist on the infamous 'Come check out my etchings'?"

"No." He chuckled. "As I told you the other night I'm an avid fly fisherman. I'm very proud of my catches—largemouth, smallmouth bass, crappie, yellow perch, trout. You name it, I have it on my wall—all top-quality mounts."

"Sounds, uh, fascinating." Ebony had fixed her lips into a stiff smile when Taffi's Aunt Norma, aka Mama Corky, interrupted. With unkempt brows sprouting out like insect antennae and a moustache that defied waxing, she was just as shaggy as her son. "My, my, but don't you two make a lovely couple."

"Mother, I was just trying to ask Ebony here for a date," Corky said.

"Smart move, son." Norma patted his arm. "It's about time you started fishing for something that doesn't have fins and scales. Well, I'd better move along then and let you two take care of business."

"Save a dance for me," Corky called out to his mother then turned back to Ebony. "Now, where were we?"

"Ebony! There you are!" Yolanda came rushing over. "Mind if I borrow her for a minute?" she said to Corky, taking Ebony's arm to drag her away.

"Where's the fire?" Ebony asked once they reached a private spot near an old sycamore.

"You owe me." Yolanda tugged at the bodice of her dress and adjusted her cleavage. "Damn, this thing is uncomfortable."

"I owe you for what?"

"For saving you from Halibut Hell, that's what. I know all about Corky. Believe me, you'll die of boredom listening to this guy drone on and on about lures, lines, baits, and tackle."

"Well, he seems nice enough." Ebony looked over her shoulder at Corky, who was several feet away munching on a piece of broccoli. When he waved, she waved back.

"Nice is good," Yolanda conceded. "But don't stand here and tell me that you're attracted to Corky."

"Well, not exactly, not yet, but who's to say I won't be someday, after I get to know him much better?"

"I think it's great that you're trying to move on. But it's a very critical time for you right now. You've got to be more selective, choose wisely. If you start jumping at any and every guy who asks you out, you'll never get over Isaiah. No one will ever measure up. Don't you see? Isaiah will remain God's gift, this . . . this paragon . . . A legend in your mind."

"I hear what you're saying. But . . ." Ebony said softly, looking down at the satin pumps dyed to match her orchard-wine dress. "I've got to be realistic or I'll always be alone. The reality is I just might be a Corky kind of girl."

"So you're willing to settle." Yolanda shook her head. "Is that what you're trying to say? There's such a thing as having a nice guy who can also rock your world. Don't you want passion? Don't cheat yourself out of that, Ebony. One day you'll regret it."

Ebony hesitated, dragging in a deep breath because her heart was so heavy. "I have to be realistic, Yolanda. Men like Isaiah just don't fall in love with women like me." She willed back the tears that threatened to squeeze forth, then marched back to join Corky and the rest of the wedding guests.

CHAPTER 36

Fresh off his plane from San Francisco, Isaiah purchased an *Examiner* and a cola to kick back during the loading delay in the baggage claim area of the Cincinnati airport. Too tired to muscle his way through the cluster of passengers poised to pounce on every vaguely familiar bag on the conveyer belt, he opted to relax and catch his breath on a nearby seat until the crowd thinned. He leaned back in a chair, sipped his soda, and scanned the front page, where he found the final installment of Ebony's Reuben Renfro profile displayed front and center in section A on page 1. He took his time and absorbed the magnitude of Ebony's gift. She was good. *Damn good.* Her prose was spare, accessible but evocative and vivid. She'd captured the essence of Renfro, the man and the multimillionaire. When Isaiah was done, he felt as if he'd spent a weekend shooting the breeze with the ice-cream mogul himself. He'd never expected anything less. Ebony was one extraordinary lady. He'd never met anyone like her and doubted he ever would again. Why it had taken him so long to recognize that bugged the hell out him. On impulse, he reached for the cell phone tucked in the side pocket of his laptop case. He wanted to call and congratulate her on a bang-up job, but thought better of it. Still reeling from the realization that he had indeed fallen head over heels in love with her, he wasn't sure how to proceed with that knowledge. Any feelings she might have had for him before he'd bolted for San Francisco without so much as a goodbye were probably shattered. He found himself dialing the number to the *Examiner* newsroom instead. Editors loved positive feedback from readers and in this case it would reflect positively on Ebony. He asked for John Hogan, the editor who had encouraged him to go after the Renfro scoop.

"Hey John, Isaiah Malone here. I see you got your Renfro piece after all. Good job."

"Yeah, that Ebony MacKenzie actually came through," John bellowed, with a strong note of surprise in his voice. "Who'd a thunk it? We ran the series over several days. Thought we'd get more bang for our buck that way."

"So when is Ebony's start date?" Isaiah asked.

"Start date?"

"Yeah, didn't you say whoever got Renfro to talk, got that staff job?"

"Oh . . . uh . . . yeah," he sputtered. "I meant to call all the job candidates and tell them—"

"What?"

"Well, it's the honchos at corporate headquarters. You see, there's this hiring freeze and all . . ."

Isaiah decided something stank. "A hiring freeze? And just when did this happen? Don't bullshit me. You know all I have to do is make a few phone calls and I'll find out. In case you didn't know, George Malone is my father. He and your publisher are very tight."

"Well, actually . . ." John paused. "Let me see, I don't exactly remember the date."

"Just a couple of phone calls to the right people." Isaiah repeated his threat.

"Uh, well . . . Actually, the hiring freeze has been in effect for about eight months."

"Eight months? So this so-called freeze was in effect when you sent everybody out on a goddamn wild-goose chase for Renfro. Son of a—"

"Wait. I thought by the time one of you got to Renfro—

that is, *if* one of you got to him—the hiring freeze would've been lifted."

"You never mentioned this to me, Ebony, or any of the others who would've killed for a job at the *Examiner*. You blatantly misrepresented the hiring situation there and you know it. You took advantage of us, exploited us." Isaiah was shouting now. People were staring, but he didn't give a damn.

"Now just wait one minute here," John protested.

"No, you wait, you lying, underhanded—"

"If you're going to persist—"

"I oughta report this to your publisher." Isaiah wasn't sure why he said that. They were probably aware of John's bull all along—probably sanctioned it. They would have no qualms about wasting desperate freelancers' time—especially those coming from a tabloid or community weekly.

"If you'll just let me finish. Ms. MacKenzie is the first in line for a job as soon as the freeze is lifted. That could happen as soon as—"

"When?"

"Well, uh . . . I don't know when exactly with the economy like it is . . . Well, you never know—maybe as soon as six months."

"Yeah, right, like I'd believe anything that leaps off those lying lips of yours." With that, Isaiah clicked off his cell phone. Ebony must be devastated, he thought, jerking to his feet. She'd been counting on that *Examiner* gig to help her family. And her life had been threatened in the process, and for what? For a job that never really existed. He stalked to the conveyer belt, now loaded with luggage, snatched up his belongings, and hopped in a taxi.

CHAPTER 37

The taxi driver parked in front of Ebony's house. "Need some help to the door?"

"I think I've got it." In his arms Isaiah balanced the boxes of Little Debbie Apple Flips, Chocolate-Flavored Crispy Bars, and Devil Crème Cakes he hoped would bring a smile to her face. He'd bypassed two florists, opting to make a pit stop at the Cozy Corner Convenience Store instead.

At the front door, he carefully maneuvered the stacked boxes to one arm and pressed the doorbell. Unsure how Ebony would receive him, even bearing gifts, he instructed the taxi driver to wait in the car with his luggage.

An older woman, who had to be the feisty, kung-fu-loving grandma, came to the door. Her white hair glowed around remarkably smooth dark brown skin. Now he knew where Ebony got her flawless complexion. She cracked the door and peered out over a security chain.

"Hello, I'm Isaiah Malone. Is Ebony home, by any chance?"

"So you're Isaiah? Well, I'll be." After unhooking the chain, she cracked the door wide enough to reveal her baggy sweatsuit. "I'm Althea MacKenzie, Ebony's grandmother, but just about everybody calls me Granny Mac." She extended her hand, grinning and scanning him up and down with obvious approval.

Paws clattered across the floor as devil dog charged toward them, barking her ass off as usual. For a weaselly female, Black Gal had *the* biggest canine balls with her snapping and snarling as if she could just gobble up Isaiah for breakfast.

Granny Mac shushed the dog. "Now cut out all that racket." Miraculously the pooch tempered her raucous hissy fit to hyper hops around her owner's ankles. "That a girl," the old woman cooed, then turned her attention back to Isaiah. "Sorry, honey, Ebony's not home right now."

"Oh," Isaiah said, peeping inside the room behind her as if he hoped to find Ebony lurking there. "Well, I have something I'd like to leave for her if you don't mind."

"All those are for her?" Granny Mac's eyes grew wide as she appeared to take note of his snack-cake haul for the first time. "She won't come up for air for days."

"When is she expected back?"

"A few hours, I'm guessing. She's just two houses down at Taffi Wilcox's wedding. See where all the cars are lining the street and driveway?"

Isaiah looked in the direction she pointed and briefly considered crashing the wedding, then decided against it. He'd stick out like a street bum in his jeans and pullover shirt at what was likely a classy affair. "I'd like to leave a note with the Little Debbies if that's all right with you," he said, thinking maybe it was best Ebony wasn't home after all. He'd made the first move by extending the olive branch, now he'd wait for her response. This would buy a little more time to think. He still hadn't come up with the right words to convince her to give him another chance to make her happy.

"You should've seen Ebony. She looked real pretty when she left here today all gussied up in satin. She might be a bridesmaid again, but my grandbaby's got it going on—as you young folks say. She's just taking her time. She can afford to be choosy, you know. She's quite a catch."

As if Isaiah needed convincing. It had taken him long enough to realize that Ebony was indeed the one and only woman for him. He felt like the biggest idiot ever for running off to Napa like he did.

Granny Mac babbled on. "But you just wait. I predict she won't be single for much longer." She winked and lowered her voice to a whisper. "I'll let you in on a little secret. Why, just the other day, Taffi's mama told me Ebony could have Taffi's cousin Corky wrapped around her little finger if she wanted. Corky's in the wedding, too. In fact, I do believe Corky's making his big move on Ebony today, right after the ceremony."

So some dork named Corky was making a play for *Isaiah's woman*? He didn't like that one bit. Maybe crashing that wedding wasn't a bad idea after all. But then the taxi driver tooted his horn, reminding him that the meter was still running. "Do you think I could bring these inside?" The stack of boxes teetered in his arms.

As soon as Granny Mac opened the door wide enough for Isaiah to enter, Black Gal bolted outside.

"Black Gal! Black Gal!" Granny Mac clutched her chest as if she were having a heart attack.

Isaiah dropped the boxes and reached to steady her. "Are you okay, ma'am? Should I call 911?"

"No! No! I don't need 911." She flailed her arms. "Please! Get Black Gal before she gets hit by a car or something!"

Isaiah took off across the lawn, then slid to a skidding halt and circled back. "You sure you're all right?"

"Yes, it's just my acid reflux, but I'll just die if something happens to my sweet fur baby! Now go! Please!"

Black Gal zipped across a neighbor's freshly cut grass, knocking over a pair of plastic pink flamingos. Just as Isaiah was gaining on her, she glanced over her shoulder at him with a look that said, *"Catch me if you can, sucka!"* then took off at warp speed.

Black Gal whizzed through a blanket of annuals edging the second yard, scrambling toward the wedding festivities.

"Damn dogs," Isaiah grumbled, barely skirting a steaming pile of poop obviously left by some fleabag twenty times Black Gal's size.

Wedding guests screamed and scattered as Black Gal zoomed in hot pursuit of a froufrou cat wearing a sparkly collar.

"Black Gal! Come back here!" Isaiah shouted, wondering why he bothered wasting his breath.

"Black Gal! Isaiah!" Isaiah heard Ebony before he saw her beautiful face.

"Ebony! You go left! I'll go right! We can probably corner Black Gal near the buffet table!"

Ebony, hitching her gown up to her shins, wasted no time taking off in pursuit of her grandmother's beloved dog.

The bride screamed, her face turned as white as her billowy gown. "Black Gal's ruining everything! Don't let her get to Grendel!"

The cat yowled, then scurried under the buffet table.

Black Gal howled, burrowing under the flap of the tablecloth to follow it.

Some tuxedoed geek with a bushy unibrow slashed above his eyes stepped forward. "I'll take care of it, Ebony."

"That's okay, Corky," she told him. "Stand back and tell everybody else to stand back. The more people around, the more freaked out and spastic Black Gal will get."

So *that* was the ol' Corkster. Isaiah smirked, delighted that Ebony had nipped his little Dudley Do-Right gesture in the bud.

"Black Gal, here girl, here girl!" Ebony pleaded, dropping on her knees to crawl under the table. Isaiah did the same. In the frenzy they bumped heads. Hard.

"Ow!" Ebony rubbed her forehead. "What are you doing here, Isaiah?" Anger flashed in the dark depths of her eyes. "You're supposed to be globe-trotting, aren't you?"

The cat climbed inside a basket of white calla lilies under the table.

"Well, I'm back."

"Obviously," she huffed. "What's the matter? Somebody dock your frequent flier miles?"

"More like somebody stole my heart."

"I repeat, what are you doing here?" she demanded as if his answer hadn't registered.

"What does it look like? I'm chasing Black Gal . . . and you."

"Me?" Finally, her hard-carved features softened.

"I came back for you because I happen to love you and there ain't a damn thing I can do about it."

"Love me? *You* love *me*?" Ebony scoffed. "Yeah, right."

Isaiah lunged toward Black Gal, who eluded his grasp with a move worthy of John Elway. The cat popped out of the basket like a jack-in-the-box and skittered away from the buffet dragging the tablecloth, which had snagged on its sparkly collar. Distracted by the platters of plump baked chicken breasts toppling to the ground, Black Gal forgot about her feline quarry and dug in. The crowd gasped as the five-tiered wedding cake followed, crashing on Isaiah, blanketing his head and chest with white.

Sure he resembled a melting snowman, Isaiah cleared crumbling cake from his eyes with his fingers as the band stopped playing and guests looked on in stupefied silence. He turned to address them. "I'd like to extend my deepest apologies to the bride and groom on Black Gal's behalf for wreaking havoc on your blessed event and demolishing your beautiful wedding cake. And on behalf of myself for horning in on your special day. But I just have to tell this woman here what's in my heart . . ."

"Why are you wasting precious time?" the bride prodded with flip ebullience. "Go on and tell her, then, would you?"

Armed with the bride's approval, he faced Ebony. "I love you. You got a problem with that?"

Smiling, Ebony scooted beside him. "No, I don't have a problem with that. Just so happens I love you, too. And try as I might, ain't a damn thing I can do about it, either."

"So whadda you say we try to give this love thang a shot?"

"I say—"

"The dog took off with the bride's bouquet!" somebody shouted.

"Wait! I've got her!" somebody else shouted. "Ow! She bit me!"

"There she goes again!" another voice yelled.

"I say... to hell with Black Gal," Ebony said, looking deeply into Isaiah's eyes.

Isaiah saw his own love reflected in her eyes and it made him feel all warm and gooey inside. "Damn straight. Devil dog's on her own." It was probably the wedding setting coupled with the love blooming in his heart, but one thought suddenly hit him like a freight train and he had never been more sure of anything in his entire life. "As I was saying before we were so rudely interrupted..." His voice cracked with emotion and the biggest lump actually lodged in his throat. "Ebony MacKenzie, you're the most wonderful, captivating, caring, smart, sexy, funny, and truly, truly dazzling woman I've ever met. Would you be my wife? If you don't say yes, I swear I'll wither up and die. I love you something fierce, woman."

"Yes, yes, I'll be your wife. Because even when you're a colossal knucklehead, I love you, too." Ebony's eyes were bright with tears as she swiped a finger across his cake-covered cheek then licked it. "Besides, how can I resist when you're looking so darn yummy covered in all that vanilla butter-cream frosting?"

Isaiah drew her into his strong arms, spreading the mess and smearing the sticky white confection all over her. As the crowd cheered, they shared the longest, deepest, breath-stifling kiss. A kiss that promised each day they spent together would be sweeter than the last.

CHECK OUT THESE SOUL SISTERS!

BUTTERSCOTCH BLUES
by Margaret Johnson-Hodge

At the age of thirty-four, Sandy Hutchinson wonders if love will forever elude her, until the day she meets Adrian Burton, a Trinidadian with caramel skin, naturally wavy hair, and eyes the color of butterscotch. Together they share a whirlwind romance—until the night of a fateful call from the hospital and she learns of his ailing ex-wife. Now, Sandy must decide if her love is strong enough to help get them through what may be their darkest hour.

A FAMILY REUNION
by Brenda Jackson

It's been fifteen years since the Bennetts were all in one place at one time, and now at a total blowout of a reunion, three generations will gather to remember old memories and reestablish deep roots. But for four special cousins, hidden desires and long-kept secrets will challenge their bond, test their courage, and change their hearts forever...

FAR FROM THE TREE
by Virginia DeBerry and Donna Grant

Struggling Manhattan actress Ronnie Frazier has come home to Buffalo for her father's funeral. In Ronnie's opinion, Celeste English already has it all as a doctor's wife and a mother. But when the sisters journey to their newly inherited North Carolina family homestead, the startling truth about Celeste's perfect life and Della's murky past begins to emerge.

TRYIN' TO SLEEP IN THE BED YOU MADE
by Virginia DeBerry and Donna Grant

Gayle Saunders and Patricia Reid have been best friends since they were children. Gayle, the beauty pampered by her working-class parents, believes a man will make her world complete. Pat, the brainy one, is the hand-me-down child whose mystery parentage haunts her. And then there is Marcus Carter, linked to both women from the moment a childhood tragedy bonds them in secrecy.

THE TURNING POINT
by Francis Ray

Desperate to escape her abusive marriage, Lilly Crawford files for divorce, then slips away from her small east Texas hometown. When her car breaks down on a back road in Louisiana, Lilly seeks help and finds unexpected employment as a caregiver to Adam Wakefield, a former prominent neurosurgeon who is now blind. As the two spend long days together, an unexpected bond develops that can offer the promise of healing...

**AVAILABLE WHEREVER BOOKS ARE SOLD FROM
ST. MARTIN'S PAPERBACKS**

I Know Who Holds Tomorrow

Francis Ray
Blackboard bestselling author of The Turning Point

Happy with her career but miserable in her marriage, TV personality Madison Reed is living a lie. To the world, she and Wesley Reed—son of one of America's premier black families—are the perfect couple: young, good-looking, and destined for greatness together. Then she gets a stunning message... Wes has been in a terrible accident, and Madison is stricken with grief and guilt. But her mourning turns to blinding pain and shock when she discovers that the tragedy not only has taken Wes away, but also the woman who was with him. And now the only part of Wes that remains is a baby girl—Wes's daughter... Through the dark days that follow, Zachary, Wes's best friend, is there for Madison, holding her, healing her. Soon Zach's loyal love begins to ease her pain. But when another secret is exposed, their future together is threatened unless they can find the key that holds the promise of tomorrow...

> "Francis Ray creates characters and stories
> that we all love to read about.
> Her stories are written from the heart."
> — Eric Jerome Dickey, *New York Times* bestselling author

Available wherever books are sold
from St. Martin's Press